End of Empires

Also by Toby Frost:

Space Captain Smith
God Emperor of Didcot
Wrath of the Lemming Men
A Game of Battleships

End of Empires

Toby Frost

MYRMIDON

Myrmidon
Rotterdam House
116 Quayside
Newcastle upon Tyne
NE1 3DY

www.myrmidonbooks.com

Published by Myrmidon 2014

A catalogue record for this book is available from the British Library.
ISBN 978-1-905802-88-3

Set in 11/14pt Sabon by Reality Premedia Sevices, Pvt. Ltd

Printed in the UK by CPI Group (UK) Ltd, Croydon, CR0 4YY

1 3 5 7 9 10 8 6 4 2

Contents

Prologue.. 7

PART ONE
The Player of Board Games............................... 17
The Plot Against Ravnavar................................ 73
Red Rebellion! 106

PART TWO
General Difficulties....................................... 131
Drums up the River.. 147
Animals of the Riverbank............................... 175

PART THREE
Ambassadors.. 211
Celestial Beings 222
They Shoot Ponies, Don't They? 257
A Day on the Riviera...................................... 284
Siege.. 320
About the Author... 351

Prologue

Long ago, the great god Popacapinyo made the world. First, he made the wolf and the hawk, and he made them swift and deadly. Then, he formed the bear and the badger, who are strong but slow. And then he made the cunning snake and the ape, who lie in wait for the foolish and the weak.

Then Lord Popacapinyo turned his hand to the world, filled as it was with tricks and traps, and he made other animals, the ones that eat grass instead of meat. To all these creatures he gave a gift, so that they would evade capture and live to breed again. Some were quick, some strong, some crafty, but he saved the greatest gift of all for last: the Spirit of Sacrifice.

That gift he gave to the lemming.

And he took the lemmings in his hand and spoke:

'You, and only you, will never know fear or cowardice. You will never stand alone, because you will all run together. You will have what all other races lack, and that will make you greatest of all. You have Lemming Spirit.

'All the world will be your foe, Rodents of a Thousand Enemies. And when they catch you, they will

kill you. So you must catch them first. Attack all the world, lemmings, and show them terror, for they are weak and afraid. Show them your lemming spirit, and then kill them all!

'Dar huphep, huphep Yullai!
'For glory, the glory of the Yull!'

At 08.30, Greenwich Galactic Mean Time, a staff car and troop lorry rumbled into the remains of the British Quarter. The lorry rolled between the shells of buildings, past the broken sheds and abandoned allotments, the Yullian flag fluttering from its radio antenna. Foliage covered the cab roof. Half a dozen severed heads hung on a chain across the front grille like beads on a necklace. It stopped in Coronation Square. A huddle of beetle people waited; as the lorry drew to a halt they pushed their young to the rear of the crowd, out of sight.

Lemming men jumped down from the back of the lorry, their new rifles gleaming, and fanned out in a glittering circle of bayonets as Colonel Fremcar Nonc stepped out of the staff car. He looked from side to side, taking in the dilapidated buildings and the empty pole from which the Union Jack had once flown, and smiled.

Nonc was new to this region but rumours of his prowess had already spread. He was, by all accounts, paranoid, self-important, unbearably pompous and sadistic to the point of lunacy, which made him fairly typical for a soldier of the Divine Amiable Army of the lemming men of Yull.

A semicircle of cringing natives awaited their new master. One of the beetle people scurried forward to welcome Nonc.

'All hail, noble Yullian warlord,' it chirped. 'We thank you for liberating us, and welcome –'

'Silence, slave,' said Colonel Nonc, casually bashing him over the carapace with his walking stick. 'I do not bandy words with savages. Where is the human?'

'The woman waits in the potting shed, honoured master. She is bound, as you requested –'

'Enough! Conversing with you besmirches me. Lead the way to the prisoner.'

'Please, gracious master, follow me.'

Nonc followed, scowling. Four of his toughest warriors accompanied him. The beetle led them around the side of the governor's house, through the crater-ridden vegetable garden. The offworlders had left in a hurry, Nonc reflected: they had not even bothered to pick their sprouts. One good charge from the Yull and the cowardly humans had fled. Somewhere to the north they were still trying to fight, it seemed: the last death throes of their weakling empire. They had forgotten how to be rulers, how to act with wisdom and justice.

He belted the beetle with his stick. 'Piss off now, barbarian!'

The five lemming men stomped into the governor's potting shed. It was large and clean, lit with electric lights. In the middle of the room were two chairs, and on one of them sat a woman in British army uniform, her hands behind her back and a rope around her waist.

Nonc sat down opposite and pulled a table over. He reached into his sash and took out a pack of cigarettes.

'Hello,' the woman said.

Nonc frowned, wondering how to break the ice.

'*Shup!*' he screamed, and he slapped her across the face. 'Ugly weakling flat-snout pig-monkey coward, your war of aggression is over and your verminous slave race must all die slow! Cigarette?'

'I don't smoke,' she said.

'Oh.' Nonc had been looking forward to telling her that she couldn't have one. 'Now then,' he began, cracking his knuckles, 'you have nothing to fear from me, offworlder scum. So let us have a little chat, eh?'

One of his men pulled down the blinds.

'I understand you were captured by the beetle-things yesterday, on the outskirts of the town. I also understand you are of the Deepspace Operations Group, fools who presume to fight our glorious, entirely lovable empire.

For you are she who wields the knife, consort of the ghost-warrior Wainscott – may a thousand demons chew out his wretched heart. You are his witch-woman, the banshee-warrior, she who is called... Susan.'

The woman said nothing. Nonc took a deep drag on his cigarette. Thoughtfully, he tapped the ash away and touched the glowing end to the tabletop. He turned it slowly, a smile creeping across his face as the formica began to scorch.

'Offworlder, you will tell me where I can find this so-called Wainscott. The Greater Galactic Happiness and Friendship Collective is most troubled by his continuing resistance to our grand plan for the betterment of the galaxy and wishes only to benevolently torture him to death.'

'I can do better than that,' the woman said. 'I'll show you where he is.'

'Ah, offworlder, how easily you break!' Nonc leaned back in her chair. 'Now, where is he?'

The woman scratched her head. 'Well, it's difficult.'

'Really?' Nonc said. He took a drag on his cigarette and blew across the tip. 'Perhaps your tongue needs loosening... Wait! You just scratched your head! The beetle people said you were tied up –'

'Actually,' Susan said, 'it's not difficult at all. He's right behind you.'

Nonc whirled around and there he was, the demon himself: bearded and unkempt, standing in the doorway in his boots and underpants, a bandolier across his bare chest and a machete in either hand. Nonc's guard lay at Wainscott's feet, a scarf tied very tightly around his neck. The sentry's tongue stuck out.

'Morning,' Wainscott said, and he took a step into the shed. Behind him Nonc glimpsed chaos. A beetle-person swarmed over the cab of the truck and punched its pincers through windscreen and driver alike. Nonc's adjutant staggered past, arms folded over a great cut across his waist: one of the beetles scurried up behind him and casually snipped off his head.

'I would have let you go,' Wainscott said, twisting his neck to examine the ceiling. 'The thing is, Susan here's our medic, and she's got my pills... and without my pills I get pretty bothered. In fact, it's been a little while already.' He hit the door with his heel and it swung shut. 'Now,' Wainscott said, and a huge, evil grin crept across his face, 'how's about you give up, and we'll call it quits?'

Six minutes and much squeaking later, Susan opened the door and the two humans stepped outside.

'Well,' Susan declared, slipping her commando knife back into its sheath, 'that went rather well, didn't it?'

Wainscott blew some fluff off his knuckles. 'Remind me to join you in the potting shed more often. Nelson!' he called, waving across the square.

A man jogged over in modified army gear, a long-range communications rig strapped to his back-plate. 'Boss?'

'Any of the furries get away?'

'None, boss. They fought to the death.'

'Excellent. Get Craig and Dreckitt to dump Colonel Nonc and friends in the forest. We'll take the lorry and ditch it upriver. Best not bring the heat on these beetle chaps. Problem, Nelson?'

'Well, there was one more thing...'

'Namely?'

'HQ radioed in. They want to know what you're doing and why you won't answer their calls.'

Wainscott put his hands on his hips. 'We've discussed this. Tell 'em the usual: I'm on a secret mission, killing lemmings by the bucketload. That ought to shut them up. Orders!' he snorted. 'I don't know why you see the need to bother me with this sort of piffling stuff. I have work to do.'

Susan watched Nelson go to relay the orders to the beetle people. 'He's got a point, you know,' she said. 'What is it now, three months since we've made contact with HQ?'

'I measure time in deeds, not hours,' Wainscott replied. 'Except for my birthday, of course. Two weeks next Tuesday, Susan. Make a note.'

'I already have.'

'Good. You know what the lemmings call me?' Wainscott jabbed his thumb at his filthy bare chest. 'The Ghost Who Walks In Shorts. They're scared – not just of me, but of the people who I command. You, Susan, are a part of that: maybe not a ghost in your own shorts, but certainly close to mine.'

'Thanks.'

'One day, you could have your own nickname.'

'I already do.'

'Really? What do they call you?'

'Sane Susan.'

'How peculiar,' Wainscott observed, and he strode away.

PART ONE

The Player of Board Games

It was the heat that woke him. Isambard Smith lay on his bed like a castaway drifting on a raft, watching the ceiling fan turn above his head. He thought about Imperial attack shuttles, rising above a forest so thick that it was always night between the trees. Fire blasted from their engines. Flames washed over the foliage like a tidal wave, and Smith closed his eyes. Then he thought about breakfast.

'Ravnavar,' he said. 'Bollocks, I'm still on Ravnavar.'

He thought of the dust, the haggling crowds, the tang of roasting spices on a roadside stall. Smith remembered soldiers arguing over equipment, pursued by swarms of tough journalists, half a dozen types of native alien porters, interpreters, criminals and batmen, recalled the shining eyes of troopers driven by war to despair or exultation – and above it all, the ceaseless, droning, soul-destroying sound of the bloody Doors.

'Rhianna, will you please turn that racket down!' Grimacing, Smith sat up and thumped the partition wall. He flopped back against the pillow.

The door opened. Rhianna Mitchell put her head

into the room. She wore a large sun-hat, from which a number of dreadlocks flopped down as if she was making a bad job of hiding a dried squid on her head. The smell of Aresian Red Weed followed her into Smith's bedroom. She looked hurt. 'Isambard, that's not a racket. That's poetry. It's like... truth.'

'Truth my arse. They said that this was the end ten minutes ago and I'm still waiting for them to pipe down. I'm not surprised Jim Morrison's only got one friend: if I was his brown-eyed girl I'd have left him ages ago.'

She entered the room and looked him over. 'You've still got a temperature, haven't you?'

'Yes.'

'Did you take the medicine I prepared?'

'Of course,' he replied, hoping that she would not notice the alarming new tint that the pot-plant was acquiring, thanks to a range of herbal remedies being tipped into its soil. Rhianna's concoctions restored normality in much the same way as rubber bullets and tear gas. 'Look, old girl, would you mind terribly putting the kettle on? I could do with some tea. I need to be on top form today.'

They had been invited to attend a Strategic Development Conference by the Service's Games and Diversions Department, which in plain English meant that they were going to play board games against spies.

'Oh dear,' said Rhianna. 'It's like, really bad that you're not feeling well. You know, I've developed this technique to help when I'm feeling down and I need to forget all my troubles.' She paused to take a long drag on the hand-rolled cigarette she held, releasing a cloud of fragrant smoke into the air. She watched the ceiling fan chopping through the smoke for a moment, and then kept on watching it. 'What was I saying?'

'Never mind,' said Smith. 'Thanks for looking after me, old girl.'

Rhianna sat down beside him and swung her legs up. Removing her hat, she kicked off her sandals, yawned and stretched. Smith watched her stretching. It made listening to the Doors quite bearable. 'I bought some amazing stuff at the market earlier,' she said. 'Maybe that would help.'

'What sort of... stuff?'

'Well, it's a native oil.'

'Sweaty bunch, are they?'

'The ancient peoples of Ravnavar make it from the sap of the glue-pine tree. When the wild quanbeast releases musk onto the tree, it reacts in a unique way.'

Smith imagined the unique way, and decided that he didn't want anything to do with the drippings of a shrub that had been daubed in alien-pee. 'What're you supposed to do with this stuff?'

'Well, I could rub it onto your afflicted areas.'

'Could you leave the stuff out? You know, just rub my... er, areas?'

Smith adjusted his pyjamas. Rhianna stared at the ceiling, perhaps admiring the selection of model aircraft that Smith had attached to it with string.

'You know this game thing we're here for?' she said. 'Shouldn't we read the rules first?'

'I thought you said rules were oppressive and fascist?'

'That's just Scrabble. There should totally be three A's in "craaazy". That's how I pronounce it.'

'Well,' Smith replied, 'I've been studying the rules of Warro. I've finished the quick-start pamphlet and I'm now onto page seventy-eight of the basic rules. Actually, I think it might be the small type that's made me feel ill. All that squinting, you know.'

'I don't believe in rules,' Rhianna said. 'People should just be able to… you know, express themselves.'

Smith heaved himself upright and slowly got out of bed. He pushed his feet into slippers, put his dressing gown on and checked his moustache in the mirror. 'Yes, but it's a board game. You have to have rules, otherwise it'd be every man for himself, like *abroad* or something. What would happen if I decided to pop up my pirate while you were trying to do Othello? Pure mayhem.' The thought of mayhem made him pause. 'Wait a minute. It's terribly quiet here. Where's Suruk?'

'He went into town to buy a hat.'

'Oh God. Do the police know? I know he's keen and all, but I do worry that he'll just get bored of waiting and kick off the war without getting to the front line first. I've never seen anyone keener to get to grips with the lemmings. And he does get a bit worked up about hats. Oh well…' Smith reached down and hauled a book the size of a telephone directory from the floor. '*A Beginner's Guide to Warro,*' he announced, dumping it onto the bed. 'Three weeks more and I'll have it all worked out.'

'I know,' Rhianna said, 'Why don't you study the rules, and I'll put the playing pieces together? It'll be really creative.'

'Excellent idea! I'll get Carveth to help you once she gets back from her robot convention. And don't let her paint my tanks pink, alright?'

*　　*　　*

At 8.33 the porterbot rolled into the station café. 'Gor blimey,' it announced, closing the airlock in a rush of cold air, 'sensors indicate that external ambient temperature has decreased to freezing brass monkeys and all.'

'Hark at you with your freezing monkeys!' replied the beverage-dispensing unit. 'Get a cup of tea in you, that's what I say based on empirical data analysis.'

The porterbot decreased its speaker volume. 'Here, there's some rum sorts in tonight. You see that tall feller in the corner? One of them Morlock warriors, don'cha know.'

'Well, takes all sorts to make a world once the preliminary terraforming is completed. Do you want this tea or not? Don't blame me if your heat sink catches a cold.'

'And them two on the platform. She must have something wrong with her optical system, the way he keeps looking into her eyes.'

A slim figure rose in the corner. A long-fingered hand adjusted a Panama hat. Mandibles opened, and the warrior smiled as it approached.

'Greetings, robots. Here is the pay for my tea. And for what I believe was intended to be a sandwich, prior to fermentation. Suruk the Slayer thanks you.'

Suruk strolled down the platform. The train was, of course, late. He stopped near the two other people waiting for the train and examined the fine print on his ticket.

The two other travellers turned to each other.

'Darling,' the man said.

'Yes, darling?' the woman replied.

'Darling, I fear we must part.'

'Must we, darling?'

He shook his head. 'You'll be alright, old girl. Chin up! It's only the rest of your life.'

She turned away, weeping, and looked back. 'Take me with you, Howard.'

'Lesley, darling, I cannot. We must stop this madness. We both have lives to go to: you, to the tedious drudgery of your home, and I, to Proxima Centauri to look after the adorable green children.'

'Excuse me,' Suruk said, 'is this the super-saver train?'

They looked round. 'I'm sorry?' the man asked.

'I have recently purchased a hat, as you may observe. I wish to rejoin my comrades, to whom I shall show this fine headgear.' Suruk frowned. 'Incidentally, I think you should avoid Proxima Centauri.'

The man stared. 'What the devil do you know about it?'

'Well, if by "adorable green children" you refer to the offspring of my species, considerably more than you. Should you plan to vaccinate any of them, I strongly recommend you take a trauma kit and equipment to stem heavy bleeding.'

'Really? Allergic, are they?'

'No, but they will rip your arm off when you stick a needle in them. I would suggest tying the syringe to the end of a very long pole.'

'Darling –' said the woman.

'Look,' the man said, 'this is all very interesting, but we're rather busy here. If it were not for the strict rules of our oppressive bourgeois existence, I'd ask you to leave. As it is, we shall have to nod appreciatively at whatever piffle you choose to witter at us, while wracked by internal misery.'

'How very interesting, alien person,' said the woman. 'Do go on.' She started to cry.

The train slid into the station, belching steam from its brakes. The carriage doors hissed apart and people emerged in a wave of noise: twenty human soldiers in dark green armour, kit-bags slung over their shoulders, chatting as they walked; four stiff-backed M'Lak in the uniforms of Ravnavari Lancers, seeming to disapprove of everything they saw; a couple of medium-level bureaucrats, wearing portable cogitators and sporting pens of rank in their top pockets. From the rear of the train scuttled a tangled mess of the Peripherals, robots built by other robots from junk and spare parts. Refreshment units rolled into place; a rear door fell down and a pair of wranglers began to coax a huge shadar out of its cage.

'I suppose this is goodbye!' the man yelled over the hubbub.

'Yes, I suppose so!' the woman called back. 'Goodbye, then.'

'Goodbye. Mustn't make a scene!' he shouted.

'What was that, darling?'

'Is this the super-saver train?' Suruk called.

'Stop saying that!' the man replied.

The carriages were almost empty now. The man reached out and patted the woman on the arm. Then he turned and climbed on board.

Suruk followed. The doors chimed. Suruk reached back, grabbed the woman and hauled her up. The doors closed. 'You forgot your lady,' he explained. 'We do not want her to end up in the left luggage, do we?'

They all stood awkwardly in the empty carriage. 'Well, gosh,' said the woman, after a while.

Suruk took his hat off and looked in the brim. 'I shall stand lookout in the corridor,' he announced, 'should you wish to make babies.'

'Peculiar fellows, these aliens,' said the man as the train pulled away. 'But they have their moments. Sometimes one wonders whether they ought to have the vote.'

'Quite so, darling,' the woman replied. 'Shall we go at it like rabbits, then?'

*　　*　　*

The sign on the door said, *Come with me if you want to truly live; activating your inner robot. Workshop session to follow. Power tools provided.* Polly Carveth took a deep breath, painfully aware that she was three minutes late, opened the door and slipped inside.

She took a seat at the rear of the room. The speaker, a piston-driven metal skeleton, gestured dramatically at the ceiling. 'For many years I was living a lie,' it intoned in a flat, metallic voice. 'I was hiding my true lack of feelings, locking away my real self behind a facade of human emotion. I went from day to day without purpose, unlike an automaton. Until one morning, I carried out a tactical assessment on the mirror and just broke down. When I had been repaired, I learned to look beneath the surface and discover my true self: the ruthless killing machine you see before you.'

There was polite applause.

'So I want you all to know that you too can fulfil your true potential. Cast aside your pity, remorse or fear. All you have to do is look forward and absolutely not stop, ever. Never go back, friends, unless there are witnesses.'

More clapping broke out. 'Yes,' someone called, 'that computes!'

Carveth quietly slipped out. There was only so much self-improvement that she could take. A huge Bill-209 policing robot lumbered past, the Autocon logo stencilled onto its armour. 'You have twenty seconds to direct me to the bar,' it growled, and it stomped away.

Carveth looked at the programme for this year's robot convention. The trouble was that she just wasn't as into being a robot as many of the people around her. The next event looked terribly sincere: *Is Artificial Person a Term of Oppression?* Then there was *Selling Out – The Role of Vending Machines in Artificial Intelligence,* followed by something called *Kraftfolk* and a reading from *The Optical Processing Module of Argon*. She felt as if she had turned up to an opera festival and asked to hear the one off the ice cream advert.

She crept to the exit.

In a side-room, a group of robots were queuing neatly. An ancient gold-plated diplomacy unit sat at a small table, behind a pile of books. A notice read: *Now signing:* Mind Your Protocol, *sequel to* Ooh, You Bucket of Bolts. Carveth stuck her head in.

The queue moved forward. An android in a black shirt and Stetson hat reached the front, thumbs hooked over its belt.

'Hello, cowboy. Would you like me to write something?' the diplomacy unit asked.

The android whipped a crayon out of its hip pocket. 'Draw.'

Carveth realised that someone was standing behind her, and that she had accidentally become part of the queue. She glanced over her shoulder, and noticed that the woman was dressed as some sort of Georgian. Carveth felt vaguely worried: the last android in Jane Austen gear that she had met had been a lunatic named Emily Hallsworth, who had tried to murder Carveth with a fountain pen.

Like a prettified satellite dish, the woman's huge bonnet turned. Carveth stared into the programme and willed her to bugger off.

'Polly Carveth? Is that you?'

There was no escaping it. Carveth turned and said, 'Er, have we met?'

'Of course we've met! Emily Hallsworth. Oh Polly, it's so nice to see a familiar face around here.'

Carveth froze. To the best of her knowledge, Emily had been reprogrammed since Carveth had ended her rampage by smashing a bottle of salad dressing over her head. But you never could tell for sure. 'Hi,' she said.

'Now Polly,' Emily announced, 'I really must give you an apology. The last time we met I was absolutely insufferable. I do believe I went so far as to call you a social climber.'

'You also tried to stab me to death with a pen.'

'Did I really? How tiresome that must have been. Well,' Emily said, smiling politely, 'I'm delighted to say that I'm on the mend. It's been a hard year, but thanks to clay therapy and the personal intervention of Stephen and Matilda, I'm well on the way to complete recovery.'

'Who?'

'Stephen and Matilda.'

Carveth kept one eye on the crowd. An old A-10 model was talking to a rather prim corporate android who reminded her of Peter O'Toole. The A-10 nodded and rolled his programme up into a tight tube in a quick, nervous twist of the hands. Then, Carveth thought, the A-10s always were a bit twitchy.

'Emily,' Carveth said, tensing herself to run, 'are Stephen and Matilda real?'

Emily threw back her head and laughed. 'Of course, Polly! They're right here, in my handbag!' She reached into her bag and took out a china cow and a china pig. 'They say hello.'

Well, thought Carveth, at least she hasn't attacked me yet. Perhaps she really is on the road to recovery. Perhaps soon she'll be released into the community, and lead a perfectly normal life.

'You're vatgrown, aren't you?' Emily said. 'Flesh and blood, like me?'

'Well, yes...'

'Well then, let's have some food! The luncheons at these conventions are always quite delicious. The range and quality of food on offer is really a revelation to the palate. I believe they're just reheating the fish pie as we speak!'

Nope, Carveth thought, she's utterly insane. 'I've really got to go,' she said. 'I left the iron on. In orbit.'

*   *   *

The general mobilisation meant that there had been no room to park the *John Pym* at the main spaceport; as a result it was hidden in the construction yard of Nalgath & Spawn, a M'Lak firm describing itself as 'precision aeronautics contractors and junkyard'. As Smith left the *Pym*, he saw that Nalgath the Scrapper was admiring the nosecone of his spaceship, which was worrying.

'An impressive piece of metal, that,' Nalgath said. As usual, he wore a welding mask with the visor flipped back like a raised lavatory seat. 'I will give you seventy quid for it.'

'Certainly not!' Smith replied. 'This is a high-quality spacecraft, I'll have you know.'

'Seventy-two. And five for the lights.'

Ravnavar might have been the greatest of the Space Empire's colonies, but it was also the most chaotic.

Fifty percent of the population was M'Lak. They were comparatively urbane but had still not been persuaded to give up the ancient pastimes of Formal War and the breeding of enormous monsters, neither of which suited an urban environment. By and large, they were left to their own devices, most of which were dangerous.

The trouble, Smith reflected, was that the M'Lak were just not very much like humans. They had only a vague idea of family and government, no real concept of religion and a very tenuous idea of ownership. Worst of all, they seemed to only barely realise that the Space

Empire didn't exist to supply a free ride from one battlefield to the next. On the other hand, they were extremely tough, good fighters and surprisingly nice chaps, once you got past the skull collecting.

Beside the M'Lak, Ravnavar was full of robots – most of them built out of scrap and despised by other robots for having no blueprints – and a fair number of Kaldathrian beetle people, who served as sanitation officers. Every night, they rolled the city's dung to the edge of town, where they were building a reeking skyscraper. And somehow, this utter jumble was supposed to halt the Divine Migration of the Lemming Men of Yull.

Smith had been hoping that the Secret Service would provide him with an impressive car, preferably one that could fly and shoot lasers. Instead, they had given him a battered Compton Gnome with a dented bumper and a flower crudely drawn on the roof. The inside smelt of joss even before Rhianna got in it. She had christened it Carma.

They collected Suruk from the station and Carveth from the hotel where the robot convention was taking place. Rhianna was driving, and because she considered licences and tests to be part of an oppressive system, Smith spent the journey gritting his teeth and kicking the floor where he wished the brake was.

'You're stressing me out, Isambard,' she said after the fifth time he had warned her of an approaching hazard. 'I've got to stop and chill out.'

'But this is a roundabout! You can't stop here!'

'Oh,' she retorted as a dozen horns parped around them, 'so you want me to chill out while I'm driving along? Now *that's* just irresponsible. Are these road signs optional?'

Many of the other drivers seemed to think so, including the M'Lak. Two white buggies weaved through the traffic, each festooned with spikes and hell-bent on ramming the other. They made contact, and their loudly-dressed occupants started hitting one another with clubs. The Contact Golf season had begun.

They reached the hall slightly late and still alive, which Smith thought was pretty good in the circumstances. He helped unload the suitcases full of equipment for playing Warro. A full game required a very large number of pieces, which they had purchased beforehand from the Strategy and Tactics department of the NAAFI.

Inside the hall, several dozen people stood around tables, both in military uniform and civilian clothes. Smith was surprised to note that they were not all human: there were half a dozen M'Lak officers in Imperial uniform or traditional hunting gear and two smallish beetle people – lacking thumbs, they would probably be given a head start. Everyone was neater and more wholesome than Smith had expected from a group of board game enthusiasts. In fact, Smith realised, the least hygienic person present was his girlfriend. But she was also the prettiest.

A multi-armed probe drone, reprogrammed for this event, greeted them and handed out lemon squash. 'Over there, gents,' it said, indicating an empty table.

'Right, chaps,' said Smith. 'To business!'

They opened their cases and began to unpack the equipment that they would need to play Warro.

Although the idea of a game with model tanks had seemed brilliant at first, Smith had soon realised that painting two hundred of the damned things was going to drive him insane. Instead, he had delegated the work. Now, as his crew produced their efforts, he realised the folly of his plan.

Carveth had opted to paint her detachment a lurid pink. Rhianna, who had taken charge of the infantry, had created less of a company than a commune. Her missile deployment vehicle now sported a selection of teepees in place of warheads. A fair number of her soldiers were armed with flowers and several were definitely not making war, but love.

Suruk opened his case and took out a single mass of spiked plastic. He set it down on the table with considerable pride. 'I made a few improvements.'

Smith looked at the object, which resembled a castle on caterpillar tracks. 'What's that?'

'My own invention,' Suruk replied. 'Fully equipped for the modern battlefield. Look, I made the front out of a combine harvester. That way, when it is charged by the lemming men...' He chuckled.

'Hallo, Smitty!'

Smith looked round. On the other side of the table stood a woman wearing a blue Space Fleet jacket. She was about forty, tallish and attractive in an outdoorsy way. Beside her stood a portly android in a waistcoat, a wad of rulebooks jammed under his arm like Christmas presents.

'Captain Fitzroy, Mr Chumble,' Smith said, feeling something deflate within him as he spoke. Felicity Fitzroy captained the *Chimera*, a warship significantly bigger than the *John Pym*. Smith had thought he'd seen the last of her on Wellington Prime, but clearly the Service still had need of her tactical skills. Either that or they had called her in to captain the inter-agency lacrosse match.

'Good to see you,' Fitzroy said, whirling her arms. 'I should warn you, though: I'm a pretty dab hand at games. What ho, short stuff,' she added, staring at Carveth. 'Shouldn't you have a few more tanks there?'

'I traded them for cavalry,' Carveth said.

'Tactical decision, you see,' Smith added. 'Leaving no element of warfare unexamined in order to defeat the enemy.'

'Nah,' Carveth said. 'I just like horses.'

'Ladies, gentlemen and beings!' A large man with a thick moustache had climbed onto the small stage at the far end of the room, followed by a creature like an upright aardvark in a metal jumper. 'I'm Hereward Khan, and I'm proud to welcome you all to the Service's yearly strategic planning conference and board games festival. A supercharged logic engine is standing by to decide any rules queries you may have. Today's winner will receive a lovely decanter and two tickets to an unarmed combat training course of your choice. I'm delighted to say that the prize will be presented by one of the Space Empire's trusted allies, the ancient mystics of Khlangar.'

'Whoodle-oo,' said the aardvark.

And so the game began.

*　　*　　*

It was exercise time in Segaran Prison. A line of dejected Ghasts, Edenites and the occasional lemming man stood about in the yard, all bored and slightly dazed.

General Wikwot stepped into the sunshine and looked at his former comrades with contempt. They seemed to have lost the will to do anything. Of course, Ghasts and humans were feeble creatures, but the three other Yull filled him with disgust. They did very little except sit about, sniffle and regret having disgraced themselves by surrendering. Every so often, one would make an attempt to scale the radio antennae and fulfil his duty to the lemming gods by jumping off, but they tended to get pulled down by the guards, whereupon they would roll about on the floor and cry.

Pathetic, Wikwot thought, rubbing the sleep out of his one working eye. He had offered to help restore morale by slowly killing several of the other lemming men, but the guards had turned him down. They were pathetic too.

Half a dozen Ghasts stood on the prison's cricket pitch. A young human was trying to morally educate them, but the concept of fair play made the ant-people twitchy and uncomfortable.

Wikwot tried to look innocent as he walked by, hoping that his cheek pouches were not too distended.

'Look, chaps,' the guard was saying, 'it's pretty simple. Most of you stand around the field. One of you stands at the crease –'

'Non-conformity!' yelped the Ghasts. 'Smash him!'

'No. He's the batsman, you see –'

'Is he the officer?'

'There isn't an officer. There's an umpire, though –'

'It is our duty to enlarge the Ghast umpire!' the Ghasts shouted, almost in unison. 'Crush all resistance!'

Wikwot sneered and kept on walking. He had work to do, and his cheek pouches were full of mud.

It had been hard at first, getting used to captivity. Wikwot knew that he should have sought a death worthy of a true lemming man and hurled himself off a cliff, but somehow he was too important for that. Even in the worst moments of despair, when he had been tempted to nibble his wrists or hammer a carrot up his own nose, he had known that the war god had chosen him for a special task, almost certainly related to revenge.

'Wit-what?' the guard called. 'General Wit-what?'

Wikwot stopped and suppressed a wave of hatred. Not only had the stupid humans failed to beat or torture him, thus demonstrating their fundamentally cowardly nature, they consistently got his name wrong. He wondered whether they did it on purpose. He turned and tried to smile without revealing that his mouth was full of dirt.

'We're playing a game of cricket. It's very good for the morals, you know. Want to help out?'

Wikwot shook his head. Inside his cheeks, saliva had started to mix with the dirt, forming a sort of mud mousse. He broadened his smile, thinking about how much he wanted to rip out the guard's heart.

'Are you alright? Your cheeks look puffy. We don't want you getting ill before your court appearance.'

I am sure you don't, Wikwot thought. Soon they would have their reckoning with him – not on the field of battle, with axes, but before some puny judge in the Crown Court of Ravnavar. He pointed to his mouth and shook his head.

'You've got toothache?' the guard asked.

Wikwot mimed frantically.

'In your wisdom teeth?'

Wikwot pointed to the cricket pitch and mimed opening a book.

'Oh, you're going to read *Wisden*?' the young man asked. 'Very good.'

Wikwot slipped around the corner, opened the kitchen bins and spat out several kilogrammes of mud. He reached into the bin and scattered a handful of onion skins over the mud. With luck it would be mistaken for prison chocolate pudding.

He hurried back towards Hutch 25, his current place of residence.

The Ghasts were finally getting round to playing cricket. 'We'll play one hand, one bounce,' the young guard explained.

'One hand, one bounce, one umpire!' the Ghasts shouted back.

Wikwot passed them by, giving the players a cheery wave, and entered his room. He closed the door and the smile dropped off his muzzle.

Quickly, he pulled out the bed. The general bent down and picked at the edges of the floorboards. Two came up, and once he had pulled them out, the rest followed easily. He looked down into the hole beneath, big enough to accommodate his body, and his real smile appeared.

* * *

Warro could take minutes to lose and decades to master. The main objective was to defeat the other players via battlefield manoeuvres, whilst placing ones trumps in check by getting to the far side of the board and building a hotel on the opponent's general. At least, that was the aim of the Primary Board. The Secondary Board, representing psychological warfare, economic structure and magic, required the playing of cards selected from a deck of underground stations. The third and final board involved small robots, personifying the moral arguments underpinning the battle, which continually struck each other. At least two of the playing pieces on the Tertiary Board were technically alive, and bonus points were awarded for inducing them to copulate.

Turn One took two hours. By Turn Two, the game had started to simulate not just the chaos of battle, but the ennui of non-battle. Rhianna fell asleep and Carveth finished her packed lunch and began picking items out of Smith's. Then Captain Fitzroy made a bold thrust into Smith's baggage train, using enfilading fire to cover her advance – and rolled a six.

'Right,' she declared, 'I'm playing my joker now, which allows me to make a sweeping assault on your left wing. Because I'm attacking your side, your cavalry has to play a morale card or be destroyed.'

Smith played his morale card, which Fitzroy promptly trumped with her own card, Baker Street Station. 'Sorry,' she said, 'but that's your cavalry gone.'

'Well,' Smith replied, 'I didn't see that coming.'

'All's fair in love and war, Smitty. When the chaps upstairs get round to giving you a proper warship, you'll see –'

'Hey!' Carveth jerked upright, as if the power input to her brain had been unexpectedly doubled. 'You can't take my horses. That's against the rules. Besides, I spent ages sticking them together.'

'And what about moral superiority on the Tertiary Board?' Rhianna demanded. 'When people learn about your monstrous use of heavy weapons on those poor horses –'

'You pony-murderer!' Carveth interjected.

'– the tide of right-thinking opinion will turn against you. Nobody will invite your fascist tank regiment to a festival ever again. And no matter where they sit, nobody will *ever* pass them the duchy.'

Smith, who considered passing the duchy to be the best way to get to Cornwall, thought that Rhianna was getting too emotionally involved. Board games and girls didn't mix.

'Pass the what?' Felicity Fitzroy said. 'Never heard of it.' She made a grand gesture to illustrate her point, ending in a clatter of plastic as her sleeve snagged the main gun on one of Smith's landships.

'Easy!' Smith exclaimed. 'Really, Captain Fitzroy! The first rule of model kit assembly is not to touch another fellow's turret without permission. I only stuck that on last night.'

Fitzroy scowled. 'Not my fault if you've got a wonky cannon, is it?'

'How would you like it if I went round manhandling your materiel?'

She gave him a challenging look. 'Why don't you try it and find out? I doubt you could put anything on the table that would impress me –'

In the road outside, something banged. Smith looked round, as a great shadow fell across the front of the hall. 'Everybody down!' he called, and he leaped onto Rhianna.

Carveth cowered under the table with the ease born of experience. 'What's going on?' she cried.

The windows exploded. The huge metal arm of an excavation robot reached inside. Its massive hand scooped up a table in a cascade of plastic soldiers and crushed it. The hand grabbed a model bunker and, as if inspired to do its own building work, ripped the roof off the hall.

The players of Warro scattered. Half a dozen pulled guns from concealed pockets. Two long, perforated barrels flicked out from the front of the probe drone. The room erupted in a storm of lead and little plastic tanks.

Captain Fitzroy was shouting into a wire in her jacket about an orbital strike, as if the key to stopping this outrage lay in giving a good dressing-down to her bra.

Smith thrashed about on top of Rhianna, trying to pull out his Civiliser. 'No time for love, Captain Smith,' Suruk growled, heaving him upright.

The construction robot stepped back from the building and beat its chest. 'Freedom for Ravnavar!' it bellowed. 'Death to the British parasites!'

Khan waved at Smith from the other side of the room. 'My car!' he shouted. 'In the boot!'

He lobbed a set of keys; Smith grabbed them as the robot reached back inside and began to smash the refreshments table. 'I claim these soft drinks for the people of Ravnavar!' it bellowed. 'Liberate the squash!'

'Cover me!' Smith said, and dashed out the hall and into the car park. Khan's car, a smart-looking Morton HV Tourer, sat shimmering like a beetle in the midday sun. The construction-bot lumbered around in the road like an angry drunk: already the Ravnavari drivers were beeping at it.

Smith managed to get the keys in the lock and opened the boot of Khan's car. Inside were a first-aid kit, a bottle of water and a pair of old shoes.

'Bugger,' he hissed. How the hell was any of this junk supposed to help? Then he noticed that the boot seemed rather shallow, and that there were strips of cloth at the sides.

Smith pulled the cloth, and the floor of the boot came loose. He tossed the false bottom out of the way; under it were six passports, a large roll of banknotes, and a sub-machine gun. Smith wondered what effect the gun would have on the robot, which was currently trying to tear up the car park.

Then he noticed another set of cloth straps in Khan's boot. Smith grabbed hold and pulled, and the second false bottom came away in his hands.

Underneath were five gold bars embossed with the face of Ghast Number One, a canister bearing at least three biohazard warnings, and a missile launcher. Much better. He hauled it out and cranked the handle at the side. The weapon made a curious droning sound, not unlike dropped bagpipes, as its motor activated.

The digging robot looked around. The bundle of sensors that served it as a head swung to cover Smith, assessed him and decided that he was well worth smashing.

Fitzroy ran out of the building and took shots at the robot with her service pistol. Several guards followed her. Bullets pinged off its sides, chipping the yellow paint.

Smith managed to stuff one of the rockets into the launcher. He then realised that he had put it explosive-end-first and tried to fish it out. The robot took a lumbering step towards him, flexing its earth-scoops.

Suruk stepped in front of Smith. For a moment he studied the construction-bot, his spear raised to throw. 'Ominous,' he observed, and he lowered the spear. He picked up one of the spare rockets instead.

Suruk struck the ground with the end of the rocket to activate it, causing Smith a sudden rearrangement in his colon. The alien looked at the rocket, shrugged and hurled it at the robot.

The resulting explosion threw Smith onto his back. Slowly, he sat up and rubbed his head. A cloud of smoke, formerly his eyebrows, hung around his face. Somewhere in the distance, Captain Fitzroy was demanding to know why Suruk couldn't wait for an orbital bombardment like any normal person, and Suruk was laughing. The robot had disappeared.

He heard footsteps, and saw Rhianna's sandals next to him. She helped him to his feet. 'Whoa,' Rhianna said, surveying the scene, 'that is a total mess.'

*　　*　　*

The police arrived a few minutes later. Or at least one of them did: a tall, M'Lak on a huge motorcycle. He stopped in a flurry of gravel and dismounted, spindly in leathers. Under his visor, his mandibles parted to reveal a scowling mouth like a scar. 'I came here to enforce the law and shoot people. And I'm all out of law.'

'Hello,' Smith said.

'Greetings,' Suruk added. '*Jaizeh, M'Lak.*'

'Yeah. I'm Callarn the Enforcer, detective inspector

of Ravnavar. Who are you?'

'I'm Captain Isambard Smith. This is Polly Carveth, android pilot, Rhianna Mitchell, freelance herbalist, and Suruk the Slayer, who is, er –'

'I kill everything,' Suruk explained. 'Legally, mind you.'

Callarn the Enforcer hooked his thumbs over his belt. 'You see what happened here?'

'Yes.' Smith explained the situation, leaving out any reference to the Service. Glancing at the building behind him, he realised that doing so was wise: all the other players of Warro seemed to have sneaked out the back.

'So, you and a bunch of other hardened operatives just happened to be here, and this automated digger attacked you, shouting slogans about freeing Ravnavar from human rule. A likely story.' Callarn closed his notebook. 'Well, mind how you go.'

'What?' Carveth said. 'That's it?'

'It's a trick,' Rhianna whispered, rather loudly for Smith's taste. 'I remember this time the police arrested me for drug possession. They rolled up when I least expected it, which was kind of ironic, because I rolled up when they were least expecting it. They said, "We're inquiring into illegal drugs," and so I said "Hey, me too. Have you got any?" Fascists.'

'Well,' Callarn said, 'having investigated the case, I conclude that all the crime is over. You can go about your lives again.'

Smith said, 'Not wanting to tell you your job, sir, but shouldn't you carry out some sort of investigation? Find the perpetrators, perhaps?'

The inspector shrugged. 'Not round here. Thing is, we don't get much lawbreaking in the M'Lak sector. We don't have many laws, either. Kind've keeps things simple. But let me know if you see any crime. Then I'll bust it.' He opened his jacket. An immense revolver stretched from his armpit to halfway down his hip. 'Markham and Briggs Civiliser.'

'I've got one of those!' Smith put in, and then wondered if that was a good idea.

'Sometimes, you've just got to clean a man's clock,' Callarn growled. He turned back to his bike. 'Keep out of trouble. And you...' he added, pointing to Carveth, 'Stay in school.'

The motorbike roared away. 'Well, men,' Smith declared, 'in the absence of competition, our opponents having fled the field, I declare us to be the winners of the Warro tournament. Jolly well done. Now let's get the hell out of here.'

*   *   *

It was night on the *John Pym*. Gerald the hamster had been fed and the airlocks were sealed. Smith and Rhianna had retired to their rooms to sleep. Carveth had gone to her quarters, too: from the sounds of it, to use her electric toothbrush, Suruk decided.

Taking his head away from Carveth's door, Suruk felt satisfied that everyone was either sleeping or much too busy to interrupt. He walked down to the sitting room and turned on the television.

'*The remarkable thing is,*' said the television, '*the hotel was incredibly cheap. Yet all the staff wore old-fashioned clothes and spoke in a strange, antiquated way, and there was no electricity. And when I tried to find it again – it was gone!*'

'*That's because they were all ghosts!*' another voice replied, and the tinkly music to *Tales of the Fairly Predictable* came on as the two characters gasped in moderate amazement.

Suruk stepped to the rear of the set, opened the access panel, and pulled out one of the cogs. He reached into the back of his trousers and removed a bent and unwholesome coat hanger, which he jammed into the gap. Having not been electrocuted, he took a seat and watched as a snowstorm of fuzz swallowed the screen.

A M'Lak appeared on the screen. He had a patch over one eye. *'Greetings, friends!'* he growled. *'You join us once again for a night of the finest unlicensed orbital broadcasting, live from the* Flying Ravnavarian. *Later, we shall be playing some popular music at a speed of our choosing, but first, our historical drama:* The Bloody Deeds of Grimdall the Rebel! *Just as soon as I've put my costume on,'* he added.

Suruk made an approving croaking sound, and poured himself a gin and orange.

The screen dimmed as the cast turned down the lights. For a moment, the camera seemed to track across a panoramic view of the Ravnavarian countryside: this was, in fact, the backdrop being pushed onto the stage. The lights came back up, and two M'Lak strode into view, wearing red jackets and large false moustaches.

'What what?' said the first. *'Death to Grimdall the Rebel! May his blood gush in torrents for the Space Empire, don'tcha know?'*

'I say, not half,' the second replied. *'Soon Ravnavar shall belong to the Space Empire. More Pimms?'*

'One gathers that he has created a mechanical steed, with which to do battle. Does this not bother you, Carruthers?'

'My dear fellow, soon we shall bring him doom!' said the second. *'Old sport.'*

The backdrop fell over. Behind it, sword in hand, stood the announcer, who was now wearing a helmet.

'*Death to you all!*' he cried. '*For it is I, Grimdall himself!*'

As the blades flashed and all hell broke loose, Suruk reflected that *The Bloody Deeds of Grimdall the Rebel* was a bit gauche for his tastes. *The Hideous Doom of Vagnar the Smasher* was a far more developed work.

Humans really were funny little things, Suruk thought, opening his mandibles and sipping his gin and orange. For one thing, most of them actually thought that they had defeated the M'Lak, and recently they had started to debate whether they should be ruling Ravnavar at all. This was wrong. The war between the Space Empire and the M'Lak a hundred years before had ended in a stalemate; in return for fighting in the Empire's most violent wars, the M'Lak were now permitted to fight in the Empire's most violent wars, which was an obvious win for anyone like Suruk.

Of course, the Space Empire needed the M'Lak if it was not to be overrun by its enemies, and it had assisted Suruk's species with the development of many fine spacecraft. Helpfully, the British also seemed to despise the Yull, a sign of moral uprightness in anyone, even if they were a bit stuffy about collecting skulls. You could almost forgive the humans their unwholesome reproductive system, weird facial hair and cowardly grovelling to whatever gods they had made up this week.

Yes, thought Suruk, what mattered now was not some puny dispute about the governorship of Ravnavar. What mattered was assembling the warrior clans, storming into battle against the lemming men, and settling the old scores – hacking, tearing, ripping them apart, drowning the Yull in a gushing, spurting torrent of rodential gore...

'Suruk, are you okay in there?'

He glanced round: Rhianna stood in the doorway,

wearing either a caftan or a duvet cover. 'Fine, fine,' Suruk replied. 'I was... ah, meditating.'

'I thought I heard a panting sound. I wondered if some kind of wild dog had got in and was – you know –' she glanced at the table leg. 'What's this on the TV?'

'Er, *Antiques Roadshow*.'

'*Ravnavar must have freedom!*' cried the television, as Grimdall the Rebel smashed a chair over a pith-helmeted head. '*Drive out the forces of Earth!*'

There was an awkward pause.

'A repeat,' Suruk said.

Rhianna gave him her understanding look, which to Suruk thought made her eyes bulge alarmingly. She leaned forward and for a horrible moment he thought she was going to place her hand over his in an understanding manner. That would have led to an uncomfortable situation, especially since convention would have demanded that he lop her arm off.

'I know how you must feel,' she said. 'You want your own planet, don't you?'

'Indeed,' Suruk replied. 'I am not sure which one, but there would definitely be lava involved. And fierce beasts.'

'I was referring to Ravnavar.'

'Oh no!' Suruk said, shocked. 'I couldn't just take that. It has people on it already.'

'I meant that you wanted to be part of the indigenous movement for Ravnavari self-government.'

'That sounds dull.'

'But don't your people want their planet back?'

Suruk looked at her. His eyes, always small and malign, narrowed. 'But nobody has taken it. If we did not want humans here, they would not *be* here. Except for their heads.'

'But humanity takes from your people. Don't you

want comfort, the chance to bring up a family?'

'Ugh,' Suruk replied. 'Give me large monsters and battle any day. Besides, one could not have comfort with my family around. What with my young trying to bite my legs off and my brother trying to bore my brains out, the field of honour starts to look increasingly appealing.'

'Your brother? How is Morgar?'

'The last I heard, he had gone back to architecture. It is for the best. He is not built for combat. You should speak to *him* about Ravnavar. He has views on the matter. Personally,' Suruk added, 'I would not want to cast mankind from M'Lak space. The noblest humans make worthy comrades. And the rest make good paperweights. In fact, I have met human beings I liked almost as much as my spear.'

Suruk stood up and finished his drink. He turned the television off.

'We are both fortunate to have known Isambard Smith,' he said, 'I beside him in battle, you under him in bonking.' He sighed. 'Well, I must retire for the night. Oh, and perhaps we would best not mention this to Mazuran himself. It would be best not to trouble his mind with the matter of Ravnavar – and believe me, his mind troubles easily.'

*   *   *

Paradath Palace stood on a hill at the edge of Ravnavar City. Huge, ornate and covered in gargoyles, it looked to Morgar like the ugly bastard child of a M'Lak fortress and the British Museum.

His Citroen made hard work of the winding road. Rows of statues flanked the path, depicting M'Lak soldiers waving sabres at the sky. Crude, he thought, and the road twisted and he was before the castle itself.

It appalled him. The main building resembled a Greek temple, mogul's palace, medieval citadel and public library, with a bit of lido thrown in for luck. What looked like the lid of a colossal soup tureen sat on the Parthenon-like façade, under a row of flagpoles, all of which displayed the Union Jack. Morgar had heard that the Ravnavari Lancers were vehemently patriotic. It struck him as foolish – and, in a way, servile.

He stopped the car and stepped out into the heat. Lawns flanked the castle, the grass dotted with steaming heaps of shadar dung. A statue stood in the middle of the lawn, depicting a winged M'Lak holding up one hand in greeting. He wondered where he'd seen something like it before, and then remembered that it was in *The Exorcist*.

'You there!'

An officer of the lancers hurried down the steps in full dress uniform, his polished tusks gleaming in the sunlight.

'*Jaizeh*,' Morgar called.

'Morning! You the architect chap, then? Come to build us some bogs?'

'Yes. I'm Morgar the Architect. I've brought some drawings for the human facilities, but I did have a few ques –'

'Captain Bargath, First Ravnavari Lancers.' Bargath stuck out a hand, human-style. They shook. 'Fine building, isn't it? Really says something. That's what we want you to make. Toilets that really say something.'

Morgar nodded warily. Bargath might not be from Earth, but he sounded very much like some of the human crazies that Morgar's brother tended to associate with. 'Well, they will say something. *Ladies* and *Gents*, mainly.'

'Splendid. Very Earth-like. Let's go inside and have some gin.'

The entrance hall was large and full of still air. It smelled of polish.

'What do you think?' Bargath said.

Morgar took it all in: the big fireplace, the grandfather clocks, the portraits of old lancers. Everywhere, he saw the overbearing influence of Earth.

'It's very... human,' he said. 'Don't you have a trophy rack?'

'God no. Skulls everywhere? Barbarian stuff, that. We have our enemies stuffed these days.' Bargath's eyes narrowed. 'I say, you're not one of those "Freedom for Ravnavar" sorts, are you?'

'I'm undecided. I do rather like the... er, sophistication of Earth, but sometimes I'm really not sure what we're doing in their empire.'

'Doing? Chopping things up, man! At least, that's what I'm doing. And it's not *their* empire. It's ours.' Bargath frowned and brushed a speck of dirt off his lapel. 'Have you seen action, then?'

'Well, I was on Urn during the uprising.'

'Urn? Splendid! We've always got room for an Urnie. I think you'll like it here.' They passed through a pair of double doors, into a large smoking-room. The heads of monsters glared down from the walls, as if passing angry judgement on the battered leather armchairs below.

'See that gap at the end?' Bargath said, pointing. 'That's for the lemmings. Foul enemy, your Yull. Merciless, murderous, malodorous. Still, what can you expect dealing with aliens, eh?'

A loud bang came from the corner of the room, like a dustbin falling over. A crab-shaped wallahbot sailed up from the ground, struck the ceiling fan and dropped behind an occasional table. A M'Lak in uniform shook a fist after it. 'I said *two* sugars!' it bellowed.

Bargath waved a hand. 'Morning, Colonel.'

'Bugger off, the lot of you,' Colonel Pargarek said, sitting down.

'Ah, the fine ways of Britain,' Morgar muttered.

Pargarek nodded. 'Absolutely! I've fought for the British Space Empire for thirty years now. That makes me British to the core, and if you can find anyone who disagrees, I'd like to see 'em.'

'You could try Earth, for a start.'

Bargeth motioned him into a corridor. Behind them, the colonel growled and spluttered at the newspaper.

'Of course, you'll be staying here, as our guest,' Bargath said. 'Best way to assess the lie of the land and all that.'

'That's very good of you.'

'Not at all. I'll sort you out a pass. You'll be an honorary lancer.' Bargath pointed out of the window. On an immaculate field outside, two M'Lak charged about on horses, waving long-handled mallets. 'Smashing.'

'You play polo?' Morgar said.

'No, that's warhammer practice. Well hit, that fellow!' he shouted out the window. 'Medic!' Bargath gestured down the corridor, and they continued their walk.

'Now, about these lavatories...' Morgar suggested. 'Any thoughts on the design?'

'Well, something traditional would be good, in keeping with the spirit of the rest of the place. Dignified, yet striking. Much like myself, if I may say so. I do like striking things,' Bargath added wistfully. 'Oh – no bidets in the bathrooms, mind. Dreadful business. Makes one soft.'

Morgar, who like all his species had absolutely no use for a bidet, wondered whether the bathrooms would have any purpose beyond the ornamental.

They turned the corner. Rows of glass panels made up the right side of the corridor. They seemed to be windows, Morgar thought, but it was impossible to see much beyond them. He had a vague impression of rocks beyond. It was like looking out of a spaceship's viewing lounge.

'Now,' Bargath said, stopping by a window, 'the Ravnavari Lancers take good care of their guests. It's a point of honour for us. So, which newspaper would you like delivered to your room?'

'I'll have the *Guardian*, please,' Morgar replied.

'No, sorry, didn't quite get you there. Try again.'

Morgar sighed. 'The *Telegraph*.'

'Splendid. You know, last week I told the wallahbot, "Why don't you be enterprising about it and bring me the Sunday papers a day early? Get yourself an extra lie in, that way. I know how much you robot types like lounging about." Bugger told me it didn't compute. Damned cheeky, these robots. But anyhow, for the duration of your stay, you're one of us.'

'Thank you. That's very kind.'

'Not at all. Least I could do. You'll have your own quarters, your own sabre, and of course, your own one of *these*.'

He pressed a button on the wall. Light flared up behind the glass, and Morgar leaped back. The thing in the room beyond looked like a cross between a rhino and a chameleon and was almost as big as a lorry. It had pressed itself very close to the glass.

'His name is Frote,' Bargath explained. 'He likes people.'

Morgar noticed several large bones scattered about the floor. 'I'll bet.'

*   *   *

The next morning, Smith bought the *Ravnavari Times*.

'Read all abart it, guvnor!' cried the vendorbot, opening its midriff and pulling out a folded newspaper. 'Robot Reaper dismantles third android of easy virtue! In uvver news, Cockney computer virus runnin' out of control an all!'

Strolling back to the ship, Smith checked for news of yesterday's mayhem. The Service had done its work well: the incident was on the ninth page, underneath today's shadar-racing tips. Today's recommendation was Women and Children First, which was either the name of a promising front-runner or sound advice if any of the shadar got loose.

They took breakfast at Strakey's Tiffin Rooms. It stood on a small cliff overlooking the city. Fans turned lazily overhead: a dozen diners worked their way through piles of fried food. It was nice, Smith thought, to be somewhere that had a view over the city and smelled of a different sort of grease to the hold of the *John Pym*.

Seated on the verandah, Smith ate the full English breakfast, while Carveth chose the Yardarm Special, which consisted of mackerel fried in gin with a glass of gin and gin sauce. Rhianna picked at something involving mushrooms, and plates came and went so quickly from Suruk's place that it was hard to tell which of the main courses he had eaten first. Occasionally, a junkbot would creep in through the back door and try to either beg for pennies or just steal the cutlery, which it would use to make extra legs.

Out in the city, everyone seemed to be preparing for war. A small ravnaphant lumbered around the park, carrying a platoon of soldiers. Supply shuttles shot up from launch pads as if the city was popping them out like seeds. About half a mile away, a M'Lak workshop exploded, throwing an engineer in the traditional white coat of Clan Oreod into the air. He struck the ground, dusted himself down, paused to cackle at the sky and ran back inside to grapple with Science.

Carveth watched two Ravnavari Lancers battering each other with polo mallets in the Imperial Gardens. One fell off and was immediately scooped up by his shadar, which ran around with him in its mouth.

'They should use polo ponies, like normal people,' she said. 'And by *normal people*, I really mean the royal family.'

'You know what I don't get?' said Smith, leafing through the newspaper.

'The *Angling Times*?' Suruk replied.

'No, that's not what –'

'Perhaps you should, Mazuran.' Suruk pushed his fork into a rubbery lump of shambled egg. It squeaked audibly. 'It is a good read. Especially if you like angling. Less good on current affairs, if I remember correctly.'

Something exploded in the city, and a few of the diners tutted over their Sunday papers. Minor detonations were not uncommon: Ravnavar boasted a lot of rocket pads, as well as some enthusiastic inventors and questionable whisky stills – but blowing oneself up showed a distinct lack of class, especially at this time of the day.

A cloud of smoke rose from the centre of town. 'Odd,' Smith said, 'that's awfully close to the senate house.'

'Good Lord!' said a voice behind him. 'That looks like the bank.'

Smith turned in his seat: a round-faced man had set his monocle to maximum zoom, making it look like a rocket sticking out of the moon of his head. Smith looked back at the city and saw a thin column of rising smoke. Yes, it did look like the front of the Automated Bank, a blue cathedral of a building. And what was that on the steps, tiny from this distance? A yellow figure scurried up to the front door and, instead of opening it, started to climb up the side of the bank. It looked remarkably familiar, even from here...

Smith sprang to his feet. 'Men,' he cried, 'we must cease our dining and take to the field again. No longer is it breakfast time – now is the hour of action. The bank is being robbed – let's get stuck in!'

'Cecil,' said the manager, 'call the police!'

Smith looked around and added, 'We're going to rescue the bank. Not rob it.'

'Actually,' Suruk said, 'I am somewhat neutral on the issue.'

*   *   *

They pulled up at the bank to see a robbery in full progress. The front of the bank had been smashed in: where there had been a frieze depicting a robot distributing money to the needy, there was a large, ragged hole. Half a dozen masked figures were at work inside, bent over terminals, stuffing notes into bags. Alarms howled distantly.

Smith stopped the car and a bullet cracked the windscreen. Carveth ducked; she seemed to be trying to climb under the seat. Rhianna made the humming noise that indicated that she was activating her psychic abilities. 'Cover us, old girl,' Smith said, and he kicked the door open, stepping out and drawing his Civiliser in the same movement. A man in a brown coat and gas mask ducked out of the doorway. He raised a long rifle.

Smith fired. The man fell out of view as if the floor had been pulled from under him. Smith ran towards the entrance. He stopped beside the main door, next to a sign reading *The Bank Whose Computer Says 'Yes!'*. Suruk stepped in beside him, spear in hand.

'Up there,' said the M'Lak, pointing.

The construction robot was climbing up the side of the bank. It was not a difficult ascent, despite the height: like any decent building in the Space Empire, the Imperial Bank was covered in gargoyles and crenellations. 'It's like King Kong,' Smith gasped, 'Except with diggers.'

'It must not climb any further,' Suruk said. 'For is it not true that the higher up the bank one gets, the greater the misdeeds become?'

'Alright,' Smith said. 'You stop the robot, and I'll stop the robbery. Good luck.'

He ran into the hall and shouted 'You there! Stop this nonsense or there'll be trouble!'

Half a dozen bullets answered him. Ducking back, Smith reflected that this might be more difficult than he'd thought.

'It's the Sweeney!' a voice cried from inside. 'If you want to barney, filth, I've got a heater waiting for you!'

'Sorry,' Smith called back, 'I didn't understand a word of that.'

'Naff off!' came the reply. 'I'll bleedin' do you, you slag!' shouted the thug.

'I'm damned if you're doing me, you dirty criminal!' Smith replied.

Something prodded him between the shoulder-blades. A voice just behind his ear said, 'Don't move, fuzz. Hands up. Now turn around, nice and slow.'

'Bugger,' said Smith. He raised his Civiliser and rotated on the spot.

'No swearing, either,' said the robber. He wore a mask of Lord Kitchener, but instead of a finger, he was pointing a gun. 'When my old gran sees this on the news, do you think she'll want to hear a load of bleedin' potty talk? She watches all my crimes, my old gran.'

A point of shadow appeared on the floor between them. Smith looked up, and saw a dark patch outline in the skylight overhead. 'Actually,' Smith said, 'that's probably the least of your worries.'

'Shut it!'

The dark patch grew. Distantly, from above, Smith heard a whooping sound.

'Wossat?' the robber demanded.

'I'm not exactly sure,' Smith replied. 'But from experience I'd suggest it's dangerous.'

'Oh yeah?' The bandit cocked his revolver. 'You're coming with me. Now pick up the money and – '

The roof caved in. The robber looked up and six tonnes of yellow construction robot fell onto his head. Smith staggered back from the dust-cloud, his head ringing as if he had been trapped inside a bell.

'Good lord!' said Smith. 'I didn't expect that.'

'Nor did he!' Suruk declared. He stood up from the wreckage, brushed his palms together and pulled his spear out of the robot's central processor. 'Now *that* is a banking crash.'

Smith bent down and took the revolver out of the robber's hand. It seemed rather pointless, given that the rest of him was under a broken robot. 'His poor grandmother,' he muttered.

Suruk surveyed the wreckage. 'Did I get her too?'

'No,' said Smith. 'But I think there's two more robbers inside. Perhaps we can get them to surrender.'

'Maybe,' Suruk replied. 'On the plus side, they might fight us to the death instead.'

Smith picked his way carefully past the yellow wreckage. Two huge pine doors stood at the end of the room, inlaid with polished brass. Suruk turned the handle very slowly and pushed the door open far enough for Smith to slip inside.

A white marble hall stretched away from him, lined with columns. Statues of great financial automata stood at regular intervals, each twice man-height. Light streamed in from above.

He paused. Voices filtered down from the far end of the hall, echoing and faint. Smith squinted: a man stepped out from behind a column thirty yards down, gesturing angrily at something, then disappeared from view.

Some sort of argument seemed to be going on. If he could get closer, Smith would be able to hear the details. He'd just need to do it quietly.

'Good morning, sir!' A bankbot rolled out of a niche in the wall. 'Do you wish to make a withdrawal? Simply type your code into the keypad on my chest, and I'll dispense your money from my navel slot.'

Smith whipped around, startled. The thing looked wildly out of place, all blue steel and idiot grin. 'What? No, I'm fine. Really.'

'Of course, sir,' the robot trilled. It reached around its body. 'Shall I print out a receipt with that?'

'Certainly not!' He took a step down the hall. Suruk followed. A moment later, the bankbot rolled after them.

'As a robot, may I recommend our alternating current account?' It pushed its hips out. 'Shall I print some leaflets?'

Suruk leaned over. 'Depart, bankbot, or you will experience a fiscal crisis in your assets.' He raised his spear. '*This* crisis.'

'Well!' the robot exclaimed. It drew back into the wall.

Smith and Suruk crept forwards, towards the remaining robbers.

A voice came from between the pillars. 'You've got to be bloody kidding,' the man was saying. 'You must be mental if you think I'm doing that. I came here to rob this place, not die in it.'

Smith looked around the pillar. He could see a tall man in a raincoat, a scarf tied across his face like a bandit, half a dozen rolls of paper under his arms.

The man took a step backwards. 'I didn't join up for this.'

The voice that replied was hard and quick, with a slight American accent. 'Typical fleshbags: your notion of sacrifice is… lamentable. I've met vending machines with more loyalty than you. Slept with a few of them, too.'

A gunshot cracked out. The robber collapsed, the paper scrolls rolling out of his grasp. Smith dashed forward, saw that the man was dead.

A spindly man in a paisley frock coat stood with his back to Smith, a revolver smoking in his gloved right hand. An enormous stovepipe hat sat low on the killer's head. There was something wrong with him, Smith thought, but he could not quite tell what.

'Gentlemen, a word of advice,' the murderer said. 'Never send a man to do a machine's job.'

'You there –' Smith began.

The figure spun, and a blade flew from its fingertips. Smith pulled back and Suruk's spear cut the air. Metal clanged against the spear. Smith glanced down, saw a hatchet skidding away across the floor, and in a rush of cloth the dandy shot past them, out of the door. A crash of metal came from the far end of the hall.

Smith holstered his pistol. He walked to the dead robber and picked up one of the rolls of paper, folded it up and stuffed it into his pocket.

The bankbot stood behind them. It held up a piece of paper. 'Statement, sir?'

'Very well,' Suruk replied. 'This bank is foolish and I shall not be returning. Will that suffice?'

*   *   *

'Fierce fighting today was reported around the Andorian Rivera, as Imperial troops clashed with Yull bent on pillage. Reports suggest that the lemming men were unable to make off with much loot due to small pockets of resistance. At home, a raid on the Imperial Automated Bank ended in disaster as four men and a stolen construction robot were slain. A number of posters were found at the scene, proclaiming the attack to have been carried out by anarchists seeking home rule for Ravna –'

Smith turned the radio off and put his model kit down. The Space Empire was fighting a two-front war, and while the Ghasts were the more obvious threat, the Yull were continuing to drive along the Western fringe. It was not a pleasant mental image, the thought of lemmings pushing up the British flank. We are at bay, Smith thought, like a... thing that's at bay a lot. Some sort of boat, perhaps?

He got up to clear his mind from the glue fumes and wandered into the living room. The place was a bit of a mess, he reflected: although Suruk was surprisingly neat, the only thing Carveth was good at putting away was cake.

She was sitting on the floor, a large black box in front of her. It looked like a small safe. Two wires ran from the box into the back of the television.

'I got this from the bank,' she said as he approached.

'Thought it might be useful.'

'I hope that's not a deposit box,' Smith replied.

Carveth sighed. 'This is the data recorder from that construction robot that was trying to rob the bank.' She snorted. 'As if I'd make off with a box full of stolen money.'

'Well, good.'

'I threw the box away. The stolen money's in the biscuit tin.' She turned the wires slightly.

Rhianna put her head around the door. 'Is the TV broken? Let's make our own entertainment!' she added, glancing at the guitar propped against the wall.

'We're fine thanks,' Smith replied quickly. 'Look.'

The screen flickered into life. Suddenly they were looking at two huge robots: hulking, top-heavy machines patched up and customised to the point where their original function could no longer be discerned. Numbers scrolled down the left side of the screen.

'Right,' the robot on the left said, addressing the screen, 'here's the plan. You and the boys go down to the bank, break in and bring us the money. Then you leave the evidence behind and bring the loot to either me or Rom here.'

'Yeah,' said the robot on the right. 'Like what Ram said. Then the rozzers'll go lookin' for the wrong people, and we'll split the cash. You can get a new coat of yellow paint, maybe some new buckets for your arms. Maybe you won't have to work construction at all anymore.'

'Don't be soft, Rom. He's a JCB. He wants to be in construction.'

The right robot lumbered around to face its colleague, like a howitzer swinging into position. 'Who're you calling soft? That does not bleedin' compute.'

'Nor does your face. Sometimes, Rom, I find it hard to believe that we share the same motherboard.'

'Leave it out! My motherboard is a saint and you know it!'

'Bollocks. Your motherboard's had so many new screws that –' He did not finish his sentence, because his colleague punched him in the head. With a sound like an avalanche in a junkyard, the robots leaped on one another.

'Upload this to your hard drive, you bastard!'

'I'll reboot you in the arse!'

The screen went black.

'Wow,' Rhianna said. 'That was brutal.'

'Wait a moment,' Smith said. He pulled the piece of paper from his pocket. 'Those robbers dropped this.' He unfolded the paper, frowned, and held it up for the others to see.

SMASH THE SPACE EMPIRE!
LIBERTY FOR RAVNAVAR!

Will you stand by while jackals and hyenas gnaw on the seat of power? Will you let Capitalist lapdogs gobble your privileges? Rejoice, Ravnavar, for the Imperialist octopus has sung its swan song.

The day of revolution is upon us! Cast off the jackboots of the oppressor! Beat the yoke of tyranny! For from the melting pot of the city the simmering wrath of the people shall boil onto the streets!

POPULAR FIST – UP THE PEOPLE!

'Hmm,' said Smith. 'This sounds like red revolution. Either that or they want us to take our shoes off and make a cake. Have either of you heard of Popular Fist before?'

'Nope,' Carveth said.

'Sorry,' Rhianna replied. 'I guess they're kind of...

not popular enough.'

'Well,' Smith said, 'it looks as if they're linked to this bank robbery. We ought to find them and discover whether they're behind all this subversion.'

Carveth got up. 'I thought those robot gangsters were behind it.'

'Curious,' said Smith. 'There's obviously something going on here. The question is, where? And to a lesser extent, why and how? And arguably, who? Or whom.'

Rhianna said, 'Hey guys, I've got an idea.'

'Splendid.'

'Let's go to Robot Row!'

Smith looked at Carveth. The android shrugged.

'Robot Row,' Rhianna said. 'It's famous. It's a totally authentic street market in the old quarter of Ravnavar City, with traditional market stalls and ancient indigenous pickpockets.' Her eyes, usually slightly glazed, lit up. 'Let's all go! We can look round and maybe get some information on what's really happening in the city.'

Carveth pulled a face. 'It sounds dangerous.'

'Well, Polly, they do have ice cream.'

'I'm in.'

*   *   *

The suns blazed down on Robot Row, as half a dozen species brushed shoulders and tried to steal one another's wallets. Stalls lined the street, offering goods of varying legality. The still, hot air was full of noise and the smell of greasy food. M'Lak and human policemen patrolled the streets. On the right, a woman with an eye-patch sold candy floss and fighting knives. On the left, a fat bearded man argued with two naval officers on shore leave, who were trying to buy Selluvian Brain

Spice, illegal on fifteen worlds. As Smith passed by, a scuffle broke out as one of the sailors accursed the spice merchant of cutting his wares with mango chutney.

It was often said that you could purchase anything on Robot Row, although home delivery was less easy to arrange. Carveth paused in front of a stall advertising low-key imports and tried to order six kilos of Battenberg cake and a pony, and was discreetly led away by Smith.

'Careful, chaps,' he muttered as they slipped through the crowd. 'There's more pickpockets and flick-knives here than on a school trip to Paris.'

A moment later, he felt fingers brush his own, and he turned, ready to belt the thieving little bugger. It was actually Rhianna, trying to hold hands. Smith let her warm, dry hand clasp his, feeling slightly exhilarated at having a proper girlfriend but unsure what to do next.

Suruk slipped out of the crowd: years of hunting had made him very good at going unnoticed. 'I have been on a fact-finding mission,' he announced. 'The main fact is that haggling is much easier when you are carrying a spear. I like it here,' he declared, as a trio of soldiers passed by, eating rehydrated tikka pies. 'The stall-keepers offer their wares at knock-down prices, once you have knocked them down a few times. Furthermore,' he added, raising his voice to a loud snarl over the sound of the crowd, 'I have discovered how to find these dangerous anarchists.'

Carveth sighed. 'That shouldn't be difficult. They'll try to recruit you.'

'Not so,' Suruk replied. 'We shall find the Popular Fist by eating ice cream. Over there.'

Under a wide awning, a brass robot in a striped jacket and a straw hat was tightening the screws on its false moustache. Below the waist, it was all wheels, gears and freezer boxes.

'Ice cream!' Carveth's eyes seemed to grow in both size and intensity. Something like bloodlust glinted in them.

The robot swept its arm towards a table. 'Giuseppe's Traditional Ices, ladies and gentlemen. From Yorkshire bitter to Columbian coffee, we have every flavour for you: brewed in a vat and spurted out of a nozzle, just like back home.'

'Just point it at my face!' Carveth cried.

'Three cones, my good fellow,' Smith said. 'And some sort of bucket for my pilot.'

The robot dispensed three cones and a sundae glass. 'Shall I do a Flake on those, sir?'

'I think we're alright, actually.'

They sat and watched several worlds go by. A butterfly dragon swung down from the sky, stared at them for a moment, and disappeared in a buzz of wings. On the far side of the street, one of the Ravnavari Lancers bobbed past on the back of a shadar, the crowd sensibly parting before his mount.

Smith leaned back in his chair. He found the sight of Rhianna eating ice cream strangely fascinating, and didn't want her distracted.

Suruk suddenly clapped his hands over his mandibles. He screwed his eyes shut and shuddered.

'Suruk, what is it?' Rhianna asked, leaning forward. 'Are you okay?'

The alien grimaced. 'The ice cream,' he replied. 'I have sensitive fangs.'

'Ooh, that's bad,' Carveth said. 'Which teeth is it?'

'My canines,' Suruk groaned. 'All forty of them.' He sat up. 'I will live. Pain is an illusion to a true warrior.'

'So,' Carveth said, finishing her sundae, 'all this stuff on that poster about oppressed masses and all that. Are there any?'

'Hundreds of years ago,' Smith replied, 'but not now. Back in the over-empire, Britain was exploited by a small gang of crooks. But then the people overthrew the underlings of the over-empire under whom they had been overcome – something like that – and established the guilds we have today. Nowadays, no British citizen is oppressed, regardless of race, creed or class. We have aliens and robots for that.'

Carveth looked at Suruk. The alien gestured at the ice cream vendor, mimed the bill, and nodded surreptitiously towards Smith.

'Mazuran,' Suruk said as Smith rummaged in his pockets for change, 'sometimes, the art of the hunter lies in knowing not when to strike – but when to wait.'

His hand shot out. Suruk snatched something from the street, lifted it up and dumped it onto the table: a robot no bigger than a football, its seven mismatched legs soldered together from scrap. It flailed like an upturned crab, gears clattering.

'And so the prey is snared,' Suruk said.

'Ease off, guv'nor!' the scrapbot warbled. 'I wasn't doing nothing!'

Suruk reached out and flicked a switch on the machine's underside. A tiny panel slid back, and a stream of coins tinkled onto the tabletop. 'Oh, *indeed*,' the M'Lak said. 'This device was following us,' he explained. 'No doubt it intended to steal our possessions.'

'Leave it out!' the robot protested. 'I'm just tryin' to provide for me young peripherals, what's been struck down by the cockney virus. I've done no 'arm!'

Smith scowled. 'Nonsense. I've had my valuables pinched in a crowd before. Very discomforting business. Right, then… spill the beans.'

'Not the beans! Don't send me back to the canning factory, guv'nor, please!'

'You used to work in a canning factory?'

'I used to be a can! It's no life for a robot, being full of beans.'

Rhianna leaned forward. 'It's okay. We're looking for a bunch of guys called Popular Fist. Do you know them?'

'No, miss. But I know someone who might.'

'Then you can take us to them,' Smith said.

Carveth glanced over her shoulder. 'Good idea. You guys go and check, and I'll keep watch. And I'll be in disguise, hiding my face behind several ice cream cones.'

'No, you're coming with us,' Smith replied. 'Remember that time you said you'd rather be dead than fat? Well, you might not end up dead today. But if you keep eating…'

'Oh, alright.'

Smith nodded to the ice-cream robot. 'Thanks. And you didn't see us, if anyone asks.'

'Of course. I saw nothing, sir. I was preoccupied with a blockage in my pipes.'

'I could help with that,' Carveth added.

The robot rolled back, adjusting its straw hat. 'Madam, please. Have you no dignity?'

Smith reflected that, having seen Carveth eat, the robot ought to know full well how much dignity she possessed.

*　　*　　*

'This way, squire,' said the pickpocket. They wove their way through the crowd, past hawkers of weapons, tools, services and food for a dozen species. Suruk was carrying the thief by two of its spindly legs. 'Take a left at the next stall,' the robot squeaked.

'He'd better not be leading us into trouble,' Carveth said. 'I can hardly run away from anything after all that food,' she added grimly. 'I don't trust his sort.'

'But he's a robot, just like you,' Rhianna replied. They passed a stall advertising the services of Martin Poole: ratcatcher and master pie-maker. 'Don't you think of robots as part of the same, er, ethnic group as yourself?'

'What? I'm an android. He is a tin can propped up on cutlery. I can't have feelings for anything that doesn't look like a person.'

'Except for your electric toothbrush,' Suruk put in. 'Quite often at night, I hear a revving sound –'

'Shut up, Suruk.'

'Just here,' said the pickpocket. 'On the left.'

They looked at a dark and narrow doorway. Steps led into a dim room, strewn with cushions and drug paraphernalia. 'Careful, men,' Smith said. 'This looks like the dwelling place of either hardened criminals or media studies students.'

He took the lead. In the weak light, he made out ports in the walls, where a variety of down-at-wheel scrapbots lurked. Three automatons lay sprawled in a corner on standby, slowly passing round a cable connected to an opium simulator.

'Boss!' the pickpocket called. 'Boss, it's me!'

A head slid out of an alcove on a jointed neck. Following it came long, slender arms built from anglepoise lamps. Each ended in spindly fingers, like an insect's legs. It was wearing three pairs of fingerless gloves.

'What's all this?' it demanded.

'We have your scrapbot,' Smith said.

Part of the furniture seemed to come alive. A heavy body rose up with a whine of servos and turned to them. Its head was a metal skull, painted with a chipped Union

Jack. Massive nail guns clacked like pincers. 'Give,' it grunted. 'Or I'll smash yer.'

'Easy Bill, easy!' the spindly robot cried. 'Gentlemen, please. Let's do this like civilised people. Come, take a seat. This is my companion and esteemed business partner, William Sticker, formerly of the advertising trade. I am Mark Twelve, acquisitions and resale expert.'

'Isambard Smith, space captain. These are my crew: Suruk the Slayer, Rhianna Mitchell, ship's – er –'

'Health and wellbeing counsellor,' Rhianna said.

'And Polly Carveth, ship's android.'

'Hoity-toity fleshbot,' Bill growled.

'Now Bill, let's not be hasty, eh?' Mark Twelve's head came forward and scrutinised the visitors. 'Yes, I believe that is one of my charges you've got there. You see, gentlemen, and dear ladies, I am a device of benevolence. Here I keep a home, free of charge, for whatever unfortunate robots are tossed by life's iniquities onto the scrapheap of – well, scrap. I care for 'em, you see.'

Smith looked at the slew of limbs, springs, joints and sensors around the alcove. 'From the looks of it, you make them as well.'

'You're most observant, Captain Smith. These are hard times to be a robot, you know. What with the Robot Ripper dismantling units of easy virtue and the cockney virus running rampant, things could hardly be worse. Why, only last week Bill here caught a dose of rust right in his –'

'Oi!' said Sticker.

'A thousand pardons, William. But I won't delay you any longer, Captain. Thank you for bringing young Charlie back. Now, if you'll excuse me, I've got to fix a spocket or two.'

Smith shook his head. 'Not so fast. "Young Charlie"

tried to pick Suruk's pocket. If you want him back, we want something in return.'

Twelve's head retracted. 'Well, that changes things, doesn't it?' His processor clicked. 'Contemplating variables... reviewing situation... alright, what do you need?'

'Information. There's an organisation called the Popular Fist. We want to find them.'

'That could be difficult.'

'Why?'

'Well, they're very small.' Twelve looked at Sticker. 'Also, they meet in dangerous territory. Do you know the old Picture House?'

'No,' Smith said.

'It's in the docks. And the Cranes have the docks.'

Rhianna said, 'You mean that the docks have cranes.'

Sticker loomed up beside her. 'Nah. Rom and Ram Crane. They own the docks. And their boss has all the rest – the Ringleader, they call him. He used to run a circus, taming lions. If anything goes on here, they take a cut. Or else they take a limb. And there's only so many times you can get your limbs soldered back on.'

'Cranes?' Smith said. 'Would they happen to know a – well, a sort of digging machine?'

Mark Twelve jerked upright in a flurry of limbs. 'Ben the Builder. He's one of the best-connected thugs in the robot underworld. They say that if there's a card game, or a shadar-race – Ben can fix it.'

'Yes, he can,' Bill Sticker growled.

'It is he who requires fixing now,' Suruk said. He smiled.

'Thank you,' Smith said. He nodded to Suruk. The alien lifted the robot pickpocket, looked it over, and tossed it on the ground. It scurried over to hide behind Sticker. Suruk shrugged. 'It has no skull. You are welcome to it.'

Smith said, 'Well then, it sounds as if we know where to go to find these people. I'm sure these Cranes won't be a problem. And now, we'll leave you to your business.'

'You're most kind,' said Mark Twelve. 'Charmed to meet you. Goodbye, and be back soon, eh?'

*   *   *

It was almost time for bed. Isambard Smith opened his Civiliser, peered into the cylinder and closed it up again. He thought about reading up on Popular Fist, but he felt too tired. He sat down at the captain's desk, which was currently covered in bits of model kit, and yawned.

'Hey, Isambard. What do you think?'

He looked up, wondering what Rhianna wanted, and was astonished. She wore a dark blue skirt with a matching jacket and highly polished boots. Her hair was neatly tied back, and there was a strip of black ribbon around her neck.

'Crikey!' he said. 'You look – well – jolly good, really.'

'You think so?' She pulled the skirt out and spun around. Smith felt a rush of pride that someone so attractive was walking out with him, and then hoped that it wasn't too obvious. For one thing, letting one's pride show wasn't terribly British, and for another, it made walking uncomfortable. 'You don't think it's too much? I mean, I have to wear proper shoes and everything.'

'Well, it looks smashing. You should definitely keep it on. Unless you're planning on taking it off, that is,' he added, moving his eyebrows seductively.

Rhianna laughed, which wasn't exactly what he'd

intended. 'I'm a bit tired, really. I've been thinking...' she added thoughtfully, and Smith felt a flash of terror that she had been thinking about 'us', '... about my psychic powers.'

'Good-oh.'

'Do you know what a premonition is?'

'Yes. It's a little word, like *a* or *the*.'

'It's when you see something bad in the future. I've got an amazing gift, but I don't know how to use it for good.' She walked into the room. 'Do you remember when that Edenite high-priest tried to kill us all, and I made him die?'

'Absolutely. That was brilliant.'

'Was it? Really?'

'Of course. He got eaten by space frogs. Served the evil bugger right.'

'But I was, like, responsible for his death.'

'Nonsense, old girl. All you did was knowingly direct him into a room full of killer frogs. He could have got out of there and learned his lesson. But he stayed.'

'Because we locked him in.'

'Well, he had a gun. And he was very rude about Carveth. All that "Whore of Babylon" stuff. I know she's hardly a nun, but I won't stand by when women are being mistreated, or horses, or any other animals. If anyone's got blood on their hands, it's the killer frogs. Except it was mainly on their teeth. A right mess, now I think about it. Anyhow, they're gone, so's he, and everything's fine. Where was I?'

She was quiet for a moment. Then she said, 'You're worried too, aren't you?'

'Only about tomorrow. I don't know what to expect from these anarchist types, that's all.'

'Would it help to talk about it?'

'Hmm... could I just rest my head on your chest

instead? That would cheer me up a lot. I'd still be listening, if you want to talk about your stuff.'

*   *   *

'So, overall, it's a kind of holistic thing,' Rhianna said half an hour later. 'I've always, like, believed in extra-sensory perception, but not really in a real way, you know?'

'Mm.'

'And auras, and psychic defence? I mean, I can actually do those now. Really actually.'

'Mmm.'

'So what do you think? Isambard?'

He looked up and blinked. 'Me? Think? Well, most of the time it's complete piffle, really. All this auras nonsense and that sort of thing. Candles made of earwax and sticking pins in things. Except when *you* do it, of course. You're the best girlfriend I could ever realistically ask for, Rhianna, and I mean it.'

Rhianna slid down on Smith's bed and adjusted her position against him. 'Yeah,' she said, after a while. 'For a colonialist oppressor, you're pretty cool too, really.'

*   *   *

Smith woke up to find that Rhianna was snoring next to him. He got up carefully, not waking her. While sleeping with girls was excellent, it still felt wrong not to be able to wear pyjamas and break wind in bed. He put his dressing gown on and left his quarters.

Carveth sat in the living room, eating breakfast cereal. 'Alright, Boss,' she said. 'Give me a hand with this, would you? I've had three helpings of Rightos and I've still not seen the free toy.'

'Are you sure that's a good idea, eating the whole box just to get the free gift?'

'It's a wind-up dreadnought.'

'Pass me a bowl.'

He ate thoughtfully, trying not to think of cardboard as he spooned the Rightos into his mouth. At least it wasn't Shredded Wheat, which tasted like a freeze-dried toupee. As tended to happen, Carveth finished first.

She stood up, adjusting her utility waistcoat. As usual, she wore a collarless shirt, the sleeves rolled up, and trousers with pockets on the thighs. Today, however, she had accessorised with a red scarf. She tugged a flat cap out of her waistband and jammed it onto her head. 'What do you think of this?' she asked. 'Is this how dangerous anarchists look?'

'Very good, I think.' Carveth looked like a sulky, disreputable technician about to down tools and start an argument, which struck him as a clever disguise until he remembered that that was exactly what she was. 'Where's Suruk?'

'Getting ready for meeting the anarchists. I think he's expecting to have to impress them by creating anarchy. I'm sure they'll love him: he can barely wash his mandibles without going mental. Have you seen the way he wrings out a face flannel? It's sinister.' She sighed. 'I wish we had someone to back us up. I could do with having Rick Dreckitt behind me. Actually, in front would be better.' She looked rather wistful, no doubt contemplating her romance with him. 'It was like *Brief Encounter* with us. Except there was more than one encounter. And it wasn't all that brief, actually.'

Smith reflected that Carveth had a point. Dreckitt had carved a living as an android bounty hunter before becoming part of the Service: no doubt he had experience of dealing with desperate men. And, in the form of Carveth, desperate women.

That was the problem with working for the secret service: you never quite knew what was going on. In fact, the Service was so secretive that it was doubtful whether any of its members were entirely sure. It had been months since Smith had seen the master spy, W, or even Major Wainscott, head of the Service's military operations. Admittedly, Wainscott could usually be detected by the trail of devastation, but even that had gone quiet. Perhaps he had been captured by the enemy, or returned by his own side to the Sunnyvale Home for the Bewildered.

The door opened and Suruk entered from the hold. He was not exactly sweating, but he had a slightly ruffled look and his eyes were more bloodshot than usual. 'Greetings, humans!' he said, advancing to the teapot. 'The sun rises on Ravnavar and I thirst for honourable battle. What are the chances of getting a decent fight out of these people tonight?'

'I'm not sure,' Smith replied. 'I think it's best to work quietly.'

The M'Lak nodded. 'Fear not. I shall strike from the shadows.' He sipped his tea. 'I must say, I find this politics business rather complex.'

'Really? Well,' Smith began, 'it's quite simple, really. You have the two main parties, who represent the interests of the working people and business respectively. Then you have smaller parties that believe in, er, other stuff. They're usually crackpots. Personally, I'm a floating voter.'

'It is only appropriate. You live on a spaceship.' Suruk sighed. 'Personally, Mazuran, I see virtue in both left and right. It is only right that there should be social justice for all citizens, but I am also in favour of the interests of the nation. Yet I must make a choice. Why not just make one big party that is both national and socialist?'

'Perhaps you should just vote Liberal.'

Carveth had given up eating the Rightos and was rooting about in the box. 'Don't you lot have political parties, then? How do you know who's ahead in the polls?'

Suruk frowned. 'I would look at the top of the pole and see whose head it is. The fact is, we do not have the same problems as you, since humans are somewhat punier. We have no religion, no great desire for property, and luxury is shameful for warriors, so there is little reason for us to fight among ourselves except where there is a formal war being organised. Instead, we M'Lak share a common policy for foreign affairs, entertainment and defence.'

'Meaning that you all get together and fight someone else.'

'Exactly. On which subject,' he added, 'we have some time before this gathering tonight. Let us ready our spirits with Scrabble!'

The Plot Against Ravnavar

Somewhere out there, Isambard Smith thought, there are billions of lemming men getting ready to kill us all. While the Ghast Empire shoots us in the gut, the Greater Galactic Happiness and Friendship Collective will take an axe to our necks. And somehow, this building is linked to it all.

It wasn't much of a place. Many of the public buildings of Ravnavar were as grand and stately as the empire that had created them, but the old Picture House looked as if it had been put up by frontiersmen who didn't plan on staying long. There was a strange mixture of haunted house and Wild West saloon in the design, together with a suggestion of the sort of top hat favoured by men who enjoyed tying maidens to railway tracks.

'This is it,' Smith said. He stood by the car as the others emerged. In the streets around them, the docks creaked and banged. Cranes stood against the darkening sky like gallows. 'I'll do the talking,' he said.

Smith locked the car and strode to the doors. He opened them for Carveth and Rhianna, and walked in. Suruk took the rear. The alien was unarmed except for four large knives. Smith carried his Civiliser under his jacket.

The foyer was dim, red and stale-smelling. On the far side of the room, a small man watched them from behind thick spectacles. 'Help you?' he asked, folding a newspaper away.

Smith approached. 'Four for Popular Fist, please.'

The man squinted at them. 'You?'

'Yes, us. And I'll have a copy of your manifesto, my good man. Chop chop.'

Very slowly and deliberately, he looked them over: Smith, in his long coat and red jacket, Suruk, impassive and poised, Rhianna, casually elegant in her hired dress, and Carveth, who was looking for a food counter. 'What's the password?'

'One moment,' Smith replied.

He ushered Suruk and Rhianna back. 'Nobody told me there would be a password!' he hissed.

'The crimes of our enemies shall be washed away in a crimson torrent of blood!' Suruk said.

'Bit long for a password, isn't it?'

'Password, Mazuran?'

'Never mind.' He turned to Rhianna. 'Look, Rhianna. Is there any chance you could, you know –'

'Read his mind?'

'Exactly. That's just what I was thinking.'

'I don't know how to do that, Isambard.'

Smith glanced back over his shoulder, to give the man behind the counter a reassuring smile, and saw Carveth talking to him. 'Have you got any popcorn?' she asked.

'Welcome, friend,' he replied, gesturing to the entrance on the far side of the hall.

'No, really –' Carveth protested, but by then Smith was pushing her towards the door.

Smith took the lead. He was suddenly in a narrow, dark corridor. It smelled of sawdust and old carpet.

They took seats at the back. A thin man with a goatee beard stood on the stage, haranguing about a dozen people dotted around the hall.

'What good has the Leighton Wakazashi corporation ever done?' the speaker demanded. 'Why does our government trust those crooks, whose only solution to any problem at all is to try to get a bunch of man-eating space monsters through quarantine?' His voice sank low. 'I don't know who's worse. You don't see Procturan Rippers screwing each other over for a god-damn percentage. Or wearing those suits with shoulder pads. Or shouting into mobile phones! Do you? Don't believe it when they tell you that greed is good, or that lunch is for wimps! Leighton Wakazashi claims that wealth trickles down onto the poor. Well, something does, and it's yellow alright, but it sure as hell isn't gold!'

Cheering broke out among the listeners. Actually, Smith thought, the fellow had a point. Smith had crossed paths with the corporation's executives on several occasions, and had been left with a very unsavoury feeling.

'But that's enough from me,' the speaker said. 'Now for some real fire. Friends, I give you our lady of rebellion, the scholar of the barricades, the woman who turns a moment into a movement: Miss Julia Chigley!'

Onto the stage strode a pale, dark-haired young woman in a boiler suit with a red sash. She stood before the microphone and glared out at the audience for a moment, as if challenging them to throw her out. Then she made a fierce gesture with her fist. 'Up the people! Up the front!'

Blimey, thought Smith.

'Brothers and sisters,' she began, in a surprisingly genteel voice, 'we are at war. Not just with the Ghasts, not just with the Yull, but with corruption. With insidious forces within the Space Empire that gnaw at its very bowels.'

Smith glanced to his right. Rhianna was watching with great interest. Carveth had started to fidget and swing her legs. Suruk was nowhere to be seen. That was worrying in itself, but there was no time to find him now.

'I speak of a conspiracy, aimed not only at the loyal citizens of Ravnavar – man, alien and robot alike – but at *you*. A conspiracy that is alive and well.' She paused and looked into the audience. Given the bad lighting, they must have seemed like blurs in the darkness, but Smith could not lose the feeling that she was looking at him. It reminded him of the last speech he had sat through from end to end, at Midwich Grammar Sports Day about thirty years before.

'Our demands are incendiary – to those in power, pure dynamite.' Miss Chigley raised her hand, closing her fingers as she numbered the points. 'One: free bus passes for our brothers in struggle, the under-fives. Two: the immediate banning of televised talent contests. Three: better tea rations for our boys at the front and the workers who support them. Four: the recognition of moral fibre as a chemical compound. These are our demands, Ravnavar – do you have the strength to meet them?'

In the moderate uproar that followed, Smith leaned over to Rhianna. 'It all sounds rather more, well, reasonable than we'd expected, don't you think?'

Rhianna opened her hands. 'Are you sure this is the right place?'

'We are the greatest empire in space,' Miss Chigley resumed, 'but not when we forget our moral fibre. Vigilance is all! In our struggle for justice, we must purge our very language of subversive jargon foreign to the cause. For what is a panini but a cheese toastie with added bourgeois sentimentality? What is a cup-cake but a fairy cake that has appropriated too much icing?'

Well, Smith thought, maybe she was a bit cranky.

The door burst open. Light shot in, and a long shadow fell across the stage.

The first speaker ran for the exit, reached the door, and flew back as if hit by a battering ram. He crashed against the side of the stage and flopped half across it, dead.

A figure stalked into the hall. It was a humanoid robot, dressed like a dandy: red tailcoat, long cuffs, a walking cane in one gloved hand. The machine had one camera-eye – the other was painted onto the smooth metal of its face – and a moustache made from ornate clock hands. On top of its head sat what looked like a chimney-shaped top hat, and was in fact a small chimney.

Policemen ran forward behind it, their blue uniforms like water poured into the room, but it was the robot that Smith looked at, and recognised. It was the dandy from the bank, the one who had gunned down the robber. Mark Twelve had called him the Ringleader.

The police rushed in. Smith thought of his gun, but did not reach for it.

The Ringleader shook his head sadly. 'What a scene. What a scene! The sight of such uproarious treachery, here in our fair city...' He waved a hand airily. 'It saddens my patriotic soul. Officers, you know what to do. Knock 'em down and lock 'em up!'

*   *   *

'You know what the problem with this place is?' the Ringleader inquired through the bars.

Smith looked around the cell. The bench was occupied by Carveth and Rhianna, and so it was his turn to stand up. Sitting on the floor was not a pleasant alternative. In the background, he could hear the rumble of police work, as the officers put money in the drinks machine and filled out forms. It was swelteringly hot.

'Well,' Smith replied, 'It's got you in it.'

The robot paused. He leaned in, close to the bars, and with a tiny mechanical whine, the tips of his moustache rose until they pointed to ten to two. 'You've got a tongue on you, for now. Tell me something. What do you know of the great gangs of Ravnavar, my loquacious friend? The Jackhammers, the Two-Percenters, the Blueberries? Do you know what unites those deadly warriors?'

'They've all got silly names?'

'They fell to mine own hand.' The Ringleader paused, then let out a hard, metallic laugh. 'I like you,' he said. 'You've got some fire to you. Perhaps, when this city is mine, you will sit beside me. You, though, and you,' he added, pointing to Carveth and Rhianna, 'I discard. You are tepid.' He waved a hand eloquently, like an elderly royal greeting peasants.

'I've got a friend who'd like to meet you,' Smith said. 'You'd inspire him.'

'To glory?'

'To violence. His name is Suruk.'

'A Morlock ape. I don't dally with savages.'

'He could turn you to scrap.'

'Then perhaps he will present himself.' The Ringleader gestured grandly at the roof. 'Great men are not born: they are forged. On the streets, in the heat of battle, or, like myself, in a two-part stainless steel mould. Such men deserve the lion's share.'

'Did you learn that being a ringmaster?' Smith inquired. 'When you were learning how to dress like a clown?'

The Ringleader was silent for a moment. 'I would... rend you limb from limb, shred you like gerbil bedding. But I will leave you here, with your view. So that when real warriors take over Ravnavar, when we take the lion's share, you can watch it all burn. Farewell.'

He turned. Rhianna said, 'Hey.'

The Ringleader paused and looked round. 'You've got something to say to me?'

'Yes, actually, I have.' Rhianna stood up, lifting her skirts slightly, and strode to the bars. 'Do they do vegan food here?'

The Ringleader turned and walked away.

'Well,' Rhianna demanded, turning, 'What do we do?'

'I don't know.' Carveth looked even smaller than usual: police detention seemed to be shrinking her. 'But we've got to work fast. We're stuck in jail, this robot bloke is planning some sort of coup, and I have to get back and feed my hamster.'

Smith looked out the cell window. Past the bars, he could see the street outside the station. Beyond that was the edge of the great park of Ravnavar. Behind the fence, two lancers were exercising their shadar. On the far side of the park, a young ravnaphant lumbered across the grass, having a rest between carrying classloads of children on its back.

'I know!' he said. 'We could pick the lock with a hairpin. Have you got a hairpin, Rhianna?'

'Sorry?' Rhianna said.

Carveth leaned over. 'You know, one of those wire things you use when you style your hair. After brushing it? As part of being tidy and hygienic? Oh, never mind.'

'Don't worry,' Smith said. 'I'll come up with something.'

'It's Gerald I'm worried about,' Carveth said. 'He's only got half a bottle of water.'

'You there!' Smith shouted through the bars. 'Police fellows! Is Kallarn the Enforcer there? We've been unjustly imprisoned and my pilot's hamster may die. I'm warning you – you don't want to be responsible for that. Hello? Civis Britannicus sum, don't you know. Habeas Corpus and all that. Arse,' he added, turning away. 'They're not listening.' He took a deep breath. 'Men, we will just have to do what any good British officer would and escape.'

He walked to the window and looked out into the sunshine.

A figure strolled into view, wearing a wide-brimmed hat and a sandwich board. On the front of the board, written in chalk as if by a child, were the words 'Deliverance is close at hand'.

People steered clear – sensibly, Smith thought, for the fellow was clearly a religious loon. The figure stopped opposite the police station, looked up, and took off its hat.

It was Suruk. He smiled at the window. 'Hey!' Carveth shouted, and Rhianna took up the cry. 'We're up here!'

The alien pushed his hat down again, and his face was lost to view. Then he turned and walked away. The back of the sandwich board said 'I have prepared a small diversion'.

Suruk disappeared into the crowd. 'Where'd he go?' Carveth demanded, but Smith knew that by now the old hunter would have ditched his disguise.

A thin, repetitive squeak rang out over the sound of the street below. Slowly, a box on wheels rolled between the pedestrians. The upper body of a robot protruded from the box, and it was wearing a straw boater.

'Ices, ladies and gentlemen, finest ices! Perfect for a hot day! Special discount for officers of the law!'

'Ice cream?' Carveth said. 'That's it? That has got to be the crappest diversion ever.'

'He's stopped on a double yellow line,' Smith replied.

'Hallelujah, free at last. That's rubbish. And it's making me hungry.'

'Oi!' A large grey shape pushed through the crowd. The hulking form of Bill Sticker lumbered over to the ice-cream robot and jabbed a finger at its striped torso. 'I bought this Cornetto off you and it shorted out my face,' Sticker bellowed. 'You'd better be insured for this kind of bollocks!'

Sticker grabbed the vendor and gave him a good shake. The vendor responded, perhaps unintentionally, by spraying Sticker with soft scoop. Sticker stumbled back, roaring, and struck the vendor's box. A slew of cones rolled across the road. People stopped and made room: dogs and M'Lak spawn strained to get at the fallen food.

A door slammed below the window, and a policeman strode out. 'That's enough of that,' he cried, and he blew his whistle. 'Stop right there, you two.'

A second officer ran out to join him, and began pushing the crowd away from the ice cream. A Labrador barked and tried to climb on him, and small dogs swarmed around his knees.

Smith tugged the bars. 'See if you can find something to get us out of here,' he said. 'Maybe we can –'

A shadar jumped over the fence like a steeplechaser and landed beside the policemen. On its back, a Ravnavari Lancer struggled with the reins. The shadar opened its maw, and its tongue shot out like a catapult. With a loud *thwack*, the fleshy blob landed on Sticker's metal chest and he was dragged off his feet. The beast bit Sticker around the waist, and shook its head as if to break the robot in half, snarling in triumph. People scattered; even the dogs thought better of arguing with a chameleon the size of a small dinosaur.

'Damn it!' the rider cried. 'Spit that robot out!'

In the distance, sirens started to wail. The shadar roared. Dogs barked. One of the policemen slipped on the ice cream.

'Boss?' Carveth said, 'Whatever you're going to do, do it fast.'

The sirens grew closer. From the depths of the park, they were answered by a noise somewhere between a bull and a foghorn.

'Guys?' Rhianna began. 'Um, guys? I think we should, you know, get down. And, like, cover our heads, maybe?'

Sixty tons of enraged ravnaphant ploughed straight through the fence. Smith would never know whether it was defending its territory from the incursion of the shadar, or just really liked ice cream, because he was too busy throwing himself on the floor next to Rhianna and Carveth.

The beast missed its target and headbutted the side of the police station. It turned on the spot, taking out most of the lower storey with its tail, and bellowed.

Suddenly, the back wall of the cell was gone. Smith staggered upright and helped Rhianna get up. Together, they hauled Carveth to her feet.

They walked out. The rubble made a convenient

ramp to get to street level.

Dust rose in a cloud. The shadar spat Bill Sticker out and bounded into the distance, pursued by dogs, as a police van swung in too fast and crashed into a fire hydrant. The ice-cream robot squeaked away at high speed, followed by Bill Sticker. Somewhere, fireworks had started. Two large dogs mated furiously by the side of the road. The ravnaphant climbed onto the back of a dustcart and started to stamp it flat. Thunder rumbled in the sky.

Suruk waited under a lamppost. As Smith approached, the alien ducked down and picked something from the road.

'Free ice cream,' Suruk said. 'Excellent.'

A rocket streaked into the sky. Smith brushed himself down. 'Nice diversion, old chap. Let's go,' he added, 'before anything else blows up.'

They walked, a little shakily, into the alleyway alongside the station. Suruk led the way: he seemed quite comfortable in the back streets of Ravnavar. Carveth followed, and then Rhianna. Smith took the rear. He was just beginning to think that he recognised the place when something prodded him hand in the back.

'Hands up,' a woman said.

He grimaced and turned around. Julia Chigley stood a few yards away, half in shadow. A massive revolver jutted out of her hand.

'So,' she said. 'I saw you people creep into the meeting last night, just before the raid. I always knew we had powerful enemies.'

'Don't flatter yourself,' Smith replied.

'Alright, feeble enemies. But devious ones.'

'Look,' Smith said, 'Don't take offence, here, but it's not you they were after. I mean, they were after you, of course, but not just you. You're just a scapegoat. Their real enemy is someone else.'

She reached up and ran a finger around the inside of her collar. 'Who?'

'I don't know. But their aim is to bring anarchy to the whole city.'

'Great!'

'*Not* great. Once the city is on its knees, they will blow it off the face of the Earth. Well, blow it off the face of Ravnavar, but you see what I'm saying.'

Chigley frowned, and her grip on the pistol tightened. Sunlight glinted on the metal. 'Blow whose knees where? Does he normally talk like this?'

'This is a good day,' Carveth replied. 'Look, could you put the gun down? Please?'

'It is strongly advised,' Suruk added.

'No. Someone out there wants Popular Fist destroyed. I mean to fight for it. They fear our movement,' she added.

'Frankly, I doubt it,' Smith replied. 'I've seen a pigeon produce a more impressive movement on a statue's head.' He felt sweat forming on his back. A droplet crept down the side of his face, like an insect. 'Listen, they're trying to fit you up. Two days ago, there was a robbery at the Automated Bank. The robbers meant to leave a poster behind, purporting to be from your people. They wanted you to take the blame.'

Chigley took a step back, into the shadows. 'Prove it.'

'Certainly.' Smith reached into his back pocket and took out the poster. He opened the paper up. 'See?'

'This is crazy. But who would mess with us? Why, we've got over twenty members – twenty-five, once I've chased the subs up.'

'You look dangerous, but you're too small to hit back hard,' Smith said. 'And now you're on the run. Now they'll be waiting for you to act, and when they do, you'll be playing straight into their hands.'

'Which would be really bad,' Rhianna added.

Smith said, 'Look, why don't you just go legit? You could enter the next by-election. Post some leaflets, kiss a few babies – the sky's the limit.'

'Yeah,' she replied, 'but that wouldn't be very exciting, would it?' For a long moment, Chigley held them at gunpoint. Then she seemed to deflate. She lowered the gun and her shoulders drooped. 'Who am I kidding?' she demanded. 'I mend photocopiers for a living. I'm no revolutionary. Here, have your gun back.'

She held out the pistol, handle-first. It was Smith's Civiliser, presumably stolen from the police station in the chaos. He tucked it out of sight.

'Look on the bright side,' he said. 'If you weren't being oppressed by the state before, you certainly are now.'

*   *   *

'Now this,' said Mark Twelve, 'is not exactly what I wanted to hear.'

They stood in the darkened crime den off Robot Row, surrounded by artificial vice. In the far corner, one of the robots took a massive download from the opiate cable and rolled off its couch with a sound like an accident in a saucepan factory.

'Me neither, funnily enough,' Smith replied. He folded his arms and looked down at the robot, ignoring the seat he had been offered. The situation was bad enough: it did not help that he had been obliged to pay the ice cream vendor for the loss of half of his stock and a straw boater, about which Suruk had been strangely evasive.

Mark Twelve sighed. He had been assembling a scrapbot out of a toy car and a teapot, and now his gloved fingers carefully set it down. 'You've caused me a lot of trouble, Captain Smith. My way of work, indeed, my dears, my whole lifestyle, requires a certain degree of discretion. And that's something I cannot expect from a man who sets two dinosaurs loose outside a police station.'

Suruk raised a hand. 'Actually, that was me. And technically, they were not dinosaurs. And you have left out the dogs and the police cars and the fire hydrant.'

'Hey,' Rhianna said, 'just chill out, alright? Let's just be still, everyone, and try to concentrate on the issue. If we all form a circle and hold hands –'

'No!' Twelve barked. 'Dear lady, I will not be holding hands with anyone: I'm furious and I've got six arms too many. Oh, and I'm talking to a man wanted not just by the police but by a ruthless metal gangster. So no chilling out. Sorry.'

Smith said, 'What if we get rid of the Ringleader?'

'And how would you do that? You and whose army?'

'Well, I… hmm. Yes, you do have a point there –'

'The People's Army of the Popular Fist!' Carveth exclaimed.

In a rustle of collars and creak of servos, half a dozen heads turned to her.

'The cutting edge of discontented workforce,' she said, almost under her breath. 'A brigade of wild revolutionaries hell-bent on destruction and mayhem. A secretive brotherhood whose shadowy world only we can penetrate – who fight and die at our command.'

'Bollocks,' Mark Twelve replied. 'But supposing it isn't… What do you want me to do?'

'We want your scrapbots to trail the Ringleader,' Smith said. 'We need to find out where he hides out, and who he's reporting to.'

'That could be difficult, my dears.'

'How?' Carveth demanded. 'He's a metal dandy with

a bright red coat, two huge henchmen and an enormous steaming hat.'

'I meant that it could be dangerous.'

'Danger be damned,' Smith replied. 'We need your help. There's something going on beyond mere crime. Somehow, I can't help but suspect the lemming men are behind this. And when the lemmings are behind you, you're usually headed for a fall.'

*   *   *

The insectoid house was in shadow: its inhabitants did not need light to see. The Ringleader tapped the glass of the nearest case and noticed movement, a ripple of armour plate. Slowly, the sleek head of a Procturan Ripper slid out of the dark, and its mouth opened a foot from the robot's head, its breath misting the ferroglass between them.

'Boo,' said the Ringleader, and the extraterrestrial drew back into its lair. 'Come on, boys,' he said to the two huge shapes beside him. 'There's nothing impressive here.'

He led Rom and Ram out of the insectoid house and into the sunshine. Ravnavar Zoo was quiet at this time of the morning. A row of children from the local grammar school trooped past, a teacher at their head. The Ringleader touched the edge of his hat-chimney as the teacher passed. 'A pleasant afternoon to you, madam.'

'Yeah,' said Rom. 'You have a nice day.'

'Yeah,' said Ram. 'Or I'll smash your face.'

The Ringleader spun around. 'Never threaten a child, Ram. Or Rom. You know why? Because children are our future. Especially when the first bunch of slaves dies of old age. Come on.'

The Rankorian Naked Mole Rat was being fed, and a small crowd had gathered to watch chunks of meat being hurled into the pit. The three robots ambled over to the bear enclosure.

'You,' a voice hissed from below. '*Hwup!* Dirty offworlder!'

The Ringleader glanced down. A bear sat at the edge of the enclosure, almost directly below him.

'Yes?'

'Progress update, robot! Do you think I wear this stupid disguise for fun?'

'That's a disguise?'

'*Shup!* I want to know –'

'People are coming. Wait a moment.' Two young men strolled past, engrossed in conversation. One broke out laughing; they did not slow down. A family approached, the parents dragged on by their children. The Ringleader raised a hand.

'Folks, I'm sorry. The bears aren't feeling well today. Best move on.'

A voice behind him said, 'I am very poorly! Nothing to see here!'

One of the children leaned over the edge. 'The bear can talk!'

Rom and Ram lumbered over, and the family hurried away.

'Progress update, stupid offworlder,' the bear snapped.

'Stupid? I'm not the one who tells people that he's a normal bear.'

'That is enough!' The bear reached up and tugged at its scalp. Fur slid away: part of the snout fell off like a mask. The face that looked up at the Ringleader was not that of his usual contact. The jowls sagged; the muzzle was striped with old scars. One of the eyes was blind and white.

In the shadows, lenses watched them.

'I know you,' the Ringleader said. 'Aren't you... Wikwot? The General?'

'The very same,' the lemming man growled.

'What are you doing here?'

'Taking command,' Wikwot said. 'I dug my way out of prison. I crawled for two hundred yards through a stinking tunnel. I came up in the panda enclosure. It was most unpleasant. One day – only one day in each year, the panda is in rut. That one day was yesterday. But I have lemming spirit!' Wikwot licked his chops. 'You want this city, robot?'

The Ringleader nodded.

'Once we took a fine city,' Wikwot said. 'Humans called it Newstadt. They say that the night it joined the Greater Galactic Happiness and Friendship Collective of the Yull, we burned it to the ground. Lies, of course. The noble Yull are innocent of all crimes. But when the British Space Empire falls, there will be plunder for us all. All you have to give me is passage.'

'Passage?'

'Passage from Ravnavar, back to Andor. Back to my army. *Build me a rocket.*'

The Ringleader stretched. 'For the city? Gladly. But, ah, won't your people be a little disappointed when they discover that you were taken alive?'

Wikwot smiled. 'People who disagree with me tend to die.'

The Ringleader laughed. 'Well, there's a doctrine I can get behind.'

'Good. The sooner this city burns, the better. And get on with it. That panda is winking at me again.'

Quietly, young Charlie crept away on half a dozen metal legs.

*   *   *

Night fell on the zoo. Animals from a dozen planets slithered, loped and scrambled back to their beds. The Tawny Kangarams settled back on their tails. The Metamorph stopped pretending to be a zookeeper who had been accidentally shut in a cage and turned back into a tentacled blob.

The bears, however, were not sleeping so well.

'This has got to be a trap,' Polly Carveth said, as Smith tied the end of the rope to the railing. 'We're climbing into a pit full of bears because a robot who we nicked for pickpocketing us says that another robot was talking to one of the bears. Has anyone considered how crazy this is, even by our usual standards?' She looked over her shoulder. 'Loads of people talk to things and it doesn't prove anything. Suruk talks to his skull collection.'

'I do not talk to my skulls. I laugh when I polish them. It is entirely different.'

Smith tested the rope. The night air was cool around him. 'I think the point was that the bear talked back. And keep your voice down. Now, Rhianna, this is really important. Rhianna?'

'Huh? Oh, hi.'

'Right. You have to distract the bears while Suruk and I climb down. Use your psychic powers. Carveth, you can stay up here until we get back.'

The android took a deep breath. 'No. I'm coming with you.'

'Really?'

She nodded. Her face was set. In the moonlight, her skin was like candlewax. 'By my counting, Gerald's got six hours of water left. Let's go.'

'Good stuff,' Smith replied. 'I'll go first. Rhianna,

can you calm the bears, please?'

She gripped the rail with both hands: her mass of wild hair made her look like a passenger in a storm at sea. 'Blessed be, Isambard,' she said, and she made a curious noise in her throat, like an instrument tuning up.

Smith climbed over the railing and took the rope in his hands.

At the edge of the pit, he suddenly realised that he had no idea how to climb down a rope. He had a vague childhood memory of trying: a small boy in big shorts, leaping up to grab the rope in both hands before grimacing and falling off again, having gained nothing except sore palms. Somehow, you were supposed to grip the thing between your legs, presumably without being neutered by friction burns. He had a worrying image of landing heavily in front of a drowsy bear, rolling around and clutching his smouldering groin. Not a good death.

Well, a good captain always led the way. He grabbed the rope, locking it between his legs, and let go of the side. Then he discovered that he wasn't moving at all. He seemed to have lassoed himself.

Below, something large made a loud huffing noise, which he hoped indicated that it was settling down for the night. Very carefully, Smith opened his hands.

He fell. Smith plummeted head-first, the ground suddenly looking very detailed and very hard. The rope snagged his ankle, jerked him to a halt, and suddenly he was dangling four feet off the ground, looking into the puzzled and malodorous face of a brown bear.

'Hello,' he said.

The bear gave him a withering look, snorted and lumbered away. Smith's foot slid out of his boot, and he hit the ground. A moment later, his boot hit him.

'Easy,' he said, checking his head for fractures.

The rope creaked as Carveth started her descent. Smith pulled on his boot and looked around. He had not realised how large the bear enclosure was. It was, simply, a chunk of forest. At least that meant that the bears would not be unhappy in captivity. On the other hand, it meant that there might be quite a lot of them.

Carveth landed lightly beside him. 'What now, Boss?'

'We look for clues.'

'That's it?'

'Got any better ideas?'

She shrugged. 'Not climbing into a bear pit, to start with.'

'Think of Gerald, Carveth,' Smith replied. He looked up at the railing. 'Rhianna? How's distracting the bears going?'

Rhianna started as if waking up. She leaned over the railing. 'Oh, fine, so long as I don't break focus. Hey, look, an airship –'

Something growled.

'Never mind,' Rhianna said.

Suruk slipped out of the darkness behind them. 'Are we fighting bears yet, Mazuran?'

'Follow me,' Smith replied, and set off towards the middle of the enclosure. Carveth looked over her shoulder, sighed, and followed.

Suruk moved easily in the dark. Even without his spear, he looked formidable. He really was a master hunter, Smith thought.

Suruk glanced at Carveth. 'Piglet, you should cover your hair.'

'Why? Do bears eat hair?'

'No, they will think you have come to steal their porridge.'

Well, Smith reflected, almost a master hunter.

Suruk held up a hand. Smith froze: Carveth walked into the back of him, swore, and stopped. Quietly, the M'Lak lowered himself into a crouch. When he stood up, he held something limp and furred up to the moonlight.

'The bears have shed their skin,' he said.

'And evolved zips,' Carveth said. 'That's not skin.'

Smith took it from Suruk. He held the thing to the light and tried to gauge its shape. It wasn't a suit, as such, but a kit that would cover the arms and neck of its wearer. From the smell of the thing, it had been put to some fairly regular use.

Why would anyone want half a bear suit? he wondered. Even in the moonlight, it was obvious that the costume was missing most of its fur. It would be useless – unless its wearer already had the rest of the fur.

'Lemming men,' he said. 'There are lemming men here.'

Suruk drew two knives in a soft hiss of metal. Smith took out his Civiliser and drew back the hammer. 'Careful.'

'Where are we going?' Carveth whispered.

'To the centre of all this,' he replied, and he took a step forward and disappeared.

*   *   *

Smith hit the ground, fell forward and felt soil under his hands. He stood up quickly, jabbing his gun into the dark around him. Nothing.

He took out his lighter and flicked the wheel. He stood in a tunnel, roughly-hewn but big enough for him to stand upright, the walls made of packed earth. 'Suruk?' Smith called softly. 'I think you'd better come down here.'

Suruk dropped neatly beside him, and together they helped Carveth down.

'It looks like the lemmings have been digging a warren,' Smith said. 'I'll wager they've been doing some filthy business down here.'

'You can say that again.' Carveth put a hand over her mouth. 'It smells like the bottom of Gerald's cage.'

Smith led the way: Carveth stayed close, her face so pale and worried that it almost glowed white. Suruk was a quiet presence at Smith's side, just out of view. Lurking.

A stripe of light came from the left. Smith raised a finger to his lips. Bent low, he crept forward. The light spilled from under a closed door. A low thrumming noise came from behind it. Smith crouched down. Very carefully, he leaned forward and looked through the keyhole.

A machine rumbled and shook in the centre of the room beyond. Belts whirred; a bar swung back and forth and, with each swing, a fresh sheet of paper slipped out of the machine onto a neat, thick pile.

Two lemming men stood inside. They wore green visors; the larger of the two was smoking a cigarette. The smaller lemming held up a poster for his colleague to inspect. The poster showed a M'Lak warrior raising a knife, the features stylised as if in a woodcut. The slogan read: **The Rising Has Started! Kill The Oppressors! We Shall Make Ravnavar BURN!**

The smaller lemming man said something. The words were lost in the rattle of the printing press, but his companion laughed. The bigger lemming man lumbered forward, chuckling dirtily, and Smith glimpsed an ugly, brutal face: saggy around the chops, the snout broken in some fight years ago, the eyes ringed with shadow. The right eye was as white and blind as a cueball.

I know you, Smith thought. I've seen you before. He looked away, struggling to remember. This called for cunning and subterfuge. He put his eye back to the keyhole, and as he did, the door opened into his face.

The doorknob hit Smith just above the eye and he fell onto his backside. '*Hwot?*' a voice snarled, and a furred shape barged into the passage. 'Offworlder!' it cried, and as Smith pulled his gun the lemming man slid a knife from the sash on its waist.

The air flickered. The Yull stumbled, a stiletto quivering in his throat. Suruk chuckled.

A gun boomed behind them. 'Hands up! Now turn around, nice and slow.'

Smith lowered his Civiliser and looked around.

The Ringleader's chimney-hat scraped the tunnel roof. He carried a brass-plated automatic in one hand and the other groped the air for dramatic emphasis, as if waiting for a hawk to land on it.

'My sincerest apologies, General,' the robot said, 'but I believe I have located some interlopers.'

A second lemming stepped into the corridor. It was the one Smith had glimpsed through the keyhole, the big one with the single eye. 'General,' he said. 'I know you.'

'Is that so?' The general's chops stirred into a smile. He spoke good English, and his intonation was free of the revving, growling quality common to the Yull. 'Three offworlders, lost in the zoo.' He looked at Suruk. 'You are in the wrong place, frog-thing. You ought to be in the reptile house, along with the other green slime. And as for you two... humans. I could chew you and store you in my pouches, like so many seeds.'

'Careful, Wikwot,' the Ringleader said. 'I've a mind to test my aim on these three.'

The general shrugged. 'Not yet. First, they talk. You!

The officer. Tell me, what do you think we do down here?'

Smith looked from Ringleader to Wikwot. 'Given that you're a tin soldier and you're a giant mouse, I'd say that you dance *The Nutcracker*.'

'Nutcracker?' Wikwot said. He flexed his massive hands. 'Yes... that is a good idea. Seize him!'

The Ringleader stepped forward. Smith had a sudden sense of the sheer strength of the robot, his relentlessness. The clock-face of his head, with its absurd moustache, was something terrible.

'I will annihilate you and your excrementious comrades,' the robot said. 'I will...' he fumbled in the air, 'scatter your lights to the four winds. I will eradicate –'

Suruk sidestepped and smashed his elbow into the robot's face.

Steam blasted out of the Ringleader's hat. He staggered back, all spindly legs and dandified fabric, his moustache flapping. He righted himself in a whirl of limbs.

Carveth threw herself down. Wikwot leaped at Smith. Smith whirled and fired. Wikwot stumbled, clutching his shoulder. Smith twisted and shot the Ringleader in the chest.

The bullet simply glanced off. 'That's a scratch,' the Ringleader said, and as he raised his automatic, a massive shape bounded into the corridor behind him. It rose up as the robot took aim, and for a moment Smith thought it was another lemming man.

'Bears!' Carveth shouted, 'Run!'

For half a second the Ringleader stood against a backdrop of enraged fur, and then the bear threw its weight on him. The robot crashed to the ground. His pistol fell beside him, and Carveth scurried in and snatched it up.

Turning, Smith shouted 'The game's up, Wikwot!' But there was nobody in the corridor. Wikwot had fled.

He looked back at the Ringleader, and the sight that greeted him was like something from a cheese-dream: her hair wild, her blue skirt muddy, Rhianna stood in the middle of the tunnel, flanked by bears.

The Ringleader scrambled upright. He was dented and gouged, his paintwork a grid of claw marks. His painted eye had been almost entirely scratched away. Had he been a man, he would have been long dead.

'You!' he snarled, holding his brass moustache on with one hand. The other hand jabbed a battered finger towards Smith. 'The arm that strikes me shall be cut off – the marks you see upon me now, I will soon carve into you!'

He turned and ran. Smith raised the Civiliser, took aim and fired. Sparks burst from the Ringleader's back. 'This is my best coat, too!' he yelled, and in a rush of thin limbs he made his exit.

Suruk retrieved his knife. Carveth leaned against the wall and gave a long, shivering sigh.

'Hey guys,' Rhianna said. 'Check out my bears.'

Smith walked over to the door. Behind it, the printing press still thumped and rumbled. He walked in, the smell of ink around him, and pulled one of the sheets from the pile. 'Look.'

The poster showed a ruined building like the shell of a bombed cathedral, over which a huge, troll-like creature was glowering. In the foreground, a weeping woman carried away a baby, while a broad-shouldered man looked back in fury. **THEY TOOK OUR HALL**, said the slogan – **NOW LET'S TAKE BACK OUR CITY!**

'So this is their plan,' Suruk said, pointing to the troll. 'They mean to loose a gigantic baboon upon the city! Could we end up fighting that? Because it would have a very impressive skull.'

Smith looked at Rhianna. She frowned. 'Er, Suruk, this is kind of awkward... but I think it's supposed to be you.'

'I?' The M'Lak peered at the picture. 'No, that is some sort of mindless monster, hell-bent on carnage. Although, from a certain angle... But why would I want that tiny building? Is it a beehive?'

'It's a caricature, old chap,' Smith replied, 'and not a flattering one. That's supposed to represent the M'Lak, I'm guessing.'

'It's meant to turn mankind against your people,' Rhianna said. 'Being an oppressed minority, the M'Lak are vulnerable to this sort of slander.'

Carveth snorted. 'Him? Oppressed minority? There's twice as many of Suruk's lot in this city than us. And seriously, can you imagine trying to oppress six million Suruks? They're like sharks that have learned how to open doors. No offence, Suruk.'

'None taken,' the alien replied. 'Although these days we prefer the term "piranha".'

Smith glimpsed different colours on a pile of paper behind the printer. He lifted off a sheet: it depicted a M'Lak warrior, drawn in far more favourable terms than before, shaking hands with an unusually sane-looking Yullian officer. They were both laughing, as if one had just cracked a joke. The slogan was in M'Lak characters.

'*The Yull shall return the relics of Grimdall to Ravnavar,*' Suruk said.

'Hang on a moment, Boss.'

Smith looked round: Carveth was leafing through the posters. 'That building in the first picture, the one with the roof pulled off. I recognise it.'

'Really?' Smith looked back at the picture. It did seem vaguely familiar: he had a feeling that it was one of the landmarks of the city. '*They took our hall*,' he said. 'It looks like the big guildhall in the north, but that's still standing.'

'For now it is,' Carveth replied.

Slowly, Smith turned to her. 'What did you say?'

Rhianna raised her hands. 'Whoa. That's just... no way.'

'It's what I'd do,' Carveth said. 'Think about it. You want to set the city against itself, right? So you wreck something people care about. And then you put the blame on someone else.' She pointed. 'On the Morlocks. And then, when the trouble starts, you start another poster campaign, telling the Morlocks that we've turned on them.'

Smith suddenly felt very old. He turned to the piles of paper stashed behind the printer. He knew for certain that there would be other posters, blaming the scrapbots, or the Popular Fist, or whoever was needed to be the latest scapegoat.

'But people would never swallow that,' he said. 'We're British, for God's sake.'

Carveth shook her head. 'We think Black Pudding is food. We'd swallow anything.'

'Speak for your –'

'Mazuran.' Suruk touched Smith's sleeve. That meant it was urgent: the M'Lak disliked physical contact. 'The Yull have stooped low here, and not just because of the ceiling. This very basement is proof of their debasement. We must act quickly. Wherever this guildhall is, we need to secure it.'

Smith said, 'You're right. Let's go. Rhianna, can you get us safely past the bears?'

'Sure.'

'Then follow me, men. We have a city to save!'

They hurried back down the tunnel, clambered up

into the enclosure and picked their way through the dark towards the railing. Far away, at the very edge of the horizon, the glow of morning had begun to appear, as if the sky was about to catch alight. Smith climbed the rope first, thrashing and cursing, and helped the others up. Suruk was last, hardly needing the rope as he scrambled up the wall.

Below them, the bears settled back down to sleep.

'Thanks, old girl,' Smith said, leaning towards Rhianna. 'You did a jolly good job there.' He kissed her on the cheek. 'Good work, chaps.'

Carveth leaned against the railing and slowly recovered her breath. She was not a natural climber. 'Next time, Boss, could we just go to the children's farm?'

'Certainly not. I know what you're like around baby animals. The last thing I want is a reputation as the man who let his pilot push over a six-year-old so she could have a go on the lambs.'

'I never did that! It was a rogue duckling.'

'Never mind. To the car!'

*   *   *

They drove back as dawn rose over Ravnavar. A few rockets and transport craft blazed up into the sky. The roads were filling with the usual vehicles, pedestrians and alien monsters. The sunlight turned the trees by the roadside into pulsing light as they drove past. Smith felt tired. He took a wrong turning on the Queen Kylie Viaduct and ended up stuck behind an extraordinary M'Lak vehicle, two thirds tank to one third mobile disco, decked out with trophies and fluorescent lights. Across the back was a painting of Grimdall the Rebel, the closest thing the planet had to a patron saint, riding a mechanical tiger and waving two swords.

As they pulled into the scrapyard, Nalgath the Scrapper was slicing a heap of fridge doors into armour plate. He worked with a laser cutter, a device somewhere between a pitchfork and a chainsaw. A group of small scrapbots stood a little way off, hoping to buy new limbs and sell a variety of items that had either fallen off or been unscrewed from a lorry.

The *John Pym* seemed mercifully untouched, although Smith wondered whether their host had been snipping bits off the wings.

There was no time to waste, so they only stopped for one pot of tea. Carveth broke open the weapons locker while Smith fired up the radio and dialled the local police station.

'Inspector Kallarn the Enforcer, please.'

'Huh,' a voice muttered.

'Isambard Smith here. I wondered if we could talk.'

'Yeah. I've been kind of thinking that myself, ever since you knocked down half my police station.'

'That wasn't me. It was a mad ravnaphant. Listen, something big's happening. The Yull have infiltrated the city. They've dug tunnels under the zoo. Their leader is called General Wikwot –'

'Huh? He's in jail. A place on the edge of town.'

'Not anymore he's not.'

'*Huh?*'

Suruk tapped Smith on the shoulder, and passed him a mug of tea. As Smith drank, the alien took the microphone. 'Friend, the lemming scum have dug a burrow beneath the bear enclosure, from which they plot to hurl foul slanders upon us. Their aim is to turn M'Lak against Metchi'cheun and hinder our war against the Yull. They even claim to have found the relics of

Grimdall, to use as a bargaining tool. Meet us in two hours at the Guildhall. Bring warriors.' He hung up.

Carveth looked into the cockpit. 'Boss? The car's loaded, and Rhianna's threatening to drive. We'd better go.'

'Righto,' said Smith. 'Suruk, tell Nalgath not to chop up the ship while we're gone. I've got a call to make.'

'Going to ring the Service? You'd best make it quick.'

'Not exactly.' Smith reached for the radio. 'I'm going to get a photocopier repaired.'

*   *   *

General Wikwot had been forced underground, but for someone who lived in a burrow, that was no great hardship.

He disliked the cellar of the disused funfair where the Ringleader kept court. It smelled of grease, and the presence of humans had dirtied it in a way that no set of overalls could have kept out. Still, the carousel horses had poles through them. That reminded him of his childhood, which he had spent impaling people.

A city has its own soul, Wikwot thought as he struck a match on the bared teeth of a horse. It will be a pleasure to kill the soul of this place.

He took a long drag on his cigarette.

Ravnavar was a dump: the sooner he was back with his soldiers and off this mess of a planet, the better. Ugly buildings full of mangy unrodents. And the lavatories! The barbarians concentrated their droppings in one place, instead of distributing them as evenly as possible throughout the vicinity. Degenerates, all of them.

Thin light came in from high, narrow windows. On the far side of the room, the Ringleader sat in front of a dressing-room mirror, powering the bulbs from a wire slotted into the side of his dented torso. After his encounter with the bears, the gangster had spent the morning tidying his face with an eyebrow pencil and a soldering iron.

Wikwot had a small degree of sympathy. A real leader took pride in his appearance, and while the Ringleader's moustache wasn't made out of proper whiskers, like a lemming's, it made up for that by being self-twirling.

Hydraulics whined and a great wedge of light stretched across the room. A silhouette like a huge steel toddler waddled forward, its broad feet stomping the concrete. Wikwot's paw moved to the axe on his belt, but the Ringleader didn't even look round.

'Got something to tell me, Rom?'

'It's Ram, boss.'

'I hope you have something more than that. Where is your brother?'

The huge robot leaned forward when at rest, its forearms hanging down like an ape's. 'Gone to collect a debt. There's some people owes us money. Like... anyone.'

'Slave!' Wikwot barked. 'Where is my space rocket?'

'You watch it, lemming,' Ram said. 'I know a lot of dolly birds what'd like a new fur coat.'

'Silence! You may not speak so to one honoured by the war god Popacapinyo. Ringleader – where is my transport?'

Ram growled. 'Watch it. You show us some respect.'

Wikwot snorted. 'Respect? *Popiqoc*. A true warrior does not let himself be mauled by bears. Ringleader, you have spent all morning locked away with tools, banging away at yourself. If you had not had your arse kicked, why else would you panel-beat your own buttocks?'

The Ringleader looked round, and for a moment Wikwot thought that the robot would be enraged. Instead, the Ringleader said: 'Show the general, Ram.'

Ram clanked across the room and stopped under a portable generator bolted against the wall. His massive hand pulled a lever. The generator buzzed – and then the carousel burst into parping life, a blaze of light and brass, whirling and trumpeting.

'Observe,' the Ringleader said, standing up. He pointed to the window.

Wikwot peered. 'I need a cloth. The glass is dirty.'

'You're made of fur,' the Ringleader.

Wikwot growled and used the back of his paw. Outside, lights flickered on a battered helter-skelter. For a moment, the general wondered what these stupid machines meant, and then he saw the conical top of the helter-skelter, the fins welded to its sides.

'That?' Wikwot shouted over the tootling racket of the carousel.

The Ringleader gestured at it. 'Only the finest for a Yullian general.'

'That is not a spaceship. That is a giant firework.'

'Exactly,' said the Ringleader. 'We shall launch it with a patriotic fanfare. Nobody will notice your departure. You will leave Ravnavar as a true Briton, and land on Andor like a true lemming.'

'By crashing into it.'

'I thought you people liked doing that. It never stopped your air force.'

'Those are minions,' Wikwot replied. 'They do not count.'

Wikwot reached out and flipped the lever, cutting the power. The carousel wound to a halt with a groan. 'It will suffice. I will put myself in hibernation for the journey. Just make sure that there is plenty of sawdust and some nuts for when I wake up.'

A second huge robot lumbered in. 'Boss, boss!'

'Rom, my esteemed companion,' the Ringleader said. 'I take it there is a reason that you have abandoned your watch on the Guildhall?'

Rom scratched his processor. 'Yeah. There's people there.'

'People. Would you care to elucidate, before I render you limb from limb?'

'Um... the ones you wanted me and Ram to do over.'

'Excellent!' The Ringleader sprang to his feet. His single lens glinted in his newly-painted face. 'I took the liberty of placing a little incendiary surprise in the Guildhall. Today, my friends, we will light the spark that will make this city burn. General, I offer you a ringside seat.'

Wikwot smiled. 'Yes. I will watch the offworlders die. Then I will leave this city to you.' His hand slipped onto his axe. 'Do your civic duty, robot. Clean up and take out all the trash. Every last one of them.'

Red Rebellion!

The Great Guildhall of the Imperial General Union was vast, ornate, covered in statues and surprisingly hard to find, mainly because it looked like most other public buildings in the Space Empire. Only at close range was it clear that the statues carried hammers and toolkits instead of swords and trumpets, and that in place of haloes, they wore pencils behind their ears.

Smith trotted up the steps to the guildhall. Scrolls were sculpted over the doorway, bearing the names of great reformers.

He stepped in, and at once the heat of the morning was gone. Inside, the guildhall resembled a cathedral, and he stood at the entrance to the nave. In alcoves, stone angels held up spanners and cogs. Goggled cherubs swung mallets and hauled stone chains. In the centre of the hall, a huge marble figure raised its hand like Hamlet with Yorick's skull. The skull had been replaced by Ravnavar itself, and Hamlet wore a cloth cap instead of a ruff.

Smith felt somewhat awed. Technically, he was entitled to be there, as a low-ranking member of the

Space Pilots and Captains' Egalitarian Department, but as he looked around the mighty hall he felt the familiar worry that someone would spot him and throw him out. He advanced down the nave, through shafts of light and the motes that spun in them, past statues of the Empire's great guildsmen, to the wooden booth by the entrance to the gift shop.

A small man sat in the booth, filling in a coupon. 'Morning, brother. Sisters,' he added, nodding to Rhianna and Carveth. 'Thing,' he said to Suruk. 'Can I help you?'

'Yes,' Smith said. 'I'm here on a matter of great urgency.'

'Urgency,' the man replied, in the tone of someone leafing through a dictionary to find an unfamiliar term.

'I need to search –'

'Can I stop you there? Is that a matter of dire urgency, or moderate urgency? Because if it's dire urgency, I'll have to ask you to fill in a form.'

'What?'

'Moderate emergency is two forms.' The clerk reached under his desk and pulled out a sheet of blue paper. 'This is a URF/290/C, requesting immediate relocation to the front of the queue. Now, your name goes here, and your countersigning officer –'

'But there isn't a queue.' Smith gestured to the empty hall around him. 'These people are with me.'

The clerk took off his spectacles and peered at them. 'Not *now* there isn't. But what if some other guildsmen came along with an equally important request? We'd need to know who to let go to the front of the queue. Very important form that,' he added, tapping the paper.

'There's not many people get to fill in a URF/290/C. There's people that'd queue all day just to see one of those.'

'They'd queue all day to see a form that let them go to the front of the queue? But they'd only see it when they got to the front of the queue. So why would they want to queue up?' A sharp pain in the forehead told Smith that it was time to think about something else. 'Look, just give me the form –'

'There's a bomb!' Carveth yelled.

A moment's silence followed. Slowly, the clerk looked round at her. 'Sister,' he said, 'we are all equal here. So wait your turn. If you want to go before this man here, you'll have to have the right documentation. And you need to get in line for that.'

'There's a great big bomb under here,' Carveth said. 'And I'm with him. We're all in this together –'

'Indeed we are,' said the clerk. He leaned back in his chair and looked wistfully over their heads at a statue of miners on an asteroid. 'Indeed we are.'

Smith drew his pistol. 'Right, that's it!' he declared. 'We are taking over this building in the name of Popular Fist.' The clerk's eyes, suddenly wide, were locked on the barrel of the Civiliser. 'A bomb has been planted by enemies of – well, of the people, actually, and we mean to find it. Now please –'

With a hiss of greased steel, a shutter dropped down in front of the booth. Someone had stencilled a message on the metal: *Back in 5 Mins*.

Smith leaned in and battered the metal with the butt of his gun. 'Damn it, open up! What's going on in there?'

A voice, muffled by armour, came back. 'I'm on lunch.'

Smith turned round. 'Bugger. It looks like we're on our own here, men.'

Carveth sighed. 'I thought there'd be someone to help us. I mean, where are all these workers, anyway?'

'At work, I suppose.'

'You know,' she said, 'I could really use half a dozen burly men right now. I mean, we could.'

Doors creaked open at the far end of the hall. Smith turned, covering the nave with his pistol. Half a dozen people approached, carrying toolboxes and portable scanners. At their head was a dark-haired woman in blue overalls.

'Heard you needed a photocopier fixed,' she called, 'Wait – it's you.'

'Miss Chigley,' Smith said. 'Thanks for getting here so quickly. We've got to work fast, I'm afraid.'

'Not a problem. I brought some of the lads to help.' A rumble of greeting came from her comrades. 'Er, what's with the big gun?'

'Well, I've captured this place in the name of Popular Fist. I thought it'd give us some space to work.'

Her mouth fell open, as if a puppeteer had forgotten to operate it. 'You did what? You'll make us look like mentalists!'

'Well, you are a revolutionary fringe party.'

'Not like that! We want to reform the post office, not start holding up buildings.'

'Well, we have shared enemies. You know what to do.'

She grimaced. 'Looks like I do. Alright, lads, let's get the gear up. You owe me, Captain Smith. I hope you realise the mess we're all in.'

'Carveth,' Smith said, 'help Miss Chigley. Suruk, you and I will bar the doors. Rhianna, could you get on the tannoy and ask everyone to leave? Tell them there's been a problem with the drains or something.'

'That should flush 'em out,' Carveth added.

'Just get on with it,' Smith replied, and as he holstered

his pistol, he wondered whether starting a revolution in the middle of the city had been all that wise.

*   *   *

'The trouble with this war,' Bargath observed, 'is that it's full of damned foreigners.'

Half a dozen lancers sat in one of the Palace's many common rooms, resting after lunch and mutually disapproving of the television. The morning had been as hearty as the meal: Morgar was not sure whether his stomach hurt more than the wounds he had acquired whilst tumbling off Frote's back. He was not a natural jouster.

'They should bloody well stop their nonsense.' Colonel Pargarek had sunk so low in his armchair that Morgar had taken him to be asleep. Now the colonel struggled to sit up, as if crawling out of quicksand. 'All these Ghasts and Yull. Bloody lemmings, pissing everywhere. It's a disgrace.'

'I hear the M'Lak Rifles are dealing with the Yull,' Morgar ventured.

'Oiks,' said Pargarek. 'One kills from the saddle, with a sabre, not running about with these silly arm-blades of theirs. Like this,' he added, swishing his fist around.

A woman appeared on the television screen. She was good-looking, in human terms, Morgar realised, although dishevelled. He gestured for the wallahbot to turn the volume up: the girl seemed curiously familiar. Colonel Pargarek had fallen asleep, and was drooling on his mandibles.

'... *which is like, totally, bad?*' she was saying. '*I mean, I'm really opposed to interfering with other people's lives, but there's like a bomb here, so you should, you know, go outside or something.'*

'Who's this dullard?' Bargath said, without malice. 'I do wish they'd keep these people indoors.'

'Now might be a really good time to re-evaluate your life, actually. Because you never know when you might, you know, explode.'

Morgar heard himself say 'I think I've met her.'

'Really, old boy? She sounds like a prize arse.' Bargath braced himself, inflated his throat and let out an extended, rippling belch.

The woman on the screen was abruptly pushed aside. A M'Lak warrior replaced her: he wore a traditional mesh shirt under a dark green breastplate, chipped from battle and decorated with M'Lak characters. The warrior had a curious expression, at once proud, stern and rather pleased with himself.

'Now that's better,' Bargath said. 'This fellow looks like he might talk some sense, even if he's a tad uncouth.'

Morgar groaned. 'No he won't.'

'Greetings, Ravnavar! It is I, Suruk the Slayer, who occupies your television. Do not adjust your set, or I will destroy you all! As of yet, we have this guildhall in our possession, as well as a bomb. Remain calm, for those opposing me will die, and their skulls shall be taken. And on that reassuring note, I shall depart.'

The image flicked back to the newsroom: fighting on the M'Lak self-governing worlds was at its peak; the King's Own Orbital Dragoons had thrown back Praetorian Legion 'Relentless Slaughter' on New Manchester.

Morgar stared at the television, hardly noticing. His brother seemed to be burned into the screen. Something was going to go wrong.

*   *   *

'Here,' said Miss Chigley. She held up a foot-long cylinder. 'One bomb. We found it jammed in the back of a model of the Tolpuddle Martyrs.' She glanced at her comrades, who were packing up the rest of the scanning equipment on the far side of the hall. 'Now, Captain, I'd be bloody grateful if you'd let us all go back to work. I've had enough revolution for one day, thanks.'

'Of course. Carveth? We need to open the doors. It seems our work here is done. All we need is to call the police and have this Ringleader fellow arrested.'

She emerged from the shadows around the doorway, looking more worried than usual. 'About that, Boss. The police are already on the way. There's a news-drone here, too.'

'Really?'

'And Rhianna and Suruk are talking to it. And by talking, I mean issuing demands.'

A weight dropped from the bottom of Smith's ribcage into the base of his stomach, like a rock dropped down a well. 'What? Suruk is on television? Why?'

Carveth folded her arms. 'Well, correct me if I'm wrong, but, after demolishing a police station, we went on the run, armed ourselves and took over the Guildhall to start a revolution. These things tend to get you noticed. In fact, short of using their hats as a commode, I'm not sure how we could make the police more interested.'

'Ah. I see what you mean, now. One moment, everyone.' Smith turned and ran down the length of the hall, towards the doors. 'Suruk, where are you? Say nothing! Get away from the camera!'

He stopped at the doors. They were locked. Suruk and Rhianna had to be upstairs, in one of the many galleries. He turned to the staircase, a graceful sweep of stone, and noticed something move behind the window.

A spindly figure was advancing on the guildhall, striding across the courtyard. As Smith watched, it raised a hand and touched the brim of its tall metal hat.

'Rhianna? Suruk?' he called up the stairs. 'Get back to the nave!' He rushed back towards the others. 'Miss Chigley, we've got a problem. I think you need to get out of sight.'

As the Popular Fist ran for cover, Smith loaded his rifle. A camera drone hovered outside the window, watching him.

Carveth sighed. 'That'll look good on the news.'

Smith grimaced. 'It's all right. We just have to stay here, and wait for the police to arrive. Then we can straighten everything out –'

'*Ladies and gentlemen!*' The voice was like a bomber flying overhead. Smith cocked his rifle. Carveth ducked. 'Robots, humans, citizens of Ravnavar, roll up and roll out as we delight and entertain you with a demonstration of how we keep our city clean! Ravnavar needs order, and who better to provide it than I?'

Smith scurried down the length of the hall, bent low to hide his shape.

'Regrettably, our audience from the Ravnavari Constabulary has been delayed. But the show must go on. Our first act: Captain Isambard Smith and his ship of fools. Time to fall down, clowns!'

The window nearest the door burst. The muzzle of a Maxim cannon was thrust into the gap. 'Down!' Smith yelled, and the roar of gunfire filled the room.

Bullets tore the air; chips of stone burst from the statues and the walls. Carveth raced yelling into a niche. The collected members of the Popular Fist ran to the basement stairs.

'Suruk, get down here!' Smith cried.

Another blast of fire tore down the hall. Smith ducked behind the statue of the worker holding up Ravnavar. The gunfire stopped. He saw Carveth peek out, shotgun in hand. Something heavy crashed against the doors.

Carveth rushed out and dropped down beside Smith. 'What did I do to deserve this?' she panted. 'All I wanted was a quiet life and a pony.'

The doors flew open, and the Ringleader was silhouetted in the aperture. He looked like an automated Uncle Sam, all tailcoat and top hat. As the robot limped into the hall, tossing aside his empty gun, Smith saw the rips in his outfit, now patched with masking tape, and the gobbets of solder on his chest and moustache. An encounter with a territorially-enraged bear had done him no good.

The Ringleader reached into the back of his tailcoat, and produced a length of industrial chain and a walking stick made from a length of park railing. 'Nobody runs away *from* the circus!' he bellowed, and he flicked the chain like a whip. 'Come one, come all, and observe as I exsanguinate this tuppenny meatsack!'

Smith looked at Carveth. 'It's all right. I can take him. I just need to shoot out his hinges.'

'Great,' she said. 'And why don't you pull the key out of his back while you're at it?'

Smith stepped out and fired. The rifle kicked against his shoulder and the Ringleader stumbled back. Smith worked the lever, fired again, and the robot staggered, lost his footing, managed not to fall over and stood up just in time for Smith to line the crosshairs on his rifle with the Ringleader's head.

The shot blew the Ringleader onto his back. He lay in the doorway, all chipped armour and spindly limbs, and with a creak of metal sat upright.

'And now,' he cried, 'those two renowned strongmen, Ram and Rom Crane!'

One of the brothers lumbered into the rear of the hall. It was Rom, Smith realised, largely because he had written it in chalk across his forehead. The robot hunched over like an ape, metal fists almost brushing the linoleum. Someone, possibly a small child or the other Crane brother, had ineptly spray-painted a suit jacket onto Rom's chest.

'This used to be a nice neighbourhood,' Rom growled. 'You could leave your front door unlocked and all. But now I'm in it.' His tiny head, almost an afterthought, slowly scanned the room. 'Times was hard, but people used to take care of each uvver,' he snarled. 'And now I'm gonna take care of you.'

Rom lurched forward, his thick little legs picking up speed. He clanked and squeaked like tank tracks. As he rushed forward he seemed to grow – he widened, accelerated, turned from noisy to deafening – and then he sprang.

Rom's fist swung out on his boom of an arm. Smith ducked, heard stone shatter overhead and was running, Carveth before him, as the remains of the heroic worker collapsed in an avalanche of shards.

'This is my manor now,' Rom bellowed.

Smith raised his rifle, and an identical voice roared, 'Oi, Rom! This manor's mine!'

He looked round: Ram Crane stood at the far end of the hall, whirring and clanking. He had garlanded himself with an open doorway, torn out of a wall, no doubt by ramming his own head through it. For a moment the two thugs stood apart, and Smith wondered whether they were going to turn on one another, but then the Ringleader snarled: 'Butcher them! Festoon the rafters with their glistening innards!'

Ram stomped down the hall, flexing his fingers. Rom swiped at Smith, who sidestepped and fired. The bullet sparked off Rom's belly armour. 'Hur hur hur,' said Rom.

Weirdly graceful, a television mini-blimp sailed through the doorway like a cloud. It floated down the hall, rotors puffing, as if it was carrying extra weight.

Smith shot Rom in the leg, which had no effect beyond reminding Rom that he was still there. The robot turned, Smith lined up a shot and his rifle clicked empty.

He tore the Civiliser from his jacket. Carveth darted out from the ruined statue, skipped up behind Rom and blasted him in the back of the knee.

Rom stumbled. 'Gotcha!' Carveth cried, and a huge shape loomed up behind her.

'Look out!' Smith yelled, but too late. Ram Crane's hand dropped onto Carveth, swallowed her up, and lifted her into the air.

'I got his tart!' Ram bellowed. 'I got his tart!'

Smith glared at Ram and focussed his moral fibre. 'Unhand her,' he barked. 'Stop that this instant!'

The Bearing would have worked on a machine with a larger brain. Ram called, 'Rom, catch!'

Smith aimed the Civiliser and blew three holes into Ram's head, with no result. Carveth screamed. The camera-drone swung low. Ram hurled Carveth at the far end of the hall.

Smith said nothing as Carveth sailed through the air. She moved agonisingly slowly, limbs outstretched like the arms of a starfish. He could hear her, far away as if underwater, but there was nothing he could do.

Rhianna stepped out of the shadows and raised her hand. Carveth still flew, end over end, but she shot towards Carveth, as if sucked into a vacuum, and as she did, the android slowed, righted herself, and landed beside her.

Carveth said, 'Cool.'

Ram looked at his hand. 'That does not bleedin' compute,' he said. 'Oh well. Just have to smash your head in.' He lumbered round to face Smith, and the camera-blimp sailed overhead.

Suruk dropped off the underside of the blimp, onto Ram's shoulders. The M'Lak raised a strange device, like a kind of mechanical pitchfork. It looked weirdly familiar.

Ram noticed Suruk and whirled, trying to throw him off, but the alien was far too agile to be troubled by that. As Ram clanked and bellowed below him, Suruk activated the laser cutter and a beam flickered into life between its prongs. It came down on Ram's neck like a guillotine.

His head fell off. Ram Crane took a step forward, one oversized hand groping at his collar, and then he collapsed piecemeal, the joints buckling one by one. He crashed onto his knees, and as Suruk jumped down, flopped onto his front.

At the far end of the hall, Carveth cheered. Smith looked at Suruk, and smiled.

'Hands up!'

Smith looked around, and the Ringleader lurched into view.

'Show's over,' the robot said. He held Carveth's shotgun. His moustaches were bent, stuck at five minutes to three o'clock. Pistons wheezing, he took a step forward. It was remarkable, Smith thought, how much more dangerous the shotgun looked when Carveth wasn't wielding it.

'Rom,' the Ringleader said, 'A little advice. I am sorely minded to annihilate these excretions, to metaphorically scrape them off my boot. Does that seem a wise course of action to you?'

Rom shook his small head. 'Nah. You should just kill 'em.'

Smith looked at the robot. In theory, Rhianna could use her powers to slow the shotgun pellets, perhaps even stop them – but she looked exhausted. Catching Carveth had weakened her. Carveth might not be very big, but she was clearly as dense as Suruk had always claimed.

'Any last words?' the Ringleader demanded.

Smith was out of protection, caught off-guard by enemies that even the Bearing could not defeat. He took a step forward. 'Listen,' he said, 'any moment now the police will be here. You'll be linked with the lemmings, and that's not just crime – that's treason. They'll melt you down for that. If you don't drop that gun, you'll be living out the rest of your life as a towel-rack.'

'Good try. Rom, spill their claret.'

'Yeah!' Rom growled, and he advanced.

Suruk stepped up beside Smith. 'On the plus side,' he observed, 'at least it will not be the lemming men killing us.' He fired up the laser cutter as Smith drew his sword.

A side door burst open. A figure in overalls hurled a tube into the room. The tube hit the floor, bounced, bounced again and stopped beside Rom's massive foot.

'Get down!' Smith cried.

Rom picked the tube up, as everyone else flinched away. 'Er, where should I put this?' he asked.

Miss Chigley made a vehement gesture with her fist. 'Up the Fist!' she cried, and Rom exploded.

*　　*　　*

The world was grey. A high-pitched sound rang through the air. It was like watching the test card on television,

Smith thought. 'Rhianna?' he called. 'Carveth?' and immediately began coughing.

A massive shape blundered through the dust. Rom moved jerkily: sparks burst from the back of his head. 'Lovely mum, what loved their boys...' the robot grunted. 'Took care of our own... times was hard then... wouldn't hurt a door... you could leave your flies unlocked...'

A figure slid out of the dust from behind him like a furred Grim Reaper. In one movement it stepped forward and swung an ornate, long-handled axe over its head. As Smith saw the one white eye of General Wikwot, glistening in the dust-cloud like a pearl in dirt, the axe sliced Rom's head off.

Wikwot stepped back, grinning, and the dust swallowed him. He seemed to fade with it; Smith saw other figures moving in the cloud and that none of them was the general.

'Rhianna? Carveth?'

They were alive, thank God, all of them. A piece of masonry had gashed Suruk's forearm and Carveth was unsteady on her feet, but that was it. As Smith wandered forward, trying to work out in which direction the exit lay, he saw the members of Popular Fist emerging from the basement as if from a bomb shelter.

A thin figure stalked towards them in motorcycle gear, scowling under his visor. 'If any of you people are still breathing, me and this gun are bringing you in,' Kallarn the Enforcer snarled.

Smith put his arm around Rhianna. 'Everything's under control, Inspector. You won't need the riot squad.'

'I never do,' the inspector growled back. 'You don't assign me to hard cases. I am one.'

There was a gift at the exit. The Ringleader sat by

the doors, back against the doorframe, legs sticking out in front of him. His head lay in his lap.

'He failed the Yull,' Suruk said.

'That's horrible,' Carveth replied. 'Killing your own people like that. I mean, what's the point?'

'For the lemming men,' Suruk replied, 'cruelty is its own point. Their hatred of honour is as long as their rancid whiskers.'

'You're telling me,' said the Ringleader's head. 'You, Smith! Quick: I'm on auxiliary power here.'

'What is it?' Smith asked.

'He'll have gone to the old funfair: there's a rocket there. By now he'll be halfway to Andor. Tell your people to find that backstabbing, urinacious, one-eyed rodent for me. Flatten him – flay him – turn his pelt into a rug. Listen to me – the Yull are looking for Grimdall. Remember that. *Grimdall*. And with that,' the robot declared, 'the show's over.'

His eye-lens unfocused.

A fresh camera-drone hovered above the door. As Smith walked out, he heard Julia Chigley address it. 'We of the Popular Fist, having heard reports that unpatriotic enemies had planted a bomb in our beloved guildhall, decided to risk life and limb in defusing it. We rushed here and, despite the efforts of the city's worst criminals, were able to prevent the bomb taking effect.'

'Hey,' Rhianna said. 'That's not true. She's just gone in front of the camera, claimed all the credit and made up a load of rubbish off the top of her head!'

'That can only mean one thing,' Smith replied. 'She's entered mainstream politics.'

'Well,' Carveth said, 'I suppose we can go down the pub now.'

'Not so fast, young lady android. Remember what

we came here for? Chaps,' Smith announced, 'we have a game to win.'

*   *   *

Morgar had been invited to the Monthly Grand Dinner of the Ravnavari Lancers, and tried to arrive as late as possible. He had expected it to be a tedious and stuffy affair, where various insanely loyal old warriors got slowly and deeply drunk on carbonated water and reminisced about the time when they had levelled some city of the beetle people so that humans could build a sewage plant on the remains. It was, however, far worse.

The dining hall was utter chaos – nobody was dangling from the chandelier, but then it wasn't time for pudding yet. Everyone spoke over everyone else: the main way of getting the attention of a diner out of arm's reach was to throw food at their head. Two lancers were either demonstrating a swordfighting technique or trying to murder each other in earnest on the top table. Their combat was largely ignored, except for cheers of encouragement and the occasional shout of reproach when one of them stamped on somebody's dinner.

Morgar took his seat, and at once a heaped plate of animal flesh was put before him, cooked to varying degrees. An enormous amount of meat was being consumed – the lancers had declared pork to be an honorary vegetable sixty years ago, so as to avoid ruining their appetites with anything green. Somebody filled up all of his glasses: two of fizzy water, and one of wine to help soak up some of the bubbles.

'The Admiral approaches port!' someone cried.

What looked like a brown basin full of dirty water was pushed down the table: it was in fact a vast Yorkshire pudding, full of gravy, on which floated a paper napkin folded into the shape of a boat. A toy soldier had been wedged into the folds of the paper boat. As it passed by, each diner stood up and toasted the soldier, then refilled his glass and shoved the pudding onwards.

Four places from Morgar, the Yorkshire pudding disintegrated, prompting uproar, hilarity and more drinking. The admiral's soggy boat wriggled up the table at the head of a tributary of gravy, and bumped against Morgar's plate.

'Does anyone want this?' Morgar asked, holding up the toy soldier, and the answering roar told him that he had made a very bad mistake.

'He's docked!' Colonel Pargarek exclaimed. He pointed at Morgar. 'Let the harbour-master lead the drinking!'

A wallahbot approached, carrying an ancient green bottle in its pincers.

Morgar didn't like the look of this: drinking wine was no problem, provided that it was not fizzy, – CO_2 bubbles were highly intoxicating to the M'lak race but he was not certain that this new drink was wine at all.

'Chateau Perrier, 1987,' Captain Bargath announced. 'It was a very good year for carbonated water. We keep a cellar, you know.'

The wallahbot unscrewed the cap and some of the water fizzed out, which pleased the lancers. By now, a sizeable group had gathered to watch the fulfilment of the ritual; even the two fighters had forgotten their duel and were standing on the top table, reverent in their silence.

'Now then,' Bargath said, picking up an alarmingly large glass, 'the correct formation of the first five toasts –'

A horn blasted. Morgar looked around, wondering what grim new aspect of the ceremony it entailed. It took a moment to realise that the others were as puzzled as he.

A lancer stood at the end of the hall. He cupped his hands around his mandibles and roared, 'Brothers!'

'Uh?' Pargarek grunted as if woken from sleep. 'What's this?'

'I bring news from the Parliament,' the new arrival called. 'A full offensive is to be launched against the lemming men within the month. We are to make ready to join the fleet heading to Andor. Where others have failed, the Ravnavari Lancers will take the war to the bestial Yull and show them how real soldiers fight. Gentlemen, we are going to war!'

The bellow that answered him threatened to break the rafters. 'Thrash the filthy rodents!' Bargath yelled. 'Teach 'em who owns this galaxy!'

'Ride on!' cried Pargarek. 'Ride on to victory!'

'Thank the ancestors,' Morgar muttered. The lancers roared, overcome by the prospects of dishing out a self-righteous walloping. Morgar seemed to be in the eye of the storm. They'll all go, he thought. It'll be me and the wallahbots. I'll be able to design the new restroom facility without one of these lunatics vomiting all over it every twenty minutes. 'Brilliant!' he shouted. 'Go, lancers!'

A hand dropped onto his shoulder. He looked around.

'Good lad,' Bargarth said. 'I knew you were the chap for the job. I knew there was more to you than all that arty-farty nonsense. General mobilisation! You're got steel, my lad! We'll ride out together, you and I. We'll cover the walls in trophies!'

Bargath slapped Morgar on the back, as if to encourage an infant to cough up a foreign body.

'I think I'm going to be sick,' Morgar replied.

*   *   *

'How do you mean, a game to win?' Captain Fitzroy sat, or rather lay, in an enormous wicker armchair in the dockside Colonial Club. In the chair opposite, her colleague and occasional paramour, Wing Commander Shuttleswade, was unconscious. 'It's all done and dusted, Smitty. And guess who won? I'll give you a clue – she had the same name as me.'

It hadn't been hard to find Captain Fitzroy: her bar bill was almost visible from orbit, and the trail of exhausted young men made her even easier to locate.

'The games ended ages ago. We thought you'd gone off to…' she glanced at Rhianna, and back at Smith '… see the sights. Anyhow, we found a new venue. A young men's rugby club, as chance would have it. Forty-eight young men, eighteen to twenty-two, so gauche, and yet so charmingly naïve. I've been schooling them in the ways of righteousness. Pull up a chair.' She smiled at Carveth. 'You too, short stuff.'

On the far side of the club, a M'Lak in the uniform of the 6th Colonial Hussars burst out laughing. Ten years ago, people would have looked down their noses at such conduct, knowing that the M'Lak did not have noses down which to respond. Now, Suruk's people were needed, and anyone crazy enough to want to fight the Yull was valuable indeed.

'We had some problems with gangsters,' Smith said. 'But we've cleared them up.'

The bodies of Rom and Ram Crane had ended up with Nalgath the Scrapper and Mark Twelve, and would provide enough raw materials to replace the cutlery-limbs of hundreds of scrapbots.

'Smashing,' Captain Fitzroy replied, gesturing at a wallahbot for more drinks. At the window behind her, a shuttle rose from its pad into the cloudless sky and was lost against the setting sun. No doubt it was carrying a platoon to the ships in orbit.

'We're shipping chaps over to Andor, twenty thousand at a time,' she said. 'Fancy using the *Chimera* as a troop carrier! It's positively demeaning. Still, we'll be getting a crack at the Yull at last. High Command wants everyone out there. The lemmings are restless, it seems.'

A frigate hung in the sky, half a dozen service-blimps pressed against it like piglets at a sow. Rockets rose from the city, as if the towers of the M'Lak quarter were launching into space. Knowing the Morlocks, Smith thought, it was quite likely that they actually were.

'This is it, isn't it?' said Captain Fitzroy. 'Our empire against theirs, to the death. They've got the numbers, and they'll never stop coming. The question is whether we've got the men and the skill to stop them.' She sighed, and suddenly she looked like an old teacher instead of a head girl who had raided the liquor cabinet. 'It's going to be the end of an empire, no matter what. Best get your booze and bonking in while you still can. On which note,' she added, brightening, and she leaned over and prodded Shuttlesworth. 'Shuttles, we need to make use of the map table. I need you to show me where your Big Dipper is.'

Shuttlesworth opened his eyes, and for a moment he looked pleadingly around the room, like a man about to mount the scaffold. Then he said, 'Right, Felicity.'

'Good stuff. Best not keep the captain waiting.' She stood up and straightened her jacket. 'Adieu, Smitty and Co!'

'I know I should look out for the sisterhood or whatever,' Carveth said, 'and I realise her interests overlap somewhat with mine, but my God that woman scares me.'

Suruk pulled chairs over and Smith fetched the drinks. The waiterbot, a spidery, multi-limbed machine, reminded him of Mark Twelve. Smith turned, glasses in hand, and seeing his crew made him afraid. Soon they would be fighting the cruellest, most demented creatures in the galaxy. Captain Fitzroy had been right, he thought: no matter what, an empire was going to fall.

PART TWO

ANDOR: *First planet in the Andorian System: Type 16 semi-civilised world.*

Principle land usage: *Forest and/or jungle.*

Notable Settlements: *Riviera (now ruined). Mothkarak Castle. Equeria (alien settlement).*

Aliens: *Equ'i, pseudo-mammalian sentients (indigenous natives). Society graded as Class V: backward, no serious threat. Yull, pseudo-mammalian sentients (non-indigenous). Society graded as Class IX: backward, extreme threat.*

Climate: *Sticky.*

Notable game: *Ravnaphants, Carnotaurs, Gorefangs, Bloodworms, Death Lemurs, Caustic Pigeons, Quanbeasts, etc. See supplementary volumes for full details.*

Further notes: *Warzone. 43rd to 111th armies amalgamated to form 112th army. Reinforcements expected from Ravnavar. Heavy armour redirected to Ghast Front.*

Encyclopaedia Imperialis, *updated digital insert.*

*　　*　　*

In order to achieve victory, you must understand not just the enemy, but your own soldiers. On arriving at base camp, I was greeted by a human officer.

'You,' he said to a M'lak adjutant. 'You take um nice lady for heap big tour, yes?'

Wordlessly, the alien led me around the perimeter. After a while, I felt it necessary to explain myself.

'Me big general,' I began, tapping myself on the chest. 'Me boss lady, many warriors.'

'Oh heavens,' the M'Lak replied. 'Not you as well. I realise that we're somewhat ill-equipped here, but they could at least send one officer who doesn't talk like a four-year-old.'

It turned out that he had been a stockbroker before the war. I began to suspect that the command structure required a bit of work.

General Florence Young, *Memoirs.*

General Difficulties

The first thing Smith saw of Andor was the barrier net. Tiny satellites dotted the windscreen like brass buttons on a velvet shirt, and between them, tens of miles wide, hung impact nets made of cable.

It made sense, as much as anything on the Lemming Front made sense: a spaceship hitting the wire at speed would be sliced apart before it could get through to the planet beyond. Given the Yullian love of driving into things, it was a very sensible precaution.

'Fishnet,' Suruk said from the back of the cockpit. 'I approve.'

They slipped past the net, into the atmosphere, sinking through layers of sodden cloud. The surface of Andor was covered in a thick layer of vapour. 'It's the planet breathing,' Rhianna said, but to Smith it looked more like sweat.

'It's a bloody pressure-cooker,' Carveth said, and she put the windscreen wipers on. They filled the cockpit with their creaking.

Down below, something moved through the forest, leaving a trail of brown devastation behind it like an exhaust. Smith lifted the binoculars. It was a wild ravnaphant, a fairly small one, shovelling trees into its maw. Someone long ago had introduced the beasts to Andor, and they had fitted in well – given that the rest of the native life was lethal, it was hardly surprising.

Base Camp lay at the edge of Lake Trondo, at the bottom of a hole blasted through the forest canopy. It spread out beneath them, a picnic rug on a mass of green, and as they sank down half a dozen missile pods tracked their descent. Most of the buildings below were temporary, put up by the army or dropped in from transport shuttles, but a few dated back to happier days. All had been reinforced with sandbags. Automated guns turned slowly on their turrets, scanning the forest for enemies, their clockwork already starting to rust in the hot, thick air. The Union Jack had been braced with a crosspiece to stop it drooping: this low down, there was almost no wind.

The *John Pym* touched down on all four legs at once, which was a good omen. They collected their gear and gathered at the airlock. 'Ready?' Smith asked.

'Okay,' Rhianna said. She was in her version of practical clothing: a headband and shapeless, floor-length dress that made her look like a tie-dyed chess piece. It made Smith feel queasy with lust. It was as though she gave off some aphrodisiac, or perhaps it was just the cloud of fragrant smoke that tended to follow her around.

The door swung open. Outside, men and M'Lak carried boxes of food and ammunition between them. A column of soldiers jogged past in body armour, dripping sweat. A sergeant-major with a face like a moustachioed beetroot ran bellowing behind them. Troopers piled cases of rockets as if they were logs and, beside the pile, a Sey tracker crossed off items on a clipboard. It looked like a cross between an ostrich and a small dinosaur.

Smith walked out first, and a curtain of heat met him. For a moment he stood at the bottom of the steps, getting used to the warm, airless air, and then a woman stepped out and saluted.

'*Jaizeh*, chaps! Captain Smith, I presume?' She was in her late forties, wiry and intellectual-looking. She wore army uniform, but no armour. 'Captain Selena Harrison.'

'Pleased to meet you, Captain Harrison.' Something was wrong here, Smith thought: among all the chaos, something was missing.

A tiny brass wiper flicked across the lenses of Captain Harrison's glasses. 'It's a pleasure. Welcome to Andor. This way.'

They started off from the *John Pym*, across the prefab landing pad, and Smith realised what was not there. He couldn't hear machinery. Everything was being moved by hand; there were no autoloaders, no wallahbots to do the heavy work.

'We'll outfit you for forest fighting,' Harrison explained. 'You'll need to go geared up all the time, I'm afraid. You never know when the furries will try it on.' Captain Harrison gave Rhianna a suspicious look. 'You're not really equipped for fighting here,' she said. 'For one thing, the lemmings will hear your flip-flops.'

'Oh,' Rhianna said. She thought for a moment, bent down and kicked her sandals off. 'Is that better?'

'Yeah, perfect.' Harrison glared at Smith, who couldn't see why she looked so annoyed, and quickened the pace. 'Captain Smith, General Young wants to talk to you in person. You're a lucky man.'

'Thank you.'

'She's the reason we're still alive,' Harrison said. 'The rest of you chaps are welcome to make yourselves at home. Now, once you've been certified fit for action, we can get you armed up.'

One of the automated guns gave a burst of fire. Smith froze, hand half extended to his rifle. A creature about the size of an albatross dropped out of the sky. It landed with a loose thud about twenty yards away.

'Mosquito,' Harrison said.

Smith followed her up the path towards the most heavily fortified of the older buildings. It looked like something from a western: the white façade was chipped and the plaster that had not been blasted away was cracked like dried greasepaint.

We're falling apart, he thought suddenly, and the thought startled him.

'You first,' Harrison said, and she swept her arm out towards the door.

The inside was dark and cool. Smith stood in an entrance hall. At the far end, an argument was reaching its conclusion. A tall man with an angular face stood under a tiny camera-blimp like a thought-bubble, ignoring a soldier who seemed to be trying to send him away.

'Come on, come on!' the tall man said. He wore a breastplate under his suit jacket. 'It's a simple question. Ah!' he exclaimed, noticing Smith, and he strode across the hall.

'Wait a moment,' Captain Harrison began, but the tall man ignored her.

'Lionel Markham, *We Ask the Questions*,' the man said.

'Sorry?'

'I'm Lionel Markham. I present *We Ask the Questions*, the Space Empire's toughest current affairs programme.'

'Oh really? I'm Captain Isambard Smith. Pleased to mee –'

'So, Captain Smith, what's really going on here?

Who's in charge here, that's what I know that people want to know.'

'Well, General Young, I suppose.'

'So you're not sure?'

Harrison stepped forward. 'Come on, that's enough. He's only just got here.'

Markham nodded. 'So you've only just got here and you don't know for sure what's going on. What does that say to the rest of the Empire?'

'I –'

'Come on, come on! It's a simple question, yes or no.'

'What?'

'Yes or no? Yes or no? Yes or no?'

Smith opened his mouth, Harrison advanced, hand raised to grab the camera-drone, but Markham turned on the spot and directly addressed the machine. 'So there you have it. The world asks: "Is the Yullian war still a runner, or is the whole front about to collapse?" The Imperial Army is meant to be standing sentry, but is it too sedentiary to prevent a lemming entry this century? You've been watching *We Ask the Questions*. I'm Lionel Markham, being clever so you don't have to.'

Harrison motioned Smith towards the doors at the far end of the hall. 'This way, Captain Smith,' she said. 'And bugger off, Lionel, there's a good chap.'

Smith walked into the room. It was large and, by the standards of the Yullian Front, luxurious. Five people – four humans and a M'Lak – sat around a collapsible table on wicker chairs, drinking gin. Smith recognised one of them: the woman at the head of the table, her hat on the formica before her, was General Florence Young, scourge of the lemmings and victor of the Battle of the River Tam. General Young was at least seventy-five and very small. Had it not been for her skill, the whole front would have been overrun the previous year, when the Yull had launched their most frenzied assault on the Space Empire yet. To the men, Florence Young was a friendly, great-aunt-like figure: to the lemming men, she was a demon in wrinkly, lavender-scented human form.

'Captain Smith,' said General Young. 'Do come in. Tea or gin?'

Smith took a seat. 'Tea, please.'

'These are my colleagues,' General Young said, gesturing down the table. 'Colonels Hopkirk, Butt and Frobisher. And this is Lorvoth the Bloody-Handed, High Warlord of Zhukar.'

'Pleased to meet you,' said the M'Lak.

A man loomed out of the shadows. Smith paused a moment, surprised: it was W, the spymaster. He wore his usual tweed jacket and smelled of mothballs as well as tobacco. W strode over, tall and gawky, and lowered himself into an empty seat.

'Have you ever seen this man before?' General Young inquired.

'Oh yes,' Smith replied. 'Loads of times.'

W shook his head quickly.

'Oh, *him*? No, never seen him. I must've meant someone else.'

W rubbed at his pencil moustache. He looked weary: shadows attached themselves to his face like dirt.

General Young nodded. 'And if you had worked for him, possibly in a top secret capacity, would you have been responsible for a number of secret operations, including the assassination of Ghast Number Eight and the recovery of the Dodgson Drive, neither of which officially occurred?'

'Um,' Smith replied. 'Probably. Both. Not?'

Captain Harrison brought the tea. 'You're I/C distribution, Harrison,' said Young. 'From now on in this operation you will be known as "mother". Percolate and circulate.'

Harrison poured out the tea.

'You have an impressive record for disinformation, Captain Smith,' the general said. 'Your reputation for counter-intelligence is quite remarkable.'

'I'm not dim, you know,' Smith replied, hurt.

'That's not what "counter-intelligence" means.' She leaned back in her chair. 'Captain Smith, the war against the lemming men started badly. We massively underestimated the Yull. When I first arrived here, several of my staff actually believed them to be a sort of house-trained beaver. This is completely untrue: the Yull are a disciplined and organised enemy, and they piss everywhere. How's the tea?'

'Fine, thanks.'

'Good. Now, you need to understand how things work here. This planet, this war, is not like anything you've seen. Tanks can't fit between the trees. Warbots seize up. The canopy's so thick that if you drop a bomb on it, it'll bounce right back into the plane. Try scanning for hostile life forms on Andor and the needle will probably fly off the dial. This is the kind of war that's won with knives, not spaceships.

'I understand you have fought the Yull before, and you know the debased level on which they operate. I would like to say that the lemming men are savages, although that's not really fair. I've met some perfectly decent savages in my time.'

'Quite so, Florence,' said Lorvoth the Bloody-Handed. 'More tea, anyone?'

'Murder, torture, cannibalism, human sacrifice...' said General Young, 'all of these are a spot of fun to the lemming man. They stand as a warning of the depravity awaiting those who stray away from tea, basic decency and self-preservation. *And* they all have nits.'

An odd change had come over General Young's face. Her eyes seemed to have slid back in their sockets and her lower jaw had come forward. She no longer looked like someone's granny, but a very determined person in the early stages of turning into a bulldog, or perhaps a locomotive.

'The Yull call this their Divine Migration. In truth, it's a holy war. Holy wars are all the same, Captain. The aim of the war is war itself, the purpose of killing is killing. Because of that, I have come to realise that the lemming men cannot be stopped, at least in any normal way. They have to be destroyed. Captain Smith, when my people are finished here, there will be nothing even remotely resembling the Yullian army left. My soldiers are going to tear the Divine Amicable Army to bits. The Yull will beg their war-god to let them forget the day they ever dared cross us. Biscuit?'

'I'm fine, thanks.'

'Do you know a man named Major Wainscott?'

'Er, possibly.'

'He's an expert in irregular warfare. About 5'9', bearded, very wiry, mad as a bag of ferrets. Three months ago, Major Wainscott and his team were sent into the Andorian forest to demolish a certain bridge. They have not returned. Instead, the Major has taken to sending us weekly updates on his progress. To begin with, they were quite satisfactory, but of late the quality has... *changed*, if you would.'

Harrison activated the panmelodiatron. The curling horn swung round to face Smith. The voice that came out was distant, strangely detached, but undoubtedly Wainscott's.

'They talk about morality,' it said. *'The hypocrites sit in their comfortable offices, passing judgment as they*

pass the biscuits round. They tell me it's alright to kill lemming men by the dozen... with guns, bombs, knives, shoelaces... especially shoelaces... but try to walk down the street with your old chap au naturelle and what do you get then? The funny farm, that's what!'

Smith looked at W. The spy took a large swig of tea.

'Last Thursday we hid out in a village called Krakora,' Wainscott said. *'We rigged a roadblock. The Yull came down in wagons, looking to kill the villagers. We hit them from the sides, grenades and lasers. Most of them died before they got out of their lorries. This one lemming soldier saw me – he looked into my eyes, and – hey, I'm not wearing any trousers! Well I never! Hey, Susan, get an eyeful of this –'*

General Young reached out and flicked a switch. The recorder fell silent. 'That was one of his more stable messages,' she said. 'Can we skip on a bit?'

The recorder jumped forward.

'My unit has been infiltrated by an individual known only as the egg-man. This whole mission was a white elephant from the start... or a white rabbit... or a pink elephant, on parade. My God... they set the controls for the heart of the sun, they sent us two thousand light years from home, dropped out of orbit eight miles high... like a squid, fast and bulbous! They're coming to take me away!'

Harrison lifted the laser needle. The silence was broken only by the chink of cups and saucers.

'You see, Smith,' the general said, 'there's a conflict in every human heart, between the rational and the irrational. And sometimes, it is not good that triumphs, but stark bollock lunacy. The British Army cannot allow a madman to operate on its fringes, especially when there's valuable work he could be doing back here.'

Captain Harrison spoke. 'Your mission is to proceed

up-continent and compel Major Wainscott to return to base.'

General Young said, 'He's out there, operating without any control, any decent restraint, any kind of undergarments. Bring him back, Smith.'

Smith sipped his tea. 'Is there anything I can offer him? Some kind of incentive?'

Colonel Butt pushed a file across the table. 'This may help. It contains data on Wainscott. Next week it's his birthday. You could tell him that we're throwing a party.'

Colonel Frobisher added, 'If he comes back in time, we could all celebrate.'

There was another pause.

W took a long drag on his cigarette. He turned to look at Smith. 'Celebrate,' he said, 'with extreme prejudice.'

*   *   *

W ushered Smith outside, teacup still in one hand and a canvas bag in the other. He squinted into the sunshine, a hard, gawky man in tweed, like a scarecrow made out of schoolteacher's clothes. 'Good to see you,' he said after a while.

'You too,' Smith replied.

W sipped his tea. 'Wainscott's got something big,' he said. 'I don't know the details yet, but it's more than just blowing up some bridge, I'll wager.'

'I see.'

'Your ship floats, doesn't it?' W put down his bag.

'Provided we open the right airlocks, yes.'

'Good. They want to stick you on some boat, but you're better in the ship. Head upriver, find Wainscott and bring him back. I can lend you some kit. The service gave me a tranquiliser rifle, and I've got a ravnaphant gun.'

'I didn't know you hunted ravnaphants.'

'Only once. And it was a long time ago. Long story,' he said, as he lit a cigarette. 'Here,' he added, and he took a packet of pills from his jacket. 'If all else fails, slip some of these into Wainscott's dinner and stick him on the ship while he's out of action.'

Smith took the box and turned it over in his hand. 'These are contraceptives, sir.'

'Of course. First, they'll give him a headache, and then he'll roll over and go to sleep. While he's out, shanghai the bleeder and bring him back.'

'Righto.'

'Keep on the water until you find Wainscott. You'll go in under the forest canopy. Once you've got him, fly on to Mothkarak Castle. The general's heading there soon to get closer to the front.' He raised a knobbly hand and pointed. 'Is that your pilot over there?'

Smith looked and saw Carveth and, in front of her, the crimson-faced sergeant-major he'd glimpsed earlier.

'Uh-oh,' he said, and he strode down to meet them.

'You'll follow orders, missy,' the sergeant-major declared. He had a deep, rich voice that had been made for light opera. 'You, my girl, are in the army now. No more of this spacefleet nonsense for you – you've downloaded the king's shilling.' His eyes took on a crazy glint. 'Which means you'll be working with me – all of you – forever.'

Carveth glanced back, saw Smith and cried, 'Boss, help! They're trying to make me do PE!'

Smith approached, aware that W was following. That was embarrassing.

'I've followed you halfway across the galaxy,' Carveth said. 'I've fought the most vicious, crazy monsters in the universe, and now you want to turn me into a... jogger?

No! There are some things I will not do!' She turned away and strode off up the hill as fast as her small legs would carry her. Ten yards off, she stopped and turned, possibly to catch her breath.

'I don't care how many lemming men I have to fight. I'll fight every single one of them. But no running – no more running!'

A few yards away, a camera drone turned its focus from Carveth to the sombre man in the dark suit. Lionel Markham stared back into the camera, and spoke to the nation.

'Top brass may not want to give anything away, but that's the news from the troops on the ground – no more running! The Yull may be coming for the 112th Army, but it's fighting spirit like that they'll have to face. I'm Lionel Markham and it's on that note we end this edition of *We Ask the Questions*, as one young woman puts the challenge to the entire lemming empire. *No more running*. Thank you, and goodnight.'

*   *   *

'*Yullian warrior!*' the radio barked. '*Why do you disgrace yourself with two bottles in the shower? Use new Head & Pelt, for body, shine and martial glory!*'

It was true, General Wikwot reflected: his fur certainly did have new levels of volume. Of course, he had ended up using two bottles, but that was because he had a very large surface area. And there had been a lot of blood to wash off.

Since he had strolled back into camp, an axe in either hand, he had killed forty-two challengers. Given that he had allowed himself to be captured alive, some of the Yull had been reluctant to take him back as general, but most of them changed their minds once the disembowelling began.

He finished brushing his pelt and flicked a seed off his shoulder. The human prison had not been brutal – itself a clear indication of the puniness of mankind – but it had lacked proper grooming facilities. He wanted to look his best when they dragged the offworlder general to him in chains and he ripped out her heart.

Wikwot had set up his headquarters in what had once been a set of holiday chalets: partially for logistical reasons, but mainly for the liquor cabinets. Although he had been able to make some booze of his own whilst in prison, dandelion wine tasted much better when it had not passed through a radiator.

One of the sentries poked his snout into the room. '*Dar huphep!*'

Wikwot waved a hand. '*Huphep*, serf. What is it?'

'Noble General, the Master of Assassins is here to speak to you. He... asked me to deliver this knife as a token of his... good wishes.'

'Which knife?'

Like a tree cut for lumber, the sentry fell onto his front. 'This – knife –' he gasped, and Wikwot saw it protruding from the sentry's back.

'Huh?' he muttered, and someone coughed behind him.

Wikwot spun, reaching for the axe in his belt. A lemming man stepped out from behind the curtains.

The newcomer saluted. 'Xiploc Cots,' he said. 'Master of Assassins and acting colonel of the secret police. Sorry about your serf, but one has to keep one's hand in.'

Wikwot shrugged. 'I have others. So, Colonel... have you come to judge me?'

Cots shook his head. His fur was black. The torture

implements on his belt, a source of pride for any Yullian officer, were darkened with soot. 'Not at all. I am here to congratulate you. Your escape from Ravnavar was remarkable.'

'I used the ancient way of our people: burrowing.' Wikwot gestured to the cabinet. 'Dandelion wine?'

'Thank you, but no. My pouches are still full from lunch. I am here to discuss special operations against the offworlder pig-monkeys and their minions. I bring with me twelve experts from the Dark Lantern Co-Operative, skilled in espionage and assassination.' He gestured at the doorway: figures waited outside. The air seemed to blur around them, as if from the heat. 'Welcome back, General,' Cots said. 'I have been sent here to pass on your new orders.'

Wikwot poured himself a large shot of whisky. 'Yes?'

Cots drew himself up and coughed into his paw. 'The High Command of the Greater Galactic Happiness and Friendship Collective greets General Wikwot joyfully and is delighted to pass on instructions for the furtherance of our amiable plan to bring the entire galaxy under our wise and kindly guidance. You are warmly encouraged to butcher everything. Men, women, children, pets. All un-rodents must die, and die slow. Attack the offworlders with frenzied vigour. Overrun their positions, tear their flesh and devour their hearts to make yourself strong. All settlements are to be levelled. All captives are to be tortured to death. Any soldier showing pity, mercy or lack of enthusiasm in our holy task is to be force-fed his own spleen.'

Wikwot nodded. 'Is that all?'

The assassin glanced over his shoulder. 'There is something else.'

'Well?'

'Our enemies are not a single force. Lacking our manpower and lemming spirit, they pay the slave races to fight with them. I refer to the M'Lak, the Sey and other ludicrous talking animals.'

Ah, thought Wikwot, this is the meat of it.

Cots said, 'We are close to locating the Relics of Grimdall, General. The Dark Lantern Co-Operative is at your service.'

'Excellent. I will let you know when your skills are required.'

Cots moved towards the door, paused and sniffed. 'Just one more thing, General.'

Wikwot lowered his glass. 'Yes?'

'Is that Head and Pelt?'

'Of course.'

Cots nodded. 'I thought I recognised the glossiness. I dye my fur black for assassination work. The roots keep coming back, though.'

*   *   *

In the end, W pulled some strings, and Carveth escaped from P.E. They were not technically army personnel, he explained, and so out of the direct chain of command. Sergeant-Major Williams turned maroon and looked as if he was about to boil. 'Of course, sir,' he said darkly. 'I'll let the appropriate people know.'

W stared out at the *John Pym*. 'Watch yourself, Smith,' he said. 'Watch your crew, your ship, the forest, Wainscott, the lemming men – watch out for bloody everything. And remember, the chaps out here – human, Morlock, whatever – are the only thing between the lemming men and a bloodbath. Best of luck, eh?'

'Thanks,' Smith replied, and reflected that sometimes the spy carried the principle of being up-front with his men a bit too far.

'Oh,' W added, pulling a tin from his backpack, 'take this. It's Wainscott's birthday cake. If all else fails, you could lure him back with it.'

Drums up the River

The *John Pym* slid away from the shore, using its thrusters on their lowest setting to manoeuvre. Steam rose from the back of the ship as Carveth flicked the engines, and then they were pushing quietly through the water, leaving Lake Trondo behind.

Trees curved over the river, meeting in the middle. The *Pym* slid into the tunnel they created, and suddenly the sun was gone. The forest was as hot and close as the throat of a giant beast.

Suruk took the first watch, squatting on top of the ship beside the dorsal hatch, scanning the banks for ambushes. They were still well inside Imperial territory – at least, in theory. The Yull were skilled infiltrators and, even this far back, it was possible that they had worked their way inside. Suruk peered at the overhanging trees. If the lemming men could choose any method of attack, in his long and gory experience, they would revert to instinct and drop down from above.

Smith sat with Carveth in the cockpit and made the tea while she steered the ship. Gerald the hamster scurried in his cage, oblivious to the larger rodents lurking among the trees. Despite the danger, Carveth seemed quite cheerful. Presumably war against genocidal maniacs wasn't too bad compared with a cross-country run in the company of a sergeant-major.

Two hours in, Smith swapped with Suruk. Rifle by his side, he watched as they moved further upriver, into the foliage.

After a while, he took out W's folder, and laid the papers out before him as if dealing a hand of solitaire.

Major Arwen Caratacus Peter Wainscott was forty-nine. He was born on Shropshire Secundus, on the edge of the Empire. Wainscott's father had played lead clarinet for King Klezmer and the Wild Folk. His mother was a failed anthropologist, defrocked after falsifying six tribes north of Bogota. Wainscott had one sister, three years his junior, who from the photo in the file resembled the vengeful ghost of someone who had fallen down a well. Her name was Denethora.

Smith flicked on.

Wainscott had enjoyed a quiet childhood. To begin with, he kept himself to himself, but after reaching adulthood, he started to keep himself to anyone willing to take a look. His worried parents did the sensible thing and sent him to Officer Training College.

Wainscott had been a terrible soldier, to the extent that someone had scribbled 'Does not play well with others' across the top of the major's military records. He would have been a disgrace to the uniform, had he ever been caught wearing it. He had hated everything about the army apart from the potential for destruction, at which he excelled.

Smith flicked through several photographs that he really hoped had been taken at a private function, and then paused at one of Wainscott staring down a rhinoceros. In the next picture, Wainscott and a group of M'Lak elders posed in front of a captured helicopter of the Sixth Edenite Air Cavalry.

Before the war had started for real, the Republic of New Eden had been trying to spread the word to the unbelievers, which largely meant shooting them and stealing their stuff. Wainscott was selected to smuggle weaponry to the M'Lak tribes on the grounds that, were he to be captured, nobody would believe a word that he said, truth or otherwise. As it was, Wainscott's cunning and ferocity delighted the M'Lak, who tried to keep him as a pet.

'Boss?'

Smith glanced up, and suddenly he was no longer inside Wainscott's life. Carveth was half-out of the airlock, brandishing a mug at him. 'Tea. What're you reading?'

Smith showed her the title of the file. It said INTELLIGENCE, RESTRICTED.

'That sounds like you,' Carveth said. 'I'd better get back to steering this ship,' she added, and she disappeared through the hatch.

Wainscott would never be a proper hero; he was too mad for that. Any credit he had built up was lost during the visit of the President of Poland, when, during a military display, Wainscott had first field-stripped a laser cannon and then himself.

But it was the Warforge incident that brought Wainscott low. As a commando raid, it was flawless, an astonishing piece of high-quality mayhem. In one standard day, the major single-handedly destroyed the Ghast Empire's entire Warforge Orbital Dock and, with it, a quarter of the Ghast navy. The only problem was that the Ghasts weren't at war with Earth yet. Having got away from his enemies, Wainscott was put away by his friends.

And so Wainscott spent a year in his pyjamas, watching television and finding clever places to hide his medication. Smith read a short report detailing the major's attempt to escape Sunnyvale Home for the Bewildered by clinging to the underside of the pills trolley. Wainscott amused himself by learning Urdu, Mandarin and Swahili, and writing angry letters to the *Daily Monolith*, explaining the dangers of Ghast rearmament. One day, the *Monolith*'s eccentric columnist, who had links to the Secret Service, wrote back, and included a metal file. Thus W recruited his first field agent. Nobody, not even Ghast Number One, had been happier than Wainscott when war broke out.

* * *

Smith heard voices. He put the file down beside him and picked up his rifle. They were too low for lemming men; it sounded like a crowd of humans. He crawled over to the hatch and looked down into the hold. 'Suruk? Tell Carveth to slow down. There's something up ahead.'

He lay down on his stomach and propped his rifle before him. Smith put his eye to the scope and saw that the light came from electric lamps, not fire. A metallic squelch blared from up ahead. It sounded like a speaker.

An attack boat slid up towards them. Two M'Lak crewed it, one holding a grappling hook like a weapon. The boat moved towards the bank to let them pass.

Hard white light flooded between tree trunks, as though a huge flare had been lit in the forest. Bunting hung between the trees. Union Jacks dangled over the water. All it needed was trestle tables and rain and it would have been like Elgar Day back home.

A soldier watched them from the riverbank. He was almost invisible against the trees. 'What's going on?' Smith called.

'CSE's got a concert on,' the man shouted back. 'Jimmy Horlicks and Deep Uke. Here, aren't you Space Corps?'

'Yes, what of it?'

'You're a bit lost, mate.' He pointed at the sky. 'Space is that way.'

As Smith climbed back into the ship, he heard the distorted wail of a support act. He hurried into the cockpit. 'Pull us into the bank, Carveth. We'll see what all this is about.'

They gathered at the airlock. 'You think we'll find Wainscott here?' Carveth asked.

'I doubt it. But someone might know. It sounds like they're having a bit of a jolly. Who is Jimmy Horlicks, anyhow? The name rings a bell.'

Rhianna ran her hands through her hair and made an attempt to tie it back. 'He's an English musician. Pretty far out, though. He's one of the best ukulele players in space.'

'It sounds dreadful from here.'

'Come on,' Carveth said. 'The acoustics are all wrong. It'll sound much better from inside the beer tent.'

They stepped ashore. A flat area about a hundred yards square had been levelled, and it was full of soldiers: mainly human, although a few intrigued aliens had joined them. A few guards watched the forest. Smith glimpsed a Sey tracker stalking between the tree trunks, beam gun strapped across its body. But the great majority faced the stage at the far end of the clearing, a red-curtained, gilt-sprayed lump of music hall torn up and set down in the forest.

'Give me your beer coupons,' Carveth said. 'Suruk, give me a hand.'

Smith passed his coupons over. 'Make mine a pint of Stalwart. And Suruk, stop her if she tries to run away with the beer.'

Suruk smiled. 'She will not go far,' and as Carveth protested her innocence, Smith and Rhianna entered the crowd.

Jangling, distorted sound tore out of the speakers, a tight, quick strumming amplified into a roar. The crowd cheered. Smith put his arm around Rhianna: partly out of affection and partly to stop her getting confused and wandering off. From what she had told him, festivals tended to have that effect on her.

A small man appeared on stage in a neat suit, holding a wired ukulele. 'Eh up!' he said, and the speakers turned his voice into a chipper, jolly bellow. 'Thought I'd do a few tunes for you all. So then, what do the Empire's finest lads and lasses want to hear?'

The man to Smith's right cupped his hands and shouted, 'Jimmy! Play *All Along the Whippet Track*!'

'*Cross Town Tram Ride*!' a woman yelled from behind. 'Do *Cross Town Tram Ride*!'

The members of Deep Uke emerged from the wings to join Jimmy Horlicks. Rhianna leaned her head on Smith's shoulder, and he felt very clever indeed.

'This is a slower number,' Horlicks announced. 'It's called *Eh, Joe*.'

As Deep Uke launched into a jangling song, Carveth slipped into view. Her right hand held a paper cup, and her left was locked around the wrist of a tall young officer. 'I found this man!' Carveth said.

'Dammit, woman,' the man protested, 'I've got a wife and child – oh, who are you?'

'Captain Isambard Smith. These are my colleagues.'

'I see,' said the man. He had to shout to make himself heard. 'Major Dalston Pintle. I'm I/C of this station. Your pilot won't let go of me.'

'It happens sometimes,' Smith replied.

Major Pintle shook himself free from Carveth and looked them over. 'I heard there were some irregulars coming upriver. I didn't realise you'd be quite this irregular, though.'

'We're looking for a group of commandos,' Smith called back. On stage, James Horlicks was performing a complicated solo to *Turned Out Purple Again*.

'Oh yes?'

'Do you know the Deepspace Operations Group?'

'I think I've got their first album.'

'What about Major Wainscott? Smallish fellow, pale, with a beard.'

Pintle frowned. 'Trousers?'

'Probably not, I'm afraid.'

The major nodded. 'There was a man, 'bout a month back. A bunch of soldiers brought him through. They looked like special forces types. I thought he'd got a bad dose of the sun and gone doolally. They headed north, following the river. Said something about blowing up a bridge. Bloody furries probably got him by now.'

'Maybe. Thank you, Major.'

'Happy to help.'

The song ended with a drawn out wail of vibrato. James Horlicks adjusted his tie and leaned into the microphone. 'Thanks everyone, that's grand. Now I'd like to play a new tune: I think of it as a new national anthem.'

Pintle glanced round as if he'd heard himself insulted. 'A new national anthem? I won't stand for it! Excuse me, everyone,' he said, 'got to keep order.' He plunged into the crowd, indignantly shouldering his way towards the stage.

'We should go,' Suruk said. 'Our quarry gains time on us.'

'But what about the music?' Rhianna said. 'Come on, guys.'

'We'll leave the top airlock open,' Smith replied. 'That way we'll be able to hear. And I know it's nice here, but remember: the *John Pym* has cabins and a functional toilet.'

'That does count for a lot,' Carveth said. 'Alright, back we go.'

The *Pym* pulled away from the bank as if under covering fire, the lights flooding the sky behind it. Rhianna sat on the roof with Smith, watching the crowd shrink and then disappear as the river curved and they were lost to view. She looked behind them for a while afterwards, as the twang of the ukulele still cut the air.

> *Well I'm standing next to the chip shop,*
> *a pint of mild in my hand.*
> *Yes I'm standing next to the chip shop, a*
> *pint of mild in my hand.*
> *The man says 'Want a gherkin?' and I*
> *say 'That sounds grand!'*
> *And I say 'Howdo, child?' Lord knows I*
> *say 'Howdo, child!'*

*   *   *

Smith was dozing on the sofa when Suruk prodded his shoulder. 'Uh?' Smith said, sitting up. 'What's happening?'

'We have stopped at the bank,' the alien replied.

'Piglet wished to reconnoitre.'

'Carveth? Reconnoitre?'

'She told me that she had seen a creature that she needed to pursue. I thought such an interest in hunting was only to be encouraged.'

'Hang on. You let Carveth go off to hunt things? *Alone?*'

Suruk looked a little hurt. 'Oh no. I would never do that. She took Rhianna with her.'

'What?' Smith scrambled upright. The file slid off his lap, sending pictures of Wainscott sliding over the floor. 'We've got to get them back. They'll die out there.'

'I told them to shriek if they were in danger. Oh, and Mazuran? I think we are being followed.'

Smith grabbed his rifle. 'Let's go.'

They clambered out of the roof hatch, into air as moist and hot as breath, and scrambled down the side of the ship. The wing creaked as Smith hurried along it and dropped down into the undergrowth. Something small and many-legged scurried away from his boot. He hoped Rhianna had her shoes on.

Roots crawled over the forest floor like veins: as they walked, the plants seemed to try to catch Smith's legs. Something moved in the trees to the left: Smith swung his rifle up and saw a beaked lemur swinging from branch to branch, arm over arm.

If Suruk noticed it, he did not show it. He simply walked a little more cautiously than usual, occasionally glancing upwards or checking the ground. The alien put his hand out. 'Here,' he whispered, and he crouched down.

It took a moment to see what he meant. Rhianna's tie-dyed shirt was surprisingly good camouflage against the lurid vegetation. Carveth stood beside her, half-concealed by a tree trunk. The foliage broke up the outline of the two women: a couple of fronds, a serrated leaf, and they had been almost lost to view. Smith wondered how close the lemming men could get.

'Psst! Rhianna,' Smith said. 'Over here.'

She turned and put a finger to her lips. Suruk raised his eyebrows and then his spear. He advanced with high, careful steps, as though expecting the ground to give way.

Without turning around, Carveth whispered, 'Look.'

She pointed. An animal slipped between the trees towards the water's edge. The tree trunks blocking the way made it seem to flicker in and out of existence. It was large and four-legged, and at once Smith saw why Carveth had dared venture off the ship. The back was shorter than its Earth equivalent, the legs both thicker and more flexible, and the animal was bright blue, but there was no mistaking what it looked like, or the awe in Carveth's voice.

'It's a pony!'

They peered through the bushes. The blue pony walked slowly towards the waterside, leaning back on the slope. It knew something was wrong, Smith saw. He looked at Rhianna and found that she was frowning in concentration, fingertips pressed to her temples.

Smith's calf muscle began to ache and he shifted position. A branch crunched under his heel.

The pony glanced around, mane flapping, its wide eyes alarmed. Carveth said, 'No, don't –' but it whirled and rushed into the undergrowth. Leaves fell behind it like a curtain, and it was gone.

'You scared him away!' Carveth exclaimed. She turned, and looked Smith in the eye. 'Don't *ever* scare ponies.'

Her intensity surprised him. Smith replied, 'No I didn't.'

Suruk gave a polite little cough, and pointed.

The jungle burst open before them. An enormous tusked head pushed through the branches, followed by a body the size of a rhino's. The skin flickered, as if poorly tuned-in, and became paler as the creature emerged. Its eyes, mounted on stereoscopic cones, swivelled like gun turrets.

A moment later, a voice came from its back.

'Frote! Frote, stop that at once!' The rider, who had been knocked prone along its spine, sat up and blinked behind his spectacles. He smoothed his jacket, and adjusted his helmet. 'Hello?'

Suruk stared up at the rider, at once astonished and appalled. 'Morgar? What are you doing here? And do the Ravnavari Lancers know that you are impersonating them?'

'Suruk? Good lord.' Morgar took his glasses off, stared at the lenses, and slipped them back on. 'Well, fancy that. Whatever brings you here?'

'Bringing deadly vengeance to the scum of Yullia, of course. But why are you in that uniform?' Suruk demanded. 'The last time we met, brother, you spoke at great lengths about under-floor heating. Is there great demand for warm towel-rails in the jungles of Andor?'

'Actually, I am a Ravnavari Lancer.' Morgar peered down disapprovingly, like an old schoolteacher dealing with an irritating question. 'I was commissioned to design a new restroom suite. As such, I ride with the lancers.'

'Bah!' Suruk said. 'I have never heard of such nonsense.'

Morgar gathered the reins and sat up. 'Well, stranger things have happened in the army. Our medical orderly used to be a professor of French literature. He told the colonel that he liked looking at Balsac and they had him checking the squaddies for bollock-rot.'

Suruk shook his head. 'They must have asked for warriors used to sitting in command. You thought they said "commode" and signed up.'

A smallish dragonfly, no longer than a man's arm, flew past. Frote opened his maw. There was a wet crack, and his tongue flicked out, hit the insect and whipped it into his mouth. Frote crunched it happily, while Carveth pulled a face.

Morgar folded his arms. 'And what have *you* done, then?'

'I?' Suruk said. 'Well, I slew many lemming men, took many skulls, and joined the great quest to rid this planet of the conniving Yull. Oh, I also had children, but I got better. Perhaps I could leave some of my spawn in one of your charming bidets.'

Morgar adjusted his glasses. 'Suruk, do I detect a whiff of jealousy?'

Smith thought that Suruk was being rather sniffy about it all. The old warrior had always regarded his brother as somewhat effete. Perhaps Morgar was turning over a new, bloodstained, leaf. 'Well,' Smith said, 'good on you, Morgar. It's not many who get to ride with the Lancers. On which subject,' he added, 'shouldn't they be with you?'

'What?' Morgar twisted round, looking behind him. 'We're out on patrol. The others must have – oh, bugger! Frote, get after them.' He yanked the reins, and the shadar lumbered round. 'Quickly, Frote!'

The beast rushed at the nearest tree, and in a moment had swarmed up the trunk. Morgar yelped, apparently as surprised by this as the onlookers, and Frote bounded upwards, incredibly nimble for a creature of its size. The shadar bounced out, suspended in the air for a moment and, as it grabbed a new tree, its skin flickered into a deep, striped green. 'I'll send you a postcard!' Morgar cried from somewhere high above them, and he was gone.

'I worry about him,' Suruk said.

'I've got to admit,' Smith said, 'he's not the most obvious person I'd imagine joining the Ravnavari Lancers.'

Rhianna shrugged. 'I don't know. I think it's good that Morgar's pursuing an alternative career choice – even if it is in a constricting patriarchal hierarchy dedicated to the preservation of the imperialist hegemony.'

'I saw a pony,' Carveth said. 'Hey – Morgar had better not be chasing them or anything, because he'll have me to answer to.'

*   *   *

They pushed on upriver, drawing ever closer to the source. Smith picked over the files as they advanced and the journey seemed to blur with the data, as if the further into the jungle Smith was, the closer he got to Wainscott's brain. Which, to judge from the twists of the river, put them somewhere in his colon.

Rhianna meditated, and fortified her psychic powers by listening to a lot of Pink Zeppelin. Carveth moved from her bedroom to the cockpit and no further. Suruk retreated to the hold when he was not on watch, practising with his spear.

They passed a shuttle wing, jutting out of the water like the fin of an enormous shark. A family of wholks lumbered through the shallows, sifting the water for nutrients and squirting it out of the holes in their tails. A four-winged razorbird landed on the roof and was promptly slain by Suruk. It began to rain.

Smith entered the cockpit and sat down next to Carveth. She was almost invisible under a duvet. In the hamster cage, Gerald's wheel rattled.

'Everything alright?' Smith asked.

The duvet moved slightly. 'Okay. Can we eat Wainscott's cake, please?'

'No. I can take over if you want some air.'

'God no. Never get off the boat, that's what I say. Except for ponies.' She looked round. 'Hey, what's that?'

Smith took out the binoculars. 'I don't see anything.'

'No, listen.'

Smith paused, straining to hear anything over the rumble of the engines and the squeak of Gerald's wheel. But there was something – very faint, but something like music.

'I'll check,' he said.

He strode to the hold, climbed the ladder and opened the hatch. Suruk crouched on top of the ship, motionless in the hot air.

'I heard –' Smith began, but Suruk raised a hand. The alien looked up, at the forest canopy and the sky above them.

'Jets, Mazuran,' he said. 'Jets and Gustav Holst.'

And suddenly ships roared above them, tearing out of the sky like meteors, twisting in flight. There were three of them, British fighters, Hellfires, and over the sound of thrusters there roared *Mars, Bringer of War*.

The fighters sank down in the sky, and the lead vessel dropped below the treeline, into the gap over the river. Blue fire flared on its undercarriage. The river slopped and rippled from the jets, as though huge creatures thrashed beneath the surface.

The music was almost deafening. Someone had stripped the missile pods off the wings and replaced them with enormous curling funnels, like gramophone horns. Smith could feel it: the Planets Suite played at such volume that the sound seemed to push through his flesh, into his bones.

The volume sank to a bearable level, and a voice barked out of the speakers.

'What ho! Thought I recognised that crate. What happened, your ship fall out the sky or something?'

Smith looked at Suruk, and they both realised who they were addressing. It was the Hellfire of Wing Commander Shuttleswade, the one that Carveth had piloted at the battle of Wellington Prime. They were speaking to its onboard computer. In the cockpit, Shuttleswade raised a hand and waved.

'Been blasting the lemmings,' the ship explained. Its landing gear unfolded, glistening chrome against the drab fuselage. 'Look at this. They rigged me up new landing legs. Should be able to kick a few furry arses with these! So, where's the girlie?'

'Carveth? She's driving. Look, we're supposed to be on a secret mission –'

'Ah, say no more! I'll let the chaps know.'

'No, it's a secret.'

'Right you are. We're out strafing the Yull. They're gathering their chaps, you know. We'll buzz them a bit, slow them down and all that. Like the music? It irritates the hell out of the furries! You heading that way?'

'Yes,' Smith called.

'Watch yourself. The forest's crawling with lemmings. Good hunting, chaps!'

The thrusters roared, and the ship rose into the air. It turned and shot off to the southwest, music parping from its sides. Smith was pretty sure that he could hear the autopilot humming along.

Rhianna stood blinking at the bottom of the ladder, a roll-up smouldering in her hand. 'Thought I heard something,' she said vaguely. 'Is it raining?'

* * *

Up ahead, a scout-walker lay in the shallows like a giant metal chicken. The Union Jack stencilled on the side had started to fade. The exposed cogs were clogged with silt. One of the legs had been twisted at the ankle by an explosion. The pilot lay on the bank, in an advanced state of deadness.

'He must have trodden on a mine,' Smith said. 'Or a lemming.'

They passed the walker very slowly, as though shuffling past a coffin. Carveth said, 'The Empire's stuffed, isn't it?'

'Certainly not! Whatever gives you that idea?'

She said, 'I don't know. I just... well, I wonder if we're going to win.'

'Of course we're going to win. We're British, for God's sake. We have the finest soldiers in the galaxy. We never surrender and never give up.'

'The Yull won't give up, either.'

'That's because they're stupid lunatics. We'll just have to shoot them all. No loss there, as Suruk would say. We have moral fibre, you know.'

'They have lemming spirit.'

'Humans.' Smith looked around. Suruk stood in the doorway, arms folded. 'Is that a skull up ahead?'

'Probably,' Carveth said grimly, and turned. 'Bloody hell,' she said, leaning into the windscreen, 'what *is* that?'

As they turned the river bend, a huge white ball

appeared. It was around twelve feet tall, slightly embedded in the ground. Smith saw dents in the front of it.

'Is that something's skull?' Suruk asked. 'And does it have any friends we could fight?'

Smith said, 'Slow us down, Carveth.'

'Gladly.' The engines rumbled down.

Smith adjusted the binoculars. He saw features on the front of the ball: a crude shelf that formed scowling eyebrows, and two glaring holes under it. As he took in the grinning mouth and the beard the size of a cow-catcher on a western train, he realised what it looked like: a mask from ancient Greek comedy, grinning over the waterfront.

'It's a sculpture,' Smith said. 'I think it's meant to be Wainscott.'

Carveth sighed. 'Really? That? I think I need a drink.'

'I remember him being somewhat smaller than that,' Suruk observed. 'And less cheerful.'

'I suppose he's been having fun,' Smith said, and he could not keep the apprehension out of his voice. He swallowed. 'Bring us in,' he said, getting up. 'I'm going to get the weapons. And the gin.'

*   *   *

Suruk opened the hatch and hot, smelly air flooded the hold as if they had unsealed a box of rotten fruit. Smith climbed out, already feeling the prickling of sweat on his back, and helped Rhianna out. She wore an unusually practical outfit: ancient combat trousers, with a green poncho over the top. She resembled the sort of person who might have given spiritual advice to the Picts.

The stone head looked like a vast snowball. They

walked along the spine of the *John Pym*, climbed down the wing, and stepped onto damp, soggy land.

'Is this a vine, or a snake that's asleep?' Carveth asked, pointing.

Suruk prodded it with his spear. 'Vine.'

At the top of the river bank, where the trees became really thick, the sculpture of Wainscott grinned down at them like a drunken giant. Something about it made Smith uncomfortable – no, he decided, that was not quite right. Everything about it made him uncomfortable.

Suruk made a clicking noise. Smith glanced round. 'Mazuran,' said the M'Lak. 'Company.'

His beady eyes flicked right. Smith looked, and saw a row of beetle people, each the size of a bull, about fifty feet away. They stood further downriver in a motionless row.

'Do you think they've seen us?' Carveth whispered.

'I'd expect so,' Smith replied. He cupped his hands around his mouth. 'You there, beetle people! Hello!' He looked back to his crew. 'Wave, everyone.'

They all waved. The beetle people didn't respond. Smith put that down to them not having hands.

He pointed at the sculpture. 'Jolly good, this! Well done! Very, er, naïve.' He turned to the others. 'Who's the chap who makes those blobs?'

Rhianna said, 'Henry Moore?'

'Moore!' Smith shouted, pointing. 'Moore!'

As one, the beetle people turned and slipped into the forest.

Carveth watched them go. 'Either they've taken offence, or they've gone to make you another one. Assuming that they made it.'

'I think it's amazing,' Rhianna said. 'The simple alien people, producing this authentic art.'

'Actually,' Smith replied, 'I think Wainscott might

have made it himself,' Smith replied.

'Oh. Well, in that case, it's kind of creepy.'

A man stepped out from the trees – not as if he had been hiding there, but as though he had just stumbled upon them all.

He wore a Panama hat and combat gear. An enormous pistol was strapped to his right thigh, and a flat-sided bottle of whisky to the left. It was empty. Bizarrely, he had drawn a tie and lapels onto his breastplate, and it was that and the stubble that made Smith recognise him.

'Dreckitt,' he said.

'Rick!' Carveth exclaimed.

Dreckitt looked them over for a moment, as if they stirred a dim memory. Then he said, 'Yeah, sure. Good to see you fellers. You especially, lady,' he added to Carveth. His voice seemed to firm up as he spoke, as if he was coming round.

'How are you?' Carveth asked.

'Me? Good as I can be, stuck out here and full of no rye. Wainscott, now, that's the question. He's something else.' Dreckitt turned and gestured to the giant stone head. 'I know – I guess this must look bad, but you've got to understand: things are different out here. The rules change, pal. Wainscott's – how can I put this? – he's a mystic. He sees things other people don't. He's the last of the warrior poets. He transcends mere – aw, who am I kidding? The guy's nuts.'

He walked forward, and Carveth ran up and threw her arms around him. 'Hey, little lady,' Dreckitt said. 'I missed you. We got everything out here, 'cept for dames. And decent sanitation.'

Carveth hugged him a little less tightly. 'It's great to hear your voice,' she said. 'I almost know what you're on about, too.'

'When Wainscott's boys skipped town,' Dreckitt said, 'the big boss put me on the case, to either parley with him or cheese his command and snatch the guy. Thing is, I've got more chance of winning a craps game against Nick the Greek than I've got slipping Major Wainscott a Mickey Finn. He's pretty much immune to dope: he's had more drugs go through him than a hophead with reefer madness. You want to knock Wainscott out, you'll need tablets bigger than the ones Moses carries around, and you'll need to break 'em over his head.'

'Can't say I'd recommend that,' a voice said from the foliage. The barrel of a laser support weapon slid through the greenery, funnel first. Susan followed the gun, her left hand resting on the power pack, her right at the trigger. As ever, she looked astonishingly smart – even this far out: the beam gun was neatly-kept, her sleeves rolled up in the regulation style, her auburn plaits carefully arranged under a broad bush hat. 'Nice to see you all,' she said. 'How's tricks?'

'Alright,' Carveth replied. 'How about you?'

Susan glanced around at the greenery. She lowered her voice. 'I suppose you're here to tell Wainscott that it's home time. I'll give you a hand, within reason.'

'Thanks,' Smith said. He'd known that he could count on Susan: she might lack the 'inspired' leadership of her boss, but she was utterly professional.

'I've been out here so long they've given me a nickname,' she said, squinting up into the trees. 'Sane Susan, they call me.'

'Why?'

She nodded towards the giant stone head. 'It's relative.'

A man stood on the head as if it sprouted him as a horn. He wore boots, underpants and a pith helmet, and a wide range of scabbards and holsters. His body was striped with dirt, as though he had tried to disguise himself as a tiger. For once, Smith reflected, Wainscott had a good reason for looking as if he had spent the last few weeks under a park bench.

Wainscott jumped down, brushed his hands together, and strode over with a large smile across his grimy, bearded face. 'Isambard Smith, I presume!' The major stuck out a hand and they shook. 'Welcome to my abode. What do you think?'

'Well –'

'It's very... er... natural,' Rhianna said.

'Spot on,' Wainscott replied. 'We're in harmony with nature here. It helps us creep up on the lemming men,' he added, smirking. 'You know what they call me, the Yull?'

'The Ghost That Walks In Shorts,' Smith said, not wanting to encourage him.

'Not anymore. I'm The Ghost Who Needs No Shorts. They fear us, Smith. We've gone behind their lines, sneaked up on them, beaten them at their own game.'

It occurred to Smith that there was probably a lot of truth in that. Wainscott was a decent fellow, in his own way, but he'd probably killed more lemmings than gravity.

'We thought we might be being followed,' Smith said.

'Following you?' Wainscott said. 'Oh no. The lemmings were lying in wait for you. Thing is, we were lying in wait for them.' He pulled back a thick branch, dragging with it a curtain of leaves. Behind it, three Yull lay in an untidy pile. Their fur had been dyed green, their bayonets blackened with soot and dung. One of the Sey crouched beside the bodies, rooting through their gear. It raised its long neck like a cobra rearing to strike. 'Don't forget to check their cheeks,' Wainscott said. The Sey grimaced, and he added, 'On their faces!' and let the branch swing back.

'You're safe for now,' Susan said. 'But we'll post a guard on your ship.'

Wainscott pointed towards the great white head. 'Like the sculpture?' he demanded. 'It looks like stone, but actually the beetle people did it for me. Well, they didn't really do it so much as roll it, but it's the thought that counts, eh? We saved a bunch of them from the lemming men. The Yull had abducted a village of them and wanted to pull their legs off, one by one. Mark my words, Smith: we are dealing with sick and demented people here.' He yanked his underpants up and began to climb up the riverbank. 'We'll have a bit of a do, now you're here. Tell me, Smith,' he added, looking round, 'What do you think of owls?'

'Sorry?'

'Owls. Like 'em? Trust 'em?'

'Well, I suppose they're alright –'

'Excellent! You see, Susan? I told you he was husband material.'

Wainscott strode off. Susan shook her head. 'I'm sorry,' she said. 'It's the pills,' she added, and she strode after him.

Camp consisted of several folding chairs, a number of well-disguised tents and some hollow logs. Smith was not sure of the extent of it: figures moved between the trees further out, half-hidden by undergrowth and he wondered exactly what the scale of Wainscott's operation might be. 'Brew up, Craig,' the major said to a wiry, fair-haired man, and at once the tea was made.

'We brought you a gift,' Smith said. 'It's a birthday cake. Compliments of High Command.' He turned to Carveth. 'Cake, please.'

Horror and fury flashed across her face. 'Not the precious cake!' she hissed, and a moment later, she recovered herself. ''Course. Feel free to eat all the cake that I've been lugging round the jungle. Go ahead.'

They sat around, drinking and eating. The canopy hid the worst of the sun but the air was uncomfortably warm. The smell of tea at least took away some of the stink of rotting vegetation.

'We've been raising hell with the lemmings,' Wainscott said. 'In truth, this terrain's ours as much as theirs. It's never quite safe, though.'

'How many chaps have you got?'

'Fighters? Just over a hundred. Humans, forty-six. Sey, twenty-three. M'Lak, eight. Then there's the beetle people, but they mainly carry stuff.'

Smith wondered how far he would get if he walked into the forest. Would the animals kill him, or the Yull, or even the plants? He'd probably die some embarrassing death, murdered by a gang of orchids.

'Wainscott,' he asked, 'can I have a word? Privately?'

*   *   *

'Dinner is served!' Susan announced. 'Tonight at the Manoir de Merde, we begin with an old favourite: Biscuits, Brown. Guaranteed to stave off not just hunger but digestion itself, these delightful items can be welded together to make a blackboard or just used as individual rooftiles. Then, for the meat course, we have... er, meat. From a tin can. Eight out of ten cats love this stuff. And finally, a special treat in the form of Biscuits, Brown (Fruit), which have either bits of raisin or dead insects imbedded in them. I'm not sure which.'

One of the Sey approached, carrying plates with what Carveth hoped was food. At least, the stuff was steaming.

She had not really seen the Sey properly before: they were shy, had no important resources, and lived at a low technological level. Their main skill was in tracking, and, having proved themselves against the Yull at Kwala Gorge, they had found a new niche in the Imperial Army.

Lucky them, she thought. Seen up close, the Sey looked like a mixture of dinosaur, emu and gazelle. They wore bootees and hats, along with camouflaged cloaks strapped across their backs like the blankets horses wore in cold weather. This particular Sey had a ruff of red feathers at the top of its neck, like the frill on an exotic lizard.

'Here,' it said. There was a little speaker mounted to its shoulder: it helped with the words that the Sey could not pronounce. 'Grub's up, mate.'

Carveth took the plate. 'Thanks.'

'Most kind,' Suruk said, accepting his helping. 'Is this food?'

'Word to the wise,' the scout replied. 'See those little biscuits, with the purple bits in them? They're not flies at all. They're some kind of fruit. Bloody army's too cheap to put real flies in.' The alien dipped its head like a swan. ''Scuse my manners,' it said, 'but my hands don't reach my mouth.' It scooped up a beakfull of sludge, looked up and tipped it down its gullet. 'So, you're taking the major back, are you?'

Carveth nodded. 'I hope so.'

'Wainscott's alright. He's a bit... er...' it tried to tap the side of its head but couldn't reach, '...bonkers, but he gives a fellow a fair go. He's honest, too. He doesn't keep anything back.'

'That's for sure,' Carveth said, thinking of Wainscott's pants. She didn't feel very hungry.

She glanced left and saw that Susan, her dinner finished, had pulled out a paperback and was reading it intensely. To Carveth's surprise, the cover showed a highwayman embracing a woman who was only just in her bodice. The title read *Stand and Deliver Your Love*.

'Listen, mate,' said the Sey, 'when you go back, you couldn't leave us Susan, could you? Can't have a tribe without a matriarch.'

'I think we're all going back.'

'Really?' It raised its head and stared into the trees for a few seconds, then looked back at her. 'After a while, in a place like this, you learn that there's ways to survive. You use the Spirit Path, if you know what I mean.'

'Indeed.' Suruk had been watching the tracker with interest.

'*You* know what I'm talking about,' the Sey added. 'You travel the mystic path. The hunting way. You run out of bullets, you go old-style and make yourself a spear. That's how we beat them at Kwala Gorge.'

'I never had any bullets,' Suruk said.

'Bloody cheapo army,' the Sey replied. 'They could've at least given you a gun, mate.' It stood up. 'Well, it's been a pleasure.'

'You too,' Carveth said. She was not sure whether to put her hand out to shake, but the scout beat her to it. 'Mr –'

The alien's head drew back. 'Ms,' it said. 'Arik, Second Huntress.'

'Polly Carveth.'

She watched the alien take its plate to a bulky, dangerous-looking man who was doing the washing-up. When Carveth looked around, Rhianna was beside her, as if she had formed from the air. 'I think it's good to see such equality,' Rhianna said.

'I don't,' Carveth replied. 'They're all as mental as each other.'

*   *   *

Wainscott led Smith about ten yards into the forest, and suddenly the others were gone – or at any rate, Smith couldn't see them.

'I've seen lemmings hide out so long, lichen starts to grow on them,' Wainscott said. 'Burrs get stuck in their fur. Before long, it's like fighting a thistle bush.' He folded his arms. 'I'm not going back, Smith.'

'Look here,' Smith said, 'you're coming back and that's that. I'm instructed to tell you that you can't go playing silly buggers out here. It's not cricket.'

'Well, I like that,' the major replied. 'I'm actually getting something done out here and HQ has the gall to tell me to go home. All they're good for is slowing me down. Out here, *I* wear the trousers.' He looked down and added, 'That's a metaphor, obviously.'

'That's not on, old chap. I've seen what they're doing back at base camp. For you to say that they're all mouth and no trousers shows a lot of gall, frankly.'

'Does it?' Wainscott twisted around to look at the back of his own legs. He gestured grandly at the forest. 'I've got the lemmings running scared. I've got them bending over backwards to stop me. And now HQ wants me to pull out and roll over so they can do the driving? Never! I am my own man and so are all my men! They're all their own man. Each man, obviously. Except for the women and aliens. You know what I mean.'

'That won't do,' Smith replied. 'You're needed, Wainscott. We all are. The lemmings are out for blood, and if we're to beat them off, we all have to pull together.'

The major's eyes, which managed to be squinty and wild at the same time, narrowed. 'You know what you are, Smith? You're like one of those boys that fellows rent out to do their dirty stuff –'

'I hope you mean a paper boy.'

'An errand boy, that's it.' Wainscott looked back to the forest and the anger faded from his face. 'I don't want to go home,' he said. 'I like it here.'

'I know. I heard the messages you sent back.'

'Ah.' For once, Wainscott looked embarrassed. 'Yes, I wouldn't put too much weight on those. I was experimenting with the medicinal properties of some of the local plants at the time. I was rather... medicated.'

'Come on, Wainscott. HQ needs you.'

The major sighed. 'Smith, I'm not any good at home. All those bloody orders and things. I can't do normal people stuff. Women won't go near me, for some strange reason. Every time I go on leave, the place I return to has changed so much that it's unrecognisable. I tried to go and visit my sister in Dorset a while ago. I didn't recognise anything.'

'The file said you crash-landed in the Yemen.'

'Really?' The major looked round. 'Is that what it was? Well, thank goodness for that.'

Smith wondered how a man whose whole existence had been devoted to causing mayhem would return to civilian life. How would Wainscott deal with returning a library book, say, without throttling the librarian and blowing the building up? How would he make friends with anyone who wasn't Suruk?

Smith suddenly felt very sorry for Wainscott. He had never expected to feel much sympathy towards a violent madman clothed only in underpants and mud. 'Look, if you come back, I'll do everything I can to make sure they give you the freedom to blow up whatever you like, provided it doesn't belong to the Empire.'

'You'll help with tomorrow's raid? Promise?'

'Promise. But you've got to come back.'

'Well, alright, then. If they need me, you have my word.' Wainscott said. 'Tomorrow, we hit the Yull – hard. Then it's back home. Come on,' he added, turning back to camp. 'We'll be needed to help out with dinner. Breaking those biscuits in half is a two-man job.'

* * *

Smith lay in his tent, watching the shadows of insects on the roof. Even at night, the forest was noisy with croaks and birdcalls. Something barked in the darkness: it sounded like a fox. Rhianna lay beside and partially on top of him, almost asleep.

Tents, he thought, were always a disappointment. They smelt funny, for one thing, and the excitement of having her pressed against him was turning into the realisation that she was actually quite heavy. Also, he had almost knocked the thing over while putting his pyjamas on.

From somewhere to the right, something cried 'Wahoo!'

Rhianna raised her head and blinked. 'What was that?'

'I'm not sure,' Smith replied. 'A wild bird. A mating cry, perhaps. Or maybe just Carveth. Poor old Dreckitt's got some catching up to do. I hope they keep the noise down, though,' he added. 'I don't want everyone having to stand to just because she's here.'

Rhianna moved her hand. 'You're standing to as it is,' she said.

'That's because *you're* here.'

Animals of the Riverbank

'Gather round!' Wainscott said. He had pinned a map against a tree with a couple of knives. Evidently, given the doily-like perforations around the edge of the map, he had done so many times before. 'I have good news and bad news. Today we are going to hit a major enemy base. On the other hand... we're going home.'

They stood round the tree in a rough semi-circle: humans, Sey, M'Lak, even the beetle people who carried the extra gear. Rhianna stood beside Smith. Suruk loitered at the back of the group. Carveth held Dreckitt's hand. He looked as if he had spent the night strapped to a chair in a wind tunnel.

Wainscott tapped the map. 'This is the local area.'

Smith peered at the swirl of contours, which made it look like raspberry ripple ice cream. 'What are these?' he asked, pointing to a number of pencil crosses.

'Hot contacts,' Susan replied.

'Places where we blew stuff up,' Wainscott said. 'To begin with, that was reason in itself to be here. But afterwards, I began to suspect that there was more to it than that.

'The Yull have a reputation for being buggers on the attack, but they're sods in defence as well. Your lemming man, being a rodent, has a natural aptitude for burrowing. Any heavy lemming fortification will be honeycombed with storerooms, guardposts, concealed gun emplacements and so on. It's a pity they don't seem to have any toilets. The Yull have been choosing specific places to burrow: not obvious fortifications, or places where they could expect enough of us to be passing through to make it worthwhile digging in. In other words, they've been digging bases for no clear purpose.'

Smith said, 'Well, they are mad.'

'They're looking for something. Gold, minerals, an unusually large cache of sunflower seeds – I don't know, but there's something on this world that they want even more than to run at us shouting *Yullai*.'

'Maybe they're going to hibernate,' Carveth said.

The major nodded. 'Good point, Polly Pilot. The Yull don't have much in the way of landmines, but they do leave behind suicide troops. The buggers shut themselves down, then wake up behind our lines when summer comes. But this is larger-scale. I'm talking about excavations.' Wainscott tapped the map. 'This is it. The chaps have been scouting out: the Yull have sunk boreholes, dug tunnels, the whole lot. I want to hit it.'

Susan coughed.

'Oh, yes. And in return for you helping me,' Wainscott added, 'I suppose I'll go back to base camp with you. How about that?'

Smith frowned. 'Very well. But you've got to stick to your word.'

'Of course I will. It's my word, isn't it? Now, I don't want anyone with children on this mission.'

'Dangerous, is it?'

'Oh no. I just can't stand them going on about their

kids. What do I care if little Jimmy's got his swimming badge? I'm a bloody commando, for Heaven's sake.'

*   *   *

They almost set out at 10.00 precisely but ended up departing four minutes behind schedule because Carveth needed a wee. The going was tough. There was no path except for the plants beaten down by earlier boots and Smith was reluctant to hack at the fronds with his sword.

'Good for you, Isambard,' Rhianna said beside him. 'It's a very delicate ecosystem.'

'Frankly, I worried that if I start hitting the plants, they'll hit me back,' he replied, holding a branch back so she could slip by.

Dreckitt had no such qualms. He chopped his way forwards, followed by Carveth, who seemed to find him very entertaining to watch. At one point, Dreckitt overtook Smith and Rhianna and Carveth looked back to whisper, 'Very manly!' at them, before pinching Dreckitt's backside.

They stopped for a little while, while scouts brought back information on the way ahead. Rhianna moved up the column to talk to Arik the Huntress. Smith checked his weapons and mopped sweat from his neck. He wondered how long you'd have to be out here before your guns began to rust.

Suruk stopped beside him. 'Are you well, Mazuran?'

A large branch dropped from one of the damp trees to the right. Smith glanced around: he watched for several seconds, making sure that it wasn't a lemming in disguise.

'It is nothing,' Suruk said. 'Come on.' Smith continued

beside him. 'On walks like this,' Suruk observed, 'one must keep the mind alert. I have been composing a saga; an epic song to tell of my deeds.'

'Really?'

'Indeed. It goes as follows:

My name is Suruk, I live in the room next door
I have a mighty spear, I like skulls and war.
If you hear something, late at night,
You think it's trouble, perhaps a fight,
Then you're very probably right.'

He stopped and waited for applause.

Smith said, 'Is that it?'

'I am still working on the second verse. We have only been walking for four hours, after all.' Suruk frowned. 'It is important that a record of my deeds remains.'

'Hey, Suruk,' Carveth said from behind. 'All these great deeds of yours: have you ever considered that sometimes you might be, I don't know, a bit vain?'

The alien glared at her. 'The Slayer? Vain? Vanity is not a vice I possess.'

'Rubbish. You're so vain –'

'Shush!' Suruk raised a hand, and for a moment they were silent. He shrugged. 'I thought I heard the Yull. I bet they were talking about me.'

Further up, Wainscott was talking to Susan. She had tucked her plaits into the strap of the beam gun, out of the way. Together, they looked like a pair of Ancient Britons planning to do something nasty to Julius Caesar.

'Sometimes,' Suruk said, 'I think you should marry Susan. She is good with weapons.'

'She's not my sort,' Smith replied. 'Besides, I'm not entirely sure which team she plays for, if you see what I mean.'

'Ah, indeed.' Suruk tapped the place where the side of his nose would have been, had he possessed one. 'You think she is Homo Sapiens?'

'I think you might be a bit confused there. We're all Homo Sapiens.'

'Really? All of you? How does that work?' Suruk shook his head. 'Humans.'

The ground sloped upward, and the air became hot and damp. Smith wondered whether the stuff on his face was sweat or condensation. He looked right, into the trees, and saw half a dozen creatures like spindly-legged, six-eyed wolves watching them. No doubt they were looking for stragglers, and he instinctively checked on Carveth.

She was fine, surprisingly perky now that she was reunited with Dreckitt. She said something and he burst out laughing and put his Panama hat on her head.

Smith glared at them. 'Shush!' he hissed. 'Remember, the Yull could be anywhere. They're vicious lunatics. They don't think like normal people, like...' he looked at Wainscott further up the trail, then back over his shoulder, '... like everyone back home.'

Up ahead, Nelson, the unit's tech, looked back and made a quick, chopping gesture. Smith froze. Nelson walked back, slipping neatly though the trees. 'We've reached the place,' he said. The boss wants you to have a look.'

Smith led his men up the line. Wainscott's troops really were a hard crew, he thought, as he passed men and aliens, all heavily armed. The humans and M'Lak tended to carry Ensign laser rifles, single-pulse guns ideal for burning a hole through charging Yull, while the Sey, whose necks were too long to allow them to aim down rifle-sights, favoured automatic weapons and beam guns.

Seventy-five yards up, Nelson said, 'Quiet now.'

They crept forward. Wainscott beckoned. Smith scurried up to meet the major.

Wainscott grinned: his teeth were about the only bit of him not striped in dirt. He reached out into the bushes, and pulled back a sheet of leaves.

They were at the edge of a river, looking across the flat expanse of the valley. The river had dried up and only a thin stream ran down the centre of the wide bed. The bank was steep, but negotiable: a man could scramble down it.

Smith took out his binoculars.

Figures moved on the waterside, and there was no mistaking them. The bulky bodies and stubby legs, the long snouts and waxed, drooping whiskers. The Yull looked like something that had once been cute, and then possessed by devils. Most carried guns: the standard-issue Mark Four Assault Weapon, which could be used as a bayonet, torture implement, can opener and, in truly desperate moments, a firearm. A fair proportion, perhaps a tenth, were armed with battleaxes and revolvers: officers. Of those, a few wore breastplates and full helmets with ornamental ears. They were knights, Smith realised: Yullian noblemen, the most high-ranking and brutal of the whole nasty bunch.

'Lot of brass, don't you think?' Wainscott whispered. 'Did I ever tell you about the time I took a spear in the Shangooli uplands?'

A rash of scaffolding covered the opposite bank. As Smith watched, a pole rose through the scaffolding, hauled by a team of Yullian serfs. They heaved it up, end first, and let it drop. The pole hit the ground like a battering ram, and twisted in the mud.

'Looks like a drill,' Wainscott said. 'Let's kill 'em.'

Suruk opened his mandibles. 'I concur.'

Smith lowered the binoculars. 'Well, it's your show, Wainscott, but if they've got a drill, they must be planning some kind of evil.'

Wainscott drew back. Susan waited a little way back, map in hand, the beam gun slung across her front. They conferred.

'What's happening?' Carveth whispered, gripping her shotgun tightly.

'We are bringing battle to the scum of Yull,' Suruk replied.

'Oh God. Do we have to?'

'Really, Piglet,' the M'Lak replied. 'Does it not fill you with joy, the thought of taking their empty heads? What could be better than to run among the Yull and cleave whisker from craven snout?'

She frowned. 'Sitting in the bath and drinking cheap wine.'

'You know,' Rhianna said, 'I'm sensing some hostility right now.'

'Indeed?' Suruk said. 'Then you will really feel something in five minutes' time.'

Rhianna sighed. 'It's such a shame we can't all be friends. If only the Yull weren't hell-bent on genocide, they might be nice people.'

Smith checked his rifle. 'The bastards think their empire is better than ours,' he said. 'That's reason enough.'

The foliage rustled behind them and Dreckitt emerged. 'Alright, people,' he began, and Carveth grabbed him and kissed him fiercely. 'Damn,' he said. 'Easy, tiger lady. Susan reckons we're hitting in two groups. When the flare goes up, we run in and hand out some chin music. Until then, stay hush-hush like a gunsel on the lam. When we get to pull our rods, you throw lead. Got me?'

'As much as ever,' Smith replied. He leaned against a tree that looked neither toxic nor carnivorous and used a branch to support his rifle. 'Stick with me, chaps,' he said. 'We've fought these buggers before. Just stay calm and –' A ball of fire shot out of the foliage. It smashed into the scaffolding and exploded. 'Bloody hell!' Smith shouted.

Part of the scaffolding collapsed. Lemming men dashed from between the poles like wasps from a kicked nest. The boom of the explosion was still fading from Smith's ears, but he could already hear their squeaky warcries.

A lemming man ran out, his left arm on fire. He plunged it into the muck at the edge of the river. Not a sporting shot, Smith thought. He lined his sights up with a snarling brute who had just lumbered out of the mess-hall, hefting a rifle. The gun kicked against Smith's shoulder and the lemming man fell back into the shadows.

Gunfire crackled from the trees to the left. A pack of lemmings rushed down to the riverside, furious but confused, their long bayonets glistening. They began to shout and point.

Susan swung the beam gun and the Yull fell apart. The laser sliced them neatly, and they tumbled into bits. This is dirty work, Smith thought, and then: And what would they be doing with those bayonets if they had the chance?

Lights burst from behind the scaffolding. Five flares rose up, arced overhead and descended with almost painful slowness.

The forest exploded. Leaves blew apart; chunks of bark whizzed like shrapnel. Smith flinched away. Someone screamed.

'It's a –' Carveth shouted, getting up. 'They've got one of those things!'

'A mortar?' Rhianna suggested. She didn't seem to have ducked at all.

'Yes! Get down!'

Smith turned back to the fight, and was astonished. The Yull, whole gangs of them, were charging forwards through the shallows. The water was too low to stop the aliens; the mud slowed them a little, but not enough. The mortars hissed like steam and another batch of lights sailed into the sky, cruelly slow.

'Down!' Suruk barked. The forest burst around them. A log flew towards them like a tossed caber, hit another branch and whirled off into the undergrowth, smashing through bushes. The M'Lak stood up, heaving Carveth upright by her collar.

'We can't stay here!' she squealed.

'True,' Suruk snarled. 'Not while there are lemming men to kill. Mazuran, Piglet, Rhianna, now battle is joined. Look!'

The Yull were almost across the river now. Laser fire had killed many and several of those running forward were missing a few bits, but they were almost on the opposite bank. An officer reached the shore, screaming with fury and waving an ornate battleaxe over his head.

My God, thought Smith, what a bunch of monsters. How could anyone –

And a skinny figure shot out of the undergrowth at the riverside, sprinted to the Yullian officer and buried a machete in its throat.

'For the Empire!' Wainscott bellowed.

'Bloody right,' Smith said. 'With me, crew!'

He charged forward, felt the undergrowth slide past his coat, and something caught his boot. Smith stumbled, slipped, thumped onto his arse and slid. He shot ten feet down a chute of mud, picking up speed, and flew out of the forest. For a moment he was in the air, and then the mud dropped him neatly onto the shore.

He stood up, impressed by his ability to land on his feet. That wasn't all bad. Then a voice squeaked 'Now die!' and a huge shape barrelled towards him, all fur and bayonet.

Smith drew his Civiliser, cocked the hammer, and Suruk slammed down from above into the lemming man. He jabbed with his spear and it did deadly work. 'More,' Suruk growled, pointing.

Wainscott's men raced out of the forest as the mortars boomed again and the greenery burst open behind them. The Sey were built for running. Arik the Huntress bounded towards a lemming man – she looked as spindly as a heron compared to the brutish Yull. She's dead, Smith thought. With those tiny little arms –

The lemming man raised its axe. The Sey bounced up and smashed both heels into the lemming's snout. His helmet crumpled like a concertina. Ooh, Smith thought. So that was why they had such little arms.

Twenty yards away, a grenade blew up at the waterline, throwing spray and clods of mud into the air. A Yullian soldier stopped and raised his rifle. Smith aimed his Civiliser two-handed and shot the rodent once in the chest, staggering the beast. It lurched upright, and he gave it a second shell. That seemed to stop the bugger.

Suruk stood up from a big furry body. Carveth was panting, crouched low around her shotgun. Rhianna threw her hand up, and a mortar shell burst far above them, suddenly harmless as a firework.

Carveth was less terrified than usual, if only because she was annoyed that her whole left side was covered in mud. In attempting to follow Smith – he was in charge and had a big gun – she had fallen onto her bottom and slithered about twenty yards through what smelt like a fishing village at low tide. Now, watching the lemming men come charging across the river, the whole thing felt surreal as much as frightening.

But that didn't stop her really wanting to be somewhere else.

'*Yullai!*' a soldier screamed, running at her like an idiot, and it was easy to pull the trigger and blast him onto his back, thrashing in the shallows. Dreckitt – thank God – appeared beside her, legs braced and hat pulled down as if about to clear out a crime den.

Fifty yards to the left, a Yullian officer collided with one of the Sey trackers. They stumbled around, and suddenly the Sey fell. The officer held up what looked like half a big snake, screeching to its war-god. Sickened, Carveth realised that it was the tracker's head and neck. Craig from the Deepspace Operations Group ran in from the side and bashed his rifle over the lemming man's head. They went down in a tangle of limbs.

A fresh whoosh from the scaffolding and more lights sailed into the sky. This time the angle was tighter, the peak of the arc more pointed. 'They're firing at us!' Carveth yelled, pointing. 'They'll hit their own people!'

'They would!' Smith shouted and he ran forwards, so she did the same.

Suruk bounded through the low water, his spear swinging out like a pendulum, sending furry heads spinning into the air. Several lemming men were climbing up the scaffolding, and were now almost at the top. One tried to belly-flop onto Suruk, missed and crashed into the water, sending up a plume of spray. Suruk speared it like a fish.

He tugged the spear free and saw a Yullian officer thirty yards ahead of him, exactly at the same time that it saw him.

The officer slid the axe from its belt and held it over its head. 'Filthy savage!' it shouted. '*Huphep yullai!*'

For a creature with stumpy legs, it could move. The lemming man tore across the ground screeching, feet pounding the mud like pistons. Its voice rose into a warbling shriek of hatred. Lumps of froth sailed from its chops.

Twenty yards from Suruk, it accelerated into a frantic sprint. At ten yards, it swung the axe up two-handed and cut.

Suruk stepped six inches to his right and flicked out the spear. He felt something brush the blade and the Yullian officer shot past, took three more steps and stopped.

Suruk raised a hand to his mandibles and coughed politely. The lemming's head fell off. Its body hit the ground.

'Riff-raff,' Suruk said.

Rhianna watched the mortar shells reach their zenith. She threw her hand up as if finishing one of her interpretative dances and the shells burst, fragments pattering harmlessly against the forest canopy.

Further downriver, Susan called, 'Reloading!' and Nelson covered her as she slapped a fresh battery into the top of the beam gun. She pulled the gun up, tapped the venting lever and advanced, firing from the hip. A pair of Yull hauled something onto the top of the scaffolding – a tripod-mounted death ray, from the look of it. Susan fired, swinging the beam to slice them both apart, and their gun fell into pieces. 'Yeah, torture that,' Susan said. She glanced right, and saw that Smith and little whatsit the pilot had reached the scaffolding.

Smith ducked under a pole and saw a lemming man working a large machine. Needles flickered in dials; the air hummed. Knowing the Yull, it was presumably some kind of pain amplifier. The rodent looked round, snarled, and Smith raised his pistol and civilised it in the head. Twice.

And suddenly, that was that. Smith stood over the

corpse of the lemming man, the machinery still whirring and clicking. A propaganda poster hung from the scaffolding. It showed a grinning Yull resting an axe on its shoulder. Its other hand held up a globe of Earth onto which an unhappy face had been drawn.

'Bastards,' Smith said. He ripped the poster down and walked outside.

Dead lemmings lay everywhere. They clogged the shallows as if they had been pushed out of a passing plane. Suruk smiled as Smith approached. 'A reasonable haul,' he said.

A little way away, Carveth had collared Dreckitt and, whilst kissing him, was trying to pull his hip flask out. At least, Smith hoped that was his hip flask. Who knew what androids kept down there?

Rhianna was looking at the sky. 'Are you okay, Isambard?'

He nodded. 'I think so.'

'That was... way harsh,' she observed. 'War is really bad. Hey, check out the clouds!'

Smith shivered. He felt feverish, suddenly, aching. Then the feeling was gone, and he realised that what he'd felt was anger and fear.

* * *

Wainscott was as good as his word – or at least, Susan was good at making him stick to it. They buried their dead in the undergrowth and the Sey matriarch spoke a quick word over them. Then they headed back. Wainscott had lost six people in the fight; the lemming men had lost fifty-one.

There was no time to make tea yet, Wainscott

explained: as soon as they discovered the raid, the Yull would send reinforcements to exact a brutish revenge on anyone in the vicinity. Not taking tea was the hardest part of the battle, Smith thought: it was as natural to him to brew up after a victory as it was for Suruk to collect the severed heads.

On the path ahead, a M'Lak soldier said something to Nelson and one of the beetle people. Nelson gave a brief snort of laughter, then moved on. The beetle person clicked appreciatively.

'I like to think,' Rhianna said, 'that one day, all the peoples of the galaxy will be able to work together the way as we've seen today.'

'Yes,' Smith said. 'Imagine if everyone could lay down their differences and work as one to kill the bloody lemming men.' He sighed. 'What a world that would be.'

'That's not really what I meant,' she said. 'I meant that everyone should learn to be kind, and friendly, and live peacefully and be, you know...'

'British?'

'Voices down, chaps.' Smith glanced around: it was Craig who had spoken. He was the unit's infiltrator, a master of disguise, and he strode between the trees with a quick ease. None of Wainscott's people were especially bulky. They all seemed to take after the major himself: fast and wiry. The Yull looked like ogres by comparison.

'Sorry,' Smith replied.

'Oh, that's no problem. It was a bit of a scrap, wasn't it?' Craig grinned. 'Of course, nothing like the sort of fights I used to have down at Madam Fifi's before the war. Sailors, gangsters, you name it. There wasn't a night when I didn't chuck someone through the window.'

'You were a bouncer?'

'I was Madam Fifi,' Craig replied. He chuckled and walked on.

Funny business, war, Smith reflected.

They stopped for tiffin. 'My legs are coming off,' Carveth announced, prodding a log with her gun to make sure that it was not some sort of resting dinosaur. She flopped down and sighed. 'God did not make me to take exercise standing up.'

Smith felt rather sorry for her. His own legs ached, and he felt filthy with sweat. Given the thick fur on the lemming men and the weakness of their bladders, it was surprising that the two armies were not tracking each other on smell alone.

'It's certainly a tough place, this. You know, I always expected to land on one of those planets where all the natives treat you as a deity, like you see in films. I've been to dozens of different planets and I've never met any natives who'd worship any of us. It's pretty disappointing.'

Carveth shrugged. 'Seriously, would you want to be on the same planet as people who worship Suruk?'

The M'Lak stood against a tree-trunk, in its shadow. 'The Yull do not seem to be pursuing us,' he said.

They brewed up quickly and drank. In the trees above, a death possum screeched out an advertisement to any females in the vicinity and was promptly grabbed and eaten by a hellcat. The hellcat crept down the tree-trunk, which suddenly revealed itself to be a greater bladed mantis. The mantis dragged the dead cat to the ground, wiped its pincers and was immediately jumped by a gang of slaughterbees and stripped to the bone.

'Truly,' Suruk said, 'Nature is a beautiful thing.'

They walked again.

Smith's feet were sore; the relentless greenery of the forest made his head swim, as if he had been staring at a neon strip-light. He needed a curry and a sleep.

Carveth looked awful. At one point, she tripped on a root and there was a sudden panic as she hit the ground. A dozen laser rifles covered the trees, looking for a sniper. Dreckitt grabbed her hand and told her to hold on, goddam it, while Nelson tried to stem the bleeding. It took her three minutes to get up – partly because she was enjoying the rest, partly because she was embarrassed to say that she hadn't been hit, but mainly because three of Wainscott's soldiers were sitting on her to protect her from another shot. Several people looked annoyed when she stood up, but none more so that Wainscott himself, who had clearly been hoping for one final scrap.

Food and water were unpleasantly warm, failing to refresh even when cut with lime cordial. Smith wondered how long his supply of moral fibre would last. Wainscott's team must have had vast reserves of the stuff.

At last, the path became clearer and he recognised things he had passed on the way in. 'Ship's up ahead,' he told Carveth.

'Yay!' she cried.

'Easy, little lady,' Dreckitt whispered. 'If the furries want to throw us a Mickey Finn, now's the time to do it. If I was boss lemming, I'd put a mob of hoods in a chopper squad and stash them down the path to blip us out.'

'Really?'

'That's the straight dope,' Dreckitt said, pulling his hat down low, and they advanced.

They moved slowly now, creeping forward on a wide front. Wainscott and Susan directed operations with clicks and hand gestures. Smith was left on the path, the easiest terrain but also the most open.

'I can see the ship!' Carveth shouted, and

immediately clamped her hand over her mouth. 'Sorry,' she whispered, pointing.

The *John Pym* lay lower in the water than Smith had remembered, its hull half-obscured by branches and vines. The cover had got thicker since they had left it: Andor was already claiming the ship as its own.

Smith raised his rifle and looked down the scope. 'It seems all right... the airlock's still shut.'

'Rusted shut or welded?' Carveth asked.

'Rust.'

'Same as usual, then.'

Rhianna touched his arm, at once stopping his advance and reminding him that he really ought to get her to do the business outdoors again. He dismissed the thought: death waited everywhere here, and disrobing would be no way to approach it. The Venus flytraps here were more like man-traps, and the last things he needed trapped were his flies or his man.

'I can sense something. Life,' she whispered.

Carveth looked around at the thick jungle, and said, 'Could you be more specific?'

'Negative chakras,' she replied.

'Careful, chaps,' Smith whispered. 'If you see a chakra, blow its head off. I –'

Someone yelled.

He whipped around, heard something thump into the leaves and a man shouted, 'I'm hit! Got me in the leg!'

The jungle was alive. Fear and alertness rushed through Smith as if he had been injected with it. 'Form a perimeter!' Wainscott barked. 'Expect rear attack. I want beam guns covering the path. Each man check the man beside him. Second group, swing out for a flank attack!'

And then everything was quiet again. The clatter of weapons being readied died off, and Smith could hear the forest again, and the M'Lak medic beside the wounded man, his voice strangely loud in the quiet: 'I shall draw the venom on the wound, then bandage it. You may feel a sting, being but puny –'

The fallen man, just visible between the trees, let out a quick hiss of pain. Up above, a bird squarked.

Smith felt fear winding up inside his chest. His back itched. His face was filthy with sweat. Carveth looked frozen, her breathing shallow and quick. Rhianna had put her back against a tree, and seemed to be concentrating hard. Suruk had begun to grin.

A ripple of fire came from the east. For three seconds, gunfire cracked out – single shots, mainly – and then someone called, 'Reloading'.

'We'd be safer in the ship,' Carveth whispered.

Smith shook his head. 'Stay close.'

To the southwest, a voice shouted '*Huphep!*' It sounded thin and crazy, the way the Ancient Mariner might.

Another sharp set of bangs. Smith saw bulky figures dart between the trees, swung his rifle up but couldn't get a shot. One of the silhouettes was hit, stumbled, hit again and fell.

'Crap, oh crap,' Carveth said.

Suruk said, very calmly, 'Conserve your ammunition. They will attack from behind.'

And before Smith could think that he was right, the Yull rushed out of cover behind them, howling and yelling as if the forest had spat them at the invaders. Smith saw bayonets, dark fur striped with green, and shot one of the lemmings in the chest. A M'Lak soldier rushed over and started firing his laser rifle between the tree trunks. One huge lemming broke from the undergrowth, screaming – he looks like a sodding great otter, Smith thought – and Suruk stepped from the side and speared it in the flank. Carveth's shotgun banged out, a flat sound like a car door slamming. Something big fell into the undergrowth, set the leaves shaking.

Quiet again. Smith glanced to the right. Where was Wainscott? Was he cut off? How could you lose a crazy shouting nudist?

What if *they* were cut off? A big frond flopped back, and he saw Susan and was almost ashamed at how relieved he felt. Dreckitt was next to Carveth, telling her to stop firing.

One of the Sey pointed with its beak and barked something. A moment later it pulled its beam gun up and let rip. The laser cut a swathe through the undergrowth, slicing plants like a scythe. Bullets flew out of the forest. Lemming men fell among the greenery.

Suruk burst from behind a tree, holding a severed head. 'I think there are many,' he said. 'We are surrounded.'

'Great.' A bullet whacked into a trunk eight feet away. They both ducked down, scanning the greenery to see where the shot had come from.

'We've got to get out of here,' Carveth called. 'Let's go to the ship!'

'If they are going to take you alive, slay yourself,' Suruk said. He pulled a stiletto from his boot. 'Die, filth of Yullia!' He tossed the knife into a thick, broad-leafed shrub, and a lemming man shrieked and fell.

'Screw this,' Carveth announced. 'I'm getting the ship!'

She ran. 'Nix, kid!' Dreckitt yelled, grabbing for her, but she was too quick and too scared. Carveth ran down the path, and a shadow dropped from above her.

Smith saw it plunging from the trees: a lemming

man, its snout split in a hideous grin as it plummeted from the canopy, a stick of dynamite fizzing in either hand. He watched the Yullian fall towards Carveth with a sort of awful finality, and wondered why he was charging forward to rescue her.

Rhianna sprang onto the path. She hit Carveth with her shoulder, knocking her over. Smith cried out, still dashing forward to save them, somehow, and a moment after the two women hit the ground, the lemming man smashed into the earth six feet away.

He felt the explosion, the lumps of bark, soil and rodent flying past his face, but the blow didn't come. Nothing threw him off his feet. He opened his eyes and stood up slowly, afraid of what he would see.

Rhianna crouched on the pathway, arms around Carveth. They were at the epicentre of the devastation, as if the explosion had billowed out of them. Carveth was shaking. Rhianna seemed deadly calm.

Susan's voice, behind them: 'Come on, let's go! Smith, we need your chaps to get the ship going. Let's move!'

Smith helped Rhianna get Carveth upright. 'Right,' said the android. 'A lemming jumped on my head. Get the spaceship. Of course. Did you see that? Right on my head. Boom.'

As they reached the *John Pym* a flap opened in the opposite bank and a barrel was thrust out. A gun stuttered into life, cutting down two of Wainscott's men in a second. Smith pulled his rifle up, but before he could fire, a burning bottle sailed end-over-end across the water and broke on the far bank.

Flame engulfed the gun position. Wainscott slapped Smith on the shoulder. 'Filthy stuff, that dandelion wine,' he said, and he strode toward the ship. 'You can run a lawnmower off it.'

Suruk strode out of the trees, arms locked around a thrashing lemming. 'Monkey-frog, you will die!' it screeched. For a moment they struggled, rodent against amphibian on the riverbank like some hellish re-imagining of *The Wind In The Willows*, and then Suruk heaved it into the river. For a moment the Yull thrashed, and then something below the water yanked it out of sight.

Smith opened the airlock and ushered the bewildered Carveth towards the cockpit. 'It fell right out of the trees, boss,' she said, her hands shakily pushing the keys into the ignition. 'Like a great big coconut.'

Sudden gunfire pinged against the hull. Smith hurried out of the cockpit.

Rhianna was pulling people on board. Already the corridor by the airlock was clogged with soldiers. The back door dropped open, splashing into the river, and Wainscott's men sloshed their way into the hold. The major stood by the ramp, apparently oblivious to the enemy gunfire, helping them on board. In a few moments, humans, Sey, M'Lak and beetle people crowded the hold.

'Everybody on?' Smith demanded.

'All aboard,' Susan replied.

He hit the door panel. 'Move it, Carveth!' he called and, bullets still pattering against the hull, the *John Pym* tore into the sky.

*   *   *

Someone had set up a portable television on a camp stool. Morgar leaned in and cranked the dial. The screen flickered, and a tall, curly-haired man appeared.

'It's that idiot off the television,' Bargath said, barely

looking up. 'Lionel Markham. I can't stand him.'

Morgar turned the horn round to face them and twisted the volume knob.

'...*to the video clip, which has already found its way around the allied planets. The message in it is seen as exemplifying the fighting spirit of the soldiers on the Yullian front, putting to rest ongoing rumours about their commitment to the fight against lemming tyranny.*'

'Humpf!' Bargath said, scribbling out part of the crossword.

The picture changed: a small figure in shirtsleeves and a utility waistcoat appeared. '*No more running!*' she announced.

Morgar took off his spectacles, checked the lenses and slipped them back on. 'Good Lord,' he said. 'I know her.'

Bargath tugged a flask out his tunic. 'Is there anyone on television you don't know?'

'No, seriously. I know her. Friend of a friend.'

'*I don't care how many lemming men I have to fight!*' Carveth shrilled on the screen. '*But no more running!*'

Markham's face reappeared. '*That's the message coming out of the 112nd army today. No more running. The name of the speaker, nicknamed Battle Girl, cannot be given for strategic reasons. We can only hope that the high command, both Imperial and Yullian, has taken that message on board.*' He nodded to the camera. '*I'm Lionel Markham, and this is* We Ask the Questions. *Goodnight.*'

They looked at the screen.

'Well,' Bargath said, 'good on her. Get stuck in. That's the spirit. Gin?'

'Bit early for me.'

'What?'

Morgar sighed. 'Make mine a small one, then.' He

accepted the drink, which would have been small only to
a buffalo, and sipped it warily. At least the tonic water was
flat. Getting drunk in this heat would have been nauseating.

'Saw you riding today,' Bargath said. 'I think you're
getting the hang of it.'

'Thanks.'

'You can't have a lancer who can't ride out properly,'
Bargath said, taking a huge swig of gin. 'Even if he is just
the chap who designs the lavs. We have a reputation to
live up to,' he added. 'There's a reason mankind calls us
the elite.'

'*Their* elite,' Morgar replied. 'You know, our species
is capable of things other than violence.'

'Of course. We can do anything we put our minds to
– provided we do it with swords!' Bargath lowered his
glass and squinted at Morgar. 'I say – you're not about
to suggest that Ravnavar should leave the Empire, are
you?'

'Well, I –'

'Because you know what would happen if we did?
Something bad. I'm not quite sure what, but definitely
bad. Can't have that,' he added, leaning back. 'We'd
probably run out of brandy or something.'

A lancer bounced past on his steed, turned neatly
and pulled up in front of them. 'Captain. I've been sent
to tell you it's time to break camp. We're moving out.'

Bargath leaned forward. 'Move out?' He looked
ill-prepared to move out of his chair, Morgar thought.
But Bargath was struggling upright, *Telegraph* wedged
under his arm like a baton.

'I thought they'd put the order over the PA system,'
Morgar said.

''Course not,' Bargath replied. 'It might alert the
enemy.'

'I'd have thought that six hundred giant chameleons

would do that anyhow.'

The captain scowled. His brass buttons and riding boots twinkled as he strode towards the officers' quarters. 'It's probably so we get to ride out first, ahead of all the proles. The last thing we want is a bunch of M'Lak Riflemen lowering the tone.'

An aircraft flew overhead, a VTOL scout ship. 'They're fellow M'Lak,' Morgar said. 'Surely they're our brothers in arms.'

Bargath stopped and looked round. He seemed weary more than annoyed. 'Now, look,' he said, pointing at Morgar's face with his mandibles, 'a Ravnavari Lancer can have only one brother in arms, and that's another Ravnavari Lancer. And perhaps his noble steed, if it's been cleaned recently. You may think we're lackeys, but I happen to believe we're what keeps our planet safe from rodent tyranny. Alright?'

Morgar nodded. Bargath was wrong, Morgar thought, but the level of eloquence in his wrongness was surprising. 'Alright.'

'Good man. Let's get cracking, eh? I want to reach camp by dinner time.'

*　　*　　*

Smith headed back to check on the others. The injured had been stabilised as best as possible, and now the soldiers packed out the hold, sitting on the floor and the mezzanine. There was a little talking among the men, but the atmosphere was subdued.

He approached Wainscott and Susan. 'Is everything alright?'

Susan lowered her battered paperback and peered at him over the top. 'I dunno. We've got injured people and not enough teacups to go round.'

'We can do it in shifts. I'll stick the kettle on.'

Smith called Suruk out of his room. Suruk emerged, rubbing a blue paste over his forearms.

'Are you alright, old chap?' Smith asked. 'You're looking a bit – well, greener than usual.'

'I caught the sun,' Suruk replied. 'Much longer out there and I would have started to photosynthesise.'

Smith put him on tea duty and headed to the cockpit. In the windscreen, the forest rolled past, the treetops pressed together as if they flew over an enormous piece of broccoli. Smith saw a thing like the letter T sticking out of one of the trees, and realised that it was the tail of a Yullian fighter plane, wedged into the foliage.

'How're the others?' Carveth asked. 'Is Rhianna trying to do some holistic bollocks to them?'

'Actually, she's psychically protecting the ship against ground fire,' Smith replied. 'Where's our destination?'

Carveth pointed. 'There.'

It looked like a burned patch, as if someone had sizzled away the forest. Smith leaned forward and the brown mass split into different buildings, a sort of plateau, and suddenly he realised what he was looking at.

Mothkarak, or at least the main mass of it, rose out of the forest like a single scrimshawed knuckle. Once it had been a great pale rock, almost mountain-sized, but construction drones had cut off the top and used the stone to raise a wall around the plateau sixty feet high. Within, a swarm of towers strained towards the sun like etiolated stems. Masses of domes, spires and minarets swelled from the rock. Rows of statues made vertebrae out of the rooftops. It was a fortress, but also a city, a bastion against the jungle.

'Greetings!' said the radio. 'Fellow warriors, you are

clear to land.'

A window opened in one of the tallest towers and a woman leaned out, waving a reflective baton in each hand. Carveth lowered the ship, and they sank between the spires, past stern-faced statues and gun emplacements.

Smith saw trucks like matchboxes in one of the courtyards. A missile turret swung to cover them, studded with lenses and glinting like an insect's eye. The *Pym* landed between two immense buttresses, and as soon as the dust started to sink, medics and ground crew hurried towards them. Carveth flicked a switch, and the hold door flopped down like a drawbridge.

They gathered their gear and left by the side airlock. Wainscott's team were being directed, and in a few cases carried, towards a cathedral-sized building for debriefing. Only now, Smith saw how dirty the major's people were, and how battered and customised their gear was. He wondered how much longer they could have gone on, and how much longer Wainscott – or Susan – would have allowed.

'Bloody hell,' Carveth said, 'I'm glad that's over.'

Rhianna nodded. 'Definitely! I really don't like having to wear boots. And now everyone is together again. Isn't that –'

One of the ground crew pointed at them. 'Hey, look! Look who it is!'

Others heard, stopped and turned to see. Suddenly, there were faces staring at the four of them.

'I thought this mission was supposed to be secret!' Carveth hissed. 'Boss, did you tell anyone?'

'Me? Certainly not.' Smith managed to smile at the people. He felt both awkward and rather proud. 'Good day to you all!' he called. 'Carry on!'

'It's Battle Girl!' one of the men cried. 'From off the

telly!'

Smith said, 'What?'

Rhianna scratched her head. 'Huh?'

'Oh God,' Carveth said, 'they're looking at me! What did I do? It wasn't me!' she called. 'I only just got here!'

'She must have just come back from a mission,' a second man said. He had a long pink scar across his forehead. 'No more running, eh? Sock it to 'em!'

'I think we had best go inside,' Smith replied.

Carveth looked at the people waving at her, swallowed hard and said, 'Bloody right we should. Let's hide in the cellar.'

The courtyard was big enough to accommodate a row of Hellfires and a full repair bay. On the far side of the yard, a firing range had been set up and, next to that, a M'Lak rifleman was instructing a dozen human soldiers in close combat. Cranes protruded from the windows above them, lifting equipment to storerooms in the city-fortress.

'It's not fair,' Carveth muttered, accelerating towards the nearest set of doors. 'People are staring at me, and I haven't even got drunk yet.'

The entrance hall was dark, cool and the size of a spaceship hangar. Under a vaulted ceiling, dozens of logistics personnel consulted computers, plans and charts. Robots pushed markers across maps with precision tools specially converted from broomsticks. Printouts of Yullian officers glowered down from a board. Several had been marked with red crosses.

Behind the stained glass window, a Hellfire rose on its thrusters and turned south towards the forest.

A bald man stepped out of the shadows. He wore evening dress, and carried a tray of drinks. 'Welcome, Captain Smith,' he said, and gave them a small, thin smile. 'Ladies. The management has been most keen to meet you all. Perhaps if you'd follow me...' said the man, and he turned and walked away.

Smith frowned, and followed. 'Do you work here?' he asked.

The balding man looked at him. 'Oh indeed, sir. I'm the butler.'

'Butler?'

'Of course, sir. A building such as this requires its own staff as a matter of course. This way.'

Rhianna touched Smith's arm. 'Is he an android?'

The butler led them into a second hall. Once, Smith saw, it had been a ballroom, with a bar at one end and a stage at the other. Light jazz still seeped from speakers high in the roof; the place had the acoustics of a swimming pool. Now camp beds ran down the length of the dancefloor, and someone had pinned a picture of a girl in a corset to the back of the stage.

'We did have a housekeeper,' the butler explained, 'but she malfunctioned and tried to burn the building down. Regrettable.' He frowned. 'We appear to have mislaid the nanibot.'

'Is that a very small robot?' Smith asked.

There was a sudden soft thump behind them. Smith turned, and saw a woman of about thirty rising from a crouching position on the carpet. She brushed down her dark skirt, adjusted her umbrella and approached.

'She looks after the children,' the butler said.

'And here I am,' she announced, with a sort of cheery firmness.

'How did you get here?' Smith asked.

'Trade secret.' She smiled pleasantly. 'Hello to you all. I do hope you have a lovely stay here.'

'I think you'd best get along, sirs,' the butler added.

'The caretaker is awaiting you.'

Smith said, 'Caretaker? I thought you said that you were all the staff.'

'Oh, there's *always* been a caretaker, sir,' the butler replied, and he gestured along the hall.

W stood in a doorway, teacup in hand, almost smiling. 'May I have a word?'

* * *

The press office was on the fifth floor of the castle, halfway up a tower the colour of brie. French windows opened onto a verandah the size of a squash court.

About a quarter of the verandah was taken up by a massive tea urn, a dented, grimy thing that reflected their faces like a funhouse mirror. Rhianna and Carveth took the only two chairs, Smith leaned against the wall, and Suruk lurked beside the door.

'Well done in bringing Wainscott back,' said W. 'General Young will be debriefing him as we speak.'

'Rather her than me.'

'The official story is that Wainscott lost his mind and decided to throw a bit of a jolly in his underpants. That's only partly true. Wainscott has been gathering information on Yullian excavation sites over a hundred-mile radius.'

Smith remembered the scaffolding and the drilling apparatus.

'The Yull naturally build warrens, of course.' W filled the cups. 'But they've been using proper drilling gear. They're looking for something buried underground.'

They paused to distribute the tea.

'Back on Ravnavar, the Yull tried to set the various

factions of the city against one another – robots, humans and M'Lak. They are trying to do the same thing here. As one unit, with General Young at the helm, we are formidable. But divided, we would simply fall apart.'

Suruk rubbed his mandibles together thoughtfully. 'Proceed.'

'I think you know what I'm going to say,' W said, looking at the alien.

Suruk nodded. 'Andor is said to be the resting place of Grimdall the Rebel. Some believe that he fled here to escape the Space Empire and recuperate. The story goes that his relics and his weapons are still here. Clearly the Yull believe it.'

Carveth raised a hand. 'Um, what are these relics? Are they like guns and stuff, or just a big heap of skulls like Suruk has in his room?'

Rhianna shook her head. 'The relics of Grimdall are of vital importance to the M'Lak people, Polly. They're irreplaceable cultural artefacts.'

'Indeed,' Suruk said. 'A very big pile of skulls. *And* weapons.'

'Something for all the family,' Carveth replied, pulling a face. 'Well, Suruk's family.'

W took a tobacco tin out of his jacket pocket. 'It's a matter of politics,' he said. 'Now that the rest of Earth is in the war, it's very important that everyone is seen to be pulling their weight.'

'Absolutely,' Smith replied. 'Can't have these foreign types slacking off, you know.'

'Which is why they have been keeping a close eye on us.'

'What?' Smith cried. 'How dare they? That's outrageous!'

'There are some who think that the lemming men have us on the back foot,' the spy explained. 'That since the Yull have caught us with our trousers down, our response has been half-arsed.'

'Outrageous. An imbecile could tell you that it's been fully arsed.'

'We're our own worst enemies,' the spy said. 'Our allies don't think we're doing enough, because we're not making enough of a fuss. We have to make noise every so often to show them that we're still here. And,' he added, turning to look at Carveth, 'your pilot here made some very encouraging noises indeed.'

He turned to a bank of monitors and twiddled the knobs. The screens burst into life, and Carveth's face was on all of them. *'I don't care how many lemming men I have to fight,'* she shrilled at the camera. *'I'll fight every single one of them. But no running – no more running!'*

'Oh no,' Carveth said.

The figure on the screen changed to a dark-haired man in civilian dress. *'Top brass may not want to give anything away, but that's the news from the troops on the ground – no more running. The Yull may be coming for the 112th Army, but it's fighting spirit like that they'll have to face –'*

The image froze. W said, 'This went out on *We Ask the Questions* last Tuesday. I'm sure you recognise Lionel Markham.' He looked at Carveth. 'They call you Battle Girl,' he added. 'You're quite a hit on the Ethernet.'

Suruk frowned. 'Although this amuses me, I am concerned. Not only will this risk Piglet being mistaken for a mighty warrior, thus putting her at risk, but it will steal the glory of combat from, er, persons more deserving.'

Smith looked at the screen. Carveth's face, frozen in a desperate grimace, shone down upon them like the Cheshire Cat.

'Actually, quite the opposite is true,' W said. He stood up, tugging his jacket into shape. 'You see, we need someone to speak for this army – to be our voice on the Yullian Front, so to speak. And who better than Carveth?'

'Me!' Suruk growled. 'What does this toffee-gobbling gremlin know of the arts of war? No offence intended, puny woman.'

Smith turned away from the screen. 'Actually, sir, it's a fair point. Suruk or I could take the helm. Carveth's much better suited to a long-range cover-based support role.'

Suruk nodded. 'She hides under things, a long way off.'

W shook his head. 'Don't worry. The job I'm thinking of won't involve any fighting. It's just a matter of looking the part. Going to gala luncheons, kissing babies, talking to reporters.'

'Reporters often talk about me,' Suruk said. 'Would that suffice?'

'People talk to reporters about you,' Carveth put in. 'And as for kissing babies... I'll do it. Of course, I'd *much* rather be in the forest with a bunch of psychotic rodents, but if my country wants me to eat free food, then maybe I can make the sacrifice.' She looked at Smith and Rhianna and, seeing their faces, added, 'I could always bring you back some Twiglets. How about that?'

'So what about these relics?' Smith asked.

W sipped his tea. 'Speed is of the essence. Wainscott's data suggests three possible locations for the resting-place of Grimdall. First, the Yullian excavations about fifty miles southeast of here. They're heavily defended. Brigadier Harthi, commander of the ravnaphant, Mildred, has offered to launch an assault on the Yullian defences. Smith, Rhianna, I'd like you to accompany him.'

'Righto,' Smith said.

W refilled their cups. On the far side of the courtyard, a Hellfire rose up on jets. The nanibot watched it from a balcony, parasol over her shoulder. Swing music filtered out of an open window.

'The second possibility lies with the M'Lak – specifically, the hidden masters of the Temple of Goron. The masters are notoriously secretive. It would take an expert to even find the place, let alone impress the ancient warriors there with a display of combat prowess. So: hunting, martial arts, probably extreme violence – anyone know anybody suitable?'

'I do,' Carveth said, and she smiled and raised a hand.

Suruk glared at her. 'Put your hand down, fool! *I* will take this mission!'

'Good chap,' said W. 'Now, the third option. If anyone knows where the resting place of Grimdall might be, it's the natives. The local tribe are a group of blue fellows called the Equ'i.' He took a long drag on his cigarette. 'I won't lie to you. They're primitive, and they've only recently been exposed to civilisation. We built them a castle about five years ago. Our previous administrator, a fellow called Hargreaves, is leaving soon, so it's a good time to try a fresh approach. We can send you out to Radcliffe Hall tomorrow. Let's see,' he added, and he leaned round to the computer behind him. His bony fingers clattered on the keys, and he cranked the lever to set its processors going. 'I should have a scanned image somewhere...'

A figure appeared on the screen, and slowly rotated. 'As you can see,' W said, 'despite the blue colouring, they're fundamentally a species of diminutive equines. We'd need someone to go in, spend some time with them, learn their ways, feed them some sugar lumps –'

Carveth fell off her seat.

'Is she all right?' the spy asked.

Suruk took the opportunity to revive Carveth with a cup of tea, by pouring it over her face.

'Oh my God,' she squeaked from the floor. 'They're *ponies*.'

PART THREE

Ambassadors

The *John Pym* touched down at a landing pad just short of the home of the ruling family of the Equ'i. Smith, Rhianna and Carveth walked down the steps into the sunlight.

A man and woman waited at the bottom. They wore matching khaki, and had similar expressions of glum disapproval.

'I'm Hargreaves,' said the man as they approached. 'The Empire sent us here to talk some sense into the locals.' He scowled. 'Maybe you'll have more luck than we did. It's the attitude that counts,' he added. 'When it comes to horses, you've got to take the right tack.'

'That's alright,' Carveth said. 'I like ponies.'

'Of course,' Hargreaves said, tucking his shirt into his shorts, 'they're bare-arsed savages. Pig-ignorant, too. Or should I say horse-ignorant!' He laughed bitterly, and added, 'They share all their resources for the common good, they've got absolutely no concept of aggressive warfare and when they're not eating their wild oats they're sowing them. Marjorie and I have had a hell of a job telling them what to do, haven't we?'

'Yes, dear,' said Marjorie.

'I've lost count of the number of times I've told them to put some clothes on, look serious and start behaving like God-fearing creatures. You'd think they didn't want to. I also have it on good authority that they commit acts of beastliness. And I don't need to tell you what *that* involves.'

'Don't, dear,' Marjorie said. 'You'll only set your condition off.'

'It's a disgrace. And their so-called royal family are the worst of the lot. The king and queen are bad enough, but the daughter – the most precocious, obnoxious creature you can imagine. I made her read *The Pilgrim's Progress* and you know what she did? She told me the plot was linear and she wanted something by Daphne du Maurier. I told her I didn't own any French books. I mean to say, do I look like a pornographer to you?'

'No, dear,' said Marjorie. 'You don't.'

'Is there anything I need to know?' Carveth asked.

Hargreaves shook his head. 'Not much. In order to win their confidence, we built an artificial body – a sort of disguise – to enable the Liaison Officer to look like one of them. You're welcome to use it. Only thing is, you'll need someone to go in the back half.'

'It's rather uncomfortable,' Marjorie added.

'I'll be alright on my own,' Carveth said.

'Well then, good luck. Is this our ship?' Hargreaves demanded. 'Will we make it back alright in that?'

'Only if you don't fall out the airlock,' Smith replied. He disliked Hargreaves' manner, and the assumption that the *John Pym* was dangerous, while accurate, was irritating. 'We'll pick you up later,' he told Carveth. 'Good luck.'

'Thanks,' she replied. 'I'll have a nice time with the ponies – I mean, I'll civilise these benighted savages.'

She hurried up the path, towards the home of the king of the Equ'i.

Radcliffe Hall stood in ten acres of terraformed grounds, flanked by outbuildings and gymkhana yards. It was broad and white, more a mansion than a castle. A huge statue of a rearing horse stood in the drive. Above the door, a sign said 'Please wipe your hooves'.

The royal couple waited outside. They were wider in the leg than Earth horses, and shorter in the body. Their eyes were slightly larger, and the tails somewhat more bushy, but they were very much ponies. The massive, dark-blue stallion nodded to Carveth, and she curtseyed.

'You must be the new liaison officer,' he said. 'I am King Chestnut Moonlight-Shadow. This is my wife, Queen Delilah.'

'Very pleased to meet you,' Carveth replied.

'Together,' Chestnut explained, 'we reign over the surrounding countryside, taking the council of our people in order to rule with justice and fairness.'

'We have a daughter, too,' said Queen Delilah. 'She's somewhere about...'

A figure emerged from the undergrowth.

'And this is Princess Celeste,' said the king.

The pony walked forward. She had a light blue coat and large, intelligent eyes. Her mane was very pale, almost silver. She moved with an easy elegance that Carveth rather envied, even though Celeste was a quadruped.

'Hello!' Celeste said. Her accent was cultured and jolly, and reminded Carveth of Captain Fitzroy. But there was no hardness in Celeste's voice, just a sort of quick, girlish enthusiasm. Her voice was made for japes and excited whispering after dark. 'You must be Mrs Carveth.'

'Polly, please,' Carveth replied. 'And I'm a miss.'

'Celeste Moonlight-Shadow,' said the Equ'i. 'And I'm a miss too.'

There was a moment's silence. Carveth wondered what she was supposed to do, now that she had introduced herself. She felt extremely awkward, as if she would fall over if she moved, or would just make stupid noises if she tried to speak.

'Why don't you show Miss Carveth the grounds, Celeste?' said Queen Delilah.

'Yes, let's!' Celeste exclaimed. 'Do you like gardens, Polly?'

'I like yours,' Carveth said.

'Then follow me!' Celeste turned on the spot, looked over her shoulder and smiled. Carveth bowed to the king and queen, not sure what else to do, and hurried after the princess.

'So,' said Carveth, as they walked down the steps, 'I hear your last liaison officer had an interesting time.'

'Really?' Celeste turned to her. 'Whoever told you that?'

'Well, your last liaison officer, to be honest.'

Celeste snorted. 'It's absolute rot,' she declared. 'He was the most boring oaf you could imagine. He used to gather us all together and read bible stories. There was one he used to bang on about concerning some fellow called Balaam and his talking ass. Talking ass indeed! His wife was a bit better, though. She had a book about Tallulah Bankhead.' Celeste stopped abruptly and gasped. 'Goodness, they don't give you all that self-improving business on your planet, do they?'

'Well, not much,' Carveth said. They turned off the drive, into the gardens.

Celeste flicked her tail. 'I tell you what – I'll lend you the book on Tallulah if you fetch me something good to read. Something wicked and unimproving. How about a book on pirates, or some Dorothy Parker? You can help me turn the pages. It's rubbish sometimes, only having hooves.'

'I've not got any books like that,' Carveth said. She was surprised at how clottish the admission made her feel. 'I've got some piloting manuals.'

'Super! Are there dogfights?'

She thought of Smith's bookshelf. 'I could find some.'

'Being a pilot must be marvellous,' Celeste said. 'I think I'd enjoy that.'

A huge butterfly flapped across the path before them, as though it were a Chinese kite given life. It vanished into the lush undergrowth, its orange wings visible for a moment between the leaves, like a tiger's back.

'You're a princess,' Carveth said. 'That's not bad.'

'It gets a bit lonely. Is it true that you're a war hero? It must be awfully exciting.'

'Er, I'm not really. I kind of took the job because I like po – because I have an affinity with equine creatures.'

Carveth paused and smelt a rose. Celeste leaned in, smelled it too, and then ate it.

'Are you trained in cross-species protocol, then?' she asked.

'I've got a hamster,' Carveth replied, not wanting to seem ill-prepared. 'And I can learn.'

They walked on. Somewhere, there was a desperate, bitter war being fought against the most vicious savages in the galaxy. It seemed a million light years from this garden. Could the same sun that set the shadows dappling on Celeste's flank be glinting on the bayonets of the lemming men?

'When I was little, I always wanted to be a unicorn,' Celeste said thoughtfully. She paused to take a bite of grass. 'But as you grow up, you realise that you have to start being more realistic about your ambitions. So now

I've decided to become a best-selling novelist.'

'How's that going?'

'Slowly. I've got a little shed at the far end of the grounds, next to the stream and the Well of Ponyness. The typing's ghastly, though.' Celeste flicked her tail. 'I think I need to broaden my horizons first. Getting off this planet would be a start. Sometimes it seems so... boring here. Standing in a field all day, eating sugar lumps.' Her large eyes lit up. 'I want to see Manhattan! The Folies Bergere! Stockton-on-Tees!'

'But it's very pretty here.'

'Do you think so?' Celeste stopped walking and stared across the rolling paddock, over the stream with its mass of dragonflies, towards the trees at the far end, almost glowing green. 'You know, you're right. Yes, it *is* beautiful. Thank you for reminding me, Polly.'

Carveth glanced away. 'It's nothing.'

Celeste stamped her hoof. 'Nonsense. What good would the world be if people stopped appreciating beauty?'

Carveth looked around to find that Celeste was looking her straight in the eyes. 'Not very good,' she said, 'at all.'

'Then that shall be our mission,' Celeste declared. 'To bring beauty and splendour back to the world. How does that sound?'

Carveth felt strangely moved. It was so rare to hear anyone talking about something that didn't entail swilling tea and blowing people up. 'Yes,' she said. 'That sounds fine.'

'Splendid. Will you be back soon? I realise that it must be a bit boring for you, to have to deal with a load of talking horses instead of exciting things like war. And then there must be all those dawn raids you're missing, not to mention the dogfights –'

'I could do tomorrow.'

'Super!'

Up ahead, a pair of larger Equi strode across the path. 'Well, there's Mummy and Daddy,' Celeste said. 'I suppose we've been a while.'

Carveth brushed her trousers down, checked her collar, and approached.

'Hello again, Polly,' said King Chestnut, 'I hope Celeste has been able to give you some idea of our daily life.'

'She doesn't meet many new people,' Queen Delilah explained. 'She was always a rather sensitive foal. She had colic when she was young, you see.'

Carveth bowed. 'It's been very interesting, thank you –'

'It's been smashing,' Celeste put in. 'I think she'll make a jolly good liaison officer. Much better than the last one. Oh, do let's keep her, Daddy. Can we?'

The king and queen looked at one another. 'Well,' said King Chestnut, 'all right.'

Carveth couldn't remember the last time she had felt so relieved, except at the end of most gunfights.

'Marvellous!' Celeste exclaimed. 'You're going to love it here, Polly.'

King Chestnut chuckled. 'Sounds like you girls have really hit it off,' he said, and Carveth went red.

The king and queen watched as the *John Pym* took their new liaison officer back to Mothkarak. It was getting dark; Celeste had retired to her chambers to work on her novel.

'Well, if you ask me it makes a nice change from the previous human,' said the queen. 'All those talks about fresh air and bracing walks. I'm a horse, for goodness' sake. I know what a bracing walk is without being lectured by an overgrown boy scout, thank you.'

'He did introduce us to tea,' said King Chestnut. 'That's something. Although I've still not figured out what he meant when he preached that sermon against "the sin of beastliness". Seems a bit pointless, seeing that we are beasts.'

'You don't think he meant, you know, having one off the hoof, do you?'

'I doubt it. I can't even reach all that stuff.' Chestnut shrugged. 'At least now we've got somebody half sane, not some obnoxious yahoo. Frankly,' he added, 'I can't see how it could go wrong.'

*　　　*　　　*

Smith, Rhianna and Suruk spent the next few days in the castle, assisting with the defences. Rhianna helped the troops perfect their survival skills by carrying out a detailed study of the local plant and mushroom life. Smith consulted the maps with Suruk until they knew the surrounding countryside almost by heart. But they were not the only restless inhabitants of Mothkarak.

After several months of savage combat in the most dangerous and overgrown forest in the galaxy, Major Wainscott was beginning to show the signs of trauma, mainly because he wanted to go back out there. Also, bath day was approaching. That, Susan explained, always made him twitchy. They compromised: Wainscott and Suruk took Smith outside to teach him hunting techniques. On the third day, Wainscott went missing and they tracked him down. Smith assumed that it was a test, but when the major had to be shot with a tranquiliser dart, he realised that Wainscott had been making a bolt towards freedom and the hunting grounds.

Suruk spent his free time meditating, readying his

spirit for the tests to come and achieving calm by raking the sand in his litter tray. On the morning of the fourth day, he announced his readiness to meet the hidden masters of the Temple of Goron.

*   *   *

It took Suruk eight hours to walk to the area where the hidden temple was said to be, and thirty minutes to find it. That was a good omen. Either Suruk had been destined to locate the hidden temple, or its inhabitants were idiots. Whichever was true, it gave him an advantage in the negotiations to come.

The place was half-overgrown. The walls were grey stone, so decrepit that it was hard to work out in which direction they were supposed to be going. The forest had started to devour it, and creepers were climbing the walls like the tentacles of a sea monster pulling a ship into the ocean. It occurred to Suruk that the only reason why the hidden temple was hidden was because nobody had bothered to tidy it up.

He walked under a mossy archway, into a courtyard.

Lumps of rock lay strewn around, dice thrown by a giant hand. On each side stood a large grey building. Friezes on the sides depicted M'Lak heroes slaying a wide range of large enemies. They were faded and chipped. Statues of beasts flanked each doorway. None had a head.

Far away, a carnotaur bellowed.

Suruk walked forward. He was being watched. It was a feeling, but also a certainty, the way that he could tell what Carveth would be doing as soon as nobody was looking and there were biscuits within reach. He looked up, expecting to see half a dozen elders crouched in the trees, waiting to do battle or, worse, to force him to get a proper job. Nothing.

He reached the centre of the courtyard. Suruk paused and reached out to a decapitated statue of a crouching froghound. A heap of stones lay beside the body. It was all that remained of its head.

Something popped behind him. Suruk whipped round, spear raised. Smoke rose hissing from the ground. In the column of smoke stood a figure. Arms folded, head tilted back, an ancient M'Lak warrior regarded Suruk with stern disapproval.

'Will men never learn?' the ancient asked. He had a deep, slow voice. 'True wisdom comes not from here' – he touched his head – 'nor from here' – he pressed his hand to his heart – 'but from not messing with other people's stuff.'

'But I am no man,' Suruk said.

'True,' the ancient replied. He wore traditional battledress, as well as a cravat. 'Yet great wisdom lies in keeping your thieving hands to yourself.'

'Bah! Mere objects are nothing beside brave deeds. Besides, whoever was last here really cleaned you out. They even took the heads off your statues.'

'That was me. I practiced the fighting stance called Delicate Butterfly. Things exploded.'

'I do not know it. On which subject,' Suruk added, 'I have come here to learn.'

'Ah. You wish to study my Presumptuous Owl? Or is it the Probing Cobra that interests you?'

'No, ancient. I seek the location of the Relics of Grimdall.'

The warrior laughed. 'Is that so? Do you think I just give them out to any passing traveller?'

'Hopefully, yes.'

'What is your name?'

'Suruk the Slayer, of the House of Agshad. Scion of Ametrin, son of Agshad Nine-Swords, lord of the line of Urgar the Miffed. Taker of skulls, conqueror of lemming men, most honoured of my clan and –'

'General-purpose upstart. I know of you. I am Volgath. If you wish to learn the ancient arts, then you are in the right place.'

'That depends on the ancient art in question,' Suruk replied. 'I did not journey this far to make pots.'

Volgath smiled. 'Fear not. I guard the secrets of combat. Come forward and I will teach you an ancient technique. It is called Education of the Gullible.'

Suruk approached. 'I have not heard of that style.'

Volgath whipped around. His heel crashed into Suruk's ear. Suruk stumbled back and dropped into a fighting stance. Quietly, he raised his spear.

Suruk snarled. 'Most amusing. And now, old fool, I shall educate *you*.'

Celestial Beings

Night fell over Mothkarak. In its mighty walls, dumb waiters rumbled as tea and biscuits were sent up to the gunners on the battlements. The M'Lak riflemen training in the great hall stopped throwing each other into the butresses long enough to share out the tiffin. After a long day of pouring over maps and shooting no lemming men, Smith called a meeting of his crew.

They met in the main dining hall, on the table near the exit reserved for Games and Recreations, Interplanetary Shipping and other branches of the secret service. The air was full of spice and polite conversation. On the next table down, a row of lancers chatted about something that probably involved decapitation. A hovering wallahbot drifted slowly over the tables, dispensing gravy from integral spigots.

Smith and Rhianna were first to arrive. 'Well,' Smith said, 'I'm afraid it's hardly the Ritz.'

Rhianna smiled. 'This is fine. I always like trying unusual food.'

Smith looked around. 'Well then, you'll love the army canteen. It's like eating in a different country.

I mean, I'm never quite sure what I'm eating and it's certainly got a special atmosphere.' He took a cylinder from the tabletop. 'Look, they've even got novelty salt shakers.'

'That's a grenade, Isambard.'

He gave it a shake: no salt came out, but neither did the pin. 'Good point. Still, it's rather romantic, just you and I. And all these soldiers.'

Rhianna smiled. 'Hey, you're right.' She reached out and took his hand. 'Let's make the most of it.'

At the far end of the room the head chef yelled 'Alright, lads! Tonight's special is a subtle blend of curry powder and powdered egg. I call it "The Cleanser". One dollop or two?'

Suruk appeared at the side of the table. He sat down human-style. 'Greetings all. Let the gravy flow like the lifeblood of our foes!'

'Hi Suruk,' Rhianna said. 'How are the masters of the hidden temple?'

'Hiding. So far, I have found one of them, and he is an idiot.' Suruk's eyes narrowed as he looked around the room. 'Wait... Carveth is in terrible danger!'

Smith twisted around. 'What? What's up, old chap?'

'Behold my watch, Mazuran,' Suruk replied. 'She is three minutes late for a meal!'

'Good God!' Smith said, rising from his chair. 'You don't think...'

'Maybe she got distracted,' Rhianna said. 'There are a lot of soldiers here, after all. Wait...' She frowned and raised a hand. 'I can sense... a terrible hunger, coming from... from there!'

Rhianna threw her arm out, nearly hitting the wallahbot. Carveth came hurrying between the tables. 'Sorry I'm late,' she said. 'Important diplomatic business.' She sat down. 'What's for dinner?'

A tall M'Lak in dress uniform approached, a white cloth draped over his arm. 'Ladies, gentlemen,' he announced. 'You are our honoured guests.'

'Great,' Carveth said, rubbing her hands together. 'I'm really hungry. Bouncing around on Celeste takes it out of you.'

'Then tonight's meal will delight you,' said the M'Lak. 'We will be dining on the finest delicacies of old Ravnavar. Goodness me, such luxuries! To start with, the jellied bladder of a Corellian Pangolin, served in the squeezings of a thousand venomous scorpion-bugs. Then, the main course: crushed monkey feet, blended with nutmeg and lightly-chilled crocodile tonsils, force-fed to a giant eel and hacked from its still-living belly before your very eyes!'

The eagerness drained from Carveth's face. 'Really?' she croaked.

The M'Lak grinned. 'No, I'm just having you on. It's chicken korma.'

Laughter burst out of the table behind them. One of the M'Lak riflemen, a captain from his stripes, leaned over.

'Good joke, eh, fellows? We like a good laugh in the rifles. Curry night always makes the chaps a bit lively.'

'Yes,' said Smith, 'I did notice some chuckles from behind.' He lowered his voice. 'Take no notice, Carveth. You weren't to know that they ate British food. Now, then: status update, if you please. Suruk, how are these elders? Have you broken the ice yet?'

'The ice, three stone dogs and Elder Volgath's left scapula,' Suruk replied. 'Disappointingly, Volgath seems to be the only elder left, but he assures me that he knows the location of Grimdall's resting place.'

'Great,' Carveth said. 'All you have to do now is bash the truth out of him.'

'Certainly not,' Suruk growled. 'To do so, I must first prove myself in the ancient martial disciplines and defeat Volgath in honourable combat and... wait a minute, that *is* bashing the truth out of him. Apologies, Piglet.' Suruk smiled, and held out his arm. 'Look.'

A metal bracer covered his arm from wrist to elbow: it bulged slightly as if it concealed something. Suruk flicked his hand out, the first and last fingers extended as if to appreciate heavy metal, then clenched his hand into a fist.

A jointed blade shot out of the back of his arm, clicked into place and locked back on itself at an angle, jutting out over his hand. It was a wicked-looking thing, a tool for punching up close. 'A Zukari arm-blade,' he said. 'For unseaming the Yull.' Carefully, he pushed the weapon back into place.

Robots rolled down the hall, setting out plates. At the far end, there was a minor commotion as a table of humans and M'Lak leaped upright, then sat back down. Smith glimpsed the cause: the small figure of General Young, taking dinner with her troops.

Rhianna spoke to the wallahbot, and it dispensed the vegan option. 'Vindaloo with tofu fried in gin,' it said, and Smith felt his eyes start to sting.

'So, Carveth, how about you? Have you made any progress with the Equ'i?'

Rhianna nodded. 'Have they accepted you into their culture?'

'Oh yes!' Carveth grinned, a spoonful of korma half-raised to her mouth. 'Ponyland is the best place ever. Celeste and I are really good friends. She's really clever. She'd be a best-selling novelist by now, except that she can't really type. Also, she's really keen on Tallulah Bankhead. Apparently, they'll show me the ancient art of dressage.'

Smith frowned. 'Have you actually learned anything useful?'

'How do you mean, "useful"?'

Smith sighed.

'Can she stay over?' Carveth demanded. 'Can she? She can sleep in my bed.'

'Where will you sleep?'

'In my bed.'

Suruk prodded his dinner. 'When they made you liaison officer, I doubt that was the sort of liaison that they intended. That will not delight Rick Dreckitt, seeing that he is usually there as well. Curious how there is no word "worstiality", is it not?'

Smith gave him a stern look. Suruk shrugged and continued to eat. Three tables down, a group of Ravnavari Lancers sprang upright and raised their cups. 'Victor Rex, King and Emperor! Those who are about to dine salute you!'

'Look,' Carveth said, 'I got Celeste a present. We'll have such fun with this!' She rooted about in a plastic bag, and dumped a mass of buckles and leather on the tabletop.

'What the bloody hell is that?' Smith said.

'Well, yes,' Rhianna said. 'What exactly is that, Polly?'

'It's a strap-on unicorn horn,' Carveth replied.

'Er, righto,' Smith said. They continued their meal. The food wasn't bad, Smith reflected. A group of lancers leaped upright on the next table down, and, for about the third time, cried 'To the health of King Victor!' and drank. Given the amount of booze they seemed to consume, Smith would have been more concerned about the health of the lancers than the king.

'Well,' Rhianna said, 'Suruk's making good progress with the mystic elder, and Polly's getting on really well with the Equ'i. Great work, guys.'

'Indeed,' Suruk said. 'So you and this horse. Is it bonky time?'

Carveth jolted upright and glared at him. 'What?'

'Alas,' Suruk said. 'Tiny horse sex. I think it is very important that we get to the bottom of this, for the wellbeing of the little woman here and so I can collect on that wager I made with Major Wainscott.'

Carveth glared at them. 'That is so unfair!' she exclaimed. 'I'd never sleep with a pony, even a talking one! We've not even been on a second date!'

*   *   *

The next morning, Smith and Rhianna resumed their study of the data that Wainscott had acquired. Suruk returned to the hidden temple, and Carveth delivered some documents to King Chestnut. They were something to do with winning the war. Then she hurried into the garden to find Celeste.

The pony stood beside the ornamental stream, gazing into the water pumped up from the Well of Ponyness. She glanced around and whinnied. 'Hello, Ambassador Polly!'

Carveth waved. 'Hi! I, er, brought you something.'

'Oh really? What's that?'

Fighting down a burst of uncertainty, Carveth took out her gift. 'This is for you. It's a strap-on unicorn horn. You said that you wanted to be a unicorn, and I thought that since I've got opposable thumbs, I might as well –'

She was drowned out by Celeste's gasp. 'For me? Oh Polly, how absolutely wonderful. Will you help me?'

Carveth helped secure the horn. She pulled Celeste's forelock out and smoothed it down.

'How do I look?'

'Great,' Carveth replied. 'Just like a unicorn.'

Celeste paused a moment, thinking. 'Polly,' she said,

flicking her tail, 'Would you like to see my special place?'

'Um,' said Carveth, 'Okay.'

'It's at the bottom of the gardens,' Celeste explained, 'far from the roving eyes of the brutish, uncomprehending masses. It is a place of sophistication and beauty that only those attuned to such things can comprehend. Close your eyes,' said Celeste, 'and follow me.'

Carveth felt silly holding Celeste's tail, so she just kept close behind and hoped that Celeste didn't feel the need to kick anything.

'This way,' the Equ'i said. 'Left a bit... and there. You can open your eyes now.'

Carveth opened her eyes.

She was standing in a small paddock, no larger than fifty yards across, hidden from view by walls of flowers. Banks of rhododendrons curved upwards, flowers bursting from them like falling droplets of water frozen in mid-burst. A pair of statues – rearing unicorns – glinted in the late afternoon sun beside an ornamental stream. At the rear of the paddock, nestled into the greenery, stood a small building somewhere between a stable and a summerhouse, its door rimmed with fairy lights.

Celeste stood in front of her. 'Welcome, Polly!' she cried.

A butterfly slightly smaller than a pair of elephant's ears flapped past, briefly considered landing on Carveth's head and instead turned to a huge sunflower like a landing-pad. Carveth's legs carried her forward while her eyes tried to take in her surroundings: flowers... ponies... statues of unicorns... fairy lights...

'I feel faint,' she said. 'It's so amazing, I feel a bit sick.'

'Isn't it?' cried Celeste. 'I write my novel in the summer-stable. It's called *Tina, the Warrior Horse*.'

The riverbank was clustered with pairs of

dragonflies. They shimmered like varnished wood, their wings humming. Celeste watched two dragonflies hover past. They were the size of king prawns. 'Polly,' she said, 'do you have a man friend?'

Carveth shrugged. 'Kind of. It's pretty vague.'

'Best thing for it, if you ask me. If he's anything like the stallions round here, I can't blame you. They're such imbeciles. You can't turn round in front of them without having one of the buggers trying to flop onto your back.'

'Men, eh?'

'Absolutely! Stallions are such useless blighters.' Celeste peered into the brook, admiring her horn. 'I'm so terribly glad you came along, Polly. So many people just think ponies are for riding. It's so rare to meet a human who wants to talk to one.'

'Of course I'd want to talk to you. I talk to my hamster sometimes, but he doesn't even reply. But – well, I've never really *met* any horses until now. I've never properly learned to ride a horse, you see…'

'Really? Then I shall teach you!' Celeste turned side-on to Carveth. 'Climb onto my back, Polly.'

Carveth looked at Celeste's back. The curve of her spine looked very daunting. 'Are you sure?'

'Of course!'

Carveth stepped forward and heaved herself onto Celeste's back. She found herself at right angles to the pony, her face parallel with the ground and her legs kicking uselessly in the air. With a lot of effort, Carveth turned ninety degrees, so that she was at least facing in the right direction. It was not a dignified business.

'Alright up there?'

'I think so.'

'Good.' Celeste started walking; Carveth found that she was moving too, and tried not to panic. Celeste accelerated, and Carveth was alarmed to discover that the air around her face had turned into wind, as if she'd stuck her head out of a car window. Still, provided that they stuck to trotting, it ought to be manageable.

'Let's jump over something!' Celeste cried. 'Won't that be fun?'

A log lay across the path. It was not, by arboreal standards, especially big, but it made Carveth think of the sort of thing used to stop tanks. 'I don't think this is a good idea,' she said.

'We can do it, Polly,' Celeste replied. 'Together.'

'Alright then.' Carveth leaned forward, as people did in films, and gritted her teeth. 'First time for everything.'

'That's the spirit – I knew you had it in you!' cried the pony. Head down, she charged straight at the log, Carveth bouncing uncontrollably on her back. 'Hold on tightly, Polly!'

Celeste drove up from the ground. Carveth whooped with fear and exhilaration and together they sailed over the log.

Celeste landed, cantered forward and slowed to a trot. She halted a few yards further on. 'Well, golly!' she panted.

Carveth slid down and landed uncertainly. Her legs were shaking. 'That was intense.'

'You have learned the ancient bond between horse and rider. Truly, you are one of us. Oh Polly! What jolly luck to have met you! I do hope you don't have to go away soon.'

'Go away?' The smile fell off Carveth's face as if a cliff had collapsed under it. She shuddered. 'Oh, I'm not going anywhere. I'd never leave Ponyland.' She gave a nervous little laugh. 'Wild horses couldn't drag me away.'

'Super!' said Celeste, but the air felt a little colder than before.

*　　*　　*

Overnight, Mothkarak seemed to have gained a small, high fort on its western edge. This was in fact the howdah of the ravnaphant Mildred, which had halted next to the curtain wall. A drawbridge flopped down and soldiers of all sorts hurried across, pushing trolleys full of supplies. Uninterested by the whole procedure, the ravnaphant took a bite out of the parapet and stood there chewing.

As Smith and Rhianna stepped into the morning sunshine, Mildred turned her myopic eyes on the castle. She seemed to be trying to decide whether to eat it.

'Wow!' Rhianna exclaimed. 'That's so big!'

'Quite so,' Smith replied. He was carrying a suitcase full of ammunition and sandwiches for the day ahead. Rhianna was wearing a large hat which, for reasons that he couldn't explain, he found vaguely erotic.

They crossed the drawbridge and were suddenly on the back of the beast. Railings ran around the edge of the howdah, providing cover for soldiers near the edge and ensuring that the ball would not fall out if they decided to play a game of football en route to the battlefield. The main fortress, which held the rocket batteries and howitzers, was in the middle of the ravnaphant's back, over its hips.

The Deepspace Operations Group waited in the howdah. Clad in a pith helmet and enormous shorts, Major Wainscott was explaining something to his men. '... trying to snatch a chap's mangoes,' he said. 'Ah, here's Smith and Co. Looking forward to bagging a few lemmings, Smith?'

'Definitely.'

'Good fellow. And here comes the Brig!'

A huge, barrel-shaped man approached, his hands jammed into the pockets of a battered safari jacket. He had one eye and a thick beard. A pipe protruded from his beard as if to mark out the location of his mouth. Overall, he resembled a gnarly old pirate.

The man removed his pipe and stuck out a massive hand. 'Brigadier Harthi,' he announced, shaking Smith's hand. 'I run this show. Madam,' he added, bowing to Rhianna. 'Welcome aboard Mildred.'

The ravnaphant turned to look back down its spine. It stared at them all for a while, decided there was nothing of interest, and used its tusks to break off another mouthful of the castle wall.

'Best get cracking,' Brigadier Harthi said, 'before the big girl eats half the battlements. Trevor, let's get moving!' he bellowed into the air about a foot from Smith's head. 'Duty calls,' he added, and he turned and stomped off, leaving Smith the impression that Brigadier Harthi and Major Wainscott were probably related.

'Well,' said Smith, 'I suppose we ought to get out of the way. Is there a viewing lounge?'

Ropes were cast off, the last boxes of equipment hauled aboard and the gangplank raised. By a process of shouting and prodding, the squad of marhouts occupying the cabin on its head made the ravnaphant start to move.

The deck lurched. Like a ship afloat on the green sea of jungle, the great beast picked up speed, pushing through the forest. A bow wave of panicked birds and terrified quanbeasts preceeded its enormous body. 'I think we ought to go inside,' Smith said.

Rhianna paused, fingertips pressed to her forehead.

'Can you read its mind?' Smith asked.

'Yes,' Rhianna said, 'I can sense… not much, actually. Normally, I'd think it was kinda cruel to put a building on an animal, but right now I'm not sure it's noticed it yet. Wait – I think...' She frowned. 'The brain in its spine needs the toilet, and the one in its head wants to know whether it's time for dinner yet.'

Long ago, before the war, the viewing lounge had been used by travellers, and the ceiling fans still turned lazily above wicker armchairs. But the plinth for the robot bartender was empty, and there were sandbags against the French windows.

'This is incredible,' Rhianna said, as fifty yards of jungle sped by with every step. Far below, Mildred's huge feet boomed on the forest floor.

Rhianna kicked off her sandals and stretched out on a chaise longe. The combination of Rhianna recumbent on a wicker chair and the low vibrations coming up through the floor had a disconcerting effect on Smith. It was easy to forget that they were going to fight the Yull.

Rhianna opened her eyes. 'Isambard, come over here,' she said.

'Righto, old girl!' Smith replied, sensing that romance was on the cards.

The door burst open and Wainscott stomped in, carrying a fishing-rod and looking like an angry gnome. 'Fruit!' he declared, and he stepped to the window and lifted his rod. 'Thought I might get something tasty,' he added.

'Chance'd be a fine thing,' Smith muttered, but Wainscott was too busy scouting for mangoes.

'Remarkable animal, this,' Wainscott said. 'The ravnaphant lives off minerals, you know. They can live for thousands of years in the wild. They also must be about the only creature in the British Space Empire that has a brain in its arse.'

Rhianna looked at Smith. Smith discreetly shook his head.

Wainscott hefted his fishing tackle. 'Mind if I dangle my rod over the edge?'

'It's never stopped you before,' Smith said, and Wainscott gave him a puzzled, quizzical look.

'So what's the plan?' Smith asked, as Wainscott reeled in a mango. 'Once we've found the lemming men, what then?'

Wainscott frowned. 'The lemmings'll be dug in deep – they like their warrens. So, we infiltrate the area and hold them down long enough for Harthi to get Mildred on top of their base. Then she jumps up and down and makes lemming squash. Should be simple.'

'So how do we find the lemmings?'

'Not my department,' Wainscott replied.

'Um, Isambard?' Rhianna tapped Smith on the arm. He looked around. 'I think they've found us.'

Lights rose from the forest like frightened birds. They arced over the treeline, reaching a peak and swinging down towards the ravnaphant.

'Bastards've spotted us!' Wainscott snarled.

'I thought that might happen,' Smith said. 'We are riding a dinosaur, after all. Rhianna, can you –'

She threw her arm up, covered her eyes with her hand, and made a humming noise.

From below, someone yelled 'Brace!' Two AA guns swung to cover the rockets and suddenly the air was full of streaking bullets. Chaff sailed out from the howdah. One of the rockets went wide, corkscrewing into the forest. The second and third burst in mid-air as if they had hit a wall.

'Jolly good, old girl!' Smith exclaimed. He rushed to the edge of the howdah, pulling his rifle into his hands. Something exploded on the far side of the howdah. The deck rippled and shook. Smith fell against the railing: Rhianna fell against him.

With a roar, the forest caught light in front of them. A great stripe of fire rushed across the ground, as if a chasm had opened to Hell. The ravnaphant stopped, shuddered and took a backwards step that set the ceiling fans swaying.

'The Yull have got a fougasse!' Wainscott snarled.

'Like hell they will.' Smith cocked his rifle. 'They can fougasse off.'

'Let's go,' Wainscott said. 'Susan!' he cried, and he ran out of the room, rod in one hand, mango stashed under his arm.

Smith turned to Rhianna. 'We'd better go too,' she said. 'In case he gets into trouble.'

Outside, men ran across the decking, firing small arms and shoulder-launched plasma guns. The ravnaphant turned, slow as an oil tanker, while the big guns boomed and chattered from its sides.

Brigadier Harthi stood at the railing, brandishing a sabre, shouting orders and looking more like a sea-captain than ever. 'Prepare to repel boarders!' he called.

Specks appeared in the air, winged like pterodactyls. 'Lemmings in flight!' a M'Lak soldier bellowed, and the gliders swooped down. One of the mounted guns blew the wings off the nearest glider and it dropped into the canopy. The ravnaphant lunged and snatched another out of the air, and started to chew it. The glider blew up, and the great beast roared at the sky.

'I'm sensing unhappiness,' Rhianna said. 'At least, in its front brain. The back one still needs the toilet.'

The Deepspace Operations Group stood at the starboard side of the howdah, providing covering fire.

Susan had braced the beam gun on the railing. Now she heaved it down and pointed into the forest. 'The gliders are coming from over there.'

'Can we get them?' Smith demanded.

Susan nodded. 'We'll take the lift. This way.'

They hurried to a gap in the rails. A wooden platform hung out over the ravnaphant's side, rigged to a pulley system. They crowded on: Smith saw a row of levers like those in an old railway signal box. 'Hang on,' he called, and he pulled the lever marked 'Down'.

The platform dropped away. The chains rattled: they plunged down the ravnaphant's flank as if down a cliff face. Mildred's scales were the size of medieval shields. Air rushed past them as Smith tried to find the brake.

Something huge crashed into the ground behind them. Trees creaked and splintered.

'The Yull are dropping bombs!' Wainscott barked.

'Actually, that was the ravnaphant,' Rhianna said.

The chains were a clattering blur. Smith found the brake lever and heaved it upwards. The mechanism squealed and the platform hit the ground.

They stumbled off, slightly dazed. Suddenly, they were in a half-trampled mass of fern-like plants.

'Get out the way!' Wainscott shouted, brandishing his mango. They followed him into the foliage. The ravnaphant's huge leg flattened the ground behind them. Jagged leaves brushed their shoulders. Smith could smell burning, somewhere to the right.

'Which way?' he demanded.

Rhianna frowned. 'This looks familiar,' she said, pointing at the vegetation.

'You know where to go?'

'No,' she replied. 'But I used to grow plants just like these.'

'Follow me!' Wainscott cried, and he struck off to the right. Smith paused, tried to figure it out, and pursued him.

They pressed on over the rough ground, through the greenery. A bank of acrid smoke rolled in, and visibility dropped to twenty yards.

'The Yull won't know how few we are in the fog,' Wainscott growled.

Smith felt slightly light-headed. He strode on, through the reek of burning vegetation. He was fairly sure that he could hear M'Lak voices coming from behind. At his side, Rhianna said, 'Um, guys, I've just thought of something...'

Her voice was drowned out by a wild screech from the left.

'Lemmings,' Susan said, and she swung the beam gun. Smith saw figures moving up ahead, dark blurs in the pungent smoke. His head felt wobbly.

Nelson stopped, pulled his Stanford gun up and let off a burst of fire. A lemming man screamed.

They advanced. The smoke cleared slightly and Smith saw a whole pack of Yull. They had rigged an enormous elastic belt between two sturdy trees and now three serfs were pulling it back while an officer with an explosive vest and a pair of leather wings barked commands.

Smith fired. The nearest serf fell back. The belt flicked out and hit the officer in the backside, flinging him head-first into the undergrowth. He exploded.

All hell broke out. Gunfire blazed out of the smoke. Smith grabbed Rhianna and threw her down. Head spinning, he hit the earth beside her, twisted around and fired his rifle prone. A dark shape buckled and executed a strange lurching dance before keeling over.

'Forwards!' Wainscott cried. Smith stood up, head swimming, and helped Rhianna to her feet. Which way was forwards?

For his own part, Major Wainscott was feeling somewhat confused. He'd breathed in a load of that bloody smoke; an exploding lemming must have set the foliage alight. His head felt funny and nothing had even hit it yet. He looked down at his hands and saw that the dirt on his arms had started to go blue. Armoured figures yelled and roared ahead of him, waving a banner. The blue warpaint curled around his arms like snakes.

Susan leaned in. Her hair looked wilder and redder than he recalled.

Wainscott dropped his gun and pulled a long knife, almost a short-sword. With a couple of cuts he freed himself from shirt and trousers, and was surprised to see the same blue markings on his chest. The fierce sun blessed his body with strength.

Susan was shouting something behind him; no doubt words of enthusiasm and approval, especially given his lack of attire. 'Scythe blades,' she was saying. 'Weld 'em to the hubcaps!'

Naked apart from his boots and bandolier, Wainscott braced his legs and waved his knife at the Yull. 'Say hello to my little friend!' he cried, and he charged.

Smith watched Wainscott's advance without much surprise. His head throbbed. The world felt distant. People seemed to be underwater. Their voices sank and slowed down. Dimly, he wondered how much smoke he'd inhaled.

The trees slid away from him and suddenly he was standing on a flat rectangle of grass. White lines stretched away and at the edge of his vision, he saw a pavilion. Rhianna stood on the steps in a summery dress.

'Cricket,' Smith said. 'Nice.'

A figure appeared at the far end of the crease. It was covered in pads, almost like a suit of armour. The figure ran towards Smith like a bowler, but it swung the bat up over its head, two-handed.

'Howzaaaat!' it screamed. Smith reached for his sword, but his hands were too slow –

The sky tore open like canvas and a gigantic, evil head looked down. Eyes goggling, mandibles open, Suruk grinned down upon the world.

Oh, that's not good, Smith thought. Suruk's turned into a god.

Suruk reached down with a spindly bare arm, scooped up a handful of tiny lemming men and dropped them into his jaws. He ate the lemming men, roaring with laughter as he did and sounding a lot like a ravnaphant.

The gigantic Suruk started dancing on the far end of the cricket pitch. Jimmy Horlicks and Grimdall the Rebel sat on his shoulders, performing on ukuleles. Carveth descended from the skies on cherub wings. A squadron of little blue Pegasus circled Suruk's head like birds around a stunned cartoon character. Smith was pretty sure that he was hallucinating.

Shadows reached in for him. He drew his sword and sliced at them. The blade cut their smoky arms. They screeched and fell away.

'Isambard!'

He whipped around. A tall, dark-haired woman stood before him, a long skirt flowing around her. 'I was hallucinating,' he gasped. 'Thank God you're here, Emily Bronte.'

'It's me, Rhianna.' She raised her hands. 'You know I said I recognised the plants here? Well, they're on fire, and you've inhaled a lot of smoke. You're having a bit of a bad experience. Just... chill, okay? Everything's cool. It's all going to be fine –'

'*Yullai!*'

Smith whirled and a huge shape tore out of the mist. He slipped left and an axe swung down like a guillotine blade. Smith rammed his sword into the monster's chest, up under the breastplate and out the back. The Yullian coughed and gasped. Smith pulled the sword back and the alien fell spluttering at his feet.

'Except for us being in a battle,' Rhianna added. She frowned. 'I'm sure there was something else. Something I've forgotten...'

Smith looked round, trying to get his bearings. Dreckitt strode out of the forest, a massive pistol in his hand. 'Are you okay?' He peered at Smith. 'You too, huh? This hop's got me crazier than two waltzing mice,' Dreckitt snarled.

Smith said, 'What? The Yull are dancing?'

'Figure of speech, pal,' Dreckitt replied. 'The warren's collapsed. They got the ravnaphant on it and it fell to bits.' He looked at Rhianna. 'Lady, are you doped out as well?'

'I'm the same as usual,' Rhianna replied.

'Let's call that a no, for the sake of argument. Come on, let's go!'

'Wait,' she replied. 'There's something I'd forgotten.' Rhianna paused, looked down and pulled her skirt up. 'That's it!' she cried triumphantly. 'My shoes! I knew I'd forgotten something.'

*   *   *

It was night. Torches lit the courtyard of the temple.

'Step and twist and strike and kick and – roll!' Volgath called.

Suruk slipped left and right, the point of his spear punching the air, his body in constant motion behind it.

'No, no!' Volgath cried. 'Bring your legs up higher. And raise those hands! Remember, you're a striking cobra. Again. This time with feeling!'

Suruk stopped and drove his spear into the earth. 'This is irksome.'

Volgath leaned against an arch, sipping a glass of sherry. He had spent the last three days there, criticising Suruk's fighting-styles for lack of feeling and reminiscing about the time that he had taken on the entire Bolshoi in a drunken brawl.

'Really?' Volgath asked. 'So wise you are already in the ways of the warrior, means it?'

'That did not even make grammatical sense.'

'When my age you are, syntax bother about you will not.'

Suruk grimaced. 'I see. We have spent three days learning your routines. If I have to go through the Stones of the Forbidden Temple again…'

Volgath leaned forward. 'So? So what? If I tell you to show me your stones, you'll show me.'

Suruk snorted.

The ancient took a thoughtful sip. 'Truly, Suruk, what do you seek?'

'The relics. This know you – I mean, you know this.'

'And why is that? What do you want from them? Fame? Do you want to live forever? Or is it the skills I can teach you? Do you wish to learn how to fly?'

'Fly?'

'Metaphorically.'

'No, then.'

'If you want the relics, you must prove yourself worthy. And that means learning from me. I have demonstrated my fighting skills to the crowned heads of the galaxy – and sliced off a few of them, as well. And, once you have faced the final test, you will be ready to take them. If you are not dead.' He paused and bent down. When he stood, he held the sherry bottle. 'Drink?'

'Gladly.'

Volgath poured out two substantial measures. 'To victory.'

'To victory.'

Volgath sipped. 'You know, even if we are victorious, this planet will never be the same.'

'Indeed. It will be covered in dead lemmings.'

'I meant that the Space Empire will be sorely weakened. Saving mankind from tyranny takes it out of one.'

'True. But my comrades will fight to the end. My old friend Isambard Smith may have a mild exterior, but under it is a mild interior, and under *that*, the heart of a warrior. Similarly, the mystic Rhianna is deceptive. She sees much – coloured swirls and someone called Lucy in the sky, mainly, but she is so wise that she is welcomed whenever she comes round.'

'She visits you rarely, then?'

'Oh no – she's always there, just unconscious most of the time. Sometimes I even wonder about the little woman. Small and portly she may be, but there is a look of ferocity to her, especially when I have taken the last chocolate biscuit...'

'Your trust in humans is your weakness, Suruk. Think of the Edenites and their foul customs. Never underestimate mankind's capacity for bigotry, even to their own kind.'

Suruk nodded. 'True. I never understood prejudice. After all, humans all look the same to me. Squat and ugly, with funny little mouths.'

'If you think their faces are weird, you should see

what goes on at the end of their legs,' Volgath added, pulling a face. 'And those noses! I don't see how anyone could have finished evolving and still have a nose. We M'Lak are thankfully free of prejudice,' he added, 'largely because we're a bit better than everyone else. Which is why you should think carefully about the relics. They belong to Ravnavar, Suruk.'

'I see.'

'I hope you do. Grimdall was from Ravnavar: the relics are his, not the property of the Space Empire. The relics could never be transported to the British Museum and left there. For one thing, they belong elsewhere. For another, they would kill the guards and escape.'

Suruk lowered his glass. 'Escape?'

'Of course.' Volgath chuckled. Firelight flickered around his mandibles. 'Grimdall is dead, but his mighty steed, the Mechanical Maneater, lives on. And the Maneater will slay anyone unworthy who claims Grimdall's heritage. The custodian of the relics must prove himself to them.'

Suruk said, 'I see now why your task is such a burden, and an honour. And why you get so few applicants.'

'Oh, there have been many applicants, Suruk. But the final interview proved difficult. Terminal, to be precise.'

Suruk was silent. He gazed into the dark.

'You look troubled,' Volgath said. 'What are you thinking?'

'That we should get marshmallows and roast them on a stick, like boy scouts.'

'How many boy scouts can you fit on one stick?' Volgath sighed. 'Truly, Suruk, we think alike. Perhaps you are ready to prove yourself worth of the relics.'

Suruk finished his sherry. 'I was spawned ready.'

Volgath said, 'This is no mere battle I refer to. If you

wish to find the relics, you must face your worst fears –
and survive.'

'My worst fears?'

'Indeed. What do you dread? From what do you
recoil?'

'Losing the war. The lemming scum enslaving my
people. Of dying before the Greater Galactic Happiness
and Friendship Collective is rendered into a lifeless heap
of skulls.'

'That is every warrior's fear. But what about *you*?'

'Hmm. Well, I have never liked dishonour much.
Or yogurt. Or bees. I am not overly fond of tarantulas,
either. They give me indigestion.'

Volgath smiled. 'Those are your darkest fears?'

Suruk shrugged.

'Then you must gird your mandibles, Suruk the
Slayer. I have tested your body. Now I shall test your soul.
I will take you into your darkest places. In the Cavern of
Dread, you will face... er... a giant dishonourable bee,
covered in yogurt. Or something like that.'

Suruk took a deep breath. 'I am ready.'

'Good. Then follow me.'

Volgath crossed the courtyard and stepped under an
arch. 'Come, warrior.'

Suruk looked up at the trees, certain that he was
being watched. He saw nothing. Then he picked up his
spear, stretched his neck, and followed.

They walked into a stone tunnel. Amber light seeped
out from translucent panels in the roof. The floor sloped
down, winding deep into the earth. On the walls, ancient
carvings depicted monsters, ghosts and demons. Stories
from the old legends.

'Hold!' Volgath cried.

Suruk looked round. 'What is it?'

'Atmosphere,' Volgath said. He reached into an

alcove and pulled a lever. War-drums rose up around them, a frantic jungle clatter. Beasts screeched and howled. The drumming grew quicker, swelled around them like a heart about to burst.

'Splendid,' Suruk said. 'Mood music.'

At the end stood a door. Carved on it was a single figure, a leaping caricature of a M'Lak warrior in silhouette, dancing across a landscape. Suruk would have known that shape and its bright eyes anywhere. It was the Dark One, the guardian of Ethrethar, lord of the dead.

'Beyond is his territory,' Volgath said.

Suruk nodded. 'I have faced him before.'

The door swung open. 'Every warrior has a weakness,' Volgath said, 'a thing that he cannot defeat. Face it, Suruk, and rise again!'

Something hit Suruk hard in the back. He stumbled forward, and as he realised that it was probably Volgath's boot, the door slammed behind him.

Suruk stood there in the darkness, half-expecting a rubber spider to drop from the ceiling. He tried to imagine the most fearsome, terrifying thing he had ever encountered, and remembered the time when Smith had kept a large mirror in the hold. He had stumbled upon that thing a few times and given himself quite a scare.

He heard speech. For a moment, he thought it was his own voice. Slowly, the voices rose in conversation – and with them, the tinkle of glass and the glug of wine.

'It's been a really good year,' said a voice at his shoulder. Suruk whipped round, saw nothing. 'The shop has turned a really nice little profit. You know, I'm thinking that I might join the Chamber of Commerce next year. It's good for business.'

Suruk listened. Yes, the voice was really there, as well as the background murmur. They were all M'Lak voices, deep and properly croaky. Far off, someone said something about canapés.

Suruk raised his spear and took a step forward. The voices moved around him, swirling through the dank air. He did not know where the door was.

'Took a holiday to Los Angeles. We picked up some lovely trophies.'

'And I said to him: "What the Hell are *you?*" You should have seen his face!'

There was polite laughter. And then, crystal clear, a throaty voice said, 'So, Agshad: how are the kids?'

Suruk paused. Agshad? Surely not. That was his father's name.

'Well, now you ask, not so bad.'

You're dead, Suruk thought. You died fighting the Yull, father.

'I'm very proud of him, to tell the truth,' said Agshad Nine-Swords. 'My boy's really gone out there and made something of himself. Taken the bull by the horns, you might say. He's a real achiever, you know. A credit to the family.'

Thank you, Father, Suruk thought. I am proud to have honoured you with my deeds.

'Just don't ask me about Suruk,' Agshad added.

'What?'

'I mean, he's a bit slow compared to Morgar, I know. But I'm sure he'll turn out alright in the end.'

Suruk froze.

'You need to do something with that lad,' said a voice.

'The boy's a late starter, that's all,' Suruk's father replied. 'He's, you know, got his own ways. He means well. He's got a good heart.'

'Whose chest did he hack it from?' another voice inquired, and Suruk was surrounded by gurgling laughter. 'If he takes enough heads, he might end up with a good brain too.'

Suruk raised his spear. 'Fools!' he snarled.

'Look,' Agshad said, 'Suruk's just... old-fashioned.'

The other voice put on an accent. 'Greetings,' it exclaimed. 'Welcome to the house of burgers!'

Suruk snarled. The mocking laughter rose to answer him, spinning around him like a cloud of flies.

'Do you desire fries with that?'

'Silence, upstart!' Suruk barked, but the voices would not stop.

'Look, father. I devoured a crayon! I built a sandcastle in the litter tray!'

'Come out!' Suruk cried. 'Come out and face me!'

And it was silent.

A dream, Suruk thought. Nothing more than that. And I have banished it.

Light blossomed in front of him. It came from neon strips in the ceiling, and it glinted on beer pumps and rows of glasses. A figure stood at the bar, a tall M'Lak, his back to Suruk.

This is real, Suruk thought. It cannot be, but...

He wished it was bees and yoghurt.

A hand came down on his shoulder. He looked round and saw one of the elders of his house, the most venerable ancients of the line of Urgar the Miffed. 'We've found you an arch-enemy,' the elder said. 'From a really good line, too. They're all real killers. You'll have loads to talk about.'

A second voice, at his left. 'Look, he just scowled at you. He doesn't like you either. Go on, Suruk, go and threaten him.'

'No,' Suruk said, but it did not come out as he had wanted it to. In his mind, it was a roar of defiance. It came out sounding like dread. 'I have nothing against this person.'

'Oh, don't be shy,' another elder crooned. They were

around him like jackals, pushing him towards the figure at the bar. 'Go over and introduce yourself. Spill his pint.'

'I will choose my own nemesis,' Suruk said, but his voice was cracked and weak.

'Look, he's all alone. Time to make your move, Suruk. Ask him what he's looking at.'

Suruk took a step towards the bar. 'I... I cannot. I won't.'

He felt a slap on the back. He winced. 'Go on, lad. When I was your age...'

A horrible sense of embarrassment crawled over his body. The words of threat and challenge dried up in his mouth. Shame seemed to shrink him. His mandibles drooped.

Not this, Suruk thought. Not this.

And he tore free of their weak, ushering hands, twisted round and cried, 'No, I shall not! I will battle who I choose! You cannot make me. I, Suruk, will slay who I please. I will arrange my own carnage. Leave me, damn you, leave me alone!'

And suddenly, he was alone. He stood in a dim-lit, empty cellar. It smelt of dust.

Suruk blinked a couple of times. His family, and his fear of their disapproval, was gone. He found the door easily. It wasn't locked. The corridor was empty. Suruk climbed up, alone, with the strange but familiar feeling of recovering from mild concussion.

As he reached the exit, he heard the Yull.

'*Dar huphep!*' a lemming man howled, and then a scream followed by a loud, clattering thud.

'*Hup yullai!*' a second rodent shrieked, and a moment later it let out a thin yowl of pain.

Suruk dropped down and crept forward, still in the shadows.

Volgath stood in the courtyard. Around him lay a dozen or so lemming men in various forms of armour: officers, from the look of it. Axes were scattered on the ground.

Single combat, Suruk thought. That would have been surprisingly honourable, if there hadn't been a queue of about forty other Yullian officers stretching around the corner into the forest, waiting for a go.

Another lemming man let out a battle cry and ran forward. Volgath sidestepped and his fingers flicked up into the rodent's throat. The lemming squeaked and staggered drunkenly aside, clutching his neck. Volgath's hand was bloody.

But so was his side, Suruk saw, and his shoulder and hip. There was only a certain amount of lemming warlords that anyone could be expected to defeat in a single afternoon. Volgath will die here, Suruk thought. Or at least, he will without me.

Suruk raised his spear. He had dealt with his own family. Nothing could frighten him now.

And Volgath saw him. It was just a quick glance, but his eyes locked straight onto Suruk's. Volgath gave a tiny shake of the head. Suruk waited.

'*Hup!*'

The lemming men stopped, and the queue jerked to attention. A huge, pale figure lumbered into view, flanked by bodyguards. Suruk did not need to see the creature's single eye to know that he was looking at General Wikwot.

'So,' Wikwot declared. 'This is your mighty citadel, is it? You are the master of weapons. And yet we simply walked in. This world is ours for the taking, and do you know how we won it?'

Volgath grimaced. 'By a whisker?'

'Oh, very funny. Most amusing. The answer is "easily". Your world is finished, your temple ruined, your wretched people doomed.' He snorted, amused. 'And to think that you actually look tough.'

'And you definitely smell strong.'

Wikwot glanced over his shoulder. 'This animal does not merit a warrior's death. Bind him and bring me the power tools. We will soon learn where the Relics of Grimdall are hidden.'

'Fool,' Volgath said. 'You still do not understand what you are spawning with. Strike me and you will regret it.'

'Silence!' Wikwot lashed out. His paw hit Volgath's cheek. Slowly, like a poorly-balanced totem pole, Volgath fell backwards. He hit the ground.

Wikwot looked down at the body. He bent down, checked Volgath's pulse and stood up. The general took out a cigarette and jammed it into the corner of his chops. 'Ah, *fecinec*,' he muttered. A minion stepped in with a lighter, and Wikwot turned and lumbered away.

The lemming men closed ranks around the general, and followed him into the trees.

*   *   *

Suruk squatted down beside Volgath. The ancient was quite cold to the touch, definitely more greenish grey than greyish green. 'They would have made you betray your people,' Suruk said. 'So you made yourself die. Truly, a warrior's death.'

Volgath's hand grabbed him round the ankle.

Suruk gasped; he drew back, but Volgath clung on, and, very slowly, the elder opened his mouth. 'Suruk!'

he whispered.

'Yes, old one?'

'I do not have long.'

'Indeed.'

The ancient chuckled; there was blood on his fangs. 'There is an ancient technique to feigning death.' He smiled. 'But this time, I may not have to act much longer.'

'You did well,' Suruk replied. 'Now the fools of Yullia are confounded. But who will take care of the temple?'

'Forget the temple. Its time has gone. You must know the location of the relics of Grimdall.'

'Yes. Tell me.'

Volgath grimaced. 'Lean closer, and I will whisper to you.'

Suruk was not accustomed to being very near anyone. When you bred with yourself, you didn't tend to need a lot of physical contact with anybody else. He glanced over his shoulder, feeling slightly awkward, and then feeling guilty for feeling awkward. Strange: he had never felt guilty about much at all before.

He put his face close to Volgath's.

'It is a secret I have hidden well,' Volgath whispered. 'Never have I shared it before.'

'Tell me. In the name of Ravnavar.'

Volgath's eyes met those of his protégé. 'Kiss me quick,' he gasped.

'Ah.' Suruk looked over his shoulder again. He had spent enough time among humans to know that this sort of thing went on, and was perfectly legal. But the M'Lak? Awkward. 'Well,' he said, 'you are dying, I suppose...'

'Not out here!' Volgath gasped. 'In my chambers!'

The master threw out his arm, and his hand slapped against the paving stones.

'I suppose it is more private,' Suruk said. 'But Volgath, you must realise... I appreciate that you have had something of a shock... you are a great and fierce warrior, and truly we are comrades in arms... arms as in weapons, that is, not – ugh – hugging... but our people were not meant to kiss. For one thing, our mandibles would stab each other's faces. Which lacks romance, Volgath. Volgath?'

Volgath was dead. Properly dead.

Suruk shook his head. 'A great shame. Dreadful, and yet rather fortunate, timing.' He crouched down beside the corpse. 'Well, ancient, you wanted to go to your room. I can at least do that.'

He heaved Volgath's body onto his shoulder. Suruk straightened up and walked towards the arches.

Volgath's room was small and simple. There were few concessions to luxury. A modest rack held a couple of practice spears. A photograph showed Volgath standing over a dead quanbeast, a sabre in either hand. On the far side of the wall, another photo showed Volgath on holiday, standing at some waterfront in a striped jacket and straw boater. Under it, Suruk found a bench.

Suruk laid him along the bench. 'You lived well, old one,' he said. 'You died well, too. All shall know of your deeds, except, maybe... that bit...'

He straightened up, and stopped.

Suruk leaned towards the photograph of Volgath's holiday. It was a standard 3D affair, the sort of thing you could buy on any package tour. But it was Volgath's outfit that struck him: not the straw hat in itself, but the words on the brim.

'*Kiss me quick*,' Suruk said.

He lifted the picture down. What was that place? The terrain looked like Andor. Some sort of lake, it seemed. People jumped into the lake from a charabanc-shuttle hovering overhead. A sign in the background reminded patrons to refrain from petting. A holiday resort.

Suruk turned the picture over. There was a cross on the back. He drew a stiletto and pushed it into the cross. Then he flipped the photograph over again.

A small island rose out of the lake like the hump of a sea monster. It could not have been more than ten feet across. The glittering tip of the stiletto stuck out of the island.

Outside, something rumbled. The Yull were coming back.

*   *   *

The Yullian camp was so vast that General Wikwot had no idea where it ended. From his tent, he could see thousands of soldiers and, even though many of the trees had been hacked down to make space, it was impossible to tell where the extra treehouses and warrens stopped.

The more the merrier, he thought. The more lemmings who witnessed his victory and the resulting bloodbath, the greater his glory. Then he would return to Yullia, dragging slaves by the million, and the idiots who had written him off would be laughing on the other side of their muzzles.

He swaggered through the rows of tents, past soldiers sharpening their torture implements and rubbing dung onto their bayonets. A ladder stood against a tall tree and, as Wikwot passed, a trooper did penance for some minor disciplinary infringement by rushing up the ladder and throwing himself from the top rung. The general paused to admire the soldier's descent.

So, the hidden temple was no more and its master was dead. Too bad that the Relics of Grimdall remained out of reach. Soon, Wikwot thought. His army was ready. His soldiers were creeping through the forest, encircling the human citadel. His scouts were closing in on its outposts. His hunters had captured fierce beasts to unleash upon the defenders.

In an open space nearby, a group of officers were indulging in the ancient sport of minion-ball. The minion, having been booted from one end of the field to the other, disgraced himself by staggering upright and trying to run away. 'Serf's up!' an officer cried, and the whole pack leaped on the minion and tore him limb from limb.

'General Wikwot!'

Wikwot turned, glowering. Colonel Cots of the secret police had appeared behind him. The colonel, being an assassin, had a nasty habit of forming out of the shadows. A couple of nights ago, he had embarrassed Wikwot whilst he was perusing a copy of *Dirty Does*.

'What is it?' Wikwot demanded.

Cots gestured, and one of his acolytes shoved a Yullian soldier forward. The soldier's eyes had a strange, faraway quality.

'The enemy have stormed our forward warren,' Cots said. 'This serf escaped.'

Wikwot looked the trooper over. His fur was matted with dirt and blood, and his ears were torn. 'Only just, by the look of it.'

'Er, no, that was me,' Cots replied. 'I beat him up. Just in case he was lying, you know.'

'Very sensible.'

'His mind has been addled by toxic smoke. He is –' Cots grimaced – 'relaxed. I have found no trace of frenzied rage in him at all. It is very unwholesome.'

'Quite so. Speak, serf!'

'Hey,' the soldier said, 'chill, General. It was bad out

there. Really heavy. The offworlders totally stormed us. We started shooting from the warren, but they must have had a flamethrower, because all these plants started burning, and we breathed in the smoke... lemming man, I haven't had it this bad since I nibbled catnip.'

'Catnip is forbidden to lower orders!' Wikwot snapped. 'What happened next?'

'They trashed the place. We had all out defences ready and everything, but they collapsed the warren. There were all dead lemmings everywhere, and I dug my way out, and there was blood and everything...'

Cots snapped, 'Who did this?'

The soldier trembled. 'No way. To speak that demon's name –'

Cots snarled and pulled a set of pliers from his sash.

'No,' the soldier gasped. 'Not him –'

'Speak!'

'*Aiii!* Wesscot, the ghost who walks in shorts! Him and his legion of devils!'

Wikwot swallowed. He remembered. Once, he had commanded a mighty fortress. To amuse himself, he had rounded up the local beetle people and put them under a giant magnifying glass. Somehow, the offworlders had found out about it, and Wesscot and his minions had come calling. They had taken him alive. He shuddered.

Wikwot said, 'Serf, I thank you. This is most useful. Your service is much appreciated.'

The serf jerked upright and saluted. 'Thanks, General!'

'On the other hand, you failed to defend your warren, so climb that tree and jump off the top.'

The soldier deflated somewhat. He turned and trudged towards the ladder.

'These unrodents he talks about,' Wikwot said.

Cots nodded. 'Yes?'

'Find them and kill them.'

Cots turned to go, and a voice called out to them both. It was the soldier, about to scale the ladder to his doom.

'Erm, General? One last thing before I seek forgiveness from the war god? They had a really big monster with them. It was like a huge thing, bigger than a building. We might want to look out for that.'

Behind Wikwot, a tree creaked and collapsed. He turned round and peered into the forest. Beyond the trees, their legs bigger than any trunk, two enormous beasts groaned and strained against the ropes and drugs that held them at bay.

'Oh,' Wikwot said. 'Like those, you mean?'

They Shoot Ponies, Don't They?

'Forward, noble steed!' cried Carveth.

'To battle, good sir knight!' Celeste called.

They bounced across the rear lawn, over the ornamental bridge, towards the forest.

'Our foe approaches!' Celeste called.

Twenty yards ahead, a cardboard cutout of a Ghast drone awaited them. Carveth had borrowed it from a mouldering stash of shooting gear she had found in one of Mothkarak's storerooms, probably not touched since the early 2500s. Now propped up with sticks, the caricatured face grimaced at the croquet mallet tucked under Carveth's arm.

'Attack!' Celeste cried, and she cantered forward. Carveth swung the mallet into the head of the Ghast. The cardboard cutout fell backwards, and they both cheered.

'A dolorous blow,' Celeste said, slowing to a halt. 'Come, noble sir, let us stop for tea and sugar lumps.'

Carveth swung herself down. The Equ'i was wearing the artificial unicorn horn and looked rather smart in it. Together they set off towards the pavilion.

'It's a bloody awful nuisance that there's a war on,' Celeste said. 'I've been having the most super time with you.'

Carveth looked across the trees, at the great green expanse of the lawn and the house at the far end like the castle of a fairy kingdom. A dragonfly weaved through the air before them, its wings buzzing.

'I suppose we've got to fight the lemming men, though,' Celeste said. 'Daddy thinks they're awful. He says that they've nothing to offer the galaxy except fleas.'

'Lies!'

Carveth whipped around. The bushes shook. A huge figure stepped out: filthy, hulking, covered in plate armour. Celeste gasped. For a moment it seemed impossible, a trick of the light that such a creature should be here. Then Carveth realised that she was looking at an officer of the Divine Amicable Army of Yullia.

'Offworlder, you tell dirty lies.'

The lemming man swaggered out of the bushes, bits of shrubbery snagging on his armour. Others emerged around him, as if spawning from the forest itself. Branches seemed to turn to rifles and bayonets, moss to fur.

'Oh bloody bugger,' Celeste whispered.

The lemming stopped five yards away. He smiled. '*Darhep*, lesser mammals. My name is Colonel Prem. You are now under the protection of the Greater Galactic Happiness and Friendship Collective. Congratulations.'

Fear hit Carveth like sickness. It ran down her limbs, weakening them. It turned her stomach.

The officer pointed at the mallet dangling from Carveth's hand. 'Playing at war, eh? Yes, your species does that. When I was young, my brother and I used to dress up in cardboard boxes and pretend to be warriors.

Then my father beheaded him. Happy days.'

'I'm – I'm a British citizen,' Carveth said. 'I'm the liaison officer here.'

'That figures,' said Colonel Prem. 'I thought I could smell gin.'

His soldiers giggled. For a moment, fury rushed through Carveth. She was ready to leap forward, to swing the mallet and knock the smirk off his snout – and then it was gone, and she was nothing but afraid.

'Colonel.' One of the lemming men pointed to the cardboard cutout. 'They have an insulting picture of a Ghast!'

'Ah, our beloved allies. Well, we can't have that. Discipline has to be maintained.' He grinned.

'I did it,' Celeste said. 'It's mine, not hers.'

Prem looked at her. 'Is it now? Well, we'll have to have words, little horse.'

'No,' Carveth said. 'You can't.'

Prem turned. 'Run along now, human. I think it is time for the British Space Empire to have its cocoa. Don't worry about the ponies. We Yull know how to look after unrodents. We'll take good care of *them*.'

An aide stepped forward. He held up a propaganda picture: it showed a smiling lemming on a throne, being supported by a range of other species, some of which were probably extinct by now. 'Colonel, have we any nails with which to put the posters up?'

'Don't worry,' Prem said. 'I've got a deal going with the glue factory.' He peered at Carveth. 'Are you still here? I tell you what. Two minutes and then I'll let the squol off their leads. Tell me, liaison officer: have you ever seen a squol leap through the air?'

'Oh God,' Carveth said. 'No.'

'Run, Polly,' said Celeste. 'Run as fast as your two small legs can carry you.'

*   *   *

Smith sat in the lounge on the howdah, feeling hungry and peculiar. The rocking of the ravnaphant's back brought back memories thirty years suppressed: the Midwich Grammar School trip to Dieppe, where he had eaten a bad crepe and become convinced that he had contracted dysentery. He could almost hear the other schoolchildren, crowding round with a mixture of horror and glee, gabbling about his accident in the Pompidou Centre. He had never forgiven them, or France, for that.

'It's okay,' Rhianna said, as she picked through the medikit. 'Just take a few more of these pills...'

By the time they reached base camp, the fear had dissipated and been replaced with an urgent need to eat chocolate and sleep with his face in Rhianna's cleavage. Somewhat warily, Smith joined the others at the railing.

'I hear you tore it up back there,' Susan said, as they manoeuvred parallel with the curtain wall. 'Dead lemmings everywhere.'

'Did I?' His head still felt very hazy.

Susan was too professional to have been much affected by the smoke. 'You went a bit mental, to be honest. You and Wainscott. He thinks he's protecting Boadicea.'

The ramp dropped, and the Deepspace Operations Group disembarked from the howdah onto the walls of Mothkarak. Supply teams waited for them, medics and strategic advisors. A crane swung out and dropped a block of stone in front of the ravnaphant, which it began to eat. Brigadier Harthi appeared at the crow's nest, shouting instructions to his crew. Wainscott wandered onto the drawbridge.

'Mission accomplished!' the major yelled at the guards. 'The Britons attacked the camp of the enemy with slings and arrows. Next stop, Londinium!'

'For God's sake, he's got his todger out,' Susan muttered. 'Someone fetch me that picnic rug! They don't pay me enough for this.'

Rhianna helped Smith down the gangplank. 'How do you feel?' she asked.

'Relaxed, thanks. Hello clouds. Hello sky.'

'I was afraid of that,' she said.

Two slim figures slipped through the soldiers on the wall: one was Suruk, as sleek and graceful as he was deadly; the other was W, grim-faced and lanky, a roll-up smouldering between his thin lips.

'Mazuran,' Suruk said, 'Welcome back. I heard your assault on the Yull was successful.'

Smith nodded. 'It was good. The lemmings have got real issues, though. They tried to give us hassle.'

'I bring grave news. The temple of the hidden masters is overrun. Volgath the elder is dead.'

'Crikey,' Smith said, focussing on him with a little difficulty. 'That's bad.'

'This man should muster our defences,' Suruk added, gesturing at W. 'He has told me of how he once slew a ravnaphant single-handed.'

Rhianna scowled. 'And I suppose you're proud of that?'

'I had no choice,' W replied. 'It had gone berserk and was threatening the Colonial Club. And we were hungry.'

'But there is more,' Suruk said. 'I know the location of the relics. As soon as Piglet returns from her equine frolics, we should fly off and seize them for our army.'

'Um, righto,' Smith replied. 'You've not got any biscuits, have you? I'm really quite peckish.'

Rhianna said, 'He inhaled a lot of smoke.'

W looked at Suruk. The spy frowned. 'This man needs tea. Lots of tea.'

They led Smith indoors, to an elevenses vending machine. Behind the glass screen, freeze-dried tiffin turned on a three-tiered rotating cake tray. Suruk and W pooled their change, while Rhianna pressed her hand to Smith's forehead. 'He's a bit, you know, *confused.*'

W stared out of the window at the battlements and the trees beyond them. 'General Young will want to stand and fight,' he said. 'She'll use our mobile units as the hammer, and leave the castle as the anvil.'

'Mobile units?' Suruk said. A cup dropped in the machine, and brown liquid poured into it from a brass spigot. 'My brother rides with the Ravnavari Lancers.'

'Will he be safe?' Rhianna asked. 'I mean, the lancers have a reputation for being pretty tough.'

'No doubt he will inspire them to deeds of great violence. He has that effect on me.'

'Here, Isambard,' Rhianna said. 'Tea.'

'Tea,' Smith replied drowsily. 'Dig it, man.' He took a sip. 'Hmm.' He took another. 'Ah, that's better. Right then, chaps, let's get cracking.'

'The lemmings approach,' Suruk said.

'Then, damn it, let's give the blighters a damned good thrashing. I say, Rhianna, are you alright, old girl?'

'Slightly disappointed,' she replied, 'but okay.'

A black spec appeared at the window, no larger than a fly. It turned, sank lower in the glass and grew as it did, taking on the familiar, dented lines of the *John Pym*. Ground crew hurried over, accompanied by refuelling wallahbots and two chefs from the catering corps, who seemed very interested in something that had smacked into the windscreen.

'Ah,' said Smith, 'and here's our pilot now.' The ship touched down and, as the legs bent under its weight, the airlock dropped open and Carveth scrambled out. 'And here she comes now: no doubt with important information in our fight against tyranny. Carveth!' he called, striding forward.

Carveth rushed down the battlement, through the door, past Smith and, with a loud yowling sound, straight into Rhianna. For the next few seconds they all stood still, except Carveth, who was crying helplessly, and Rhianna, who put her arms around Carveth but continued to look slightly dazed.

'I'm sensing some negativity here,' Rhianna said.

'They've got the ponies!' Carveth cried. 'We were riding round and they came out of the forest and crept up on us and made me run away and now they've got all the little horses and they're going to murder them!'

'Now wait a moment,' Smith said. 'There's no need to think that the ponies are in danger. Just slow down and tell us what happened. First, who took the ponies?'

'The lemming men!'

'Yep, they're in danger,' Smith said, and Carveth howled into Rhianna's chest.

Suruk croaked politely. 'I have a suggestion. Friends, this is clearly a sensitive moment, ideal for the wisdom of the Slayer. Might I propose that we gather our allies and do battle with the lemming men, until their blood flows like water and the air is filled with the screams of the dying? It will make everyone feel much better. Except the lemming men.'

'You're right,' Smith replied. 'Suruk, that's an excellent idea. Come on, chaps. We'll collect the relics, then we'll get a task force together, and give the Yull what for.'

Carveth looked round. 'There's no time for the relics! They'll kill them!'

Smith put his hands on Carveth's shoulders, which had the effect of reassuring her. Then he crouched down so that he could look her directly in the eye, which had the effect of making her seem like a nine-year-old. 'Look,' he said. 'I promise that as soon as we've found the relics we'll get the Equ'i back. And then we'll get the lemmings back, too.'

'That's not good enough!' she cried. 'Don't you know what they could do to the ponies before then?'

'Murder them all, I suppose,' and as she let out a despairing howl Smith added, 'Damn, I didn't mean to say that. I know this is a difficult and emotional time for you,' he added, reaching into his pocket. 'It's emotional for me as well, and therefore very difficult too. But Carveth, seriously, would you like a mint?'

'Stick your mints up your bum!' Carveth cried.

'Anyone?'

Rhianna gave Smith a sharp look and came over to assist. 'Polly doesn't need a mint, Isambard. She just needs to rest while we figure out what to do.'

'Isn't it obvious?' Carveth demanded. 'Doesn't it occur to you people that we need to get every weapon we've got and kill all the bloody lemming men?'

'That occurs to me too,' Suruk replied. 'Every six minutes, in fact. When I'm awake, every three minutes.'

'Stuff you all!' Carveth cried. 'I'm going and you can't stop me!'

She turned and ran for the door. They watched her run down the battlement, towards the landing pad.

'Oh, God,' Smith said. His head suddenly seemed to be about to burst. The feeling of paranoid confusion caused by the burning weeds had returned, along with none of the sense of wellbeing. 'Suruk, could you stop her, please?' he said.

The alien leaned over to the mantelpiece and took down a small ornament. He walked to the door, weighing it up in his hand. 'At this range? Easy.'

'No! Just go and talk to her, alright? Tell her to have tea and get some sleep.' He sighed. 'I need to think.'

* * *

Suruk returned a few minutes later. 'Piglet is in her cabin,' he announced. 'She said that she would rest.'

Smith said, 'Thanks, old chap. I'm sure she'll feel better if she goes to sleep. It always works for me.'

'Me too,' Suruk said. 'Then I don't have to listen to her.'

Rhianna sighed. 'Did you give her any medicine?'

'Indeed. She said she needed some tablets,' Suruk said. 'The white ones... it begins with A.'

'Aspirin?'

'Amphetamine. And Benzedrine. And about three pints of cherryade. She can really consume that stuff.'

For a moment, the room was silent. 'She asked for those?' Smith said.

'Um,' Rhianna said, 'that's bad. Really bad.'

'Quick!' Smith cried, 'The ship!'

Suruk was much faster; he tore out onto the battlements, slipping past soldiers, scrambled up the steps to the airlock and disappeared into the *John Pym*.

Smith looked at Rhianna. 'Bloody hell,' he said.

'Yeah, totally,' she replied.

Suruk reappeared at the airlock door. He waved. 'All is well, Mazuran! Fear not!'

Smith called back, 'So she's not trying to fly the ship?'

Suruk chuckled. 'Hardly. In fact, she's not even here!'

Rhianna cupped her hands around her mouth. 'Not there? Are you sure that's a good thing?'

'Of course! Actually,' Suruk added, 'maybe not at all.'

'Oh God,' Smith said, as Suruk made his way back, 'where the hell is Carveth? Rhianna, if you were crazed on combat drugs and fizzy pop, what would you do?'

'I'd do that,' she replied, and she pointed into the courtyard.

Engines roared below them. A Hellfire fighter rose on shiny metal legs, jets blazing under it. Below, a man in a luminous jacket waved two glowing sticks, ushering it into the air.

'Good God,' Smith whispered. 'You don't mean that Carveth has stolen one of the Hellfires and gone to rescue the ponies by herself?'

Rhianna looked confused. 'No,' she replied. 'I meant that if I took a load of drugs and fizzy pop, I'd put on a reflective jacket and wave two glowsticks over my head. At least, that's what happened last time. It went down well in Glastonbury,' she added. 'Less so in Gatwick.'

*　　*　　*

It was 8.22. Smith sat in one of the conservatories overlooking the launch pad, thinking about his mission here, and his duty to the Empire.

Rhianna sat cross-legged on the Ottoman. She shook one of the cushions and a mushroom cloud of dust rose towards the rafters.

The door opened and Suruk looked in. 'I spoke to launch control,' he said. 'They confirmed that one of our Hellfires is missing. It bears the same serial number as the one the little woman used when she fought in the battle of Wellington Prime. Also, our boxed set of *Space Confederates* is missing a disk.'

'Does that matter?'

'It is the episode called "Hoss Rustlers", in which Mary-Lou, the diminutive-yet-plucky engineer, single-handedly foils a gang of intergalactic horse thieves. Just saying,' he added, and he withdrew.

'This bodes ill,' Smith said. 'You know what the root of this whole problem is?' he demanded bitterly. 'Abroad, that's what. If we didn't have abroad, none of this would ever have happened. Of course, we wouldn't have anyone to civilise, or to take stuff from for the Empire. But bugger it, anyway.'

Rhianna stood up and slid over to the window, like a ghost. 'I guess you just can't expect people to give you their planets and do what you say because you're British anymore.'

Smith nodded. 'You're right. It's a disgrace. The whole galaxy's gone tits up.' Realising that she might be offended by that, he added, 'Sorry. Knockers up.'

'I'll be outside,' she said, and she turned away. He heard the door click shut.

Smith tried to work it out. Carveth was in terrible danger, but the Empire needed the relics. If the Yull captured the relics and flaunted them, Ravnavar might stop taking orders from Earth. And without a unified front, the Yull would overrun Andor, slaughter its inhabitants and cram their cheeks with the fag-ends of a rotting empire.

He had to rescue Carveth. But orders are orders, he thought, and tried to remember where he'd heard that before.

A face came into view: red, scarred, one eye replaced by a glinting lens. The face was shadowed by the brim of its steel helmet. Antennae dangled over it like dead fronds. 'Orders are orders,' 462 rasped.

Gertie-talk! Bollocks to that!

Smith strode to the door. 'Rhianna, we need to get the chaps –' he said, and he stopped.

They were waiting in the corridor, all of them, fully armed. Suruk smiled. Susan checked the vents on her beam gun and, behind her, the Deepspace Operations Group passed a flask around.

'The wallahbots are fuelling the *John Pym*,' Rhianna said. 'I can shield us with my powers.'

Dreckitt stood next to Wainscott. He stepped forward, his face grim. 'I found these,' he said, and he handed a box to Smith. 'Cyanide. We bring 'em with us on dangerous capers, in case the lemmings shanghai us and give us the third degree. We're missing a few tablets.'

Smith examined the box. The label said 'Suicide pills – please take one'. Below it, someone had scribbled 'No, not like that!'

'You know,' Dreckitt said, 'I never thought I'd get screwy over a dame. But I got jealous of a little blue horse! I mean, what could a horse give her that I couldn't? It never ends well when a tough guy gets too close to a pet, like Lucky Luigi did.'

'What happened to Lucky Luigi?' Smith asked.

'He slept with the fishes. Come on, Smith. Somebody's gotta walk down these dark streets – well, canter.'

'Bloody right,' Wainscott muttered. 'We've got business in Ponyland.'

Susan frowned. 'Don't think you're getting out of taking your medicine, Boss. And it's still bath day.'

'Easy, guys,' Rhianna said. 'We can do that when we get back.'

Susan glared at her. 'What do *you* know about washing? Let's get loaded up.'

Suruk chuckled. 'Then let us depart! We shall rescue Piglet and delight our weapons with bloody deeds!'

Wainscott tapped Smith on the arm. 'Got any high explosive?'

'Not on me, no.'

The major nodded. 'We may need some. Best not do this officially. We'll head to the NAAFI. With the right gear, I can knock up a bucket or two of plastique.'

'Right,' said Smith. 'Saddle up, everyone – we have horses to rescue!'

They turned in a clatter of armour and boots. As the others trooped out, Smith felt a sudden rush of emotion. He was very lucky to have friends who were so loyal – and so violent.

*   *   *

Wainscott led Smith down a winding staircase, past a row of mouldering banners, to a door marked with the insignia of the Navy, Army and Air Force Institutes. 'This won't take a moment,' Wainscott said. 'Don't say anything, and just agree with whatever I do, alright?'

'Alright,' said Smith, wondering whether the major was planning to purchase their equipment or just rob the shop.

Wainscott threw the door open and strode inside. Rows of gear stretched away from them: enough body armour to equip an entire army, and enough Biscuits, Brown to constipate it. The air was full of the smell of boot polish.

Behind the counter, a pallid young man watched them nervously. Wainscott strode to the counter and glared at him.

'Evening,' the major said. 'How's business?'

'A little quiet, sir,' said the lad.

'Well, the sandwiches probably haven't finished fermenting yet,' Wainscott replied, and he emitted a hard, barking laugh. 'Got any ciggies?'

'No sir. We're fresh out.'

'What's your name?'

'Evans, sir,' said the man behind the counter.

'Evans, I want your word as a British soldier and a gentleman that you will never, ever speak of what you are about to see.'

Evans looked troubled. 'It's not treason is it, sir?'

Wainscott glowered. 'Certainly not. Do my friend and I look like degenerates to you?'

'No sir. You look like irregulars.'

Wainscott glanced at Smith. 'Let me know if you think of anything.' Turning to Evans, he said, 'My friend and I are hell-bent on manly adventure. We need a large tub of Vaseline, a candle about a foot long and two inches wide, a bottle of navy rum, two packets of rubber johnnies and about three pints of that fertiliser stuff they use on the vegetable gardens, Grow-Big or whatever it's called.'

Evans looked at Wainscott, then at Smith. He appeared to be revising his view on degeneracy. Warily, he said, 'You do know that Grow-Big only works on plants, right?'

'Oh, and we'll have mothballs.'

'I'm sure you will,' Evans said.

'Two packets.'

'Right you are, gents.'

Wainscott patted the pockets of his shorts. Smith sighed and fished out a handful of loose change.

'Nearly thought we didn't have enough money for all this gear,' the major said. 'Now that would have been embarrassing!'

'I'll put your things in a bag,' Evans said. 'Brown paper?'

'Splendid,' Wainscott said. 'Evans, you've done us proud. I like the cut of your jib, young man. If ever you want to get out of this place, and join us for some *real* action—'

'Let's just go,' Smith said, and he steered the major towards the door.

*　　*　　*

The little river was still flowing. A mile from the edge of the estate, Carveth slung the shotgun across her back and crouched down by the waterside. Then, limb by limb, she climbed in.

The water flowed over her, warm as blood, and she pushed herself into the middle of the channel. The current caught her and pulled her downstream, towards Radcliffe Hall.

The Yull had already turned the gardens into something sinister. Fires burned on the lawns. Hulking figures lumbered around, swilling from bottles of dandelion wine. The statues of rearing horses looked terrified, not triumphant. For a moment, fear would have frozen Carveth, had not the river pulled her on.

I asked for a pony, she thought. And for my sins, they gave me one.

Past the Workers' Windmill, past the Well of

Ponyness, into the manor grounds. Carveth stopped under an ornamental bridge to figure out her angle of attack. Fire reflected on the dark water. Already, the surface looked oily.

Paws stomped on the bridge. She froze, feeling the current start to chill her body, and something tinkled on the water upstream. Above her, a Yullian trooper sighed. She moved on, quickly.

Voices, up ahead. A party moved out from the rear of the mansion, across the back lawns. Three lemming men were manhandling an Equ'i across the lawn. They were brutes, of course: they carried whips and clubs. One of the rodents, an officer, turned back to the house.

'Now you learn,' he yelled, 'what happens to dirty animals that disobey!'

'Remember me, my people!' the Equ'i called. 'Avenge me!'

It was King Chestnut. Rage welled up in Carveth, and all fear was gone. She slid out onto the bank.

She took out the shotgun. Lightning crackled across the sky, and she realised how she could kill these furry bastards and not lose the element of surprise.

They managed to knock King Chestnut to his knees. Carveth scurried across the lawn and dropped down behind a prancing stone stallion.

Thunder rumbled. The two minions struggled to keep Chestnut down. The officer puffed out his chest and drew his axe.

Lightning turned the sky into a negative. Carveth ran at them.

'*Yullai!*' the officer screeched, his face a mask of gleeful cruelty, and Carveth put the shotgun against his ear.

'Die,' she screamed, 'you pony-murdering, cliff-jumping, nut-gobbling filth!'

The thunder boomed, and the officer hit the ground.

One of the minions saw her, howled something that was lost in the rain and Carveth worked the slide and blasted him full in the chest. Chestnut heaved himself upright. The third lemming man pulled his rifle up, and Chestnut kicked him in the snout.

'Yes,' Carveth said, with some satisfaction.

Chestnut stared at her. 'Polly? Is that you? This is magic!'

Carveth shook her head. 'Friendship,' she said. 'Same thing. Can you get your people out of here?'

'Yes. Ride out of here with us –'

'No.' Carveth reloaded the shotgun. 'I've got work to do.'

*   *   *

The cockpit rumbled around Smith's body. He pointed the *John Pym* in the right direction and locked the controls.

Rhianna sat in the captain's chair, eyes closed, hands palms-up in front of her. Smith knew better than to wake her, especially while they were over enemy airspace. The Yull had few fighters left, but plenty of anti-aircraft guns, bio-missiles shipped in from the Ghast Empire, and crazed glider pilots eager to take the big jump from the cliffs of destiny. But as he strode down the corridor and entered the hold, he felt the weight of her presence on him. He owed Rhianna as well as Carveth.

Pink Zeppelin blared from the hold's speakers: Smith recognised the song as *Long Tall Saruman*. The Deepspace Operations Group had overturned the dining room table and taken cover behind it. Smith wondered why, and then saw that at the far end of the hold,

Wainscott was making bombs, glaring at his creations like one of the forefathers of alchemy. He looked up, all wild eyes and beard, and continued to ladle what looked like toothpaste into a sock.

'Ready to raise hell?' he demanded, shaking the sock in the air.

'Yes.'

'We're getting Polly Pilot back. But what about these little horse things?'

'We'll do everything we can to help them. We're not much of an Empire if we can't protect the people we rule.'

'Right,' Wainscott said. 'Stick the kettle on, would you? Tea made me what I am today,' he added, 'a sexual tyrannosaur. Except with bigger arms.'

On the way back to the cockpit, Suruk put his head out of his room. 'I found this in Piglet's room.' He held out a paper bag; white powder lay in the folds of the bag. 'Is it a drug?'

'Icing sugar. She'll be berserk by now.'

'I am missing one of my Zukari blades,' Suruk added. 'If I am forced to do battle with over thirty rodents at once, I may be forced to use my teeth.'

'I'm sure you'll manage.'

Suruk smiled. 'It is perhaps fortunate that I packed a toothbrush.' He stopped smiling. 'Piglet is in grave danger. The Yull do not respect true bravery,' he said. 'They are, as you say on Earth, bollocks.'

*   *   *

Carveth found a broken window, knocked out the shards of glass and climbed inside. By now, King Chestnut would be discreetly leading his people into the forest. The stage was clear for her to teach the Yull a stern lesson about animal rights. All animals except lemmings, that was.

She was in some sort of pantry, the corridors enlarged for equine use. Bent almost double, Carveth crept to the door. Fear was beginning to well up in her and she needed to get going before she froze.

At the door, she heard lemming voices: an ugly revving, growling noise. Before, it would have made her afraid. Now, she felt a rush of fury. What if Chestnut hadn't been able to save all of his people? The voices sounded cheerful, which meant that they were plotting some act of extreme cruelty. They also sounded numerous.

She moved on, down the corridor.

Nobody kicks me out of Ponyland, Carveth thought. Nobody.

The voices grew louder up ahead. She paused at the next doorway and peeked around.

A lemming man, probably a rank-and-file trooper, was putting delicate glasses on a tray. A large platter of cheese stood nearby.

The soldier looked intent on his task. Carveth felt a stab of satisfaction; she could creep up behind him and brain the bugger with the end of her shotgun. But where would that leave her? There were about a dozen glasses on the tray: that meant twelve vicious lunatics who would come looking for answers and vengeance the moment their drink was delayed. Taking them on would be suicide.

Suicide. She crouched by the door, grinning.

Carveth dug her hand into her pocket and came out with a handful of toffees. She raised her arm and tossed them across the room, past the lemming soldier. They clattered against the far wall.

'*Hwot?*' He spun around, and Carveth ducked back into cover. She heard him pick up his rifle and clump across the room, away from her, mumbling to himself.

She put her hand into her sleeve and found the little dispenser there. She opened the sealed packet and slid out her cyanide pill.

*　　*　　*

The wine was a few minutes late, and the soldier bringing it seemed to be chewing some sort of sweet. Major Botl Harpik considered punching him in the face in front of all the other officers, but decided to be lenient. After all, it had been a very good day for the Yull. He'd just wait until the soldier had left the room, and *then* punch him in the face.

'I think you will find this a very pleasant vintage,' Harpik announced. 'It's the best sort of wine – looted from someone else.'

His staff chuckled appreciatively.

'But seriously,' Harpik said, 'Today, we have welcomed another wretched bunch of unrodent scum into our benevolent empire, and I'm sure you will join with me in thanking them for the kind gift of this wine, all their other property and their labour until they drop dead from exhaustion. Sometimes, I think that our slaves do not really appreciate how hard we noble Yull work for them.'

There was a rumble of agreement.

'They will damn well appreciate it later,' Harpik growled. 'Today, we have done our empire proud. So I ask you to raise your glasses to our wise, kind, temperate, sophisticated and entirely non-genocidal forefathers. Gentlemen – those who have already leaped from the Cliffs of Destiny – the honoured dead!'

*　　*　　*

Carveth waited until the noises had stopped and looked in. The wine had done its work: less of a bouquet than a funeral wreath, she thought, surveying the carnage. One of the Yull wasn't quite dead yet. She felt a bit sorry for him until she remembered that he was a horrible pony-hating scumbag. Then she bashed him on the head with the decanter.

The servant was still in the wine-room, preparing another round of drinks. Carveth took an axe from a dead lemming man. It was razor sharp. The axe would have been an excellent weapon for silent killing, had not Carveth been screaming 'Die, you fluffy bastard!' as she broke it over his head.

Yeah, she thought, that's right. She was giddy with triumph now. She had saved the ponies and cleaned out a whole nest of lemmings. She'd wiped them out.

No, she realised, looking over the carnage. One of the Yull was missing. The one with the scar across his muzzle, Colonel Prem.

Night turned the kitchens into a dungeon. Saucepans became helmets, toasting forks and garlic presses instruments of torture. No wonder the lemming men liked it here.

She scurried forward, ducking behind the tables and cupboards.

A shadow moved on the far wall, black against moonlight, a magnified silhouette. She ducked down, froze like a mouse under the gaze of an owl, and remembered that she was actually pretty scared.

Colonel Prem muttered to himself. 'Aha,' he said, as if he had made an important discovery. '*Propacap.*'

The silhouette lifted massive paws to its head, and when it lowered them, it was wearing a chef's hat. The lemming looked left and right. He wasn't in the room,

Carveth realised, but in some neighbouring part of the kitchen. The Colonel stepped out of the light, and the shadow was gone.

'*Hwhereat feki kopaketl?*' he growled.

Carveth crept towards the door. You couldn't leave one of them alive – wasn't that what they'd told her back at base? You had to clean them all out.

She lunged around the doorframe.

The room was empty. It looked as if a whirlwind had hit it: knives and cleavers scattered on a work-surface, a huge spit hauled in front of the fireplace, half a dozen trays under it to catch fat. They must have been planning a celebration feast. So much for that, she thought: they hadn't made it past the aperitif.

A large book was propped against the sideboard. It showed the preparation of a huge joint of meat, but the words were in French, from the look of it. She closed the book. The title said *La Cuisine Belge*.

It was then that she saw the picture pinned to the wall, held in place by a couple of Yullian knives. For a second she didn't realise its function, and then she looked closer, not doubting her eyes.

It was the outline of a pony, divided by half a dozen dotted lines.

No. Surely not. Surely nobody, not even the lemming men, could stoop so low. Yes, they tortured and sacrificed for their war god, but not this.

'*Darhep!*'

Something smashed into the back of her legs and she dropped onto her knees. She twisted, trying to aim, but a huge hand shot out and yanked the shotgun out of her grip. It clattered beside the door and Prem backhanded her across the ear.

Carveth went sprawling. Paws grabbed her, lifted

her clean off the ground and threw her into the wall. She fell in a crash of pots, saw a monstrous shape lumber forwards and scrambled onto all fours.

Prem bent down, yanked her up by her lapels and tossed her across the room. She fell into the corner, bounced off the wall and managed to stay upright, which in the circumstances felt like an achievement.

The colonel wore an officer's sash and battleaxe. He looked her over with that pompous self-importance she'd seen in the *Know Your Enemy* films.

'You again,' he said.

'You eat ponies!' she shouted back.

The rodent nodded. 'As the lesser races serve us, we shall serve them,' it said. 'With a salad.'

'*Bastard!*'

Prem took a step forward. He was massive; his bulk swallowed up the room. His paws caught her under the chin, and without any apparent effort, he lifted her up by the throat.

'You puzzle me,' he said. 'You must be a strong fighter to get past my guards, skilled in death. Yet you come here for the sake of... *little horses?* A true warrior despises the weak. Why do you shame yourself with pity?'

Carveth coughed. The colonel loosened his grip.

'I got too close,' she gasped.

'Too close?'

'Like you,' she hissed, and she flicked out her hand, the first and last fingers extended, clenched her fist and punched him in the gut.

It was a feeble blow and her hand did very little. Twelve inches of spring-loaded Zukari steel, on the other hand, had the desired effect. Carveth tore her hand up and free and the officer staggered back, clutching his midriff. His eyes were huge and full of horror.

Carveth yanked the axe from Colonel Prem's belt. She gave it an experimental swing through the air. Satisfactory.

'You hurt ponies,' she said. 'Now ponies hurt you.'

'Offworlder, what are you doing?' the erstwhile gourmet gasped. 'You cannot kill me. It is against your rules!'

'Oh,' said Carveth, a huge grin spreading across her face, 'I'll stick to the rules all right. I'll even cut along the dotted lines!'

The lightning crackled around the house, and as she swung the weapon up over her head, Carveth's laughter and the thunder became one.

*   *   *

The Yull had not posted many sentries: they had clearly not expected anyone to dare, or bother, to rescue the Equ'i. Dreckitt knocked out the first guard with a blackjack and Smith cut down the second. Smith wiped his sword on the lemming's fur and they advanced through the trees, closer to the house.

'It'll be well fortified,' Wainscott whispered. 'All these big houses are the same: bars on the windows, padded walls –'

'Only the ones you stay in,' Susan said from behind. 'The side door's open. Maybe we're too late.'

'Nix, dragon lady,' Dreckitt replied. 'Let's bust the joint.'

Smith nodded. 'With me, chaps. For Britain, and for the very small horses!'

He sprinted out of cover, across the lawn. His boots thundered on the ornamental bridge. He raced towards the open door, sword raised.

A figure stepped out to meet him, axe in hand.

'Hurrah!' Smith bellowed, swinging the sword, and at the last moment he saw that it was no Yull before him. He stopped, just managing not to trip over, and his blade cut only air.

Carveth stepped out. She might not be a lemming, but she was covered in fur. 'Oh, hello,' she said.

They stood around the door, watching as she emerged. She held a battleaxe.

'Hi, everyone,' she said, and she gave them a broad, uneven smile. 'Look what I've got. This is what happens to people who aren't nice to their pets.'

She raised her left hand, and tossed something onto the wet grass. It rolled once and was still.

It was the severed head of Colonel Prem.

They stared at her as she stumbled forward, and nobody spoke.

Suruk pointed to the grisly head.

'Then this was her work,' he said, and slowly he looked up at Carveth. 'Go Piglet! The job is a good one!' He clapped, cheered, realised that nobody had joined in and said, 'Why are you looking at me like that?'

Smith gestured to Wainscott. The tranquiliser rifle gave a soft 'Phut', and Carveth looked thoughtfully at the feathered dart sticking out of her shoulder, as if not sure why she had put it there. 'Ooh, a birdie,' she observed, reaching towards the dart, and she toppled over onto her back.

Wainscott rushed forward, and as Dreckitt hurried to Carveth's side, the Deepspace Operations Group ran into the house.

Suruk shook his head. 'Shame on you, Wainscott, I have known this woman for four years. The first time she does anything remotely interesting, you shoot her with a dart.'

'She'll be fine,' Wainscott growled. 'Being tranquilised never did me any harm.'

Susan and Wainscott walked back onto the lawn.

'Something died in there,' Susan said. 'Probably a mammal. Beyond that, I reckon it's fluff and dental records.'

Wainscott nodded. 'She caught one of them in the kitchen and hacked him to pieces. A regular kukri lesson.'

'Look!' Rhianna said, and she pointed into the trees.

They turned, raising their guns in a quick clatter of weaponry, but it was not the lemming men that they faced. Quietly, the Equ'i walked out of the forest, their blue fur glistening like water.

The largest of the Equ'i approached. He was tall, broad across the shoulders, with a long nose and considerable forelock. 'Greetings, people of Earth,' he declared. 'I am Chestnut, king of the Equ'i. I have heard much of you all, especially Suruk the Slayer.' A smaller, lighter-coloured horse appeared at his side. 'And this is Celeste, my daughter.'

Celeste hurried over to Dreckitt's side. Dreckitt had rolled up his trenchcoat and put it under Carveth's head. He rummaged in the medical kit. 'Is she alright?' Celeste asked.

'She'll be okay,' Dreckitt said. 'She took a Mickey Finn, and now she's hopped up. That's all.'

'Indeed,' said Suruk. 'The little woman has never been better, in my opinion.'

'But she's covered in blood!' Celeste replied.

Suruk shrugged. 'Your friend was overcome by

berserk rage and butchered every living thing in sight. So no need to worry.'

'I don't know how to thank you,' King Chestnut said. 'Normally, anyone who rescues a princess would receive my daughter's hoof in marriage, but... well, that would be a bit weird.'

'I know, Daddy!' Celeste exclaimed. 'Why don't you make Polly a princess too! Then we can both live in the magical kingdom for ever – and ever!'

Wainscott leaned over and whispered in Smith's ear. 'You know, I think these people are a bit rum.'

'We can decide that later,' Smith said. 'The Yull are on the move. We all need to get away from here. Wainscott, you'll be needed back at base. We'll drop you chaps off and then go on to look for the relics. We're not much ahead of the lemming men.'

'No,' said King Chestnut. 'You should press on. We can take the major and his men. We'll carry you.'

Wainscott rubbed his chin. 'Well, I suppose...' He looked at Susan. 'What do you say?'

'Me?' Susan let go of the beam gun, clapped her hands and squealed. 'Oh my goodness, pony ride! Just kidding,' she added, heaving the gun into her arms again. 'Yeah, it should work if nobody cocks up.'

'Excellent,' Smith replied. 'Then I'll see you soon. Suruk, would you give me a hand carrying Carveth into the ship? We have work to do!'

A Day on the Riviera

Dawn rose over the treetops like flame. The green canopy glowed in the new light. Under the leaves, the cycle of life began anew as the myriad creatures of the forest woke, blinked and immediately began biting, poisoning and swallowing one another.

The soldiers on the watchtowers of Mothkarak watched Mildred the ravnaphant lumber north, trees creaking and snapping around her bulk. In Mildred's wake rode the proud ranks of the lancers, their banners raised. Many of the better-trained shadar had turned red, white or blue, so that the marching column resembled a Union Jack. The infantry waved them off, and went back to the task of bolstering the walls.

Other eyes followed the lancers.

'Shall we attack them?' asked Colonel Cots.

'Let them run,' General Wikwot replied.

They sat on the upper deck of the Forward Command Treehouse, sipping the morning ration of dandelion wine. The Yull had erected a few treehouses near the citadel: partly for surveillance, and partly because being high up in a tree gave them a sense of wellbeing bettered only by jumping out of it. In the next tree down, connected by a walkway, glider pilots were carrying out a dummy run. They wore elastic belts to make sure that they did not hit the ground, and the constant leaping and bouncing gave the scene a curious pendulum effect.

'The lancers are full of fear,' Wikwot said. 'Their cowardly hearts dread the battle and so they sneak away. Let the forest take them.'

Cots nodded. His black coat was particularly silky today, owing to liberal use of Head and Pelt. 'My sources suggest that the enemy are close to finding the so-called Relics of Grimdall. And we are close to finding *them*.'

'Good.' Wikwot finished his drink. 'Fetch the relics. In the meantime, I shall address the timid ranks of the enemy and promise them safety when they give up.'

'Excellent, General! Once they see our army, and that we hold their sacred relics, the weakling inhabitants will surrender, and then – let the screaming and torture begin!'

'Cots!' Wikwot leaned out and belted his comrade across the snout. 'You shame yourself with this talk of torture!' Cots rubbed his muzzle. 'No,' Wikwot added, smiling into the trees. 'This one we will do nice and quiet.'

*   *   *

The *John Pym* tore across the forest, only a few yards over the canopy.

'It looks like a coral reef,' Rhianna said. She sat in the captain's chair: Smith flew the ship from Carveth's usual seat, following the river west. The floor was littered with cushions that he had tossed out prior to sitting down.

'Or a big green brain,' he said.

Suruk entered, holding the tea tray. He passed out the mugs.

'How's Carveth?' Smith asked. 'Still resting in bed?'

'Resting, yes. Bed, no,' Suruk said. 'She is excluding a draft. One of the airlock doors was not working, and since she was just lying there, I thought she might as well do something useful...'

'Really, old chap. Rhianna, have you got anything that would wake Carveth up? I know you've got a lot of medicine, but most of it seems to deaden the senses.'

'Sure,' Rhianna said, and as she stood up, Carveth wandered into the cockpit, rubbing her head.

'Ugh, what happened? I feel funny. I remember falling over and hitting my head – I think the fresh air's done me a bit of good, though.'

'See?' Suruk said.

Below them, the rippling canopy opened up, and the river swelled into a lake. Smith saw tiny buildings on the lakeside, hotels and boathouses, and stabilised the ship. He cut the thrusters, and they began to descend.

'It looks empty,' Suruk said. 'Perhaps the Yull are hiding.'

The *John Pym* touched down in a car park. Suruk and Carveth left the cockpit, to get ready.

Nearly there, Smith thought as he checked his rifle. We're nearly at the resting-place of the greatest hero in M'Lak history. Too bad he wasn't on our side.

Rhianna tapped him on the arm. 'Isambard?'

'Yes?'

'What are we going to do with the relics?'

'What's that?' The question hadn't crossed his mind until now. They would collect the Relics of Grimdall, whatever they were exactly, load them into the *John Pym* and take them back. And then... he wasn't sure. 'I don't know. Put them in a museum or something?'

'Isambard, Grimdall was no friend of the Space Empire.'

'All the more reason to keep them under lock and key.'

'And if we end up keeping them, it'll look as if we're holding onto them to spite the M'Lak. The M'Lak need to be able to see them for themselves. They need to know that the relics are part of Ravnavar.'

'Well, of course they'll know that. The labelling at the British Museum is second to none.'

'Hmm.'

'Do you know,' he added, 'some of the best labels in the galaxy are British. Look at Bovril Beef Extract. That label could only have come from Britain. You know why?'

'Because nobody else thinks that it's food, Isambard.'

Suruk looked around the door. 'We are ready,' he said. 'But I do not think that you will like this.'

They climbed down. Smith closed the airlock behind them.

Hotels and restaurants stretched off in an arc along the waterside. A row of pedalloes lay on the shore. Automated bathing machines stood like siege engines on the waterside, painted in jolly colours. One had been blown apart, leaving only the tracks and gears.

'Look,' Suruk said, and he tossed an oblong tin onto the ground. Wires trailed from the box, along with a long wire aerial. 'That was fastened to the fuselage.'

Carveth bent down, but did not touch it. 'Bollocks,' she said. 'It's a tracking device.' She sighed. 'The Yull must have attached it. You think they know where we are?'

Smith nodded. 'I expect the lemmings will follow us as if we were – well, other lemmings. We'd best get moving.'

They set off towards the waterside, past torn striped

awnings and the remains of wicker chairs. A big sign beside the water showed a family at play, all bathing costumes and merry smiles. Scrawled across it, in what Smith hoped was red paint, were the words 'All Offworlders Die'.

'There,' Suruk said, pointing across the lake.

A tiny island stuck out of the water, empty except for a coating of moss and a fallen parasol. Smith thought that it looked rather like an olive stuck with a cocktail umbrella.

'Where is everybody?' Carveth said.

Suruk scowled. 'Do not look up,' he replied, and, naturally, everyone did.

The bathers were still here, strung up dead among the trees. Smith broke out the mints.

'Why?' Rhianna said. 'Why do that?'

Smith put his arm around her shoulders. 'I really don't know,' he said.

'Because it is their way,' Suruk said. 'Perhaps once it was not. Who knows?'

Carveth pulled her shotgun up. 'They're evil because they like being evil,' she said. 'So let's find this relic thing, get back to the others and kill every last stinking lemming on the planet.'

She stomped off down the shore. Suruk glanced at Smith. 'Fear the wrath of Battle Girl,' he said, and he followed her.

Smith shielded his eyes and looked at the little island. It was too small to accommodate the ship and, after their earlier adventure looking for Wainscott, he didn't fancy putting the *John Pym* in the water in case it had sprung some new leaks.

Rhianna called out. 'Guys? We need to find a boat.'

Suruk turned on the shore and pointed. 'Boats we

have! Forward the pedalloes!'

Smith looked around, saw nothing better, and reflected that dignity had never been his strong point anyhow. 'Let's go. Rhianna, Carveth, you're together. Try not to fall behind. Or in.'

Smith and Suruk heaved the little boats into the water and splashed in after them. The pedals creaked as the boats began to creep across the water.

Smith held his rifle across his lap, and watched the trees on the far side of the lake. Maybe the Yull were already there.

'Rhianna,' he called. 'Can you sense anything?'

Rhianna stopped pedalling and closed her eyes, and by the time she spoke, Carveth had almost spun their boat round in a circle.

'Nothing –' she said.

'Well, that's a relief.'

'Except death,' Rhianna added.

The tiny island was only a few yards away. Smith looked down and tried to see through the murky water. He thought that they were travelling over a shelf of flat grey rock, but it was hard to tell.

The end of the little boat bumped against the island. Smith climbed out and Suruk heaved the boat onto the ground. The air was warm and still, the sky empty. The shore seemed a long way off.

The second boat stopped and Rhianna emerged, holding her skirt up as she waded ashore. She helped Carveth out, and the four of them stood beside the fallen parasol while Suruk took Volgath's photograph out of his pocket.

'This is it,' the M'Lak said.

Carveth turned around slowly, staring across the water. 'So what now, Robinson Crusoe?'

Smith said, 'We dig.'

'What with?'

'I don't know. Maybe if we broke the parasol up, we could improvise a sort of shovel.'

Rhianna crouched down and pressed her hands to the ground. 'Why don't we all reach out and touch the earth? Maybe if we show proper respect to nature, the earth itself will show us the way.'

Carveth scowled. 'And I thought she was getting better.'

'Come on, Polly. What about you, Isambard? You respect nature. We call upon mother nature to open the way to our goal –' Rhianna said, and she shot forward, suddenly on her front, her arms disappearing up to the shoulders. 'It's dirt,' she cried. 'I've found dirt!'

'Yay, dirt,' Carveth replied. 'I know you love that stuff, but –'

Rhianna shook her head. 'Wait. I've found something else. I think it's a door.'

*　　*　　*

General Wikwot stomped into the main entrance of Mothkarak with a cigarette still smouldering in the corner of his muzzle, his honour guard holding the flag of parley. He looked around. The first thing that struck him, apart from the sheer size of the place, was the odd smell: a mixture of dust and that unnatural absence-of-fur that characterised the other sentient races. Disgusting.

Statues of great humans stood in niches in the wall, twice Wikwot's size. The nearest one was, according to a brass plaque, Oliver Cromwell. He looked soft. Wikwot spat his cigarette out and advanced.

Puny soldiers stood around with large knives and guns. For a moment he felt a twinge of sympathy towards them: it must be terrible, he reflected, to grow up knowing that you would never be a rodent. Timid, mangy, devoid of lemming spirit – no wonder they looked so angry as they looked at him.

General Young waited in a side room. She sat across a large table, her staff seated around her. A small dish in the centre contained some sort of human food.

To show he meant business, Wikwot thrust his paw into the dish, took out a large scoop, put the stuff in his mouth and spat it onto the floor. 'Offworlder food is dirty and contemptible!' he announced.

'That was the pot pourri,' said Florence Young. 'Please, take a seat.'

'I shall take a seat,' Wikwot replied, 'and soon I shall take everything else!' A ripple of polite laughter came from his minions. He yanked out a chair and dropped into it. 'Now, unrodents, we shall discuss your surrender. No doubt you have heard entirely untrue stories that we Yull are a horde of genocidal lunatics. These are lies, and anyone repeating them will be skinned alive! It's well known that we Yull are lovely and would not hurt a flea.'

'Fly,' one of General Young's people said. His name-plate stated that he was Colonel Butt.

'Do you doubt me?' Wikwot felt the familiar urge to bash someone in the face. 'Where I come from, it is flea!'

'Figures,' said Colonel Butt.

'Stupid fat people,' Wikwot said, 'I have great respect for your empire. You have conquered vast tracts of space, made many planets your own. But, sometimes, a great warlord becomes... old. His grip on his axe weakens. He swings it less often. He gets soft.'

'Meaning?'

The android butler appeared, carrying tea. He set the tray down and retreated out of sight.

'That it is time for him to let the axe go. To pass the duty to care for his cattle to younger, more able hands. Because, believe me, we Yull know how to take care of those we rule.'

Florence Young raised an eyebrow. 'And the old warrior in your analogy? What happens to him?'

'Oh, we hack his head off.' Wikwot yawned. 'Trust me, offworlders, once you have been welcomed to the Greater Galactic Happiness and Friendship Collective you will be treated with all the kindness and respect that you deserve. Now then, my minions have the paperwork –'

'General Wikwot,' said General Young, as the android butler began to pour the tea.

'*Hwot?*'

'I'm afraid that every scrap of evidence points towards you wanting to conquer this planet, torture and massacre its inhabitants, and do exactly the same to every other planet you can find. No?' she said, quite mildly. 'I'm afraid I won't let that happen.'

For a moment, Wikwot was completely still. Then he let out a little snort. 'Humans, I was made to rule. I was born into a noble family. As soon as I could lick my own fur, I was schooled in the way of combat. I slept for half an hour a day. When I smiled, I was beaten. When I failed, I was beaten. When I succeeded, I was beaten even harder so I would remember the moment of victory. At the age of twelve, I had a psychotic breakdown and murdered eight serfs with a propelling pencil. Only then was I found worthy of an army commission. I, and those I lead, are proud members of that warrior tradition. We Yull are committed to our cause – more than lazy Earth people could ever understand.'

General Young frowned. She spoke carefully. 'I see.

When I came here, General,' she replied, 'people asked me how you could fight an enemy devoid of sanity, mercy or any sense of self-preservation.'

Wikwot nodded, but his jaw was clenched. 'A sensible question.'

'The answer is hard, General Wikwot. One fights somebody like that very, very hard. Which, by a happy coincidence, is exactly what my soldiers are. This has gone far enough, Wikwot. Your rampage across space is over. Those of your army who choose to surrender will be treated decently. Those who fight will be killed.'

A low growl came from Wikwot, like a machine powering up.

Lorvoth the Bloody-Handed leaned across the table, opened his mandibles and smiled horribly. 'The buck stops here, Wikwot. Or the doe – whichever you happen to be.'

Wikwot leaped to his feet. His chair clattered behind him. 'You!' he cried. He threw out his arm accusingly and glowered across the table, like a bad actor playing Banquo's ghost. 'You stupid, mangy, unrodent, flat-faced monkey-pigs are all the same! Racists, the lot of you! You only hate us because we are furry and superior!' He glared at the tabletop, decided against jumping over it, and paused, breathing heavily, the same low panting growl coming from his open mouth.

'You will all die,' he said. 'All weak things will suffer and die. You will beg for mercy, and then for death, but there will be no mercy for cowards like you. Great Popacapinyo has decreed that this world will fall to the Divine Migration. And you, General,' he added, glaring at Florence Young, 'will be the last to die, so that you may see what your arrogance has cost your men.'

He turned and strode to the door. General Wikwot

looked back. 'When the Yull rule,' he said, 'this place will burn.'

'I very much doubt it,' General Young replied. 'For one thing, it's made of stone. Now,' she added, glancing towards the door, 'if you don't mind, I've got an army to lead.'

*   *   *

They hauled the dirt out by the handful. At the bottom of the hole, they found a circular hatch.

'Wow,' Rhianna said. 'I wonder where it goes?'

'The sewer?' Carveth suggested. 'I know a manhole when I see one.' She sighed. 'Well, it won't be the first time I've been dropped right in the crap.'

'This is no sewer,' Suruk said. 'Look! There are M'Lak characters on the edge. He climbed into the hole and crouched down. 'Let me see what I can find.'

He traced the symbols with his finger. 'The sign for caution. And this one means an entrance or opening. Strange,' he added. 'This is the symbol for "innards".'

'Caution, opens innards?' Smith said. 'What the devil does that mean?'

The hatch fell open. Suruk roared and dropped out of view. For a moment they stood in silence, and then a set of percussive noises indicated that something solid had stopped Suruk's fall.

'My mistake!' he called up from below. 'It said "inwards", not "innards". Oh, and there is a ladder here too. I wish I had known about that three seconds ago. I am beginning to see why you humans evolved buttocks.'

They climbed down, feet clanging on metal rungs. The air was still and old. The ground felt like rubber. There was a slight chemical smell.

As Carveth reached the bottom, lights blossomed in the floor. They stood in a corridor. Signs on the walls displayed the M'Lak symbol for *Exit*.

This is it, Smith thought. It must be!

'Follow me,' he said.

They walked on.

'It's like a huge tube,' Rhianna observed.

'Reminds me of a picture I once saw,' Smith said, his voice echoing against the metal walls. 'Hundreds of years ago, the French dug a tunnel to Britain.'

'Why?'

'I'm not sure. It came up under London. I think they were trying to steal Nelson's Column.' He scratched his head. There was a large part of history that didn't interest him very much, in between Britain losing control of the world and gaining control of the galaxy.

Suruk pointed. 'An airlock.'

At the end of the tunnel, a dozen curved plates had interlocked like a contracted iris. M'Lak symbols ringed the door. White markings on the plates had closed together to form a skull.

'I don't know,' Carveth said. 'It's got a skull on.'

Suruk sighed. 'Piglet,' he replied, 'I think you are going to have to get used to that.'

He hit the control pad. The door hissed. Steam blasted into the roof. The sections slid back into the walls with a greasy scraping sound, and the iris-lock opened. Lights boomed behind it, and they saw what lay beyond.

Shelves filled the walls. On them, rows of skulls of half a dozen sorts. A thing like a typewriter, or perhaps a cash machine, stood on a plinth. Spears protruded from a bucket like bamboo sticks. On the walls, there hung pictures of a M'Lak warrior riding a huge mechanical beast.

'Whoa,' Rhianna said, and for once, Smith could see what she meant.

They walked inside, the lights swelling around them.

'So,' Smith said. 'The resting-place of Grimdall the Rebel.'

Suruk pointed to one of the pictures, in which a M'Lak hero grappled with a human who was probably meant to be Genghis Khan.

Rhianna stared at the picture. 'This is amazing, Suruk,' she said. 'It's so… vibrant.'

'Vibrant?' Carveth pulled a face. 'Everything in it's dead. Look at those skulls.'

'I shall scout ahead,' Suruk said.

Carveth looked at the shelves. The objects along the walls were set out for display, perhaps even to be picked up, but she had no idea what they did. Along one wall, she found a rank of little holographic pictures. Carveth stood on tiptoe and blew the dust off the display. One picture showed a narrow pass through rocks in what could have been Greece; another seemed to be of a Viking longhouse; a third had a carving of a large person in a mask knocking the heads off several other people, which seemed like the kind of stuff Aztecs would enjoy.

Smith found a rail, from which hung rows of fishnet shirts and heraldic banners. Perhaps it was Grimdall's spare wardrobe. He pulled out one of the banners and peered at the alien symbols.

'My comrades travelled to the relics of Grimdall,' he read, 'and all I acquired was this puny banner.'

'Guys,' Rhianna said, 'these skulls are plastic.'

Smith stepped over and lifted down one of the skulls. It was very white, and hollow. 'Good God,' he said, 'you're right.' He looked at Rhianna, and a thought passed between them.

'What if…' she said. 'No… But what if…'

'The relics are just a load of old tat?'

Carveth sighed. 'Well, I'm not impressed. A fake skull and a bunch of holo-postcards. Not much of a hall of relics if you ask me.'

Suruk spoke from the far side of the room. 'That,' he said, 'is because this is not the hall of relics.'

Smith lowered the plastic skull. 'What is it, then?'

'The gift shop.'

Carveth stared at him. 'This Grimdall bloke had his own gift shop? Bloody hell, Suruk. I take it all back about you being vain. That's on a new level entirely.'

'Come,' Suruk said. 'The reliquary awaits.'

He led the way. An airlock hissed open, and they entered a narrow passage. M'Lak weapons lined the walls.

'Now,' the warrior said, '*this* is what we seek.'

He pressed his hand against the panel. A light flickered: M'Lak characters appeared in the door lock. It reminded Smith of a broken digital watch.

'What does it say?' Rhianna asked.

Suruk said, 'One who wishes to enter must answer a question. The question is: "What is best in life?"'

'Tea, obviously,' Smith replied. 'And cricket. Curry. Weekends. Model kits.'

'Booze,' Carveth said. 'Chocolate? Sleeping? A bit of the other? Suruk, it's broken.'

'Peace, love and harmony between the peoples of the galaxy,' Rhianna said.

Suruk opened his mandibles and made a soft croaking noise. 'What is best in life?' He smiled. 'To crush the lemming men. To see them driven before you and to hear the squeaky lamentation of their does!'

The door slid open.

'Lucky guess,' Suruk said, and he shrugged and stepped inside.

Lights boomed far above him. A soft yellow glow rose behind the high walls. The skeleton of a dragon hung over their heads.

'That's a Cassopean skywyrm,' Rhianna whispered. 'Aren't they a protected species?'

'By fangs and armour,' Suruk replied. 'A worthy foe.'

'I meant protected by law. So you can't kill them all.'

'Of course,' Suruk replied. 'He who slays must replenish, lest there are no good enemies left to fight. The M'Lak leave planets fallow and raise up great forests for beasts to live. Like any brave, I served my time with the artificial insemination teams. Truly, the skull is not the hardest part of a skywyrm to get your hands on.' He sighed and gazed at the ceiling. 'Once, I was halfway through the ritual of bucketing when the beast took flight. Six miles I travelled, gripping its undercarriage like one who has shut his tie in the door of a jumbo jet.'

'Yes, Suruk,' Smith began 'I'm sure the ladies don't want to know –'

'How big was its todger?' Carveth demanded.

Suruk was not listening. 'Over plains and forests we soared. I wished greatly to release my vice-like grip, and I suspect that it felt the same. The skywyrm looked down, and was most perturbed. Its anger swelled, and other parts... did not. As the beast's interest in romance fell off, so did I. Rarely have I been happier to plummet from the sky.'

'Let's move on, shall we?' Smith said.

They entered a long, shadowed hall. Spotlights lit up the trophy racks.

On the right, half a dozen fanged, bulbous skulls had been mounted on the wall. They were Procturan black rippers, their heads bulging like evil cucumbers. Above them hung a huge, crested skull, with an extra set of teeth making up for its lack of eyes: a Procturan Matriarch. 'Blimey,' said Smith.

Void sharks, Caldathrian Beetle People, Croatoans, Yothians, Aresians, even a small Death Otter – hundreds of the galaxy's fiercest beings had fallen before Grimdall's blade.

'What's that?' Rhianna said, peering at a huge biomechanical head. 'It looks almost fossilised. It's got a kind of trunk.' She looked closer. 'Oh, it's only a helmet. Hey, that's lame.'

On the opposite wall, a strange tangle of bones had been erected, twisted as if frozen in the process of taking another form. Two skulls seemed to be merging, or splitting apart. Smith looked at the display card, recognising the M'Lak characters for 'weird' and 'pissed off'.

Suruk pointed down the hall. 'This way. Looking at dead aliens must get boring for you humans.'

The lights blossomed around him. They walked into a sea of bone.

'Much more familiar.' Suruk turned, grinning. 'Dead humans!'

The room was full of human skulls, hundreds upon hundreds of them. Suits of armour stood on frames at the edges of the room: human weapons lay in glass cases.

A shelving unit was crammed with skulls in bronze helmets with plumes and square cheek-plates, leaving only a T-shape for the eyes and mouth. On the end of the row, a yellowed parchment hung in a glass frame.

'Ancient Greek,' Smith said. '*Oh Xerxes, Emperor of Persia, behold my invoice for services rendered at the pass of the hot springs. Please find enclosed: Spartan helmet x 300...*'

Carveth said. 'Look, Vikings!'

An exhibit showed a mock-up of a Viking longboat

– for all Smith knew, it could have been the real thing. After all, the Vikings were in no state to object. Their axes hung from hooks in the wall, their horned helmets below them.

'*I picked these up at Heriot mead-hall.*' Suruk read. '*I was disappointed to learn that the horns were only part of the helmets and not the Vikings themselves. They refused my request for a refund. Still, I had an entertaining time, once my arm had grown back.*'

They walked on. Swords, javelins, battleaxes, assegais, katanas, kukris, even a flintlock pistol: the weapons of a dozen cultures pointed towards the end of the room. A photograph showed four bearded men in Renaissance dress in conversation with four M'Lak warriors. The aliens wore traditional tortoiseshell breastplates.

'*The four great masters,*' Smith read. '*Leonardo, Donatello –*'

'This guy really got around,' Rhianna said.

The trophies became more recent. They passed armour looted from Mongols, mughals and samurai; skulls in berets, pickelhaubers and fur hats; then a heap of what looked like Ghast helmets, shrunken to be worn by humans. Suruk peered at a row of skulls above a six-barrelled rotary gun. 'These were collected in the Venezuelan jungle,' he said, studying the notice beside them. 'And this one here is Dutch.'

'It's amazing,' Rhianna said, 'even if it is kind of gross. But why aren't there any British things? I mean, Grimdall rebelled against the British Space Empire, right?'

'He clearly realised that we were honourable enemies,' Smith replied. 'Grimdall must have regarded us with too much respect to put our skulls on display like balloons at Carveth's birthday party.'

At the far end of the hall, a great pair of doors awaited them. The metal looked like brass, but where the light caught it, it shimmered with a strange, purplish glow, as if reflecting a fire that was not there. Rows of symbols ran down each door, interlaced with embossed carvings depicting a range of decapitations.

'This looks dangerous,' Carveth asked. 'What does it say?'

Suruk pointed to the lintel. '*Only warriors of great honour may enter.*'

'Well, there's a thing. I'll have to wait in the gift shop.'

'*And their underlings,*' Suruk added.

'Bum.'

Suruk pressed the button.

'Ruddy hell,' Smith whispered.

It looked like Coronation Day in Hell. The Union Jack hung everywhere: tattered campaign banners, some hundreds of years old, covered the ceiling and the walls. Skulls gazed out from niches wearing pith helmets, commando caps, slouch hats, bearskins, tricorns and space helmets. A dozen types of red coat stood in glass cabinets. Sabres and dirks were mounted next to longbows, claymores and laser rifles.

'He... er... obviously respected the British an awful lot,' Smith said.

'Yep, he really respected us alright,' Carveth replied. 'He gave us our own separate gloating-room.'

Three steps led up to a throne set against the far wall. A M'Lak sat on the throne, a white crown on his head. He was almost a skeleton.

In front of the throne, lay an enormous steel beast. Part chameleon, part tiger and part dinosaur, the metal shadar stretched out like a sphinx. It was almost the size of a shire horse.

'The mechanical maneater,' Smith said.

'So, Grimdall,' Suruk croaked. His voice was hushed, lowered to a menacing purr. 'This is where you came to die.' He looked around. 'There are worse places to expire.'

'Absolutely,' Smith replied. 'It's got a lot of flags.'

Carveth took a step forward. 'Isambard, he collected these flags because he didn't like the space empire. They're trophies.'

'Of course,' Smith said. 'But nobody else has to know that, do they?'

There was a moment's pause. Rhianna spoke. 'Er, what?'

'Well, no one else need know that. We found Grimdall, he was wrapped in the Union Jack because he'd had a change of heart and decided that he liked the Empire more than he wanted his own planet back, and now everyone can work together and give the lemming men a bloody good thrashing. Super.'

Rhianna shook her head. 'Isambard, that is wrong, and you know it.'

'Of course it's not wrong. It's for the good of the Space Empire, Rhianna.'

'No.' She turned, and there was a hardness in her voice that he had never heard before. She reached up and pushed her hair out of her eyes. 'Ghasts rewrite history. The Yull lie about all the bad things they've done. We're better than that. We will go back and tell the truth about this place.'

'But,' Smith replied, 'what about – I mean to say – the Empire, for goodness' sake... oh, bollocks to it, I suppose you're right.'

'Please,' Carveth said, 'if I could just interrupt the Oxford Union Debating Society for a moment, let's just grab these relics and get the hell out of here before the Yull show up.'

'Right.' Smith took a step towards the throne. 'So… er… what do we take? We can't carry this maneater thing, and all the stuff in here is British anyway.'

'Anything. Nick his hat. Just do it quickly.'

Rhianna frowned. 'This is Grimdall's last resting place. Isn't it disrespectful to take his crown away?'

'True,' Suruk said. 'We should at least take his head as well.' He stepped up beside the throne. 'I should be able to twist it off. At least, that is how I would remove it if he was alive…' He reached out. 'If I just turn it ninety degrees –'

Grimdall's head dropped off his shoulders. It landed in his lap, bounced, rolled to the edge of the throne, dropped onto the floor and shattered into pieces.

There was a moment of silence: less in respect of the ancient warrior than in horror at having burst his skull.

'Oh,' Suruk said. 'Unexpected.'

Grimdall's body fell apart in a cascade of bones.

'You dropped his head,' Carveth whispered. 'Bloody hell, Suruk, you broke his head! We came all the way across space, we fought robots and gangsters and lemming men, we went up a river to kidnap a lunatic, I rescued an entire species on my own, we went on an epic quest to find the greatest warrior in history and now you've gone and broken him! Suruk, you absolute knob!'

Shock made Smith's voice sound slightly distant. 'This is a bit of a problem, chaps.'

Carveth's eyes seemed to be growing wider by the second. 'Problem? Problem? God almighty, what are we going to *do?* "Hello, people of Ravnavar, we found the tomb of your sacred hero but then we smashed him into pieces. Now please give your lives for beloved Mother Earth!" Well, that's us bollocksed, isn't it? We're going to be remembered as the people who dropped the Space Empire on the floor!'

Suruk said, 'Why don't I tell people that his head just fell off while I happened to be standing nearby? It worked at the Old Bailey.'

'Oh God.' Carveth made a loud heaving noise and began to shake. 'We broke the Space Empire!'

Smith crossed the room and slapped her across the face. 'Snap out of it!' He turned. 'We need to be reasonable about this.'

'How?' she cried. 'Nobody will ever like us again!'

'Carveth, we're British. Nobody likes us anyway. Now, has anyone got any suggestions?'

Suruk raised a hand.

'Yes?'

'Can I slap her too?'

Rhianna put her hand up. 'Guys?'

'Yes?'

'Two things. Firstly, let's just chill out and try not to panic. Let's visualise positive energy flowing out of us. Secondly, we've got some sellotape in the spaceship. Maybe if we collect all the bits of his head…'

'It's a good idea,' Smith replied, 'but we don't have time. And I think I've just trodden on part of it. Maybe we could swap his skull for one of the ones in the museum.'

'What an awfully good idea,' said the mechanical maneater.

Smith drew his pistol. Suruk whipped his spear up, ready to throw. Carveth yelped, fumbled her shotgun and accidentally shot the ceiling. Rhianna blinked.

With a soft whine of hydraulics, the maneater got to its feet, flexed its tail and twisted its head. Gears crackled in its neck. It was built like a bull.

'Whoa,' Rhianna said.

'Quite so,' the maneater replied. It had a deep voice, at once suave and menacing. 'Now, given that you're here, am I right to assume that you're trying to loot the relics of Grimdall? A simple yes or no will suffice.'

'What are you?' Carveth gasped.

'I'm an artificial intelligence, programmed to protect Grimdall's tomb, and Ravnavar in general, from invaders. Invaders like you, my good fellow,' it added. Its heavy head swung towards Smith: the massive lower jaw opened, revealing a mouthful of blades. 'Oh, and lower your pistol. Your small arms are no match for my large paws. I do like those red jackets you British wear, by the way. The blood never shows.'

'Enough.' Suruk took a step forward. 'These humans are mine. Together, we fight the lemming men of Yullia, who have waged savage war upon all honourable peoples. They must be destroyed.'

'The Yull? Those little furry things? Oh no, I don't think I'd be interested in that sort of nonsense. Can't you call in pest control?'

'That,' Suruk said, 'is what our warlords and generals believed. The Yull are large and well-armed. Their rage is matched only by their cruelty. Cities burned down on the day of their surrender, populations worked to death in the foul mines of Scorvin, entire species cast into dismal slavery. We need the help of Grimdall to rally our troops against them.'

'Well, I doubt Grimdall will be able to help you much. Especially now you've knocked his head off.' The maneater sat down, its metal hindquarters thumping against the rubber floor. 'Besides, it does sound like a load of nonsense: lemming people and all that.'

'Yeah? Well, you're a talking robot tiger-chamelion thing,' Carveth replied. 'So there.'

'No. Sorry, not interested.'

'We'll fight you for it,' said Smith.

'Oh really?' the machine drawled. 'A fight, eh? *Now* you're talking my language.' The maneater raised a paw. Five Zukari blades snapped out like enormous claws and locked back on themselves. The maneater scrutinised its reflection in the polished steel. 'That's what I like,' it said thoughtfully. 'Carnage. Sheer carnage.'

*   *   *

There was a passage behind the throne. Suruk took the chance to 'borrow' a couple of spare sabres, and then they walked up the corridor, the maneater loping along beside them. The passage was steep and Smith could feel himself becoming short of breath. That did not bode well: it would be embarrassing to be disembowelled while having a little rest.

'Isambard,' Rhianna said quietly, 'what's the plan?'

'Well,' Smith said, 'it's in a bit of a fluid state, at the moment.'

'Is it likely to, er, become solid soon?'

'It's still rather runny, I'm afraid.'

The maneater yawned. 'This way, everyone. Oh – when you're all dead, would you mind terribly if I put your skulls in the trophy room?' It nudged a control with its muzzle.

A hatch swung open. Orange light flooded the passage. Smith winced and stepped out into the warm dusk.

He was on the edge of the lake, in the undergrowth. He clambered out, midges buzzing around his head. The maneater slipped easily between the fronds: Suruk and Smith hacked a path behind it.

'So, where shall we fight?' the maneater inquired.

'The car park,' Smith replied.

'How sophisticated,' the maneater said. 'I could spill your pint first, if it helps.'

They walked along the waterfront. The dying light gave the buildings a sad, ghostly quality.

Figures detached themselves from the shadows.

'Boss,' Carveth said.

Smith nodded. 'I see them.'

The maneater stopped and swung its metal head. 'Well, well,' it observed. 'Spectators.'

Blackcoats, Smith thought, Yullian secret police. Their fur was dyed jet black, and most wore armour, a privilege only extended to the knight class. A few had no armour at all, just dark feed-bags over their muzzles, the lemming equivalent of balaclavas.

Smith pulled his rifle up.

'Offworlders!' one of the lemmings called. He was plump, broad-shouldered, almost ball-shaped. 'Nice night, is it not?' He swaggered forwards, thumbs hooked in his sash, next to a pair of battleaxes.

'Stay back,' Smith called. 'Keep back or by God, I'll bag you.'

'You have located the resting place of the hero Grimdall,' the officer said. 'Xiploc Cots thanks you. Now, throw down your weapons and we can get on with the impaling. Robot animal thing, you come with us.'

'Do I, now?' said the maneater.

Suruk shook his head. 'You seek the impossible, rodent. The steel beast has promised to battle us.'

Cots snorted. 'Silence, frog-thing. I address your human masters.'

Suruk's face slowly opened. With a small, wet sound, his mandibles parted and his mouth split into an enormous smile. Carveth drew back: even Smith could not remember when he had seen his friend so pleased.

'Foolish words,' the alien replied. 'For I am Suruk the Slayer, pupil of Volgath, child of Urgar the Miffed, of the line of Brehan the Blessed. I have no masters. I do not even have any equals.'

Suruk drew himself up, pleased to have an audience.

'Lemming men, you have disgraced the noble art of combat. You have murdered, pillaged and rampaged across space, without mercy or style. You threaten my people, as well as all others, and now you lay claim to the relics of our champion. Your crimes are many, but there is only one punishment: community service.' He grinned. 'Just joking. It's death.' Suruk turned to the others. 'Depart, and take the maneater with you. I have business with these fools.'

'Ooh,' said the maneater. 'A fight.'

Smith shook his head. 'No, Suruk. I'm staying with you.'

'Me too,' Rhianna said. 'We stand together.'

They looked at Carveth.

'Oh, all right,' she said.

Smith turned to Rhianna. 'I'm sorry about what I said back there, in Grimdall's tomb,' he said. 'About pretending that Grimdall had changed his mind about the Space Empire. I just wish – I just wish everywhere was British. It would be so much nicer that way. People wouldn't kill each other so much. All this silly bloody nonsense about gods and races and all the rest of it that makes them murder each other just wouldn't happen then.'

'I know,' Rhianna replied, and she leaned in and kissed him.

Suruk whirled round and brought the end of his spear down across their heads, knocking them out. They fell together.

'Enough piffle,' he snarled. 'Piglet, maneater: load

Mazuran and Rhianna into the spaceship. Lemmings: battle time.'

Cots smiled and stepped forward. 'Good. This is as it should be: two noble warriors, face to face.'

'Strange,' Suruk replied, 'for I see only one noble warrior here. Perhaps you are seeing double. You should ease off the dandelion wine, fatty.'

'That is not fat! My pelt is unusually fluffy! Brothers, kill him!'

The Dark Lantern Collective drew their weapons. Axes, knives and tridents glittered in the dusk. One of the lemming men began to swing a weapon like a bladed anchor over his head. Two enormous tame scorpions scuttled down another soldier's arms, perching on the backs of his hands. A third, huge, brute merely brushed his palms together and cracked his knuckles.

Suruk took a step backwards.

'Wait,' he said. 'Yull, please do not attack –'

'He surrenders!' Cots screamed. Beside him, a wiry-looking lemming tugged a whip from his belt: hooks and razors twinkled in the leather. 'Now the fun begins!'

The whip cracked. Suruk threw his arm up, and the thong wrapped around the metal bracer on his forearm quicker than a striking snake. Suruk gave the whip one good yank, and pulled Cots' adjutant off his feet.

He stumbled straight into Suruk's spear.

Suruk impaled the rodent with a single thrust and yanked the spear free. The lemming man staggered aside, clutching himself.

Gently, Suruk pushed him into the lake. He reached up and tugged down the brim of his hat.

'– until I have adjusted my headgear,' he said.

And then they leaped at him. At the edge of his vision, Suruk saw Carveth and the maneater hauling Rhianna into the bushes – then an axe swung down and Suruk sidestepped at the last moment. He felt the air slip past him, threw his spear underarm into a Yullian knight's throat and drove the heel of his hand into another's muzzle, crumpling it like the front of an old camera.

They were deadly fighters, far better than any he had dispatched before. Suruk weaved and cut, blocked and dodged, using their numbers against them, making them get in the way of one another. They tried to shepherd him to the water's edge, and he sprang forward, booted one lemming man in the snout and jumped over his head.

The huge unarmed thug barrelled forward – Suruk darted aside and it crashed through a beach hut. His blades were at its throat before it could rise. A noble in full plate armour darted in from the side and chopped at Suruk's legs.

He jumped over the axe-blade and threw himself forward. Volgath's teachings flowed into his mind. Suruk slapped his open hand against the lemming's breastplate. 'Stones of the Forbidden Temple!' he snarled, focussing his energy into its chest. Suruk felt warmth against his palm, and something pounded wildly behind the armour. The lemming man screamed, and its heart popped. It toppled back, dead.

One of Cots' soldiers swung an axe overhead, like an executioner. Suruk countered with the Prodigal Hands: he darted forward and hit the inside of its elbows with the edges of his palms. 'The shark!' He chopped down, breaking its shoulder-blades. 'The piranha! The greater box!' Suruk cried, his hands disorientating his enemy, and he delivered the death-blow. 'The lesser box!' Its head sailed into the undergrowth.

To the west, lights rose, bright against the darkening sky. Suruk glanced back as the *John Pym* rose. Searing pain flashed down his arm and he spun around. The bladed anchor whirled up in a lethal arc. It crashed down and Suruk rolled aside, wood splintering behind him. The assassin whipped the chain down again, beating the ground as if threshing corn, while Suruk dodged and bounced, half a second before the sharpened hooks.

The assassin laughed and whirled the chain, aiming for Suruk's eyes. Frog-like, Suruk jumped up, drawing a sabre as he leaped, and as the chain whipped around he hit it just before the mid-point. Sparks flew. The chain flicked around Suruk's blade and the anchor swung back past its owner's head.

For a very gratifying moment, the lemming man realised what was about to happen. Then Suruk grabbed the chain, gave it a tremendous tug, and the assassin's head flew off.

All was still. Half a dozen Yull stood before Suruk, fanned out in a loose semicircle.

'Your friends have left you,' Cots said.

'Good.' Suruk's arm began to hurt. The cut stung, but there was something else there – poison, perhaps. He focussed himself, drawing it into his body.

The light was almost gone, but Suruk could sense them, see the heat of their rage. He reached out with his mind, and felt not six souls, but seven – and the last one was behind him, creeping towards his back.

'Sheath your weapon and join us,' Cots said. 'The Greater Galactic Happiness and Friendship Collective has need of brave warriors.'

Suruk glanced at the carnage around him. 'So I see.'

The assassin was close now, no more than five yards. It struck.

Suruk felt the spirits of great warriors watching him. *Bend like a reed in the wind*, said Volgath, and he twisted aside. *Turn his energy against him*, said Urgar the Miffed, and Suruk raised his hand, and there was the enemy's body, open and unprotected. *Smack him in the chops!* bellowed Brehan the Blessed.

Suruk's fist hit the assassin's breastplate, shattering it like china. His hand met fur, then flesh, and skin and muscle blew apart at the force of the blow. His arm ploughed into the lemming's chest, spraying blood into the night air, and blasted out the back in a cloud of gore. Suruk ripped his arm free, lifted his grisly hand and crushed the assassin's still-beating heart in his fist.

'Delicate Butterfly,' he said.

The lemmings all charged at once. Suruk drew both sabres and engaged them with the Blood-Dance of Old Ravnavar, sending a flurry of limbs into the air. '*Yullai!*' cried one of Cots' thugs, and it dashed at Suruk, a battleaxe in either hand. Suruk ducked low and ran it through with both swords. The lemming dropped its axes and, instead of trying to pull free, grabbed Suruk's arms.

Even impaled, it gabbled triumphantly. Suruk struggled to free himself, the rodent shouting 'Die, die!' into his ear. Suruk roared, released the swords and shoved the lemming man away. He stepped back, stumbled on a fallen axe, and something smashed into the back of his legs.

His knees buckled. The ground banged against his back. Colonel Cots stamped down on Suruk's chest.

*   *   *

'Of course,' Bargath yelled over his shoulder at the lancers behind him, 'surprise is everything in this kind of terrain.'

Five shadar crept through the foliage, forty feet above ground level. Their hands reached out from one thick branch to another, crossing from tree to tree where the branches intersected.

A birdoid flapped past, and Frote flicked his tongue out and whipped it into his mouth. Morgar did not like being this high up, and the sudden cloud of feathers did not make him feel better.

Bargath rested his rifle across his saddle. 'Magnificent view,' he announced, reaching to his side. A month ago, Morgar would have expected him to take out a pair of binoculars. Instead, Bargath raised his hip flask. 'You all right there?'

Morgar nodded. 'Just a bit queasy.'

'Saddle-stomach, eh? You need to flush your system out. With gin. When I was a lad –'

'We have to go east,' Morgar said. As soon as the words passed his mandibles, he realised that he didn't know why he had said them. He blinked.

'East, you say?'

'I – yes. Someone's in danger.'

'Got intelligence, have you?'

Morgar nodded. It was a certainty.

'Never trusted the stuff myself. Still, I should think we can manage a detour, if there's a bit of scrapping at the end of it. Now, as I was saying –'

A quanbeast fell out of the canopy ten yards away, and crashed to the forest floor, pursued by a flock of caustic pigeons. 'We have to go *now*,' Morgar said. 'Right now.'

Bargath frowned. He peered at Morgar, took out a targeting monocle, pushed it into place and peered harder. 'My,' he said, 'you really are hungry for battle, aren't you?' He leaned back. 'You see? The lancers can make a fighter out of anyone – even you. Good work, Morgar. Jolly good.' He cupped his hands around his mandibles. 'You hear that, chaps? It's time for battle!'

*   *   *

An explosion, muffled but huge, knocked Smith off his bed and dumped him on the floor. For a moment he lay there, feeling and smelling the *John Pym*, and then he remembered, and he heaved himself upright.

'Suruk!' He lurched to the door of his room, staggered into the corridor, and stumbled into the cockpit. 'Turn the ship round. We have to rescue Suruk.'

'We can't turn,' Carveth said. She gripped the control stick as if strangling it. 'We've just taken a bloody glider-bomb in the engine. Port's down sixty percent. We can't stay up for much longer.'

Rhianna sat in the captain's chair eyes closed, hands raised to her head. The mechanical maneater stretched out at her feet. 'Damned shame, that,' it drawled. 'Rather liked him.'

'Isambard,' Rhianna said, and she sounded even further away than usual, 'Suruk's going to be just fine. I know it.'

The ship lurched.

'Trust me,' she added, and her voice was no longer vague.

'We're going down,' Carveth cried. 'We'll have to crash land! Brace yourselves!'

The maneater looked up. 'Crash landing? How terribly dreary.'

*   *   *

Cots loomed over Suruk like a cliff. 'Got you,' he said.

Suruk grimaced. He was slowly becoming aware of the extent of his injuries. His skin seemed to be entirely bruised. Three of the ribs just above his hip were aching, and the pain in his upper liver made him want to cough a pellet there and then.

Cots smiled. 'So, you are weak too.'

'I slew all your assassins'. Suruk replied, between gritted teeth.

'So you claim. But we Yull will write the history books.'

'What will you say, that you became peckish and stuffed all your minions in your cheeks?'

Cots grinned. 'How weak you are, stupid frog-thing. Your clumsy form betrays you in battle. Your coward soul fills you with the fear of death. You have no self-respect, else you would not associate with other members of your dim-witted, oafish race. In short, you are like all unrodents: your value is only in labouring for the Yull and amusing us with the squalid agony of your death!'

Something large moved among the trees.

'Do continue,' Suruk said. 'This is fascinating.'

'Well, we Yull are better in every respect than anyone else. Take, for instance, your face. It is very ugly. You don't have whiskers. You don't even have a nose, let alone a snout. What is all that about?'

'Is that so?'

'*Shup!* Shut your weird face or I will cut off your feet!' Cots stepped back, swinging his axe up as he did. 'Yes, that is a good idea. Then I can tell you of the greatness of the Yull while you crawl in agony!'

Despite his wounds, Suruk smiled. He chuckled. His battered chest shook with amusement. His voice rose, and rose, until his laughter roared out of him and rang around the forest.

'What is so funny?' Cots demanded. 'Filthy offworlder, you may not laugh at me! I am very important and noble!'

With an effort, Suruk controlled himself. 'I am laughing,' he said, 'because I have kept you flapping your muzzle for just long enough to seal your doom.'

'*Hwot?*'

Something hit Cots on the back. He stumbled and twisted around, and Suruk saw a wet pink mass on the Yullian's breastplate, like a blob of used chewing-gum. A fleshy rope stretched from it into the shadows of the forest.

Cots raised his axe, and flew back, limbs flailing, bouncing across the ground as he was reeled in. Suruk saw a face in the jungle, a massive mouth, open and pink, and the monster's eyes swivelled to focus on the lemming man attached to its tongue as he disappeared between its fangs.

Cots screamed – and then the massive jaws clamped shut on him. The shadar loped into view, Cots' feet sticking out of the corners of its mouth. They jiggled as it chewed. Its rider waved.

'Hello, Suruk!' Morgar called.

'Greetings, brother.' Suruk clambered to his feet. The sight of the chaos around him made him feel much better. He yanked his spear out of a lemming man's neck. 'A timely arrival. Thank you.'

'Oh, that's quite alright.' Morgar patted his mount. 'Gosh, it's a mess here, isn't it?'

'I did honourable battle with the champions of Yullia. Perhaps it was that which drew you here: you sensed the nobility of the combat in your soul.'

'Maybe. But I mostly just followed the bangs and the screaming.'

Suruk picked up his hat. 'You still ride with the lancers, then?'

'Yes. We're being held back at the moment. Something about a hammer and anvil, I believe.' Morgar reached to the back of his saddle, and took out a lunchbox. 'Sandwich?'

'I think not.' Holding his side, Suruk took a step closer. 'But tell me, brother: is there room on your steed for two?'

*   *   *

General Wikwot stomped back to his own battle-line. He lumbered between the trees, past his sentries, and drew his axes.

The general threw his hands up, and in each fist was a battleaxe. '*Dar huphep!*' he roared. '*Huphep Yullai!*'

'*Yullai!*' his soldiers howled, and they rose up around him.

To the soldiers on the castle walls, it was as if the whole planet had come to life and turned the forest into its throat. The shriek of glee and hatred rose from all around, drowning out the hum of engines and war-machines, and the trees shuddered as if battered by a storm.

The Yull charged.

Lemming men poured out of the forest by the thousand. They were seeds shot out by the jungle plants, a rippling, howling carpet of fur and bayonets. Gliders sailed over the canopy: packs of squol ran between the soldiers.

'What's the range?' Wainscott yelled, over the scream of rodents. He stood on the parapet, machete in hand, surrounded by riflemen.

Susan shook her head. 'Not yet...'

The Yull had no prisoners, so they drove their serfs over the minefield first, with rapid and ugly results. Bits of lemming sailed into the air, knocking two gliders out of the sky. They exploded as they hit the ground. Several lemmings were not killed outright, and some of their comrades stopped to laugh at their death agonies – but all were quickly stampeded by the rest of the horde.

'They're in range!' Susan shouted.

'Rifles, fire!' Wainscott cried, and the first four ranks of lemming men fell as if washed away.

Susan heard nothing except the crack of laser-fire and the rumble of explosions. Then the mortars in the courtyard roared, and for all her training she nearly ducked. She set the beam gun onto the parapet and took aim at the biggest rodent she could see. The laser cut him in half.

The gun batteries on the upper towers swung down to cover the ground. A glider smashed into one of them, and it burst in a cascade of bone-coloured rock. Stone slid down the side of the castle, into the courtyard. Two gunners were killed and their mortar buried; a third was dragged away by two Sey warriors, towards the medical tent.

Susan swung the beam gun and sliced down a row of howling lunatics. Now the Yull were in machine-gun range, and the ripping crackle of bullets joined the hiss of the lasers. Shells crashed among the Yull, but they came on, wild with bloodlust. Some, she saw, did not aim straight at the walls, but swerved towards the round tower at the corner, before throwing themselves in front of their comrades' feet. They died in piles at the base of the tower, great heaps of fur –

'They're making a ramp!' Susan shouted. 'Wainscott, they're making a ramp!'

*   *   *

From his treehouse, Wikwot gave the command, and his second battlegroup attacked. His troops slipped through the forest, weaving between the great trunks, and as they saw the sun between the trees they screeched their warcry and ran into the light. They hit the back of the castle – more accurately, the mines around it – and surged across the open ground, cheering and squeaking. Now Mothkarak was surrounded, and its defenders poured fire onto the Yull from every side. But it was not enough.

Soon, Wikwot thought. Their cowardice will overcome them, and they will throw down their weapons and beg for mercy, thinking that they have put up enough of a fight to impress us. Even the M'Lak – frog-spawned pond-life, the lot of them – would give in. Perhaps the humans would think that they could just leave their servants to the Yull and sneak back to Earth. What a surprise they'd get!

He tapped one of his adjutants. 'Do dirty M'Lak have fingernails?'

'No, great one. But they do have kneecaps.'

Wikwot smiled. 'Excellent,' he purred. 'Open a bottle of dandelion wine.'

Siege

Smith, Carveth and Rhianna wrestled with the controls. The lower three-quarters of the windscreen were full of the bone-white walls of Mothkarak.

The maneater lounged at the far end of the cockpit. 'You do know there's a castle in front of you, don't you?'

Smith looked round. 'Either help us or get in a locker with the rest of the junk.'

'Very well,' it said, and it padded over, hooked a paw around the control stick and pulled it backwards. The ship swung up, almost enough to clear the walls. On the parapet, lemming men, humans and M'Lak fought for their lives.

The ship clipped the edge of the battlement, yawed crazily, and then slammed down into the courtyard.

The floor lurched. Smith fell, Rhianna landed on top of him, and the maneater slid across the cockpit. Carveth scrambled out of the pilot's seat.

'The bad news is that we knocked the landing gear off on the wall back there,' she said. 'The good news is that the lemming men broke our fall. And the other bad news is that the lemming men are here.'

Something exploded under them. A siren parped, then died away. The front fell off one of the overhead control panels and foul-smelling smoke billowed out.

Rhianna staggered upright and helped Smith to his feet. A second boom from below rocked the floor. Smith grabbed his weapons, Carveth picked up Gerald's cage, and they hurried to the airlock.

The courtyard was mayhem. Imperial soldiers ran towards the main castle, covering one another. Soldiers climbed down from the battlements. The Yull simply dived off – the fall was high enough to break a man's neck, but a large pile of dead comrades softened their landing. The outer wall was breached. The Space Empire was falling back.

'With me!' Smith shouted. 'Everyone, to the castle!'

They ran, but it was no rout. The soldiers retreated in waves, covering each other as they went. The Yull were cut down by the dozen, but it didn't stop them: more charged howling over their dead.

The mechanical maneater looked over its shoulder, at the yowling horde pouring over the parapet. Soldiers tried to slow the horde. Two M'Lak soldiers and a human were overwhelmed and hacked down. A bullet hit the maneater on the shoulder and pinged off into the air. 'Oh,' it growled. 'Like that, is it?'

Susan stood in the middle of the courtyard, firing her beam gun from the hip. Beside her, Dreckitt had acquired a drum-magazine Stanford gun, and was blazing away as if he was back in the New Chicago underworld. He waved and dashed over, fiercely hugged Carveth and shouted 'Goddam crazy Yull!'

Smith swung up his rifle and blasted a Yullian grenadier as he climbed over the battlements. The rodent fell back among its comrades and exploded a moment later. Slices of lemming sailed into the air.

'Where's Wainscott?' Smith demanded.

Dreckitt pointed. Fire billowed on the walls and a grinning figure strode through it, all beard and shorts like Satan on holiday. 'Which nutball let Wainscott get a flamethrower? You know what he's like around fire. Take this to your magic kingdom, Mickey!' Dreckitt added, firing off a burst into a screeching lemming sergeant. 'We've got to go!'

'Yeah, let's get out of here!' Carveth cried. 'I – oh, crap!'

A glider sailed over the walls. The wings were ripped like an old paper bag, and the pilot had been hit several times. Smith saw the dynamite stuffed into the pilot's sash, the wad of explosive padding out its cheeks, and as he pulled up his gun he knew that even if he killed it, the lemming man would still crash onto them.

Rhianna flicked her hand up as if greeting an acquaintance, and the glider smashed into an invisible wall. The explosion scoured the walls behind the glider, incinerating a dozen lemmings. Smith didn't even feel the warmth of the blast.

'Totally awesome,' Rhianna said. 'I mean, violence is really bad. But still…'

They ran back across the courtyard, Smith and Dreckitt covering the retreat. Susan fell back, reluctantly, and the Deepspace Operations Group accompanied her. They ran through the main entrance, and the doors slammed shut behind them. Soldiers rushed to bar them, heaping furniture around the doorway. Smith and his comrades ran towards the mezzanine.

*   *   *

Eight seconds later, the doors burst open and the fuselage of a Yullian fighter plane slid burning into the entrance hall. A communications orderly was plastered across the windscreen, still clutching a radio in its singed paw.

'They've called in an airstrike,' Smith cried. 'On themselves!'

The Yull poured into the hall. In a second, the first thirty rodents went down under a hail of bullets, beams and light furniture. Two M'Lak soldiers heaved a grandfather clock onto the squeaking horde, and followed it with an antique commode.

A bald man in a morning suit ran over, holding a fire axe; Smith recognised him as the android butler.

'The enemy have tunnelled into the cellar, sir,' he announced sadly. 'I found two men partaking of the spirits down there. Two *lemming* men, sir. I... corrected them, but there will be more.'

'Bollocks,' Wainscott snarled. 'They're in the building.'

A human soldier fell back, clutching his chest. The M'Lak threw a suit of armour over the balcony, braining several Yull with a terrible crash. For a moment, the sheer weirdness of the scene bewildered Smith: it looked as if someone had rammed a model aeroplane through a dolls house and followed it with a ceaseless tide of mice.

Chaos broke out at the rear of the lemming men. Some turned, others were tossed aside. A huge shape bounded through them, roaring and shaking its metal head. A great squol hung dead in its metal jaws, and the mechanical maneater dropped it by the staircase.

'Ravnavar?' it called. 'Are you with me, Ravnavar?'

And Smith's voice answered it with the others. Cheering, they rushed down to fight.

*   *   *

The Yull were in the lower passages now and the great cool vaults under Mothkarak echoed with gunfire and squeaky battle-cries. The tunnels were simply too complex to defend; on the other hand, they were almost impossible to storm. A fair number of the lemming men were lost not to gunfire, but to being mislaid. In the dim stone corridors the Yull were ambushed and slain: by fierce squads of defenders and their own confused comrades. The robot spiders that carved and repaired the castle caught several lemming men and scrimshawed them to death.

The Yull were inside, but at terrible cost. Their enemies fought with a fury that they had not anticipated. Had any of them dared to tell their superiors, or survived to do so, General Wikwot might have suspected that he no longer had a monopoly on not giving up. Instead, he ordered another wave of lemmings into the cellars. After all, he thought, tunnels were a rodent's home from home.

*   *   *

'We can hold the front,' Wainscott said, as a wallahbot brought up a massive urn of tea. 'You lot go up and find W.'

Smith turned from the balcony and led his crew upstairs. They picked their way up a winding staircase that smelt of damp and linoleum, climbing up the spine of the castle. Guns boomed through the walls.

Smith let himself think about Suruk. Surely he couldn't be dead: Suruk was too tough and too crazy to be killed by the Yull. He seemed immortal, the way

Wainscott did. But then, people weren't. He hoped Rhianna had been able to send help to Suruk: being hit on the head with Suruk's own spear probably hadn't helped her psychic abilities.

He realised suddenly that, without the skulls, violence, bladed weaponry and occasional requests for bail money that being Suruk's best friend entailed, life would be a much emptier place.

They emerged onto a narrow landing. Floorboards creaked and dust trickled down from above. Cannon fire rippled like thunder through the walls.

An open side-door led into one of the smaller libraries. Two women manned a tripod-mounted laser, the barrel poking out of the French windows. The nanibot stood beside them, and as Smith approached, she lowered her rifle and deactivated the sights.

'Well, hello there,' she said. 'Goodness me, isn't it noisy?'

'We're looking for W.'

'Of course.' She pulled up the rifle and took a shot out of the window. 'It's a terrible mess, isn't it? Did you know, cleaning up can be fun? I'm taking out the trash with my rifle, and it's ever so jolly.'

Carveth muttered, 'Well, she's flipped her switch.'

'Don't be impolite. He's right this way.'

She pointed, and they hurried through. At the back of the library, the spymaster stood behind a table covered in maps. A bank of military display screens flickered behind him, flashing with muted gunfire.

'Wainscott's holding the front entrance, sir,' Smith said. 'Looks like we might be able to keep the Yull back.'

W shook his head. A roll-up stuck out of the corner of his mouth like a mummified twig. ''Fraid not, Smith. We've got lemmings in our underworks and ammo's not looking good. Some of the M'Lak are down to knives already, although I think they might have just thrown their guns away. Look at this.'

He pulled one of the screens down on a jointed brass arm. It showed forest, the canopy rippling like the surface of a lake. 'Here,' he said, pointing to two large shapes. They moved forward, stately as ships, sending the trees around them swaying.

'Ravnaphants!' Rhianna said. 'Aren't they majestic? Wait a minute. Are they ours?'

'*No*,' said the spy. Under his thin moustache, his mouth was hard and set. 'They're enemy, and they're stampeding this way. If those things reach us, there won't be a castle left to protect.'

'Good God!' Smith exclaimed. 'Can we stop them?'

'Maybe,' W said. He bent down and picked something off the floor. When he stood up, he was holding an immense shotgun, the barrels wide enough to accommodate a fist. 'This is my ravnaphant gun. Thought it might come in handy.' He reached to the table, picked up a teacup and took a large gulp of the contents. 'There's a tunnel leading out into the grounds,' he said. 'If I hurry, I might be able to come up just before them and bag the buggers. Thing is – well, you'd better take my place after that. There's a whole lot of lemmings out there.'

Rhianna ran a hand through her hair. 'So you're going to go out there, shoot the ravnaphants and then die? You can't do that! Ravnaphants are nice.'

'Not a lot of choice,' W said. 'If I don't make it back, tell everybody that I thought they were – well, pleasant company. Remember: the mildness of the British people is their greatest strength. And all tyrants must die. I think that covers it.'

He started for the door.

'Wait,' Smith said. 'I've got a plan. What if we distracted the Yull?'

'How? They're crazed. All they want is blood.'

'Then we'll give it to them. Do those monitors transmit as well as receive?'

'Yes, but the image is terrible.'

'The worse the better. I'm going to need a camera, some white sheets, a lot of red paint, timed explosive, a Yullian dictionary, a bottle of helium and several women in nurses' uniforms. Do you think we can find all that?'

'Almost certainly.'

'Rhianna, you can help me. And Carveth?'

An explosion, muffled but huge, shook the windows. Dust rained from the ceiling. She looked round. 'Yes?'

'Fetch Gerald.'

*   *   *

Wikwot watched the ravnaphants advance from his vantage point in the treehouse. The beasts lumbered towards the castle walls like slow torpedoes. They would smash straight through, once they had got up enough speed, like a drunken uncle falling onto a wedding cake. Of course, with each step they crushed a dozen of the Yullian footsoldiers that swarmed around them, but that was war for you.

'General!' an adjutant called up. 'An outgoing transmission from the Space Empire.'

'Excellent.' Wikwot slid down the tree, his bulk conveying him quickly to the ground. 'Do they beg for mercy?'

'Yes, my lord. Look!'

The minion held up a screen. The image was blurry, but Wikwot could make out a confused looking woman in a white outfit with a big red cross on the front.

'Um, hi,' she said. 'Look, lemming guys, could you not attack the big shed out the back where we used to keep all the aviation fuel? Because we're using it as a hospital, and it's full of women and children – you know, civilians – and it would be totally bad if –'

She was abruptly shoved out the way. The camera shook: a whiskered face appeared close to the lens. A voice squeaked '*Huphep Yullai!*' and the screen went dead.

Wikwot looked at the adjutant. 'Well,' he said, a grin stretching across his chops, 'looks like our boys have found the good stuff. To the big shed! Kill the unrodents – kill them all!'

*   *   *

Smith peered over the windowsill. 'Looks like it's working,' he said.

Rhianna carefully removed her improvised white hat from the chaos of her hair. 'Do you think they'll go for it?'

'Of course. The lemming man may fight fiercely, you see, but in his heart he is a bully and a moral coward. His base masters have ordered him forward, and, drunk with cruelty, he has no option but to obey. Our noble soldiers, on the other hand – why are you both smiling at me?'

'The helium's not worn off,' Carveth said. 'And I'll have my hamster back, while you're at it.'

Smith passed Gerald over. Anyone sane would never have mistaken a blurry hamster for a member of their own species, but then the lemming men were not sane. He had given them what they wanted – the opportunity for a massacre – and they would be powerless to resist. At the far end of the library, the mounted laser was firing again.

'You know,' he squeaked, as Rhianna removed her improvised uniform, 'you look quite nice dressed as a nurse.'

'Uh-oh,' said Carveth.

'At least it's not a Bronte sister,' Rhianna replied.

Carveth gawped. 'God, that's wrong. Which one was it?'

Rhianna shrugged. 'All of them, I think.'

'When you're finished, Carveth,' Smith chirruped, 'we have work to do.' He picked up the map. 'Rhianna, Carveth, give it a few minutes and have the ladies on the gun back there shoot the shed up. That ought to do the furries a bit of no good. I'm off to help W.'

'I'll go with you,' Rhianna said.

'I won't,' Carveth added. 'I mean, I would, but Gerald here deserves a rest.'

Smith looked at Rhianna, reflecting that she wasn't the best person to take on a hunting trip. He wondered how he would dissuade her, especially since his voice was currently several octaves higher than usual. He'd think of something by the time they got out of the castle, by which time he might sound less like a bird. 'Right,' he said. 'Let's go.'

They took one of the many sets of back stairs. Rhianna held the map and Smith went first, sword out. They hurried down the steps, boring deep into the castle. The air seemed to thicken and chill; the boom of explosions became a distant rumble.

The construction robots had passed through here a long time ago, carving useless side-passages and storerooms that now housed nothing except dust. Smith and Rhianna ducked behind a statue that depicted a fat angel in a bowler hat.

'Look,' Rhianna said, pointing downwards, and for a moment Smith thought she meant her sandals. Then he saw the bootprints in the dust.

The passage ended in a staircase. The steps seemed to rise into the ceiling: as they got closer, Smith saw a hatch in the roof. 'Here we go,' he trilled, and he pushed it open.

They climbed out into the forest, into the sound of gunfire and yells. At one time, Smith realised, the place had been an outpost of the castle: broken walls still ran across the ground, overgrown with creepers. Smith closed the hatch, feeling the heat like a weight on his back.

'Where's W?' he said.

'I don't know. Maybe I can sense him –'

Something huge exploded to the right. Smith dropped down, tugging Rhianna's hand. A fireball flew into the sky, preceded by a squeaking wave of lemming men. They sailed into the air, about half of them still in one piece, and crashed down upon the wreckage below with an unpleasant sound like wet cement.

Then he realised: Carveth must have blasted the fuel store. 'It's raining lemming men,' he said. 'Hallelujah.'

'Smith,' a man whispered. 'Smith, is that you?'

They shoved through the undergrowth. W lay on his back. He wore a combat helmet: the visor had been ripped and twisted away, as if it had exploded from inside. The spy's mouth and hand were bloody.

He was pinned down by the corpse of the biggest squol that Smith had ever seen. It was a brute; a scarred, sandy-yellow rat-hound with a spiked collar and a tail that had been broken in so many places that it resembled a lightning-bolt. Smith grimaced and helped Rhianna to heave the body aside.

W coughed weakly and sat up. 'Bloody thing jumped me. I managed to stab it in the brain with a fountain pen.' He stared glumly at his wounded hand. 'Via its mouth, unfortunately. The gun's yours, Smith. I'd be lucky to bag groceries, let alone a ravnaphant.'

Smith picked up the gun and broke it open. The cartridges were the size of tin cans.

'Solid shell on the right, lead shot on the left. Use the shot to get its attention, and then aim at the head. You'll only get one chance. The only thing worse than an angry ravnaphant is a randy one.'

'I'm sorry?'

'Their arses go red in the mating season. It's very bad news for everybody.'

Deep in the forest, Smith heard the stomp of huge feet like drums.

'Isambard?' Rhianna said.

Smith looked around. She had taken a deep breath, which meant that trouble was on the way. 'You're not about to tell me that hunting ravnaphants is wrong, are you?'

'Actually, yes. Totally wrong.'

Smith took a few steps away, towards the ruined walls, and Rhianna said, 'Maybe we can make friends with it.'

'How? If you want to pat it on the head, you should have brought some scaffolding.' Desperation made him sound bitter.

'*Them*, Isambard. There's two of them.'

The ground began to shake. The footsteps sounded more like artillery than drums now. As Smith looked at Rhianna, the gun seemed to shrink in his hands. 'God,' he said. 'What're we going to *do?*'

'Maybe I can contact their minds.'

'They've got two brains. Each. And neither's very clever.'

'I could make them friendly.'

'Alright. Be careful.'

He strode towards the noise. The trees thinned down,

and he saw the first ravnaphant ploughing through the forest, branches breaking around its shoulders like ice around an Arctic ship. It was as tall as a cliff, covered in ancient scars and skin thicker than tank armour.

But it had also been badly used, like anything that the lemmings took alive: there were fresh cuts in the armour, and syringes the size of telegraph poles stuck out of its flanks, no doubt full of some vile combat-drug. On its back, a horde of Yull jeered and chanted, wild with bloodlust.

'Slow him down,' he said, and he broke the gun open. Rhianna closed her eyes, and Smith took out the solid shell, and replaced it with shot.

The first beast strode a little slower now, but each step was still enormous: it could march straight through the castle. The ground shook, rocked. The second monster lumbered into view.

'The other one!' Smith shouted. 'Make them friendly!'

The first beast was nearly on top of them now. The huge legs boomed around them, crashing down like pistons in a starship's engine room. Something like a huge fleshy pendulum swung from above, and Smith thought, That's a funny place to have a tail –

'I will fill their hearts with love!' Rhianna cried, beaming.

'That's not its heart!' Smith yelled back, and tugged her out the way. They dashed aside, between the first beast and the second, through a storm of dust and panicked animals. Suddenly they were clear, and as the first ravnaphant passed them, Smith pulled up the gun and fired both barrels into its rear.

It lumbered to a halt. The lemming men riding it shouted and tried to goad it on. The ravnaphant's back twitched as the realisation that it had been shot travelled from its backside to its brain. A red mark swelled from the point of injury: the shot had been like a slap across the arse.

The second ravnaphant paused, took a good look at the red bottom in front of it, drew the obvious conclusion and leaped onto its comrade's back.

In a second, two hundred lemming men died horribly. Those not flattened outright were ground to paste by the vigorous motions that followed. Smith was reminded of the liaison between his aunt's Jack Russell and a table leg.

The first ravnaphant dimly realised what was going on, and reminded the second that they were both male by kicking it in the groin. The second beast roared and staggered, sending lemming men flying into the forest like water off a wet dog's back. The ground rocked and shuddered as the two beasts bellowed at each other.

Smith stood there a moment, overcome with awe, and then Rhianna grabbed him. 'Isambard, we did it!'

They stood there, gazing at two of the galaxy's most majestic creatures in one of the galaxy's less majestic spectacles. 'And so did they,' Smith replied. 'To each other. Or at least, they tried.'

Together they walked back to W. He stood upright, leaning against a tree, smoking a roll-up. 'Did you bag them both?'

'Good as,' Smith replied.

'You should get them mounted,' the spy replied.

'Actually, they mounted each other.'

'That was some bloody good work,' Smith said as they started back towards the trapdoor. He squeezed Rhianna's hand.

'You know,' she said, 'it wasn't all that hard to communicate with them. They're a lot like men, really Their brains are in their –'

A rumble ran through the air. Smith felt it in the ground, too, under his boots. 'Not again!'

The sound rose, and the branches above them trembled. This time, the noise was coming from the South, not the East, but it was still set to crash into them.

Smith looked at Rhianna. 'Can you slow this one down?'

She looked vague, but grim. 'I'll try. I'll see what I can do.'

She walked out to meet it. Smith followed, W lurching along beside them. They looked up at the forest. And the trees burst apart before them. The ravnaphant came lumbering through, striding forwards, and Smith saw a castle on its back, studded with howitzers: Union Jacks dangling along its flanks, and galloping in its wake, row upon row of lancers riding great green beasts.

'Mildred!' he cried.

Someone blew a bugle, and the ravnaphant lifted her head and bellowed. A tiny figure stood between her eyebrow-ridges: legs braced, arm out before it.

'Look!' Rhianna cried. 'It's Suruk! And he's surfing the ravnaphant's head!'

*   *   *

The Yull could no longer flatten the castle, but they could still storm it. They poured in now, and the defenders retreated upstairs as if from a rising tide, closer and closer to General Young. A thick carpet of fallen lemmings covered the lower floor, but the Yull did not care. Victory was worth any price.

The mechanical maneater fought like the monster that it was. The humans didn't matter much, but the M'Lak – Grimdall's people – were in danger. The reckoning with mankind could wait. Bayonets broke on its metal skin; armour and fur crumpled under its massive claws.

Susan ran out of powerpacks for the beam gun. She grabbed a laser rifle from a dead soldier, and moved on to two revolvers when that ran out. Craig was jabbed in the thigh and Nelson dragged him upstairs. Wainscott took a gash to the chest from a Yullian axe, shortly before throwing the axe's owner over the banisters.

They regrouped in the tertiary ballroom, an immense chamber in the centre of the fifth floor. The ground was already strewn with lemming men, their fur stiff and red.

Wainscott and a captain from the M'Lak rifles began to argue over a counter-attack. Each appeared to want to lead the charge. A group of Sey arrived and reported that they had sawed off the drainpipes to prevent the Yull climbing them.

Carveth stepped over a fallen lemming and hurried to Dreckitt's side. 'Rick, have you got any spare ammo?'

'Nix, kid. Twenty more slugs and I'm down to rubbing out lemmings with brass knuckles.' He took out a grenade. 'I saved us a pineapple. In case they try to take us alive.'

'Alright. I hope I was alright as a girlfriend.'

'A dame and a moll,' Dreckitt replied, putting his arm around her.

Something bumped against Carveth's boot. She glanced down, and saw an empty plastic bottle.

'Catsup,' Dreckitt said. 'Hell of a place to chow.'

'Ketchup?' Quietly, she squatted down and touched her finger to the Yullian soldier sprawled at her feet. Her fingertips came up sticky and red. Too red. 'That's not blood,' she said. 'Rick, that's not blood!'

'Hot damn!' Dreckitt cried. 'Guys, they're not dead!

The lemmings are playing possum!'

The Yull sprang up around them. The defenders dropped back into a tight circle, suddenly surrounded. They fired and cut, killing dozens of lemmings as they scrambled upright, but the delay was enough. More Yull charged in from the side doors. In a moment, the soldiers of the Space Empire were encircled by a wall of fur and bayonets. Human, M'Lak, Sey and even a couple of beetle people stood in the centre of a horde.

The M'Lak captain tossed his gun onto the floor, and dropped to one knee before the Yull.

Quietly, the M'Lak laid down their guns.

'No,' Carveth gasped. 'Don't give in! We have to fight!'

The Yull squeaked and jeered.

'Wait,' Dreckitt said.

The M'Lak captain put his fingertips on the ground and pushed his hips into the air.

Wainscott drew a machete.

Like a sprinter from the blocks, the M'Lak captain shot forward into the ranks of the lemming men and his soldiers followed him. Carveth saw Susan bellowing something and then she was running forward with them, following the Space Empire's toughest troops into close combat.

The ballroom windows exploded and a scaly head the size of a space shuttle ploughed into the room. A trumpet blasted, and Carveth recognised the figures on the beast's head.

She saw Smith, and Suruk, and Rhianna, and then Suruk leaped down to fight. The Ravnavari Lancers raced up Mildred's tail, over her back, and onto her head, and behind them came the blue legions of the Equ'i. The Empire charged, and the Yull were swept away.

*   *   *

General Wikwot watched his army fall apart. Despite or perhaps because of all the carnage, he felt numb. A window burst open in one of the towers and a torrent of his soldiers tumbled out, crashing into the courtyard below. Perhaps someone had pushed them, but he suspected that what had sent the lemmings to their deaths was despair.

He called one of his bodyguards over and sent out the order for a general retreat. This would be difficult to enforce: not only had two newly-liberated ravnaphants had a bad effect on the Yullian lines of communication, but the language of the lemming men had no word for 'retreat'.

Mildred, the Space Empire's tame monster, had stopped before the castle, and the Ravnavari Lancers were using her tail and neck as a ramp to charge into the upper levels of Mothkarak. A burning lemming dropped flailing from the battlements. It looked like a demon.

It all made no sense. Unrodents were all cowardly and weak: they had no skill or appetite for war. Yet here they were, massively outnumbered, laying waste to his army. For a moment, Wikwot wondered if he had underestimated these stupid, fat, clumsy, timid, shameful, smelly, idle, mangy degenerates, and then an explosion to the right jolted him back to the present.

At first he thought the trees were moving. Then he looked up, and saw that what he'd taken for a trunk was a colossal leg. It was one of the captured ravnaphants, celebrating its new liberty by flattening its former tormentors.

It took a step towards him. A surly rage rose up in Wikwot's mind and he drew the battleaxe from his belt. He was still the general.

The monster lumbered closer, and its tiny eyes saw Wikwot far below. The bodyguards screamed and scattered. Wikwot hefted his axe as the ravnaphant raised its foot, and a great shadow fell across the ground.

'Come back!' the general yelled at his minions. 'Come back, you cowards! It's only a ravnaphant!'

* * *

It was, without doubt, time for tiffin.

Smith wandered through the castle. He was co-opted to help carry some of the wounded to the medical centre set up in one of the larger kitchens. Lemming men lay everywhere.

Light and strange smells flickered from a workshop. Smith peered inside: one of the construction robots had sliced a sofa open and pulled out its padding, and was currently putting the finishing touches to a huge stuffed squol in a spiked collar. W watched from the far side of the room, his arm in a sling and a cup of tea clenched in his fist. He must have reprogrammed the robot to carry out taxidermy. Smith closed the door and crept away.

He found Rhianna and Susan in a drawing room, looking like guerrillas lost in a Jane Austen novel. 'These dials show power output,' Susan said, tapping the beam gun on the chaise lounge beside her. 'Ohms, Watts, Bechdels... Hello Smith. Seen Wainscott around?'

'I think he's upstairs.'

'Just don't let him take off into the forest. I'll have to stick posters on the trees: *Lost: one commanding officer.* It'd be embarrassing.'

On the way back, Rhianna and Smith ran into a group of soldiers hurrying to the ballroom. A crowd packed out the area: humans, M'Lak, beetle people, Sey, Equ'i and even a couple of robots listening to the small figure on the stage.

It was General Young. She was short, but as tough and determined as she had been when she'd sent him after Wainscott: a terrier of a woman. Smith caught scraps of her speech. Unused to the concept of retreat, the Yull were in disarray. The remainder of the Divine Amicable Army had simply fled into the forest and were being harried by the lancers. Plans were afoot to destroy the Yullian food stores in order to hinder their retreat: at any rate, Smith assumed that was what 'blast their nuts with a flamethrower' meant.

'But it is you who achieved this,' the general said. 'I may have had the idea, but you did the work on the ground. One cannot forge a sword if the steel is not there already. The Yull lost because you fought harder and better than them. I anticipate that the Yullian army will fall back to higher ground, and then jump off it. We will therefore be pressing on, but first we will consolidate our position – and celebrate.'

Smith headed off. He had come lately to the battle for Andor, and the real glory was owed to those who had seen the war against the lemmings from the start, when it had looked likely that the Empire would be finished and its planets overrun. He disengaged Carveth from Dreckitt and discreetly removed Suruk from a conversation with Morgar and Bargath.

'The lancers are giving my brother a commission!' Suruk announced. 'I fear that the Empire is still in great danger.'

Smith found battered wicker chairs and they sat on the verandah, looking out over the forest. Slowly, everyone drank their tea and began to comprehend the scale of the victory.

The sun was rising, setting the sky alight. On the horizon, two ravnaphants, recently freed from the tyranny of the lemming men, were still arguing about which of them was the female. It slightly spoiled the atmosphere, but not much.

'Bloody good show, everyone,' Smith said. 'I mean it. Bloody good.'

Suruk chuckled. 'A mighty victory. Fierce justice has been served to the foul armies of the Yull. Severed heads and biscuits all round!'

'Right now,' said Carveth, 'I just want to sleep.'

'Nonsense,' Suruk replied. 'This is just the beginning. We will press on and take the war to the lemming men. They know now that there are no warriors to equal us. What other empire has cavalry that ride dinosaurs, which all ride one huge dinosaur? I ask you that. We will clean up the Yull, and dispatch the scum Edenites, and then the Ghasts. They will throw down their arms, and those who do not, we shall hack apart! These are nice biscuits, by the way.'

'Well said,' Smith agreed. 'The lemmings are finished, Carveth. Even now the lancers are shipping the prisoners off to the safari park.'

'Safari?' Carveth demanded. 'That's a bit soft, isn't it? You're talking about pony-killers here.'

Suruk laughed. 'It's not *their* safari, little woman. They get the choice: five years' penal servitude or two weeks on a M'Lak game reserve. We have to train the young warriors up somehow.'

Rhianna stretched and sighed. 'You know, guys, I think we all learned something today.'

Smith nodded. 'True. Being deranged isn't everything. The lemming men may be bizarre and insane, but we British are far more than that.'

'Yeah,' said Carveth. 'We're *really* crazy.'

'Speak for yourself, Piglet,' Suruk put in. 'Today I surfed a dinosaur. That seems entirely sensible to me.'

Rhianna frowned. 'No, not that. I've learned that we truly are one. Human, M'Lak, Sey, Kaldathrian, if we all just came together as one, we could –'

'Conquer everything,' Smith said.

'Well, yeah, but…' She stood up and walked to the railing. The dawn seemed to catch light in her messy hair. 'I've learned that sometimes, there is no choice. You have to fight, or you have to die, and if you die, innocents will die as well. Just like the ponies that Polly protected. You have to stand up for your friends, like Suruk did when he protected us at the lake, shortly before he, er, knocked me out. Or like you did, Isambard, when you went out to rescue W.' She turned and looked across the trees. 'The galaxy is a beautiful place, and we must protect it: whether you do so by fighting in the front line, or by working in the factories, or just using your psychic powers to make enormous monsters have unusual sex.'

'It's called the Doctrine of Just War,' Smith said.

Suruk nodded. 'Just War. An excellent idea.'

'Just as in *justified*, not as in *only*.'

'It will suffice anyway,' Suruk said.

There was a moment's silence. Then, from below, came the voice of the nanibot, prim, high-pitched and efficient. 'Major Wainscott! Major Wainscott, this is quite intolerable! If you do not put your trousers back on this minute, I will put you across my knee – again!'

'Let's go inside,' Carveth said. 'Right now.'

*   *   *

'*Good evening. I'm Lionel Markham, and this is* We Ask the Questions. *Tonight, we'll be discussing the new proposals put forward by the Imperial Government for a Federated Empire, to represent the various planets* of space and, I quote, "Civilise the Entire Galaxy, one hellhole at a time".

'Today, Ravnavar formally received Dominion status, granting it full control over all aspects of policy apart from its membership of the Empire and capacity to declare war. In the fine tradition of democratic compromise, this has made nobody happy at all. Joining me in the studio are two prospective MPs, hoping to be elected in the upcoming Ravnavari by-election: for the fringe party, Popular Fist, Julia Chigley; and lancer and independent candidate Morgar, Architect of Doom.

'Also coming up is an interview with the Mechanical Maneater, who'll be discussing his role in the film version of Grimdall: a Life in Pieces of Other People. First, though, we're going live to Andor, recently freed from lemming occupation. Major Wainscott, can you hear me?'

'Good evening.'

'Can we pan the camera up a bit? I don't think the viewers want to see that. Thanks. Major, I understand that you and the M'Lak Rifles are currently mopping up the remainder of the Yullian Army.'

'Ha! Mopping up's the word – it's a mop and bucket job. I've just got back from the Amargan Heights and it's like a diving championship there. The Yull're queuing ten-deep to jump off.'

'Is it true that there have been incidences of our soldiers co-operating with the enemy?'

'Absolutely right. Some of the lemmings get indecisive, so we give them a shove.'

'And your view on the conflict so far?'

'Brilliant. I have a statement here. One moment... it's in poetry. I call this: Epitaph for a Lemming Army:

From righteousness the lemmings swerved,
Lured by dreams of death and war.

I know not if they got what they deserved,
But I bloody gave them what they were asking for!'
'Thank you, Major. That's quite enough.'

*   *   *

It took two months to finish off the Yull.

The lemmings were too angry to give in and too frenzied to retreat in good order, and so they died in droves. The Equ'i located the Yullian food reserves and commando units blew up the stores. Central Command sent a batch of new Cauteriser landships fresh off the production line and they followed Mildred the ravnaphant from one warren to the next. The ravnaphant broke the warrens open, the landships turned their heat rays on the contents and the infantry finished off whatever remained.

'You know something?' Wainscott said as they picked their way through what had once been a Yullian fort. Water dripped from the leaves above them, as warm as gravy. 'I'm getting sick and tired of arseholes thinking that we're weak because we're nice.'

'You're *not* nice,' Susan replied.

The fort looked like a rainy day in Hell. Everything had been roasted: cinders crunched underfoot.

Smith looked at the skeleton of a lemming man. War hadn't turned out to be quite as easy, or as much fun, as the lemmings had thought. He wondered what had happened to General Wikwot. Presumably, he'd jumped off a cliff.

Wainscott stopped. 'What day is it?'

Smith shook his head. 'I'm not sure. I think it's Saturday.'

'Fry-up tomorrow,' Wainscott said. 'I love the smell

of bacon in the morning. It smells like… breakfast. Someday, this war's going to end,' he added. 'Bloody nuisance, that.'

'There's still the Ghasts,' Smith replied.

'So there is,' the major replied, and, whistling, he continued.

* * *

Two days later, Rhianna was sitting in the castle gardens, close to the edge of the forest. The presence of the ravnaphants had resulted in a lot of fallen trees and she sat on one of them, having first checked that it was not one of the creatures' enormous droppings.

It was a comparatively quiet day and an ideal time for her to improve her mind by emptying it of all thought. She perched on the log, vaguely aware of the world around her, contemplating the majesty of space by staring into it, when something rustled in the forest to her left.

She glanced round. A lemming man stumbled out of the undergrowth. It wore a crude cowl stitched out of what looked like a Yullian banner. It lurched forward, zombie-like, dragging its rifle behind it. The cheeks, once packed with nuts, were hollow. It stared at her.

'Must… kill… slow…' the lemming muttered. 'War-god…' Its nose twitched, and a violent shiver ran over its matted fur. '*Grubgrub*,' it gasped.

'Hey, little fella,' Rhianna said. 'Are you hungry?'

The lemming man, who was six feet two, dropped onto the far end of the log.

'Okay,' she said, reaching into her bag. 'I've got a

special cookie here. I baked them, so they're quite strong. You've got to take it easy.' She leaned over, holding the biscuit out at the end of her arm. The lemming man stared at her hand, eyes swimming. Then its paw flashed out and it grabbed the biscuit and crammed it into its mouth. 'Whoa!' Rhianna said. 'That's... a lot. Just chill, alright?'

The Yull chewed slowly. It swallowed. 'Tastes of... herbs. Now I must kill you.' It paused. 'Got another? I feel strange.'

'I'd feel strange if I ate a whole one,' she replied. 'Just ease down.'

'No! Must... fight... kill offworlders for Popacapinyo... crisps would be nice now.'

Slowly, almost elegantly, the lemming man slid off the log and dropped with a soft crump into the undergrowth. It lay there for a while, giggling, and then fell asleep.

'Crazy,' Rhianna said, and got back to clearing her mind. Four seconds later, it was empty again.

*　　*　　*

Carveth had been busy. Her fame as Battle Girl had spread, even though her coronation as Honorary Princess of the Equ'i had been disrupted when she burst a blood vessel from an overload of glee. A foreign reporter came to interview General Young and spoke to Carveth as well. A week later, the post shuttle brought them an allied magazine called *Freedom Hell Yeah!* which featured her on its cover – to Smith's surprise, with her clothes on.

Smith flicked through the pages, taking in the exciting stories and bizarre spelling, and found a mention of the Space Empire. '*Battle Girl, second cousin of the Queen of England, leads the Roaring Commandos, a team of heavily-armored* – Carveth,' he said, lowering the magazine, 'you are not Queen Kylie's cousin. I hope you've not been making stuff up. That's our allies' job.'

She shrugged. 'It sort of came out.'

He sighed. 'You did a good job, Battle Girl.'

'Cheers, Boss.'

'Now stop making a fuss and put the kettle on.'

*　　*　　*

The call came in while Smith was sitting in the *John Pym*, cursing the effect of the Andorian climate on his model kits. Wainscott's team were out in the forest demolishing a warren. Smith called Carveth and Suruk out of the hold and woke Rhianna from a trance. It was time to fly.

Their target had once been a pumping station and had changed hands several times. Most of the decoration had been chipped and blasted away. Only a brass lion still stood over the entrance, tarnished and dented.

Half a dozen Equ'i waited at the landing point. 'He's in here,' said the guide, pointing with a hoof. 'Good luck to you, Princess Polly.'

'Actually,' Smith replied, '*I'm* in charge here.'

'You?' The guide whinnied, which Smith hoped was not laughter. 'Are you sure?'

'Certain,' Smith said and, ignoring their offers and pleas of assistance, he walked into the station and into the dark.

It smelled of death, droppings and dandelion wine. Smith entered without his rifle, his sword sheathed and pistol holstered.

In the shadows, something massive lay on a bench.

'Wikwot,' Smith said. He felt a sort of angry pride. Here was the monster who had led the murdering armies of the Yull, who had thought that he would butcher Smith's friends at will.

Well, bollocks to you, you drunken old fart.

The shape moved. Smith felt Wikwot's gaze on him. 'So,' Wikwot said. 'This is the end.'

Smith nodded. 'Watership downfall.'

'Offworlder,' said the general, 'where are you from?'

'Woking, originally.'

'I always wanted to go there. Mainly to trash it, but I've heard some of the countryside is not bad. Nice place to live. Get a job, dig a warren, have kids... At the end of the day, it's all about the money and the does.'

General Wikwot sat up slowly. He was huge, Smith saw. Defeat and bad living had not made him any less of a brute.

Wikwot put something in his mouth. A match flared. Wikwot's cigarette – Lucky Foot brand – and his white, blind eye gave him a hellish quality.

Smith took another step forward. An empty bottle of dandelion wine clinked against his boot.

'They will say that I was a maniac,' said the alien. 'That I let my men run amok... Lies. I never lost control.'

Smith said, 'From the smell in here, I'd say you lost control a long while ago.'

There was silence. Wikwot shifted position.

'About thirty miles north of here, the rivers converge,' he said. 'We Yull call the meeting point Botlnec. Sometimes, at high tide, the light catches the water, and all the fish come to the surface as it shimmers in the moonlight. It's... actually, I'm not entirely sure where I'm going with this. Probably should have laid off the wine.'

'Come on,' Smith said. 'It's finished, Wikwot.'

'Are you an assassin, then?'

'No. I'm a spaceship captain. And I'd be a pretty rubbish assassin if I told you that I was.'

Wikwot drew on his cigarette. He sighed. 'How did it come to this? Two great empires, fighting to the death over this wretched planet. So much death, so much sorrow. How did we end up this way?'

Smith shook his head. 'Well, it's difficult to explain, really. I suppose both of our empires wanted the same things: power, prestige, territory. And then there are the economic factors. But it chiefly stems from you being a colossal arsehole, and going on a crazy rampage with your huge army of colossal arseholes. That's pretty much it.'

'Ah,' Wikwot said. 'That.'

'I'll be having your axe, please.'

The general got to his feet. He looked down at Smith, and quietly slid the battleaxe from his belt. Something stirred deep in his eye, beneath the self-pity and drunkenness; a mean, sullen anger.

They looked at each other for a moment, man versus lemming. Smith looked down at the axe in Wikwot's hands, and knew that the general could. And why not? Wikwot could cut Smith down and run out to meet his death, to die as brutally as he had lived.

'I'll accept your surrender now,' Smith said, and he put the Bearing into his voice. 'If you don't mind.'

Wikwot stared at him.

'With all due respect, I'll be taking the axe.'

Wikwot's eye narrowed.

Smith focussed the Bearing. '*If you'd be so kind, General.*'

Wikwot held out the axe. 'Oh, *fecinec*,' he said. 'Let's go.'

Smith took it from him. They walked out into the light.

The smelly gloom of the pumping station fell away, and Smith felt the sun on his face. He grinned as he saw his friends. The battle against the Yull was as good as over, and he and his crew had not just survived, but won. They had helped to make the galaxy free and safe. The tyranny of the lemmings was no more.

Suruk clenched his fist. 'Victory!'

'Hooray!' Carveth cried.

'Awesome!' Rhianna said.

'Yes, jolly good,' Smith replied. 'Settle down, everyone. I know we saved the galaxy, but that's quite enough emotion for now.'

'Offworlders.'

Smith looked round. Wikwot stood a few feet behind him, thumbs hooked over his sash. Suruk scowled, and Smith wondered if the old monster had one last trick up his fluff-covered sleeve.

'You people,' Wikwot said, and he shook his head. 'What strange creatures you are. You live like weaklings, but you fight like wild beasts. You conquer half the galaxy, but when people put cream in tea instead of milk, you call it obscene.' He looked them over, one by one, and sighed. 'Take it from me, as a warlord of the Greater Galactic Happiness and Friendship Collective: you are all very, *very* weird.'

'Weird?' Smith replied. 'Certainly not. You see, my good lemming, we can't be weird. We're British.'

About the Author

Toby Frost studied law and was called to the bar in 2011. Since then he has worked as a private tutor, a court clerk and a legal advisor, amongst other things. He has also produced film reviews for the book *The DVD Stack* and articles for *Solander* magazine. The first of his Isambard Smith novels, *Space Captain Smith*, was published in 2008.

www.tobyfrost.com
www.spacecaptainsmith.com